PRC

THE

QUEEN

Recent Books by Steve Burt

Dumb Jokes for Kids series #1, #2, #3 (2022)

New England Seaside, Roadside, Graveside, Darkside (2021)
New England Book Festival Best Young Adult

New England Christmas Sampler (2021)
New England Book Festival Award Best Spiritual

The Bookseller's Daughter (2019)
New York Book Festival Grand Prize
New England Book Festival Award Y.A. Fiction
Mom's Choice Awards gold medal Teens

FreeK Week (2014) FreeKs teen detective series book 3
Florida Book Festival Grand Prize
Mom's Choice Awards gold medal Teens

FreeK Show (2012) FreeKs teen detective series book 2
New England Book Festival Best Young Adult
Mom's Choice Awards gold medal Teens

FreeK Camp (2010) FreeKs teen detective series book 1
New York Book Festival Award Best Young Adult
Mom's Choice Awards gold medal Teens

Wicked Odd (2005 collection, out of print)
Independent Publisher Award (Ippy)

Oddest Yet (2004 collection, out of print)
HWA Bram Stoker Award for Young Readers

Even Odder (2003 collection, out of print)
HWA Bram Stoker Nominee for Young Readers

Odd Lot (2001 collection, out of print)
Benjamin Franklin Award Mystery/Suspense

A Christmas Dozen (2000 collection, paperback out of print))
Foreword Book Award

PROTECT THE QUEEN

Steve Burt

Copyright © 2023 by Steven E. Burt

Inquiries should be addressed to:
Steven E. Burt
17101 SE 94th Berrien Court
The Villages, FL 32162
352-391-8293
passtev@aol.com
www.SteveBurtBooks.com

Paperback: ISBN 979-8-9877213-0-8
Printed in the United States

Interior design by Dotti Albertine
Cover by SelfPubBookCovers.com/DANIELA

Acknowledgments

My thanks go out to a great team of Beta readers: Jan Droegkamp, Jan Justice, Myra Symonds, Lee Ireland, and Lorraine Grey. They caught typos, issued challenges, offered questions and suggestions, and were a great help in moving this from draft to finished book.

Special thanks as always to my lone Alpha reader (like an Alpha dog), Jolyn Joslin, who has been able to manage her editor and wife roles successfully. She chewed on this novel for a year, chapter by chapter, revision by revision. She also literally fed me when I had to put in the four- to eight-hour writing stretches most days and nights over eleven months.

I am also grateful to my California book designer Dotti Albertine, who has been with me since 2000. She's a consummate professional, and I highly recommend her.

Thanks, also, to my fans—especially Claire Bernash—who for three years pushed me to take on the challenge of writing a sequel to *The Bookseller's Daughter*, which I had thought was a single-out novel.

The cover was created by artist Daniela and purchased through SelfPubBookCovers.com. I also recommend them and have used them for other book covers, including *The Bookseller's Daughter, New England Seaside*, and *New England Christmas Sampler*.

Special Dedication

Herb Nelsen was a Mainer with a warm smile and an easy laugh. He could fix or build anything. He installed the 30-foot-lomg that transformed our three-season room, fixed our kitchen lighting, and patched our leaky roof—all while in his eighties. In February, at 87, Herb died. He loved my *Bookseller's Daughter* and wanted a sequel.

Last summer I met his son Peter, also a fan of *The Bookseller's Daughter*. Peter is a builder/handyman cut from the same cloth as his dad, same affability and easy smile. When we were eight days without hot water (an inexperienced repairman tried), Peter rescued us. He also shingled our roof, which we'd put off for years.

The real rescue came after an April 30 windstorm sent the top half of a centennial pine harpooned our three-season room's roof and floor, also destroying my desk and chopping my writing chair off at chest level.

Peter was there the next day, covering what he could, moving 40 cases of books to the main unit, arranging for a crane to extract the tree. He replaced the roof structure and rebuilt the room in two weeks. We got to camp and found a home better it was than before the disaster.

So now I'm in my new chair at my new desk, looking out windows Herb installed for the room Peter resurrected, and I'm typing THE END on *Protect the Queen*. With thanks I dedicate it to Herb Nelsen and Peter Nelsen.

-Steve Burt, June 6, 2023
Bears Den Park, Wells, Maine

CHAPTER 1

"Wells Police and Fire. What is the nature of your emergency?"

"Marcy? Is this you, Marcy?"

"Who's calling?" she asked. "And how can I help you?"

A man's voice. "This is Harp Gagnon, out at Spiller Farm."

"Hi, Harp. Everything okay?"

Spillers' was a well-known organic farm on the West Branch Road, the rural portion of Route 9A connecting West Wells and Kennebunk. They also had a well-stocked meat and produce store that sat on the north side of Branch Road opposite its U-Pick berry patches. Visitors found parking tight—a small hard-packed dirt area between the building and a small, active duck pond. Motorists sometimes had to wait for a line of cows to cross the road. A patchwork of fields occupied the rolling hills to the south side of the road, orchards the hills to the north. The farm, orchards, and store *employed family members, locals, and a handful of legal immigrants and* migrant workers.

Harper Gagnon was one of Spiller Farm's field supervisors. He'd been Marcy's classmate at Wells High who had gone on to Paul Smiths College in New York to earn a degree in forestry, with a minor in Spanish. When he finished, he had come home to Wells and taken a job at Spiller Farm. He not only spoke the language of the field workers but created and taught an after-hours class: English as a Second Language.

Harp cleared his throat, as if embarrassed. "Hate to bother, Marcy, but something weird going on here. In our back north orchard. Didn't seem like much the other day, but now it may be worth filing a report."

"A report?" Marcy asked. "On the phone, or do you want an officer to come by and check it out, write something up for the record?"

"Well, I don't know. Can I do both?"

"How about you start by telling me your story, Harp."

"Okay. Well, it could be vandalism, but it could also be robbery—or do you call it theft or larceny?"

"Don't worry about the cop terms. Take a breath and start at the beginning. But first tell me: is anybody hurt?"

"Hurt? No. But scared."

"Scared of what?"

"Not exactly sure. But it started Monday morning."

She grabbed a freshly sharpened pencil from a pewter tankard filled with them and poised it over her steno pad so she could take notes. The call was also being recorded.

"Actually, there were several incidents. We thought we could handle it ourselves."

"Just tell me, Harp."

"Monday morning two guys on my crew, Max—his name's Maximillian—and his brother-in-law Jose were checking one of the north orchards way back away from the store. They found a tree partly stripped."

"Stripped?" She wrote the words *tree stripped* down and underlined them. "Or picked?"

"Both," he said. "The apples were gone, but whoever or whatever did it took some of the leaves and bark off the fruit-bearing branches."

"Deer?" Marcy asked. "Teenagers? Homeless people?"

"Well, here's the thing. The missing apples came off the top, what you might think of as the crown of the tree. Deer and people reach up and grab from the low branches. And there's no way anybody—not even a little kid—could climb up from the ground, weave his or her way through the branches, and get to the top. They'd need a boom of some kind, a cherry-picker."

8

"Do large birds take apples—like hawks, eagles, crows?"

He ignored her question. "Let me get back to the story. That was Monday morning. On Tuesday morning we found another tree stripped. Same pattern—top of the tree. It was one we'd checked Monday morning, and it was okay then."

"Okay. Go on."

"A little while later that day, Tuesday, Jorge—he's another of my workers—found two rows of Brussels sprouts uprooted."

Marcy made a note. *Brussels sprouts uprooted.* "Missing? As in, somebody came in with a machete and cut a stalk of sprouts?" She had seen them sold on the stalk at farm stands and farmer's markets.

"No, not cut. Uprooted as in, ripped out by the roots. Not tossed aside like weeds from a flower garden. And not necessarily malicious, like vandals. Simply ripped out and removed from the premises."

"Is there more?"

"Yes. Tonight."

"What happened tonight?"

"Max and Jose and Jorge. I sent them back into the orchard after supper. Gave them each a camouflage tarp and told them to split up and hide under them, keep watch."

"Did they catch somebody? Teenagers?"

"After 6:30 it was dark, and they were hunkered down under the tarps. They heard something above them. Over the trees. A loud humming."

Marcy heard a man's voice in the background now, excitedly speaking in Spanish. Then a second voice, also in Spanish. The two talked over each other. Harp didn't have to translate it, though, because he already knew the basic storyline.

"Jose says it was like a hummingbird's wings beating—except it was a deeper sound."

More Spanish in the background.

"Max says he was afraid, but he looked out from under his tarp anyway and saw a large dark figure." More Spanish. "*Grande*. Big. Bigger than a man. Dark. All shadow. Floating over one of the trees. Balancing—I think he means hovering. Like a drone but shaped like a huge person." More Spanish. "Jorge says when it turned its head, the eyes were like lava, glowing red." More Spanish. "Jose says it has a horn like a rhino."

Instead of taking notes Marcy found herself holding her breath. The passion—the terror—in the Spanish-speakers' voices was draining—immobilizing—her.

More Spanish. Harp was translating as best he could now.

"Jose says it was a dragon—looked like a dragon—from the parades in his home country. He was terrified, and he's ashamed that he didn't try to scare it away. All three of them hid until the humming noise stopped. And when it did, they crawled together out of the orchard, crawled with the tarps pressed tight over them, hoping the dragon wouldn't swoop down and carry them off. When they reached my office in the back of the farm store, they were all shaking."

"Did you go back to the orchard with them?" Marcy asked.

"They refused to go back, at least not tonight. They're talking about leaving."

"Leaving their jobs? Are they really that scared?"

"I think they are. Two of them wet their pants."

"Harp, let me get a car moving. Thad Richards is less than a mile away at the rec park. I'll tell him to meet you at the farm store in two minutes."

She dispatched Thad and scratched a note on her steno pad, then texted Aaron Stevenson and his buddy Cliff Bragdon, the two cops who had encountered the swordsman that summer. *Rubber suit back? At Spiller's?*

CHAPTER 2

The next morning Maryann Keegan parked her Subaru in front of Annie's Book Stop and focused on her store's front display window. Slatted crates and bushel baskets were festooned with cornstalks. They spilled out gourds, pumpkins, and colorful books. AJ and Keegan had done a nice job decorating it. The front-door sign announced the change from summer hours to fall hours.

Annie's Fall Hours
9-4 Fri/Sat
Or by appointment

Her cellphone said it was 8:05 a.m. Thursday. She texted *I'm at the store.* A moment later the answer: *Passing Chase's,* the roadside farm stand on Route 1. Before she could unlock the store's front door, a red Jeep turned off the main drag onto Wells Highlands and eased in next to her Subaru. Aaron Stevenson unfolded himself and stepped down onto the blacktop. He wore running shoes, a light blue Maine Marathon tee shirt, and silver-striped blue sweatpants with a matching jacket.

"Morning, Aaron," she said, and pushed the door inward. The overhead tea bell fastened to the doorframe above tinkled its welcome.

"Sorry I'm late, Ms. K," he said, reaching into the Jeep. "Aroma Joe's drive-thru was slow." When he pulled his head out of the driver's side, he had a cardboard coffee carrier balanced on one palm, two large paper cups secure in the carrier with a pastry bag between them. "Black and blue," he said, their shorthand for black coffees and blueberry muffins. With his free hand he gave the pastry bag a shake, then added his patented disarming smile.

They made their way through the bookstore to the back workroom, where Maryann flipped a wall switch. A pair of ancient four-foot fluorescents in a hanging metal fixture flickered above the six-foot work table at the room's center. She toed the kick switch of a power strip, energizing the desktop computer and the printer/copier.

Aaron had been in the work room before. His sister AJ and Maryann's daughter Keegan—who never answered to her given name Dauphine, only her last name, Keegan—were childhood best friends and now high school seniors waiting to hear about college acceptances. The two of them had worked summers at Annie's. Aaron, too, had filled in on occasion in high school. He felt at home in this back room, had drunk a lot of coffee and made a lot of small talk here

He also knew the story of the Keegan family, how Maryann's father had died of a heart attack, leaving her and her sister Zelda a house and some insurance money—which they used to buy the bookstore from the previous owner who wanted to retire. Maryann left her librarian job in Boston and moved home to run the Book Stop while silent partner Zelda went off to the University of Maine at Orono. In her senior year Zelda got pregnant but just before childbirth had suffered a brain hemorrhage, with baby Dauphine Keegan being delivered by emergency C-section. Zelda died without revealing the name of the father. Aunt Maryann immediately adopted Dauphine, becoming the mother to her newborn niece. Aaron's younger sister AJ was Daupine Keegan's—she preferred to be called Keegan—best friend. So Aaron was practically a member of the Keegan family

Now he and Maryann sat across the table from each other on high wooden stools, each nursing a black coffee and a blueberry muffin.

"Aaron, this morning you said you were calling from the station. Were you coming off shift? Keegan said she thought you had three days off."

"Nice to know Keegan's keeping up with my schedule. She's right. I worked yesterday, so now I'm off three days."

Maryann broke a piece of muffin off and put it in her mouth. She raised her coffee cup in a motion that urged him to get to the point. "Can we get to the point, please? You called this meeting."

"Sure. I was there because Marcy Stonestreet texted this to me last night. My phone was off and I was asleep." He showed her the text.

Rubber suit back?

Maryann almost spit out her coffee. "Faucon is back? How does Marcy know about him? Does she know about Luna, too? If she knows, then who else knows?"

"No, no, no, and no," Aaron replied, shaking his head. "Marcy doesn't know anything. And nobody else knows anything, either."

"But you said—

"Marcy used the term *rubber suit* because that's where the Stonehedge report left it in July. There was no mention of Faucon or Luna. Only you and Keegan and AJ and Cliff and I know who was there and what happened. If you recall, we pitched that story about a sword freak or maybe an actor wearing a rubber suit and a jet pack. That's about as much as anybody else could believe. Saying it was a live gargoyle—or two gargoyles—fighting would have landed us all in therapy."

Maryann said, "Okay, so if only the five of us know about Faucon and Luna, why would Marcy think the rubber suit guy is back?"

Aaron told her about the report Thad Richards had taken at Spiller Farm from Harp Gagnon and three field workers.

"The laborers' descriptions," Aaron said, "glowing red eyes, rhino horn, deep humming sound, reminded one of them of a parade dragon."

"That's got to be Faucon," Maryann said. "Luna—the females—have green eyes. And her Allagash clan doesn't have the horn on the forehead. Faucon's French Alps clan does."

They sat quiet for a minute.

"Why is he back?" Aaron asked.

"He probably never got far after Stonehedge. Luna sliced off three of his toes and Keegan buried that ax in his back. His broad wing and his shoulder are probably still a mess. It's not like he could stop by the ER."

"We made him leave his weapons," Maryann said. "He escaped by using those short hummingbird wings, which must limit his distances."

"But he could have gone north in short hops that way," Aaron said. "He'd have eventually gotten back to their clan. Why didn't he?"

"Two possibilities I can think of. One's obvious: he doesn't know where Luna went. If she contacts us, and if we try to go to her, he can follow."

"What's the other?" Aaron asked.

"His weapons. He may need his sword and *poignard* either to save face or to try and claim the throne."

"There's a third reason," Aaron said. "Revenge. You and Keegan not only helped Luna, you also disarmed and humiliated him. You hurt him physically and wounded his pride. Ambition—his desire to steal a throne that's not legitimately his—that's a strong motivator, but don't underestimate revenge. You and Keegan may be the reason Faucon is still around."

CHAPTER 3

After he left the Book Stop, Aaron drove to Cliff Bragdon's house. The chair in the dooryard by the front porch was empty, but on the little wooden table next to the chair sat a glass, a plastic pitcher, and a paperback.

A good sign, Aaron thought. *He's following doctors' orders, taking it easy.*

Cliff was into his third month of medical/disability leave from the department now, thanks to the injuries he'd sustained in July when Faucon dive-bombed him atop the Stonehedge crypt, slamming him across the chest with a heavy sword and knocking him eight feet to the forest floor. Aaron had told his friend numerous times that broken ribs, a bruised chest, a shattered collarbone, and a steel-pinned upper arm took time to heal. But as the summer moved on to fall, the muscular twenty-five-year-old had grown increasingly impatient.

From behind the house and barn someone shouted, "Out back."

Uh-oh, maybe the empty chair isn't such a good sign after all.

Aaron parked the Jeep and walked the packed dirt driveway between the house and the barn. It opened up onto his friend's side business: firewood. Strewn about were dozens of limbed 10- to 30-foot tree trunks that were drying and waiting to be cut. A wood chipper stood close to a three-sided enclosure constructed of old boards and overflowing with a mountain of wood chips. An old Farmall field tractor squatted nearby, a hydraulic log splitter behind it. Aaron could see that Cliff's inventory was low for late September, maybe fifteen cords of dry, split firewood stacked on oak pallets. Between the firewood and the back of the barn was a Ford F-250, magnetic sign on the driver door: Cliff Bragdon, Firewood Cut, Split, Delivered, with a phone number.

He found Cliff sitting on the truck's tailgate. His face was flushed and sweaty. In the truck bed were a half dozen pieces of split oak.

"That red Jeep of yours isn't a great sneak-up vehicle," Cliff said.

"Nope," Aaron agreed, and sat on the tailgate, too. "But then again, I wasn't trying to sneak up. I come bearing turkey foot-longs from Subway."

"And a Snapple?"

Aaron set a plastic bag between them and divvied up the subs and drinks.

Cliff twisted the top off his Snapple and took a long drink. "I can't throw a few pieces of firewood into the truck without getting winded."

"That's from pushing against the pain. Exertion is one thing, exertion against pain is even harder."

"I know that. My physical therapist explained it. I think I've also lost muscle mass from inactivity, and I feel weak. That freaking garglee did a number on me. He hit me with that sword like it was Thor's hammer. It was like a cannonball in the chest."

"But if you think about it, he didn't stab you straight on or slice you. He hit you with the flat of the blade. He did it to disable you. Lucky you're still around to talk about it."

"Good point—no pun intended—but it's not getting this firewood split and delivered."

"That's why we have friends. Know how they always say, 'Anything I can do to help? They mean it, but we're always too proud or too embarrassed to ask. Keep busy with something less physical. I'll get some of the off-duty cops, EMTs, and firefighters to volunteer a little time. Maybe a few high school kids. AJ and Keegan will have an idea who to ask."

Cliff took a bite of his sandwich, making his face look rounder, glummer, and sulkier.

"So what else is this about?" Aaron asked.

CHAPTER 4

By the time Cliff arrived at five-thirty with the pizzas, Maryann had paper cold-drink cups, paper plates, and a stack of napkins on the trestle table. Aaron sat across from Keegan and AJ, filling them in on the previous night's activities at Spiller Farm.

"So does this mean gargoyles are vegetarian?" AJ asked. "There were chickens, ducks, geese, and cows there for take-out."

"Sounds like you've discussed things to death," Cliff said, and laid the triple stack of pizza boxes on the end of the table. "Bet you started with the scary stuff and are now down to the silly stuff."

"When Aaron started telling us what happened at the orchard," AJ said, "Ms. K went around locking the windows and doors."

"Did not," Maryann protested.

"Did, too, Mom," Keegan said.

"They should have been locked, anyway," her mother replied.

Cliff pulled a kitchen chair up to the end of the table. When he saw the girls' brows wrinkle at his seating choice, he put a hand on his ribs. "Still sore. The chair's easier than getting in and out of your picnic benches." He set a cardboard six-pack carrier on the table and lifted out a bottle of Geary's Pale Ale. "Aaron? Maryann? I hit Hannaford before I picked up the pizzas."

Aaron raised a hand and Cliff slid it along the polished tabletop table like a movie bartender. Aaron barehanded it and popped the top.

Maryann gave the no-thanks sign but grabbed the remaining four and said, "Fridge," then walked away with them.

"I assume you had the gun discussion?" Cliff asked.

"Yep. It went nowhere," Aaron said.

"Not surprised. You try to interest the ladies in mace, pepper spray, maybe bear spray?"

19

"Cliff," Aaron said, "I suggested all those and more, including a cane with a hidden sword in it."

"So you failed in your mission, Officer Stevenson?"

"Mightily. What finally defeated me was Keegan's argument that she's got her trusty Louisville slugger upstairs."

"She didn't bring up the ax she used the first time?" Cliff asked. "Or the sword she captured from him?"

"No, I didn't," Keegan cut in. "Just the bat. The others are too violent. I hope to never use the ax that way again."

Cliff said, "But let me point out, Faucon did break in here once before. And that was with all the windows latched and the doors locked. Didn't he smash the deck door and ransack your bedroom?"

AJ came to her friend's defense. "He was after the books Luna ordered. He wasn't after Keegan or Ms. K. If he'd come for them, he'd have met the Louisville slugger."

"Back to the gun question," Keegan said. "You and Aaron have stressed to us that breaking and entering isn't a shoot-able offense."

"Besides," Maryann said, back from the kitchen now. "If Faucon wanted to come after one of us now, he'd more likely chase us down outside, and at night, since *gargouilles* are slow in sunlight. To my, Keegan's, and AJ's point, Cliff—keeping a gun here in the house doesn't make sense. But we appreciate your and Aaron's concern."

Cliff looked around the table at the three females and saw Aaron's head hanging and his eyes glued to the table in front of him. "Alrighty then," he said. "Good discussion. Shall we eat?"

"My thoughts, exactly," Maryann said, and they dealt out the three boxes, flipped open the lids, and fell upon the pizzas like starved hyenas on an ailing antelope.

After everyone had downed two or three slices each, their mouths were once again available for talking. Keegan led off.

"We know Faucon's hummingbird wings work, because Harp's orchard workers heard a hum and caught him hovering. And one of his broad wings—Luna said they sometimes call them great or glide or angel wings—is damaged, thanks to my ax. So why couldn't he fly home to his Allagash clan in short hops? Why is he still here?"

"He can't go back without his weapons," AJ said. "He's embarrassed."

"I think Faucon is waiting to see what happened to Luna after the battle," Aaron said. "He left without knowing if Luna found her sister's nest. Which means he doesn't know Luna, Maryann, Keegan, and AJ hatched the eggs. He doesn't know there are three legitimate heirs to King Cyrus's throne."

"Don't forget revenge," Cliff said. "He must hate Keegan and Maryann for foiling him."

"Not buying it," Maryann said. "He'd have tried to get back at us by now. I think he's sick and injured."

"So let's go back to Luna," Aaron said. "You three drove her north with the three baby gargoyles and waited for her to get her two friends. Then they took the kids and flew off to who-knows-where."

"They're in hiding," Keegan said. "If they take the two females back to the clan, they'll be culled—killed—to protect the male heir's right to succession. Their only choice, for the three of them and the babies, is to go into hiding while they make a plan."

"Any word from her?" AJ asked.

"Not a clue," Keegan said. "And we have no phone number, no email, and no mailing address. Which is probably wise, if she doesn't want anybody to know about the babies."

Cliff looked down the table at Maryann and Keegan. "So we've got Faucon making stupid mistakes, drawing attention to the existence of a gargoyle race, while we wait for Luna to contact you two?"

Maryann and Keegan shrugged. Then Keegan said, "For me and Mom and AJ, I don't think it's so much about the hiding or revealing of a secret race. It's more basic. We want to know how they're doing, the babies we helped birth. We had to kiss them goodbye the next day, and we don't know if they're okay. We don't care if one is the heir to the *gargouilles* throne. We just want to know that our babies—our nieces, nephew, grandchildren, whatever they may be—are okay. We don't see kings, queens, princes, and princesses. We just see babies—our babies."

"Keegan also wants to hear from Luna for another reason," Maryann said. "Before she and her friends flew off, Luna told us that Keegan's birth father—who, we now know, had the same white streak in his hair—knew my sister Zelda at UMO. His name was Jan, pronounced *Yon*. We'd like to know if there's more Luna can tell us, so we can find him."

"I've been going crazy online, checking UMO's graduating classes for someone named Jan," Maryann went on. "And before you ask, yes, she has been in touch with the registrar, who can't seem to find a student named Jan in the 1990s. Which is why we'd like to see if Luna can remember a little more that could be helpful. If we had a last name, we could do a data search of the Netherlands and contact him."

Aaron, Cliff, and AJ looked sympathetic.

"Want me to try?" Aaron asked. "I could also get Stedman on it. He's still out on medical leave. He's got connections. But for now he doesn't know Faucon and Luna are gargoyles. He doesn't have to know. All he has to know is: this is a paternity thing, a 20 year-old missing-persons cold case."

Keegan didn't say no. Maryann nodded yes. "Any help would be appreciated."

"Okay," Aaron said. "But I'll need your cooperation. And Keegan's."

"Meaning what?" Maryann asked.

"Any of your sister's papers, documents, and letters—those she received or those she wrote to you."

"I have a few letters," Maryann said, and looked across the table at Keegan. "Keegan's got some things, too."

The banana box, Keegan thought. *The internship notes. And Zelda's little wire-bound notebook that had my name in it—Dauphine—before I was born.* She made a mental note to go through it again before she went to sleep, in case there was some clue she had missed. Then, at some time in the future, she'd share it with Aaron and probably with Detective Stedman.

CHAPTER 5

By the time the table was cleared and the thank-yous and goodbyes were said, it was eight o'clock and full dark.

Keegan mock-warned the departing guests, "Don't stop for strangers."

Maryann added a song lyric, "And don't sit under that apple tree with anyone else but me."

AJ, Aaron, and Cliff groaned and rolled their eyes.

"Seriously," Maryann said. "Be careful. He's out there."

As soon as the others were out the door, Keegan said, "Let's hit the attic, Mom. Your show's not on for an hour. I want to pull down any Zelda boxes you've got stashed away. Shouldn't take us long."

They went upstairs and Maryann opened the attic door, then reached around the doorframe and flipped a switch. Three 40-watt incandescent bulbs blinked on, giving the attic's contents—despite things being well organized and stacked—a fuzzy look. There was an illusion of a room, but it was really just a rectangle organized around a floor of nailed-down plywood sheets and bordered by three-foot knee-walls made of cheap paneling. The space wasn't cluttered, but it was crowded: old bureaus, a cedar wardrobe, three antique oak dressers, an oval full-length mirror, a pair of blond end tables, an assembled six-foot Christmas tree with lights but no decorations on it, and plenty of cardboard boxes stacked three and four high and pressed back against the knee-walls. They walked together down the center under the roof's ridgeline until they reached the far end.

Maryann stopped and gestured. "Zelda's corner is what Dad always called it." She peeled back a dusty bedsheet, gave it a shake and coughed. "Probably shouldn't have done that."

Keegan turned on her iPhone flashlight. What she saw—stacked and arranged almost in a square, as if on four shipping pallets—was a collection of cardboard boxes, suitcases, furniture and lamps, a skateboard, a tan file cabinet, and a photographer's tripod.

"It was Zelda's space even before she went off to college. I added a few more things after she died—like the banana boxes I gave you this summer."

Keegan stared at her birth mother's corner. She'd always known it was there in the attic, but without a living emotional bond to the woman who had died as she was about to give birth, it hadn't drawn her to explore. Maybe because she had a mother—Maryann—curiosity alone wasn't enough. But now that she had some hope of finding her biological father, she was drawn to seek him out, too, through her biological mother.

"Which of the boxes are from her college years?"

"Those four across the top. Mostly college papers, notebooks, and textbooks, as I recall. I taped them shut and marked them with a Z. You already have her summer internship files—the Wells Historical Society project—that were in the blue-and-yellow banana box."

"Okay, I'm going to take the college boxes to my room."

"How about we start with two for now?" Maryann said. "You know where they are, you can get them anytime."

They took the two boxes marked *Z UMO Sr* and *Z UMO Jr*, turned out the lights, and closed the attic door.

***

Keegan lay sitting up on her bed but didn't open either box. Instead she pulled out her journal, thought back to the July evening when she and AJ and Maryann had said goodbye to Luna and Luna's sister's newborns. She wished now that she had written it down right after Luna and her two friends—or were they accomplices—flew away with the three gargoyle hatchlings. Now she had a chance to try and get things recorded accurately.

She wrote: *Luna told me that Jan (she pronounced it Yon) had the same white streak in his hair that I have. She didn't recall his last name, but she was pretty sure he was from Holland. She didn't say Netherlands, she said Holland. (*Look up the difference.) Luna said it was Z's senior year and Jan may have been at UMO for his teaching certification. (*Why would he get a U.S. certification if he was teaching in Holland/Netherlands?) She said he was about 20 or 30 years older than Z (making him about 40 or 50 then, 60 to 70 now). Luna says she saw him but never really met or talked with him. She has no idea if Jan knows about me.*

She added: *Luna thought Jan was a very common Dutch name like John or Jon in the USA. I called UMO Registrar several times, but she hasn't been able to find a UMO student with first name of Jan in 1990s. And no Dutch foreign students ever with that name.*

Keegan reached down beside her bed and grabbed her college sit-up study pillow. It had been Zelda's in college and had somehow not gotten stashed with her mother's other college stuff in the attic. The pillow was now close to 20 years-old. She flipped it over her head and into place behind her hips and lower back. She often used it when she sat on the bed and read.

She set her journal aside and opened the Z UMO Sr box, then started pulling out Zelda's 8 ½ x 11 wire-bound notebooks. She browsed one, set it on the floor, and did the same with a second and a third and a fourth. Nothing jumped out at her.

Until the genealogy course notebook. On the inside back cover Zelda had scrawled *Jan* and a phone number. Keegan marked the place with a yellow sticky, noted what she'd found in her journal, and moved on to examine more notebooks. Before she reached the bottom of the box, her eyelids grew heavy and she nodded off. She heard a familiar voice that wasn't quite her own and wasn't quite Maryann's whisper *Dauphine.*

Chapter 6

A sliver of moon lit the hardscrabble clearing in front of the cave's entrance. Decades old pines towered above a skirt of underbrush, forming a natural stockade fence. Fifty yards away, where the flinty soil met the exposed rock dome of the cave, water bubbled out of the ground, a natural spring. They had chosen this hiding place because the meadow was easy to watch from the cave's entrance. And it was long enough for takeoffs when they used their broad angel wings. The cave and the clearing in front were high, remote, and defensible, while also giving the three *gargouilles* access to hunting and foraging grounds.

The three hatchlings were three months old now and had become toddlers, bouncing and balancing and falling over like baby condors on the apron of dirt at the mouth of the cave.

Luna and Yvette sat outside on their haunches, looking like two mothers chatting at a playground playdate, watching the infants. The squatting posture also left them looking like statues their ancient race had inspired—grotesques and gargoyles, those sculpted stone 'guardians' hiding Paris's tallest buildings' rainspouts. They looked on as their three charges navigated the soft dirt and the crunchy gravel, tripping on rock outcroppings and catching their toes in the clumps of grass and low bushes that were new to them. At six weeks they were less clumsy using their hands and arms, but they hadn't a clue about what to do with their budding hummingbird wings or the heavier angel wings that, as they grew heavier, would press down on their shoulders, threatening to make them look like hunchbacks. Little did they know those same broad angel wings would later help them soar like eagles.

One little female waddled after the other, catching her foot on a root first and then on a jutting rock. She fell forward, her thickly helmeted head catching the heel of her sister, who also pitched forward.

"*Soyez prudents, mes enfants*," Luna said in French, and Yvette echoed it in English. "Be careful, my children." But neither adult rushed to the fallen pair. Experience was necessary for growth. Tripping and falling would harden them.

There was another sibling, too, a male. None of the three little ones was Luna's, Yvette's, or the Welsh *gargouille* Bronwyn's, whose turn it was to hunt and forage.

The two pudgy females, Regine and Mathilde, lay on the ground like downed novice cross-country skiers, chortling and laughing, straining and struggling to gain their feet again. Their brother Paladin preferred to hang back near the cave entrance and observe, gaining secondhand experience. The three infants-turning-toddlers had come from the eggs of Prince LeClair and Luna's sister Diana, both of whom were *morte.*

Of the newborns, according to the patriarchal tradition of *les gargouilles*, only the male, Paladin, qualified as an heir. The three adult females shared a different opinion. They were appalled that female hatchlings—not all, but those in the nest containing heirs to a clan throne or the king's throne—by patriarchal tradition, had to be "culled," murdered at birth, to eliminate any potential competition for the birthright males. Luna and her friends saw Regine and Mathilde, not just Paladin, as successors to King Cyrus, who was nearing the end of a typical gargoyle's lifespan.

The problem was—except for five humans in Wells, Maine—Luna, Yvette, and Bronwyn were the only *gargouilles* who knew of the existence of Diana and LeClair's children. Which was why the six of them were in hiding in a cave in the Maine wilderness. At least for now.

If Faucon, Cyrus's adopted grandson—*Luna saw him as the pretender to the throne*—found out that the eggs had been found and hatched, and that a male heir, Paladin, existed, he'd certainly seek him out and kill him. If the rest of *les gargouilles* found out, they'd carry out the tradition—*culling*—killing any females before they could become challengers. The patriarchal tradition was deeply embedded.

So, for the time being, Luna and her friends had no choice but to hide out. The fewer who knew, the safer they were.

***

The three babies and their protectors weren't the only *gargouilles* active that night.

Faucon could see from his hiding place in the treetops that a half dozen migrant laborers armed with shotguns had taken up positions around Spiller's orchard. The local fruits and vegetables would no longer be easy picking for him. So he headed east toward the coast.

***

Bronwyn, the Welsh *gargouille* who had been adopted into the Allagash clan, was also active, seeking food for her friends Luna and Yvette and the three infants back at the cave. While Faucon hunted and foraged near Wells and the Kennebunks, Bronwyn flew over the fields, forests, ponds and streams a hundred miles north and east of Wells. She collected crabapples, late-season blueberries, potatoes, nuts, and the occasional salmon or trout. While the babies needed mashed fruits, berries, pulverized roots, the three adults could gorge themselves on raw fish, potatoes, and apples.

***

Gargouilles were also active near the US/Canada border, where the Allagash clan had occupied an underground fifty-room cavern for almost a thousand years.

Angelina, a square-jawed Argentinian *gargouille*, had fled her clan during a bloody coup and sought refuge with the Allagash clan. King Cyrus, already past three hundred and fifty years old, took her in as a masseuse and maidservant. Tonight she entered his quarters, a twenty by twenty candlelit room deep in the massive clan cavern, carrying the king's meal: smashed raw potatoes, quartered apples, and pink salmon flesh. She set it before him on a small plank table.

"I have little hunger," he said. "I can feel myself growing older and weaker, as if I am becoming a shadow." The ancient warrior's once-powerful glide wings hung loosely from the backs of his shoulders like two weathered pieces of canvas. His chest, once bursting with muscle, looked deflated now, the skin covering his collarbone and breastbone loose and saggy like the jowls under his jawbone.

Angelina set the meal down, said, "You have to eat," and stepped back. She placed her hands on the cords of his neck and gently massaged them.

"I am sorry I did not know you two centuries ago," he said, "after my mate Giselle went to ground with our eggs."

"LeClair and Champaigne," she said, "the twin princes." She planted a light kiss on the back of his head.

"*Oui*," he replied wistfully, and reached back to give her hand an affectionate pat. "And where are they now? They should be where I am and I should be where they are. No father should outlive his sons. And no leader his heirs."

"*Si*, it is sad," she agreed. "On nights such as these, daughters could be a comfort."

"*Sans doute*," he said, his voice heavy. "But kings and clan chiefs have only sons. It is the price of leadership."

"The price of leadership?" she said, her voice edgy and with less sympathy in it now. "Or the cost of ambition? Fathers make choices. In each clan's royal bloodline—if the males wish to ascend—they make choices. They return to the nest when it is time, and they choose to bring home the males that hatch. And they destroy the females. Is that not as violent as the bloody coup I witnessed in my home clan?"

Cyrus's shoulders tensed and he stepped forward, pulling away from her touch. Without turning to face her, he said, "Leave me. And leave this clan."

"You cast me out? What have I done?"

He turned to face her, his eyes fiery red with anger. "Has Luna poisoned your mind? You have called me—*your clan chief and your king*—a murderer."

"But—

"Gather your things," he said, fighting to keep his voice low and his outrage under control. "Quickly. Leave tonight with your life."

"But where will I—

"Go!"

Hurt and terrified, Angelina shuffled as quickly as her short legs would carry her out of the king's quarters, hoping she could be in the air before he changed his mind.

CHAPTER 7

Dewey Carpenter loved surf fishing in Wells, Maine. His wife Francine loved cruises. So did two of her girlfriends. So every September, a couple weeks after Labor Day, Dewey and Francine left their Worcester, Massachusetts ranch house and went on vacation for a week or 10 days—but not together. They'd run through a checklist with Kimmy, the stay-in-your-home dog-sitter, then hug and kiss their overweight yellow labs Mac and Cheez goodbye and climb into their respective vehicles.

Francine took her minivan so she could pick up her friends for the cruise. Dewey took the Silverado with its waterproof bed liner that stretched from back of cab to tailgate as tight as a trampoline. Beneath the liner were items he had packed days ahead of time—the exact same stuff as the year before and the year before that: a duffel bag, a backpack, fishing gear, a sleeping bag, a Coleman lantern, a pair of foldup aluminum-and-canvas chairs—one at sitting height, the other beach level—an ice chest, and an inflatable fishing kayak with a thin life preserver and a telescoping, double-ended aluminum paddle. After a detour through a Worcester Dunkin drive-thru for a large coffee and a couple of glazed donuts, he'd set out on the two hour drive to southern Maine.

Which is how, at two in the morning, long after the Drake's Island Beach's parking lot gates had been closed and locked, Dewey Carpenter came to be dozing in his low canvas chair in front of the dunes, 20 feet above the high-water mark and a long stone's throw from the rock breakwater that kept open the channel to Wells Harbor.

A gray Army blanket covered Dewey's legs and torso, and, as the night grew chillier, he dozed with it pulled it up over his shoulders. Two fishing poles lay to his left. He had used the sand to his right as a cup-holder, jamming a bottle of Jim Beam into it, two fingers of liquid remaining in the bottom. Between his knees sat a Styrofoam ice chest, its lid a few feet away. A pair of good-sized bass stared up out of the cooler.

Dewey had arrived at nine p.m., two hours before high tide. By midnight he'd hooked the two bass, one from the river channel between the breakwaters, the other from the sandy shoreline. Shortly after that he'd settled into his chair with his pal Jim Beam to stare up at the Atlantic sky and smell the ocean.

He snored lightly, then snorted, waking himself up. For a moment he forgot where he was. Then he smelled the salt air and heard the light waves lapping at the water's edge somewhere far in front of him. It was time to carry his poles and chair and ice chest back to where he'd tied off his rubber kayak near the closed parking lot. He would paddle inland to where he'd parked the Silverado, load up and get back to the motel. He could ice the fish and sleep 'til noon. Then he'd have the afternoon off, seafood at Fisherman's Catch or Billy's Chowder House, grab a quick after-supper nap, and repeat the evening plan.

Then Dewey heard something up the coast. His eyes tried to pinpoint the sound, which was like the hum or thrum of a tie-down strap on the back of his pickup when he was transporting. He looked toward the shoreline a quarter mile north, seeing in the distance the familiar lights of Kennebunkport, Ocean Avenue, and the Walker's Point compound of the elder President Bush. The humming stopped and, by the light of the stars, a sliver of moon, and the yard lamp of a Drake's Island rental cottage, Dewey thought he could see a shadowy bent-over beachcomber—a sight more common in daytime and not at all in the middle of the night. He sat unmoving in his beach chair, huddled under his Army blanket, staring at the dark figure.

It shuffled. Then it stopped, bent down to the water, straightened up—though it still appeared hunched—and shuffled forward again. Coming along the water's edge toward the breakwater. What was it doing?

Dewey looked away for a moment, glanced to his right toward the buoy off the upper breakwater and the light at the end of the breakwater. When he turned to look toward Kennebunkport again, a glowing red light—like a channel marker—shone where the beachcomber's head sat atop the slumped shoulders. Not one red light but two—like glowing coals. Were they staring at him? Then they blinked out and the figure shuffled farther along.

Dewey felt suddenly chilly and pulled the Army blanket closer. Without taking his eyes off the dark shape of the beachcomber he reached out from under the blanket with his right arm and grabbed Jim Beam by the neck. He moved his arm slowly, raising the bottle to his lips while watching the stranger. He swallowed hard, a big warming gulp that spread through his chest and shoulders and down to his bowels.

The night visitor advanced slowly along the waterline, moving forward like an arthritic grandparent, occasionally turning from the ocean to glance toward the dunes, which was when the light from the stars reflected off the blood-red eyes. Whoever it was down in the lapping waves and foam, he or she didn't seem to notice Dewey where he sat stock still against the dunes, sipping slowly, nervously now.

The figure reached the place where the solid sand became a rock ring, a tide pool that, as the tide ebbed, left crabs and snails and a few lobsters and small fish trapped. The visitor—who looked like a huge gray, muscular hunchback—waded awkwardly among the rocks, working hard to keep his or her balance. The night visitor bent carefully and scooped around in the captured seawater then stood upright again—with something in its grasp. A fish? A softshell crab? Seaweed or kelp? Whatever it was that was lifted from the tidal pool, it went to the shadow figure's mouth. Each and every time.

Dewey finished his last swig of Jim Beam and set the bottle aside on the sand.

The red eyes glowed again, directly ahead of him—50 yards ahead of him—at the waterline. Looking his way. Had it seen the bottle move—caught a glint of moonlight off the glass?

The beachcomber shuffled out of the tidal pool and started advancing slowly from the waterline toward the dunes. Toward Dewey's fishing camp. To say hello? To share a smoke or a drink? To shoot the breeze—two lonely beach bums out at two a.m.?

Dewey didn't think so. He could probably outrun the arthritic old grandfather if he had to. But what about his fishing poles, his chair, his blanket. And his Jim Beam bottle. He never left trash on the beach. It was evidence that he was sneaking across the harbor after closing time.

As the night visitor cut the distance in half, Dewey closed his eyes, feigned sleep. Nobody would be so insensitive as to wake a sleeping night fisherman.

He heard the visitor's heavy feet draw closer, kicking sand in front of them like a fat man in heavy boots might do, shuffling, forcing his legs forward.

And then the noise stopped, and he knew whoever it was, was standing directly in front of him, almost toe to toe, as if calling him out. Staring down at him with those glowing, blood-red eyes.

Dewey didn't want to look. But he heard the Styrofoam cooler crunch, and he couldn't help himself. He tried to open his eyes only a slit, but once he saw what stood before him, they flew wide open in shock. A reptilian creature with a horn in the center of its forehead held his two fish up by their tails—one in each hand—almost proudly, with a sardonic grin. Then something behind its arms appeared—wings that began to vibrate at incredible speed. Dewey felt the breeze mussing his hair and drying his eyes, pieces of sand grit glancing off his cheeks and forehead, accompanied by the same deep loud hum—a thousand angry hummingbirds, he thought—the same sound he'd heard from a distance when this thing was a quarter mile up the beach. He would later describe it to the first town cop as some sort of giant bat with a vaguely human-like face— maybe a vampire—then, to the cop's sketch artist, as something akin to a bearded dragon. The humming sound intensified and then—still clutching the two large fish—the creature shot straight up and away, leaving Dewey suddenly sober, with a hammering heart and a racing pulse.

CHAPTER 8

It was mid-morning Friday when Aaron turned off the main drag next to the Moody Post Office and took a right into Elly Stedman's cul-de-sac. As soon as he turned the corner onto the detective's street he could see the stocky cop walking a garden hose along the edge of his driveway, soaking a line of potted mums.

"Morning, Sarge," Aaron said when he got out of his Jeep.

"Aaron," Stedman said, and kept watering.

"Your chrysanthemums are beautiful. Healthy. I love the rust-colored and the purple. You gonna stick 'em in the ground or leave 'em out?"

"Dig 'em in along the front of the house in a week or so, before any predicted frost. It'll gain them a month."

"How're the ribs?"

Stedman patted his side. "I can feel 'em when I step on a shovel. Or lift these pots when they're full of water." He doused the last mum in line, a bright white one, and manipulated the hose nozzle to stop the flow. "Let's go to the shop."

The house was a boxy four-bedroom, one-bath modular Stedman called his snap-together home kit, financed by Uncle Sam in exchange for four years of Navy duty. The walls and roof had arrived from New Hampshire early one morning and by evening had been hoisted into place, bolted onto the waiting foundation, and fastened together. In less than a month the plumbing, electrical, and finish work were done and Stedman moved in. A year later he added a two-car modular garage, to which he added a center wall that divided it into a one-car garage and a workshop.

Aaron followed Stedman into the shop, which smelled like pine shavings with a hint of whatever on-sale coffee Stedman had just brewed. The workbench and tools occupied the common wall. A long rubber work mat lay on the cement floor in front of the bench and a tan nine-by-twelve area rug covered most of the rest of the floor, a brown swivel rocker/recliner with threadbare arms and a well-worn seat anchored one end.

What Stedman referred to a his "entertainment center" took up most of the long exterior wall: an old digital clock radio with giant red numerals, a 40" TV on plastic feet, and an Acer desktop, separate speakers, and an HP printer/copier/fax. All of the equipment was arranged on a half dozen tongue-and-groove floorboards Stedman had stretched across three paint-spattered sawhorses. A gray roll-around office chair faced the desktop. There was also a black metal folding chair with a large black stencil on its back: Wells P.D.

"Sit," Stedman said, nodding to the chairs.

Aaron took the folding chair and Stedman set his coffee next to the keyboard then sat, working to muffle a groan as he eased himself onto the office chair.

"Time for you to tell me what's going on," Stedman said, and turned to face the computer. He rested his hands at the edge of the keyboard.

Aaron said nothing.

"Okay," Stedman said, and his fingers took to the keys, typing as he talked. "You're here this morning because Annie Fitzgerald called me, our art student and on-call sketch artist extraordinaire. She told me you were sniffing around the station early, even though you're off for a couple days."

"I like to—"

"I'm still talking," Stedman said firmly, his computer screen now displaying his email Inbox. "The reason Fitz got called to the station is because a half-in-the-bag fisherman stumbled in the station about 3:30 a.m., babbling about a vampire stealing his two striped bass. Rob Hustus took the report—said it reminded him of the Spiller Farm orchard story—

and kept the fisherman around until Fitz could come in with her iPad to sketch this so-called vampire."

Stedman opened a file and an image appeared on the screen. It showed a drawing of a figure with glowing red eyes and a horn in the middle of its forehead.

"Is that your Stonehedge guy?" Stedman asked. "With the jetpack?"

Aaron stared at the monitor. He hadn't really seen the gargoyle Faucon up close, because it had been dark when he dropped between him and Keegan and head-butted him into la-la land.

"Yes," Aaron said. "I was there when Fitz was sketching that one."

Stedman opened a second jpeg attachment.

Aaron squinted at it. "The orchard?" he asked. It looked like Faucon again, this time hovering at a distance.

Stedman didn't wait for him to acknowledge the red-eyed figure. "After you left the station, Fitz called Harp Gagnon and his farm workers and asked them to come to the station so she could draw what they saw. She'd heard about the flying purple people-eater everybody had discounted. Nobody thought it warranted a sketch."

Aaron said with a weak smile, "No department's going to put out a BOLO for theft of fruit."

Stedman didn't laugh.

Aaron cleared his throat and said, "When I saw Fitz doing the fisherman's sketch, I didn't know about the Spiller crew. I mean, I knew about the incident from the report, but I didn't have the drawing for a comparison. Now I guess they're similar enough that we can say it's a composite of the perp."

Stedman turned his office chair toward Aaron. "This isn't some actor in a monster mask and a jet pack, is it?"

Aaron tried to look impassive, inscrutable, then admitted, "No, it's not. It's not an actor. It's not a human."

"Hmph," Stedman said, without revealing much. He went back to typing on his keyboard and brought up the stop-and-go store surveillance video from the security camera at Annie's Book Stop three months earlier. A hunched figure in a dark robe, hood, and V-is-for-Vendetta mask filled the frame of the bookstore's front door.

"You and I have seen this footage before," Aaron said. "It's what led us to the York Historical Society Gift Shop stakeout this summer that landed you in the hospital."

"What I'm asking is, do you agree that the bookstore thief who flattened me is the same person—or thing—the workers encountered at the Spiller's orchard and the fisherman saw at the beach?"

"Yes."

"So this flying thing is also the one who stole Geoff Swett's rare Civil War book from Toil and Trouble?

"Yes," Aaron said.

"Which doesn't explain why he did it, but it explains why we found no ladder marks on the ground at a second-story burglary. The guy, the apple thief, can hover."

"Yes."

"Anything else to add," Stedman asked, "since we're putting pieces together?"

Aaron scrunched his lips, considering. "I filed a report the same night as the Swett break-in, one from the dishwashers at the Maine Diner. The kids said a super-goose or a pterodactyl flew over and glared down at them. It had glowing red eyes—like Fitz's drawings. Back then I had no reason to ask them to work with Fitz on a sketch."

Stedman tilted back in his office chair. "So this is definitely not some independent film actor in a monster suit with a jetpack. If I hear you right, you're saying it's not a person, not a human being?"

"Correct. Remember the books we read about Joshua Chamberlain's Civil War scouts, The Night Hawks?"

"Confederates called them harpies and banshees," Stedman said.

"Yes. And one of the Spiller Farm workers called it a dragon. The Maine Diner dishwashers said it was a flying dinosaur. The fisherman says it was a vampire."

"They're all describing the same thing with different metaphors," Stedman said.

"Exactly. Keegan figured it out first, then her mother. Cliff and I were a little slower."

"You know? You know and you didn't say anything?"

"I'm telling you now," Aaron said.

"Okay, so tell me, already. What's left? Godzilla? The Terminator?"

His name is Faucon. He's a gargoyle."

Elly Stedman's face was a question mark. "A gargoyle?"

"Yep. And he's not the only one."

CHAPTER 9

After Aaron left, Stedman called Maryann at the bookstore

"Maryann? Elly Stedman."

She said good morning and asked the expected questions about his recovery.

"Let me cut to the chase, Maryann. I know your Stonehedge story about the rubber mask and jetpack is a cover. Whatever that thing was—gargoyle or something else—it's what bulldozed me and put me in the hospital. The difference between us is, I never saw it. You did."

In the background Stedman heard the tea bell over the bookstore's front door tinkle. "Customer," Stedman said into the phone. "I'll wait."

"Hi, Donna," Maryann said away from the phone. "Need help, let me know." Then she was back, "Elly," she whispered impatiently. "Just what are you calling about?"

"We need to talk about this, so we're all on the same page. You, me, Keegan, AJ, Aaron, and Cliff."

"Talk about what?" she asked.

"You know." He waited.

A brief pause, then she said, "By talk, you don't mean at the station, do you? Officially?"

"Something tells me you wouldn't. So, how about at the bookstore or your house?"

"Off-the-record, right? Nobody'd believe it, anyway."

"Maryann," he said, and worked hard to form his words. "That thing I never saw—it almost killed me. And Cliff. And Aaron. I need to know the whole story. I need to know what the rest of you know."

She still didn't fold, so he played his hole card.

"Aaron told me about the gargoyles."

A brief pause, then, "Be here at the store at four o'clock. I'll text Aaron to pick up Keegan and AJ at school. You call Cliff."

***

Cliff's empty firewood truck pulled up in front of the Book Stop at three-forty-five. He parked and walked inside carrying a rope-handled Reny's bag in one hand, a few paperbacks in it, a square Entenmann's box in the other.

"Leave the books here," she said, and he lifted them onto the counter. "Take the Entenmann's to the work room. Mr. Coffee's set to go. Push the button."

Aaron arrived next and parked by Cliff's truck. Keegan and AJ got out and paraded in with him.

"Break room?" Keegan asked.

"I prefer to call it the work room," her mother said.

"Perspective, Mom," Keegan said, mugging for Maryann, and led AJ and her brother to the back.

Elly Stedman was last, strolling in at three-fifty-nine with iPad in hand.

"Lock it behind you," Maryann directed him. "Meet you in the work room."

While the others poured their coffees and grabbed coffee cake, Stedman propped up his iPad so he had a keyboard and standup monitor. Everyone looked his way.

"Okay," he said. "I need to know the actual story, not the Jason-in-the-hockey-mask version."

They just stared at him.

"Now that Aaron told me we're dealing with gargoyles— yes, it sounds crazy when I say it out loud—it's the only way things make sense. The floor is yours. You have my attention."

"Are you here as a cop?" Keegan asked. "Or as an individual?"

"Does it matter?" he said.

"Matters to us," Keegan said. "Didn't you ever watch King Kong or Jurassic Park?"

"What?"

"She means," Maryann said, looking directly across the table at him, "are you going to alert the government so they can go after them? Put them in chains or in cages or keep them in a zoo as a newly discovered species?"

"No. I happen to be a cop, but this isn't an official investigation. I'm here as me. Clearly Aaron and Cliff aren't here on official business, either, or they wouldn't have withheld as much information as they have."

The others simply sipped their coffees.

Stedman said, "Police reports the last couple of days—weird, unexplainable reports—suggest we're dealing with the same character, or should I say creature, who steamrolled me and put me in York Hospital. I'm finally getting to the end of a three-month medical leave."

"So, just to be clear," Keegan said. "Whatever we share tonight isn't for the police or other authorities, right? It's just to satisfy your own curiosity?"

"I'm not trying to 'out' an ancient race that has remained out of sight for thousands of years, if that's what you're asking."

"They haven't hurt anybody," AJ chimed in. "They seem to go out of their way to not hurt or kill humans."

"Tell that to my ribs," Stedman said.

"And my ribs, collarbone, and arm," Cliff added.

"And my nose and forehead," Aaron said.

"Look," Keegan said. "If Faucon wanted to kill you at the Historical Society that night, he could have. He could have run his sword through Cliff at Stonehedge, too, but instead he used a sideways swing to knock the wind out of him. And rather than stab Aaron at close range with his thrusting dagger, Faucon head-butted him with that rhino horn."

"Okay, okay, this isn't the time to argue that," Stedman said. "Let's deal with the present. Aaron's been on top of things at the station. Aaron?"

"It appears to me that Faucon is stuck in this area, whatever the reason. Keegan perforated his wing and shoulder with her ax at Stonehedge, which may limit him to those short wings—hummingbird wings. That's why the farm workers at Spiller's orchard heard the hum and saw him hovering above the apple tree. He's hungry, and he's got to turn to local food sources. His wounded upper wing keeps him from diving like a hawk."

"Which would also explain why Faucon walked up the beach and stole two bass from a fisherman at Drake's Island," Cliff said. "He couldn't swoop down to grab his own catch."

Keegan asked Aaron and Cliff, "You haven't had any reports of missing livestock, though, have you—no sheep, cows, goats, chickens, dogs, cats?"

"No," Aaron answered.

Stedman said, "Since I'm the newcomer in the mix and trust is apparently an issue, why don't I tell you what I know? You can fill in the blanks along the way."

His narrative began with what they already knew. In July he had been the detective called to investigate a late-night, second-story break-in at Geoff Swett's Toil & Trouble book business, which bought and sold rare and unusual books in online auctions. Aaron had been the first to respond to the triggering of a silent alarm. Several nights later, Stedman was called to investigate a burglary that Cliff responded to, this one at Maryann's bookstore. And later that day the Keegan home was forcibly entered and ransacked.

"It was Faucon who hit the Book Stop and my bedroom," Keegan said. "He wanted the books Luna ordered. She had thought they might help her find her sister's eggs. And, by the way, the proper term is *gargouille*." She enunciated the French

45

word: *gar-gwee*. "Gargoyles are statues that disguise drainpipes on buildings like cathedrals."

"Sorry," Stedman said. "Pardon my French. *Gargouilles*."

Keegan went back to her story. "Faucon followed Luna here. He was afraid she might be successful in locating Diana's grave and her eggs. If Luna could get to them before their—what'll we call it, *expiration date*—there was an outside chance she could hatch them. Some of them, anyway. Their father LeClair was the next-in-line to the *gargouille* throne, but he died. Faucon seems to think he has a claim."

"Faucon and Luna were after the same books," AJ said. "Because they thought they'd lead them to the eggs."

"Which were LeClair and Diana's offspring," Stedman said. "I read about him and his brother Champaigne in the *Night Hawks* book, so I'm able to put a few of the pieces together."

"LeClair was the heir," Maryann said. "Champaigne was the spare." She explained how Faucon's father Drago had given his life to save both princes during a battle in WW1. "But they both eventually lost the battle with the effects of mustard gas. LeClair died on the voyage home. Champaigne maybe twenty years ago. But before Champaigne died, he tried to pay his brother's and his debt to Drago's family—by adopting Faucon."

"Hence Faucon's spurious claim to Cyrus' throne," Stedman said.

"Exactly," Keegan said.

"Okay, for now forget this *gargouille* kingdom's politics and lay out for me what really happened at Stonehedge. The police report begs a lot of questions."

They described what happened—each of the five from a different perspective: Keegan and AJ using a Come-Along to winch open the granite crypt's roof, their encounters with the sword-wielding Faucon, Keegan discovering the secret tunnel, Maryann locating the eggs, AJ and Keegan and Maryann helping

Luna hatch them, and finally the release of Luna and the three newborns near the Allagash wilderness.

"Luna went and got two friends to help her," AJ said, but we had to keep our distance and never met them.

"So you haven't seen any of the *gargouilles* since this summer?" Stedman asked.

The three of them shook their heads sadly.

"We miss them," Maryann said. "I want to know they're okay."

Cliff said, "Aaron and I got free rides to the hospital, so we've never even seen them. I'd like to see what a baby garglee looks like, pick one up."

"Cliff!" Keegan said. "It's pronounced gar-*gwee*, not gar-*glee*. Work on it, please."

Stedman shook his head. "Wow," was all he could say. "What a story. Just wow."

They finished the coffee cake and shared the rest of the coffee. Then Stedman brought them back to order.

"So we assume Luna and her crew have left the area," he said. "But Faucon is still around, which is a problem. He's injured and he's hungry. He eats fish, vegetables, and fruit."

"But no livestock or human flesh," Keegan pointed out. "So he's not a danger."

Stedman clicked his keyboard. "I want to show you this."

Faucon's image—Fitz's police sketch done for the fisherman—appeared on the screen. Stedman turned the iPad so everyone could see it. Then he showed them the second sketch—more distant—that the Spiller Farm apple pickers had come up with: a red-eyed, dragon-like shape hovering above a tree.

"That's him," Keegan said, and AJ and Maryann agreed.

"Okay," Stedman said. "You may not think he's a danger, but here's where he becomes a problem. It's not that he's attacking humans. It's that, until now only you five had seen him. Nobody else—not around here, anyway—has seen a real live gargoyle. Excuse me, *gargouille*. Until the last couple of nights. Now we have drawings. Coming from one source, it might be discounted—three superstitious men from a different culture seeing something after dark. Or from the other source—an inebriated fisherman trying to explain how his fish got away. Even taken together, the stories aren't terribly credible."

"Regardless of the sources," Cliff said, as if a light bulb had come on. "Now there are pictures. Official pictures."

"Exactly," Stedman said. "But, as Aaron jokingly said to me this morning: by now the chief has reviewed those reports and she's not going to put out a BOLO—for the civilians here, that's a Be On Lookout—for an apple thief or a fish thief. And for two minor misdemeanors, there's no way she'd put those sketches out to the public."

"Sounds like *Jaws*," Cliff said, and when the others looked sideways at him, he explained. "You know, *Jaws*? The sheriff tells the powers-that-be there's a great white shark prowling the waters. But they don't want to spook people and lose tourist dollars, so they tell him to keep a lid on it."

Aaron reached for the last few crumbs in the Entenmann's box. "So we should expect more sightings."

Maryann said, "Even if he heals enough to head for home, what if he encounters humans along the way?"

"He leaves a trail," Keegan said. "A public record."

"And," AJ said. "It leads anybody who wants to follow right to the other *gargouilles*."

"Which may be where Luna and her friends took the babies," Maryann pointed out.

The group pondered silently for a few minutes until AJ said, "So what do we do, Ms. K? Find him, feed him, and fix him so he can get home?"

"Maybe," she said. "It's a better than reading about him making more public appearances."

CHAPTER 10

Stedman's last-minute meeting had thrown people's Friday night schedules off. Maryann and Keegan got home after seven o'clock and were famished, so they turned to their Friday night backup plan. Maryann threw together two platefuls of garden salad with leftover sliced chicken on top. Keegan quick-thawed two frozen bagels, buttered them, sprinkled with garlic powder, and ran them through the toaster oven. Within 15 minutes of walking in, they were at the trestle table chowing down and sipping tumblers of sparkling water on ice with lime wedges.

"Here's to an elegant meal on the cheap," Maryann said, and they clinked glasses.

Keegan responded with, "Stedman's not bad-looking."

Maryann's fork paused between her plate and her mouth. "What?"

"Detective Stedman," her daughter said. "Elly. I said he's not bad looking. And he seems nice. Maybe a little shy around women."

Maryann's mouth hung open, but not in anticipation of the salad. She lowered the fork and rested it on the plate.

"What?" Keegan said, frowning at her mother's surprise. "Oh, come on, Mom. That meeting wasn't totally about Faucon and Luna. There were times when I was explaining something and—even though he was sitting across from me and listening to what I was saying—he wasn't looking at me. He was sneaking glances at you."

"Why would you think that, Miss Keegan?"

"Because I could see him, Mom. I caught him looking—a couple of times—and he knows I caught him looking. Come on, don't tell me you didn't see it. You must have. The man's got a crush."

Maryann blushed. "Really?"

Keegan placed her palms on the table and leaned in, locking eyes with her mother. "No question about it. But he doesn't know what to say, isn't sure how to ask you out. The guy may be the world's smartest detective, but he's clueless about women."

"He does seem a little shy." She pushed some salad around on her plate, then speared a small chunk of chicken and lifted it to her mouth.

"Shy? Mom, if it continues, *you'll* have to ask *him* out."

Maryann giggled as she chewed.

Keegan bit off a chewy piece of her mock garlic bread and watched her mother's lips curl coyly. She raised her tumbler, said, "Mazel tov," and they finished eating mostly in silence.

***

There wasn't much Keegan could do about Luna, the babies, or Faucon, so she decided to spend the rest of the evening in her room, sifting through more of her birth mother Zelda's college boxes. The night before she'd found the name Jan—which Luna had said was Dutch and pronounced YON—alongside a jotted-down scribbled phone number. She'd thought about the number much of the day, wondering what to do about it. After all, it was from the 1990s, and the foreign student who might be her birth father had presumably returned to Europe. He would no longer be at that Maine number, which had likely been a dorm or an off-campus apartment, so she didn't dial it. She feared it would lead nowhere, and as long as she didn't know for sure it was a dead end, there was hope. She set herself a deadline—Monday. *It's a simple thing. I'll call the number Monday.*

She dug into the carton containing Zelda's senior year materials first, flipping through the textbooks to see if anything had been scribbled in the margins. Finding nothing of interest, she piled the books on the floor next to her night table.

The notebooks were a slower go, because everything was written in Zelda's hand and grabbed Keegan's attention. Her mother had taken notes, penned short essays, and committed herself to writing her own thoughts and opinions.

One notebook page had a draft of an op-ed piece on middle-class privilege, probably for consideration by The Maine Campus, the university's student-produced newspaper. Keegan wondered if the final version had been published. She was seeing for the first time what her mother thought, believed in, and fought for. She was pretty sure back issues of TMC were archived electronically, and would be available as far back as the late 1990s or even earlier.

She opened the notebook for Zelda's French novels course and halfway through came upon a note-to-self her mother had boxed in at the top of a page: *TMC idea—bias prejudice fear bullying. How Do We Treat Folks from Away? e.g. Luna, Jan.*

There was the Dutchman's name again, the man who might be her father: Jan. Keegan mouthed the name without speaking it aloud, hearing it in her mind—Yon, Yon, Yon, Yon. Still no last name, this time without the phone number that might or might not have to do with him, the one she would risk calling on Monday.

She looked again at the key words and the working title: *bias prejudice fear bullying. How Do We Treat Folks from Away?* She thought back to the story Luna had shared about Zelda defusing a tense situation near a fountain on campus. A crowd of students had come across *la gargouille* dressed in her daytime disguise—a variation on a medieval nun's garb augmented by a hood and veil that must have reminded the ignorant students of a Muslim burka. As the catcalls and veiled insults increased, Zelda had parted the waters and approached Luna, then pulled out a pen and notebook. She was suddenly— credibly—a reporter for TMC preparing to interview a famous Middle-Eastern scholar. The crowd dispersed.

51

The working title *How Do We Treat Folks from Away* was clever. Mainers often referred to non-Mainers as being "from away." Even if a person was born elsewhere and moved to Maine at two months-old, they didn't qualify as native-born Mainers. They were still 'from away." And to some, that justified treating them differently, as second class citizens. *Same is true of America*, Keegan thought. *How Do We Treat Folks from Away? How Do We Treat Folks Who Are Different from Us?*

She wondered if, like the op-ed draft she had found earlier, the words in the boxed square had gotten no farther than an article idea or had they seen print? And had Jan from Holland, a white Northern European, but an outsider to America and Maine, a person from away, been picked on in some way? Would Zelda—with Jan's permission—have told Jan's story in print to illustrate her point? Even if his name were changed in Zelda's piece, Keegan felt certain she'd be able to see through it. And she'd learn a little more about the man who might be her birth father.

She set the notebooks aside and went to her computer.

CHAPTER 11

Fifteen miles away in Springvale, outside Sanford, Jim and Carol McCusker were already asleep. Locals referred to them—and other newcomers who had bought up the ailing dairies along Hanson's Ridge Road—as the New Age farmers. The term wasn't derogatory, it just meant that times had changed and so had farming.

The New Agers retained the old structures—barns, silos, and outbuildings—but adapted them for specialty farming and niche markets: herbs, mushrooms, organic fruits and vegetables, ostriches, alpacas, bison, non-GMO grain-fed pork, beef, and poultry. Despite their different approaches to farming and marketing, the New Agers shared three things with their predecessors: a strong work ethic, a commitment to stewardship of the land and resources, and a belief in the old adage *early to bed, early to rise.* Jim and Carol McCusker weren't the only ones asleep by ten. All of the old Hanson's Ridge farmhouses and barns were dark.

The dairy the McCuskers had bought didn't stray too far from the property's original purpose. They didn't deal in milk cows and milk products, but they did raise cattle, pigs, and chickens—meaning organic, non-GMO, grain-fed beef cattle and pigs and chickens—which they slaughtered on premises and sold to specialty markets and to what some still called health food stores. Because raising beef cattle wasn't so different from raising dairy cows, the McCuskers' dooryards and barnyards appeared to passersby to have changed little from their predecessors' operations. The flatbed trucks, tractors, hay wagons, and tow-behind farm implements—seeders, cutter bars, hay rakes, balers, corn choppers with attached thrower chutes— had transferred in the turnkey sale.

In the back upstairs bedroom that was farthest from the passing lights of Hanson's Ridge Road the McCuskers snored lightly. Bert and Ernie, their matched herding Shelties, dozed by Carol's feet, their chins on their forepaws. Carol and her husband had put in a long day chopping corn and putting it up in the silo.

The dogs were the first to sense an uninvited guest on the property. They sat up in tandem, the way they herded, ears up, eyes focused on the window and beyond.

Ernie eased quietly off the foot of the bed and padded to the window, leaving Bert to guard her mistress. He stood watching the barnyard a moment, then growled low. Bert slid to the floor and joined her mate. They placed their front paws on the sill and pressed their snouts to the pane. They growled, louder now, enough to draw Carol out of her sleep.

"What is it, you two? Raccoons, fox, deer?" She spoke gently to them as if humoring a child, her voice trying to soothe. "Oh my, not another bear?"

In their five years on Hanson's Ridge, the McCuskers had seen plenty of night animals from their kitchen and bedroom windows and from their back porch. The Shelties had alerted them countless times—usually by growling, which indicated something passing through or eating in a nonthreatening way. On occasion they might yap if a coyote or fox prowled the pasture or barnyard, posing a threat to smaller animals like the chickens but not to humans. And then there was their loud, frenzied barking—the evening the bear came up on the porch at suppertime and tried to paw open the screen door.

Ernie yapped and Bert growled, so Carol didn't know what to make of it. She pulled back the covers and climbed out of bed, gently shaking Jim awake as she did.

"Jim, the dogs are talking."

Both dogs yapped now, and when Carol got to them and knelt she could see the pane was wet from their nostrils and the sill from their slobber. She tried to figure their line of sight so she could see whatever it was they had spotted.

"I think they're barking at the old silo," she said. An ancient glazed-tile silo stood apart from the three modern ones that abutted the main cow barn. It was a relic, the only thing remaining of the 1920s barn that had burned in 1972, but it was still serviceable. Wood burned, tile didn't. Which had left the tall orphan silo fifty feet behind the replacement barn.

It was the tile silo they had blown chopped corn into that day, half filling it. In the morning they would start again. In the meantime Jim had left open the loading door at the top, just under the round peaked roof, so the steaming silage could vent.

"There," Carol pointed. "By the back of the corn wagon. See it?"

After blowing the final load of corn up through the vertical steel tube and over the lip of the silo's uppermost door, they had walked away, leaving tractor and wagon until the morning.

"Is that our bear?" Jim asked.

"Looks more like a big man," she said. "Maybe a little hunched. And he's got leg problems. Look how he shuffles."

Bert and Ernie dropped back into low growls.

"He's bending down," Jim said. "And he's back up. Got his hands to his mouth."

She squinted. "He's doing it again. Down and back up. Could he be eating spilled silage off the ground?"

"I believe he is."

"Hobo?" she asked.

"Homeless person. Hobos rode the freight trains."

They watched. Bend. Retrieve. Stand. Eat. Repeat.

She straightened. "Let's go. We can't let this happen. The man is starving." She stepped back from the window. "Throw on some clothes."

Five minutes later they opened the back door. In one hand she held the dogs' leashes, in the other a plastic sandwich bag containing two hastily made peanut-butter-and-jelly sandwiches. He carried a flashlight.

"Where'd he go?" were Carol first words when they reached the tractor and wagon.

Bert and Ernie yapped at the silo roof.

Jim ignored them, checked under and around the wagon and tractor, then walked the dogs around the base of the silo. Back by the wagon, they resumed yapping at the roof.

Carol shrugged and motioned with the sandwich bag. "The dogs say he's up there."

Jim shook his head. The heavy silo loading door was still open the way he'd left it. "Can't be. With that guy's knees or feet, there's no way he could've climbed the ladder. And what would he do once he got up there?"

The ladder going up the outside of the old silo was made up of nineteen twelve-inch-wide iron steps that resembled giant staples, the points of each cemented into holes drilled in the tile. The ladder ended to the left of the door, just below the bottom of the conical roof. It was designed so a farm worker could climb it, reach out with his right hand, grip the hatch handle, and open the hatch door. Closing and latching it was trickier, because it was a farther reach to the right to get a hand on an open door.

Jim had left it open at the end of the work day because wet corn gave off nitrogen dioxide, which could be as deadly as bleach. It didn't fade for at least three or four days after fresh-cut silage was blown in. If he and Carol had been blessed with children, they'd have either closed and latched it or restricted the ladder access.

"Dogs are still barking up," Carol said. "You want me to go up?"

"Why would he go up there, Carol? Dessert?"

"Not funny, Jim. How about a safe place to spend the night?"

"If he did, how would he climb out?"

56

"Don't know," she shrugged. "But Bert and Ernie say he's up there. And the sooner we check on him, the sooner we get back to sleep."

Jim let out an exasperated breath, made his hands into a megaphone, and yelled, "Hey, if you're up there and you're hungry, my wife brought sandwiches."

The dogs quieted down.

"Okay, I'm coming up," he called, and clicked off the flashlight then jammed it into his back pocket. The sandwich bag went inside his shirt front, against his bare tummy. "Wish me luck," he said, and placed a hand on the bottom iron step.

"Luck," she said, and the Shelties returned to yapping. Before he reached the second rung, she yelled at the silo door, "Hey, mister, come out and have something to eat. It's not safe in the silo. There's gas. We've got food. You can sleep in our hayloft. I'll feed you in the morning, too." Then, trying not to sound desperate, she added, "Mister, please come out. We have no interest in calling the police."

Jim kept climbing, and in three minutes reached the door. No one greeted him, so he pulled the flashlight out and started by scanning the wider grounds around the silo in case a shambling bearlike hobo was crossing the rows of corn stubble on his way to the woods.

"Anything?" Carol called up.

"Not outside. I'll look inside now."

To the right of the ladder was an extra iron step the builders had installed, this one three feet below the bottom of the door. Jim stretched his right leg over to it, planted his foot then moved his right hand to the sill of the open door. When he had a secure grip, he moved his left hand and foot across, so that his chest pressed against the door sill.

"Be careful, Spiderman," he heard Carol say from the ground.

He peered into the warm, fetid void and called, "Hello."
Barely an echo. The plastic sandwich bag felt warm and sticky
against his stomach. He flicked the flashlight on again and
directed the beam down on the little hills of steaming chopped
corn, moving the light in a grid pattern. He saw no one but
repeated the search just in case he'd missed a hand, foot, or head
sticking out of the soft corn. Only silage.

He breathed a sigh of relief. Carol didn't have to call the
police. Nothing to report. Whoever they had seen had moved on.

"Sorry," he called down over the still yapping Shelties.
"Nobody home."

"Better close it then," she said. "In case he comes back.
Just to be safe."

He snapped off the light and slipped it into his side
pocket. Then with his left hand firmly gripping the sill, he
reached with his right and gripped the hatch handle. The heavy
metal door creaked on its hinges as he pulled on it.

"Wait," a deep voice said from very close. Inside the silo.

Jim turned his head from the door and tried to locate
where the sound had come from. Slightly above him, not below
in the silage. Inside, under the hollow domed roof.

"Do not close the door, *s'il vous plait.*"

Please? French? Jim's eyes and ears tracked the sound.

What little light entered the silo from the outside came
from the two barnyard pole lights, which didn't shine in below
the silo door, only above it. The voice had come from among the
turret roof's wooden support struts. Jim glanced up and saw two
glowing red eyes peering back.

Vampire bat was his first thought, though he'd never
seen one. *A huge one.* Then a question. *Hanging? Speaking?* It
was too much to comprehend. He found his heart suddenly
racing, his lungs fighting for air. He strained to close the door,
and when it was almost shut he heard the voice say, "Leave it!"
But he closed it anyway and pulled down the metal hatch handle

that tightened the seal. Then held onto the lever, putting all his weight on it.

"All closed up?" Carol asked, unaware that he had something trapped inside.

He trembled all over, his legs felt weak, and his arms shook with exhaustion. He was afraid to let go of the handle, because he knew there was another just like it on the inside of the door. In his pants pocket the flashlight felt like it weighed ten pounds. When he sucked in his breath, the sweaty sandwich bag slipped past his beltline and down the inside of his pants leg and out the cuff, falling to the ground.

Carol heard the sandwiches hit the ground near her with a splat and called up, "Are you alright?"

"Call 911," he rasped out. "We got something trapped in the silo, something bad. I think I can hold it. Hurry. 911."

Through the dogs' yapping and growling Jim could hear his wife excitedly telling the dispatcher what was going on and where to send help. Then "They're on their way. They're still on the line."

"Shoot video," he said. "Even if you have to hang up, shoot video."

That's when he both heard and felt a deep hum inside the silo. He felt the vibration in the door handle. Then he felt upward pressure on the metal latch, a force working against his hand and his weight—like when he arm-wrestled his older brother. Except this force was coming from the other side, the inside handle. Whoever was arm-wrestling him on the other side was twice or three times stronger than his older brother had been, and it was his older brother who always won.

Jim placed both hands on the handle so all his weight was pulling down on it. He felt the handle start to lift him.

"Carol," he screamed. "I can't hold it. Shoot the video." A pulsing light caught his eye—far off up the road. A police car, he was sure.

The handle moved steadily until he knew the hatch was about to open. He reached back for the main ladder, grabbed tight with his left hand and let go the handle with his right. The door pushed open and as he glanced up at it, in his peripheral vision he caught a glimpse of a huge black blur shooting out the door.

CHAPTER 12

Keegan's online search began with *U Maine's Fogler Library*. She knew that most university libraries in the new millennium were more than repositories for books, periodicals, and the institution's student theses and dissertations, literary magazines, and yearbooks.

DigitalCommons@UMaine was a database that allowed her to access *Archives:TheMaineCampus*, which made back issues of the student newspaper viewable. Keegan went right to her mother's UMO years to see if any of Zelda's ideas or notebook drafts had made it into print.

The first issue Keegan brought up was *Volume 116, Number 65,* dated Wednesday, April 7, 1999, when UMO's hockey team won the national championship. *Black Bears Take It All* read the front-page banner headline. A story headline to the left read **Championship Game* and under that *Gustafsson scores in overtime.* Parallel on the far right another headline announced **Mayhem* and beneath it *Students' post-game celebration results in campus vandalism.*

The issue was heavily laden with hockey-related stories, but there were also the regular sections: Campus and Community, Features, Profiles, and Reviews: books, films, music, and food. Neither of the opinion pieces on the Editorial page was by Zelda Keegan.

Keegan scanned the remaining pages. A shrunken image of the New York Times Daily Crossword was there, edited by Will Shortz, whose name she recognized from NPR. And plenty of ads for off-campus businesses: restaurants, pizza parlors with free delivery, used furniture stores, and recycled clothing shops. The next-to-last page featured columns of classified ads.

One of the display classifieds caught her eye. It was boxed and asked: *Need help in a language? Call us at the Language Tutoring Office. French, Spanish, Portuguese, Italian,*

German, Russian. It listed a room number in a campus admin building and gave a phone number. Keegan jotted down *tutoring office* and noted the phone number.

She got through four semesters of TMC archives. None of the Op Eds or articles remotely matched the content of her mother's rough drafts, and she couldn't find Zelda's byline anywhere.

Friday, September 17, 1999 was a typical seventeen-pager. The Language Tutoring Office's classified was there again. The office address had changed from the April ad—their location probably bumped around by the administration—but the phone number was the same. On the bottom right of the classifieds page was a boxed announcement: *Applications for spring semester student teaching/internships now available at Student Teaching Office, 130 Shibles Hall, 581-2456.*

Hadn't Luna said she thought Jan from Holland had been seeking some kind of teaching certification? Maybe he'd been a student teacher or an intern. Would the office have a record of him that included his last name? She wrote down the full wording of the announcement along with the phone number.

Now she had three calls to make on Monday.

Chapter 13

Luna and Yvette heard a *whoosh-whoosh* in the dark sky over the pines. They were almost certain it was Bronwyn returning—unless Faucon or Cyrus's scouts had somehow found them. Luna drew her sword from behind her neck while Yvette corralled the toddling *gargouilles* together and herded them a little farther into the cave.

It had to be Bronwyn. She had been out fishing and foraging for them, and so far as they knew, Faucon and the king not only didn't know where they were hiding, but they didn't know the eggs had been found and the babies hatched. But still they had to be careful, because the three female *gargouilles* were the only thing between *les enfants* and those who would destroy them.

Luna hid beneath the cave's overhanging ledge and listened. The series of whooshes suggested this was a small *gargouille,* about her own size, with a far shorter wingspan than Faucon or most males. The flapping stopped. The flyer had gone into a glide and would soon pull up and land.

Luna stepped out from the overhang and saw the approaching *gargouille* bank smoothly over the tall pines before it lined up with the cave entrance and skimmed the meadow. It was Bronwyn, with two large lumps hanging from her midsection like bombs under a Messerschmitt. She tilted her wings to slow her approach and Luna saw a slight wobble—the lumps at her waist were heavy—and watched as her friend shifted her feet from behind her to a forward sitting position like a like a large waterfowl landing on a lake. The turned her wings from horizontal to almost full vertical, braking. After taking two catch-up steps for balance, she stood on the hardscrabble before Luna.

"*Difficile* with those," Luna said, pointing to the sacks tied to Bronwyn's waist. "Where did you find them?"

"A potato farm. They begged me to free them." She unhooked the burlap sacks and set them at Luna's feet. "A feast tonight. Potatoes, corn, blueberries, acorns and hazelnuts, two kinds of fish, squash, peaches, apples, and two of those melons humans call cantaloupes." She let out a loud breath. "Heavy."

Yvette and the hungry babies—Regine, Mathilde, and their chubby brother Paladin—wobbled out and knocked the potato sacks over, spilling their contents. Yvette wrangled them away while Luna and Bronwyn unpacked the groceries.

Luna extended the same special talon she'd used to slit the baby *gargouilles'* eggs to hatch them and slit open the squashes and one of the melons.

Yvette pulverized the hazelnuts and acorns on a round, flat stone then mixed in sweet blueberries, apples, and corn kernels to make a soft paste for the still toothless infants.

They fed the children the soft mash before laying into the raw fish for their own meal. Occasionally they'd share bits of it with the babies and watching their eyes widen at the taste and texture of this new thing they found themselves sucking and gumming.

When everyone had finished, the three adults lay on their sides in a little triangle, each shouldering a drowsy *enfant*.

After a few minutes, Luna broke their reverie. "We cannot continue this way."

"What way?" Yvette asked.

"This way. Night to night, day to day. What Bronwyn found for us tonight is wonderful, but it will not last more than two nights. Back at home, because there are many fishers and foragers who work together, the clan has plenty of food for the winter and beyond. If it were only the three of us caring for ourselves, we could survive. But we have three growing children as well. The colors of the leaves are changing and winter will be close behind."

"We need a better supply of food," Yvette said. "But we cannot return to our clan."

"Not to ours, not to any of the clans," Bronwyn said. "The royal line has never allowed females. They may welcome Paladin but they will cull Regine and Mathilde."

Luna said, "I have been thinking about it. We must leave this cave and move indoors. Soon. Before it is too late."

"What do you mean?" Bronwyn said. "The cave is indoors."

"It is. But these little ones are growing and need more to eat. We cannot keep up. Not through the winter. Not without help."

"Help?" Bronwyn said. "Only a different clan can offer us both safety and shared food. On all the continents we inhabit, there is not one that will take all six of us in if they find these are Cyrus' grandchildren."

Luna said, "You forget the humans."

"The humans?" Yvette asked, incredulous.

"*Oui. Homo sapiens*," Luna said. "Long-lost cousins."

"Cousins we do not like," Bronwyn said. "Cousins we cannot trust. Long ago one put an arrow in my father."

Luna lifted her arm to reveal the partially healed scar on her ribs. "Faucon—*un gargouille*—did this, not a human. Do not judge someone by their race. Had it not been for a human swinging her ax, Faucon would have beheaded me. And it was three human females who helped me birth these precious little ones we now hold. They hid them and fed them and tended my wounds."

Luna's two closest friends stood speechless for a long moment. Then Yvette asked, "Will they help us again?"

CHAPTER 14

Aaron's cellphone rang at seven a.m., waking him. He found it on the nightstand and checked the Caller ID: *Stedman.*

"Morning, Sarge?" he mumbled. "What can I do for you?"

"You can call Bragdon then get dressed. Casual, no uniforms. I'll be out of my place in ten minutes, heading your way. I'll grab three coffees and a dozen around the corner then pick you and Bragdon up, in that order."

"Where're we going?"

"Sanford. Springvale, actually. Hanson's Ridge. Be ready."

***

Cliff climbed into the backseat and, before Aaron could pass him the donut box and his coffee, asked, "Where are we off to?"

"Springvale," Aaron answered. "Faucon may have made an appearance at a farm out there last night."

"Anybody hurt?" Cliff asked, chewing a hunk of donut.

"No," Stedman said. "Scared the farmers, though. A couple."

"Springvale's in Sanford's jurisdiction, not ours," Cliff said. "How're we getting this?"

"Sanford P.D. responded," Stedman said. "Buck Soule—you guys know him—took the report. Then this morning the farmer's wife called Wells dispatch, who called me. I called her back and got this invitation to meet with her and her hubby and the dogs."

"The dogs?" Aaron asked.

"Bert and Ernie, a couple of Sheltie herding dogs. They started the barking after the couple—names are Jim and Carol McCusker—went to bed. Jim and Carol had been loading corn into the silo all day. They looked out and spotted somebody eating silage off the ground next to the corn wagon, figured it was a homeless man, so they went out with sandwiches. By the time they got to the wagon, the guy was gone."

"Flew the coop," Cliff said.

"Low-hanging fruit, Bragdon," Stedman said, and went on. "The dogs barked up at the silo loading door, which McCusker had left open overnight to vent. He climbs up the ladder on the outside of the silo, looks in and finds a pair of glowing red eyes staring back at him from the rafter beams under the dome. Thinks it must be a giant bat, so he closes the door to seal it in and has his wife call 911."

"Bet Faucon didn't appreciate that," Aaron said.

"Guess not. He muscles the door open from the inside and blows past the farmer, leaving him hanging on up there for dear life."

"But no confrontation, right?" Aaron asked.

"I didn't say that. I said no one was hurt."

"So, there *was* a confrontation?" Cliff asked.

"Not exactly," Stedman said. "McCusker says the giant bat spoke to him. Asked him *politely*—in mixed French-English—to leave the door open."

"So it was definitely Faucon," Cliff said.

"I wonder if he told Buck that for the report," Aaron said. "If not, it's just a bat flying out of a silo."

"I'd still like to know why she called us. You. Wells." Cliff said.

"Before this silo thing she had read that dumb article online, the one about the Drake's Island fisherman. She remembered the guy's description: red eyes, low hum, rush of air when the guy fish thief disappeared. It sounded like her husband's description. She figured we had an open file and were working on it."

"Do we?" Cliff asked.

"Not an official one," Stedman said. "Just the one we three have in our heads: apple, fish, corn thief."

"Doesn't sound like a file," Cliff said. "I'd call it a menu."

Stedman and Aaron groaned.

***

Aaron spotted the wooden sign by the RFD mailbox—*McCusker Farms, Organic Meats & Produce, Springvale, Maine.* The once white farmhouse had suffered more than a few of the sandblasting winds that whipped across Hanson's Ridge. The main house's clapboards needed scraping and a fresh paint job, and it from the weedy front yard and bare porch that the front door didn't get used much.

Stedman drove around back and parked in the dooryard beside a dusty older Dodge pickup that had once been white but was now grayish with accents of fender rust. The business information on the driver's door matched the roadside sign.

They climbed out and stretched. Cliff brushed donut sugar off the chest of his Bragdon's Firewood shirt and Aaron smoothed his jogging jacket. They looked out past the barn at the silos. The upper loading door of the old one that stood apart from the others was wide open.

Two small collies came happily yapping from the barn, followed by a woman in high rubber boots, an oversized red tee shirt, and a pair of jeans held up by suspenders. Her hair was brown and tied back in a ponytail. The dogs took up positions between their mistress and the three cops.

"This must be Bert and Ernie, and you must be Mrs. McCusker," Stedman said, and gave his name.

"Carol," she replied. "Your partners-in-crime look like Aaron Stevenson and—guessing from the writing on his shirt, Cliff Bragdon."

"You should be a detective," Stedman said. "I can see how you got Cliff's name, but how'd you come up with Aaron's?"

"Wells basketball star, right?" she asked Aaron. "Six or so years ago?"

"Ancient history," Aaron said.

"Maybe so, but I saw you play Sanford a few times. You were fast, had kangaroo legs, and could hit the corner shots. You deserved all those accolades. Football, too." She smiled and Aaron blushed.

She started toward the house again, cooing in her doggy voice, "Bert, Ernie, they're okay." Then, "Let's go inside. Don't mind if I don't shake hands, gentlemen. I've been mucking." She and Bert and Ernie led the way up onto the porch and into the house.

The kitchen was on the left, a square room painted dull yellow, with a black-and-white chessboard floor that looked like tile but was ancient linoleum now cracked in places where it had begun to lift up. Four straight-backed maple chairs surrounded a square wooden table.

"I have fresh coffee," she said, and without waiting for an answer, poured them each a mug. She passed them out, said, "Sit, please," and sat on one of the end chairs, mug in front of her, the Shelties flanking her. From her side pocket she produced a cellphone that went next to her mug. The cops chose chairs and sat, Stedman adjacent to her.

"Mrs.—

"Carol," she reminded him.

"Carol," he began again.

"Let me save us some time, Detective Stedman. I think this flying thing—maybe a deformed flying human, for all I know—is desperate for food and shelter, and must be a long way from home. Whoever or whatever visited us last night, I don't believe is out to hurt us."

"And you base this on what?" Stedman said.

"We saw him eating raw silage, so he was obviously hungry. He hid in the silo rather than fly away when we came out. We saw him walk and bend over, and think he may be injured. He speaks French and English, which tells us he's intelligent, in some way educated, able to communicate. And the way he spoke to Jim—politely, asking him to leaving the door open—that tells me he's not violent or aggressive."

"On the phone you told me the basic story. Is there anything you told me that you didn't tell Officer Soule last night?"

"The part about the bat in the silo asking Jim to leave the door open. Jim told me after Buck took the report. He said it sounded crazy, and he was pretty sure he'd heard it, but he was starting to wonder himself."

"So Jim just told you?" Stedman asked. "And you believe him?"

"Have the two of you talked about amending last night's report?" Aaron asked.

"We did, but we decided against it. You can see what kind of people we are. We own an organic farm. We're environmentally conscious. We support the York Animal Shelter. We don't want to be responsible for getting a posse after this creature."

"E.T. go home," Cliff mumbled, and Stedman cringed visibly, raising a bridge of fingers to his forehead.

"No, no," Carol McCusker said. "He's right. Jim and I do want E.T. to go home. To get there safely. We really do." There were tears in her eyes now.

They heard the back door creak open and turned in their seats to see a man in blue jeans, scuffed leather work boots, and a sun-faded flannel shirt. Bert and Ernie rose and went to greet him. He bent down and petted them.

"Hi," he said, and removed a green John Deere cap and hung it on a hook by the door. "Jim McCusker." He stepped in and shook hands with the visitors. "If you feel my hands vibrating, it's because I just got off the tractor." To his wife he said, "Fresh load ready for the silo."

"I'll help you when we finish here," Carol McCusker said. "Pull up a chair. Perfect timing." She stood and poured her husband coffee then sat back down.

Jim grabbed a chair from the corner and found space between his wife and Aaron. He took a sip of coffee and glanced down at his wife's cellphone. "You show 'em yet?"

"Waited for you," she replied. "Ready?"

"Yep."

She picked up the phone and said to their guests. "I shot video. Not much, but a couple seconds. And no, we didn't share it with Buck Soule last night."

"Video?" Stedman asked, his eyebrows hunching.

"Yes," Jim said. "But if we show you, you have to tell us what it is." He punched a button and turned the screen toward the cops, who were already leaning in close over their coffee mugs.

They watched, then played the four seconds of movement over a dozen times.

"See the little horn on the forehead?" Carol asked. "It's not a nose. It's above the red eyes."

They nodded.

"I think the side view of it coming out shows a vibrating wing under the arm," Jim McCusker said. "Must be one on the side we can't see. Then there's what looks like a hump on its shoulders. Reminds me of an angel."

"Can't say I've ever seen anything like this," Stedman said. Aaron and Cliff said nothing. "If you'd be willing to text me a copy of the video, I can put it up on my desktop screen and slow it down."

"Actually, Detective Stedman," Carol McCusker said, "I'd rather not share it. You three have seen it, and that's enough. I don't want to take any chances it could get out, so I think it best that Jim and I keep it. Right, Jim?"

Her husband nodded.

"Then why did you show it to us?" Stedman asked.

"Not so you could catch it," Carol answered. "But so you could see what or who that fisherman saw, and those apple pickers. We wanted you to see that we're dealing with a scared, maybe injured, clearly hungry human-like being who just wants to get home. I called because something told me you have a better chance than we do of helping him get there."

Aaron said, "But—

"You don't need the video for that," she said, and stood up, pocketing the phone. Then to her husband she said, "Jim, let's get that corn in," and he rose and grabbed his John Deere cap. "Feel free to finish the coffee," she said to the three cops, and ended with, "Bert, Ernie, let's go." The four of them walked out to the barnyard, leaving the three stunned cops at the table holding their mugs.

CHAPTER 15

It was mid-morning Saturday and the sun was out. For most humans—particularly those in Maine—that meant engaging in a variety of activities. For *gargouilles* it meant sleep or tasks that could be done away from the harmful rays of the sun.

The three cops had already put in a few hours at the McCusker farm in Springvale and were on their way back to Wells. Maryann, AJ, and Keegan were at Annie's, stocking shelves, creating displays, and dealing with customers. Behind Cliff Bragdon's, unbeknownst to him, more than twenty volunteers—off-duty cops, firefighters, and EMTs along with their families and a few school kids—were cutting, splitting, and stacking cordwood for his firewood delivery business.

In Maine's old North Woods, inside the cave, Luna and her two friends had settled into their race's birdlike sit-squat position, huddling close together in a configuration resembling a prayer circle. It allowed them to sleep and refresh while offering a sense of security to *les trois enfants* dozing in their midst. Remaining upright kept them more alert to, and ready to respond to dangers that might threaten their little family.

Bronwyn was the most exhausted after foraging and fishing all night to bring home the two sacks of food. Luna and Yvette, though they hadn't hunted, were also exhausted after a night of corralling, herding, feeding, and comforting the inquisitive and rambunctious siblings who snored and snoozed at their feet. Unlike the adults the children's skeletal structures at this age allowed them to sleep on their backs or sides or stomachs—wrapped up in one another's arms and legs like a pile of tuckered-out puppies.

The night hadn't all been work, it had also been rewarding, and Luna, Yvette, and Bronwyn had enjoyed watching their adopted babies' antics. Now there was something deep and satisfying about the contact of their six bodies, as if together they were parts of a single entity.

"Luna," Yvette said softly, also giving her shoulder a little shake.

"Mmm?" Luna answered.

"It is time to put the willow bark on your wounds again. The poultice is helping you to heal."

"Mmm," Luna agreed, and started to turn away from the children.

"Stay. I have it ready beside me." Yvette felt the cave floor behind her until her fingers found the bowl-shaped stone with the paste. Every day she pounded the bark and the leaves and wetted them, mixing them together so there would be enough medicine for four applications to Luna's wounds. Faucon's thrusting dagger had pierced her upper torso, exited her back, and continued through one of her lower wings. She could still flap her angel wings, allowing her to glide and soar and ride the thermals, but her hummingbird wings weren't quite ready for hovering and quick forward or backward movements. Yvette's willow poultice helped with abscesses, ulcers, and fever.

"Can you see?" Luna asked.

"No need to see. Your wounds are in the same places they were earlier." She dabbed paste on her thick fingers and applied it. When she finished, she said, "Let's sleep again. I will wake you in the afternoon and apply more of it."

"*Merci*, Yvette," Luna said. Then she added, "Today we sleep, tonight we make a new plan."

***

Because of the silo incident, Faucon didn't spend his Saturday in a cave. The farmer had trapped him. Almost. When the man closed the door and turned the latch, Faucon had no idea if there was also a handle on the inside. So he'd dropped from the roof beam down onto the soft silage then used his hummingbird wings to rise and hover by the door. He'd felt around and located the inside lever, which he tried to lift. When it wouldn't move, he called on his wings for more lift and pressed upward, feeling it slowly give way to his pressure. When it stopped at the top of its arc, he pushed open the heavy door and shot straight out into the cool night air, catching a quick glimpse of his captor clinging to the ladder on the skin of the silo.

Coming out of the silo he'd seen flashing lights in the distance, leaving him no choice but to make a beeline for the woods that bordered the cornfields. From there he flew north as quickly as his short wings would take him for fear that *les gendarmes*—the police with the flashing lights—might arrive and hear the vibrations if he moved too slowly.

But the escape from the Sanford/Springvale area, because he couldn't use his upper wings, ate up much of the night and left him desperately searching for a haven from the sunlight. No more silos or barns.

By the time the dawn glowed far out on the Atlantic, he had run out of the usual options—barn lofts, caves, unlocked cellars. A lakeshore below looked promising—dozens of seasonal camps and cabins. But some had lights on—humans using them for the weekend. He dared not risk someone walking in on him asleep in a closet or a shower. Humans were too quick in turning to firearms. Besides, even if he escaped them, outside the sun would be waiting.

With the darkness evaporating he looked below and spotted a vast wooded tract with an old logging road that ran from a secondary road to a clearing far in the woods. He rode the currents and gradually dropped closer to investigate the clearing. No lights. No cabin or house. Just a concrete foundation with no timbers or flooring. He glided lower, closer, and spotted weeds around the foundation. No one had worked on the project for a while, which was promising. But with nothing covering the cellar, there was no real shelter from the sunlight. The very thing that plants, animals, and humans needed to survive would sap his strength, char his skin, and bake him to death.

He landed near the home site, retracted his wings, and wobbled in a circle, trying to keep the weight off the foot with the severed toes. He saw trees in every direction. The road or driveway, if it was to eventually become one—judging by the weeds in the middle of it—gave no evidence of recent traffic. A small bulldozer sat rusting on its treads close to the edge of the forest, but there was nothing about it that suggested a hiding place out of the sun. The forest floor, deep in the woods, might be his only option.

Then his eye caught a slender green building not far from the bulldozer. It was smaller than the potting shed he'd used for three nights the month before, but it offered possibilities. He hobbled toward it, the gravelly surface hurting his sore foot. He extended his short wings again and reached the little building in one short, low hop.

The fiberglass shell stood at seven feet high and more than a yard wider than his broad shoulders. The door was plastic, and when he opened it, the floor inside was six inches above the ground. He looked into the darkness and saw an odd-shaped donut, an oval plastic chair that had a huge hole in it. He stepped back, let the door clap shut, then read the English wording on it. *Portland Potties: for People on the Go.*

He understood now what he was seeing. The little house had been brought in to the construction site, either to meet the sanitation need of a work crew or a lone owner building his dream cabin alone. For *gargouilles*, it wasn't an issue, but humans balked at relieving themselves in the woods. Faucon opened the door again, winced as he forced himself to step up on his swollen foot, then with effort climbed in. There was a little fecal smell from the chamber that came from under the seat, but it was old, not fresh. He closed the solid plastic lid, which helped a little, then turned sideways, in front of the throne—the only way he could fit and lower himself into the sit-squat position he needed for sleep. Even with the lid closed, some odor remained, but he realized it wasn't from the little house itself. It was from his swollen foot. He turned his head to the right and tried to sniff behind his shoulder to see if the smell might also be coming from there, from the wound the bookseller's daughter had cleaved with her ax.

He settled into position and tried to relax and sleep, his mind drifting back to his childhood and the French Alps clan his father Drago had led, and to their family. He saw—no, he *felt*—himself wrestling with his brothers Lafayette and Fantome. He could feel and hear himself laughing as they grappled and tested their short wings—zig-zagging, crossing, feinting, and crashing into each other in the air. He could hear his father's deep laughter as he howled at his children's antics. He and Fantome and Lafayette had been under a year old then, he was certain. What he felt was that he'd been part of something: a family, a clan, an ancient race. And right now, hiding in a human outhouse, he missed it.

Then, as he was drifting off, there came an even earlier memory—a brief flash. Four of them—infants barely able to wobble around—were snuggled together in a corner. Lafayette, Fantome, Faucon—and a fourth, the smallest one who didn't appear in his later memories, the one whose eyes were not red. Had they been green? Where had their playmate gone?

CHAPTER 16

Stedman, Aaron, and Cliff were almost back to Wells when Stedman's phone chirped. He checked Caller ID and answered then put it on speaker

"Hi, Marcy. You're off dispatch today. What's up?"

"Off, yes, but still in the loop," Stonestreet said. "In case you haven't heard, our Drake's Island fisherman blabbed."

"I know. A woman I just talked to said she saw it. One of those little online articles."

"Bigger," she replied. "Big Brother really is watching."

"What do you mean?"

"The Feds. They want the file."

"You mean the police report?"

"No, the whole file. In particular, the sketch Fitz did."

"You're kidding. Was it Agents Mulder and Scully who called?"

"Don't joke," she said. "There's more."

"Oh, crap. What?"

"Stiller Farm. They want that file, and Fitz's sketches."

"Dammit. Is that it, Marcy?" he asked. "Tell me they didn't ask about the Toil and Trouble burglary or the Annie's break-in."

"Not yet."

"The York Historical Society stuff?"

"Maybe later. Want to know my theory?" She didn't wait for him to bite. "It's the visuals. That's what got them interested. It's what connects Stiller's Farm and the fisherman."

"Marcy, you should've been a detective. Anything else?"

"Not for now. Welcome to the X- Files." She hung up.

Cliff asked, "Which is worse, a posse of bounty hunters who want Faucon's head for a trophy room or a team of Feds out to dissect him or weaponize him?"

"Too many movies, Cliff," Aaron said.

"We'll see," Cliff answered. "Not everybody's going to be as nice as Mrs. McCusker."

***

They made an early lunch stop at Shain's of Maine and got back to Cliff's farmhouse a little before noon. The volunteers had all gone home, but they found stacks of firewood by the back of the barn and the tracks of firewood elves everywhere. They had even piled a cord of dry oak in the F-250. Cliff was visibly moved when he saw it, more so when Aaron told him the groups and individuals involved.

"Can you guys come in for a beer?" Cliff asked.

"Thanks, no," Stedman answered. "I want to get to the Book Stop and update Maryann."

"What kind of beer?" Aaron asked. "Allagash White?"

"Of course," Cliff replied. "I can give you a ride home later."

They said goodbye to Stedman and headed inside.

***

The Keegans' Subaru was the lone car in the Book Stop parking lot when Stedman drove in. He found Maryann was sitting behind the checkout counter reading a book.

"Detective," she said.

"Elly," he said softly. "Please."

"Elly."

"Keegan and AJ here, too?"

"In the back. Slow for a Saturday.""That's because Aaron, Cliff, and I were out of town."

She gave him a quizzical look.

"We're half your business in the off season." He smiled shyly. "Surely you must have noted a drop in mystery, thriller, and police procedurals today."

She gave a polite chuckle. *Is he flirting? Was Keegan right?*

79

"I've got something to show you," he said, changing gears abruptly. "If you can leave the front desk, we can go to the work room so Keegan and AJ hear this, too."

She marked her page, set the book on the counter, and got off the stool. "The tea bell will keep watch." She stepped from behind the counter and she gave him a playful pout. "There's still time, you know."

His eyebrows crinkled. "Time for what?"

"To salvage today's sales figures of mysteries, thrillers, and police procedurals." Then she added, "What'd you think I meant?" and led the way to the work room.

He stifled a nervous giggle and followed her back.

"Girls," she said. "Detective Stedman has something to share with us."

Keegan glanced up from the desktop computer, AJ from her phone.

"I now know what Faucon looks like," Stedman announced.

"The sketches?" Keegan asked.

"Better. Video," he said.

"Video?" Keegan exclaimed. "How? Who? Where? Let me see."

"Aaron, Cliff, and I saw it. But the person who shot it isn't sharing it." He gave them the Cliff Notes version of the silo story.

"And you're sure it was Faucon, not Luna?" Maryann wanted to know.

"Red eyes," he said. And he was using the short wings. You said one of Luna's was injured."

"But he got away?" AJ asked.

"Probably into the woods. The farmer's wife only caught a couple frames of Faucon blowing out of the door. Understandably, her focus shifted to her husband hanging from the ladder. Faucon disappears to the right." He told them that the farm couple didn't want the video or the story to get out, because they want Faucon to find his way safely home.

"They know he's a *gargouille*?" Keegan said.

"They don't know what he is, and when they asked us what we were seeing in the video, we didn't give anything away. She's guessing it's something not human but in many ways human-like, related."

"She thinks he's a missing link," AJ said.

"Maybe. But there's more." He told them about the curious Feds asking for files. "I think they especially wanted the sketches."

"So we're lucky, Elly," Maryann said. "The farmer and his wife are keeping the video secret."

He heard his name. His first name, not Detective or Officer or Sergeant or Stedman. She'd said it.

"Even without the video," he said, "the danger is in this third story getting out—or the next sighting. Once the media and the public link the fisherman story and the orchard story to the silo bat …"

"Fox News," Keegan said. "Entertainment Tonight."

"Then Faucon gets cast as Frankenstein," AJ said. "Angry villagers, torches, pitchforks."

"Or worse," Maryann said. "The modern equivalent. Deer rifles, shotguns, and AK47s."

"Do you think the Feds will come to Maine and let the dogs out?" Keegan asked.

"Literally and figuratively," Stedman said. "This isn't a good time to be a wounded *gargouille*."

"You mean Faucon or Luna?" Maryann asked.

Stedman didn't answer.

CHAPTER 17

It was an hour before dusk, too early for Faucon to venture out to fish and forage. In the cramped porta-potty he rested in his sleep-squat position, neither asleep nor awake but in that middle ground where dreams and memories mingle.

He found himself back in 1917 in the Alps, when his father Drago's *gargouilles* fought alongside King Cyrus' blended Allagash/French-Canadian contingent. Their swords and *poignards*, coupled with their ability to hover and maneuver quickly dart in any direction, proved ideal for close-quarters fighting during clandestine nighttime raids behind German lines. Once they dropped down among the enemy soldiers, their medieval weapons gave them the advantage over rifles, bayonets, and machine guns, and they wreaked bloody havoc.

Faucon, barely forty then, was strong of body, but he hadn't fully developed his battle skills. As the youngest of three brothers and third in line to Draco's clan throne, he was chosen to accompany the Alps force as an aide/trainee.

He had adored and idolized his father, a *gargouille* of incredible size and strength. But as soon as he saw the twin princes LeClair and Champaigne, he knew he was seeing the gods of war. He coveted their gleaming swords and *poignards*.

But the Germans' weaponry—rifles, machine guns, and artillery—and their seemingly endless supply of infantry soldiers, along with their capacity for relentless daylight advances, had taken a toll, forcing *les gargouilles* farther and farther back into the Alps.

He remembered—*saw*—the ice tunnel in which his companions were sleeping. They were exhausted after a night of deadly forays against the enemy. It was daytime and bright sunshine reflected brightly off the snow, so he and his comrades had no choice but to shelter and try to sleep. But the enemy could move forward in daylight, and they possessed a weapon the *gargouilles*' swords had no answer for, could not counter or even see—deadly mustard gas. It seeped into the ice tunnel where they slept. His father had been a hero, carrying LeClair and Champaigne out. But the twin princes' lungs were damaged by then, and in his dream state Faucon could again hear them hacking and coughing. Many *gargouille* fighters died from the gas, and as he and his father and others evacuated the princes they heard the gunshots in the long tunnel behind them. The German foot soldiers had breached the low end of the ice tunnel and were finishing the job.

Faucon once again saw the glacier they had fled across. With the sun beginning to take its toll, they reached a gaping chasm that stretched between them and an escarpment on the other side. *Fly*, he heard his father order the survivors around him. *Fly across and retreat into the high mountains.* Then he felt his father's touch on his shoulder again as if it was yesterday, and heard him say. *Faucon, my son, go with them.*

He remembered the icy air biting at his face as he spread his upper wings and flapped high over the chasm, hearing far below the roar of a glacial stream. He found himself once again in the center of a group of seven other retreating *gargouilles*—whoosh, whoosh, whoosh—fleeing the glacier and striking out for safety. And then came the feel of the icy outcropping returned, and the clawing of his nails as the pads of his feet slipped and he fought for purchase. He could feel his steps as he made a wobbling turn so he could look back toward the glacier and his father, who towered over the two prone princes.

He saw his father, the enormous rhino-horned warrior with the more than seven-foot wingspan, pick up LeClair and cradle him in his arms. He took a couple of steps, extending his angel wings as he moved, and lifted off across the chasm. Faucon could hear the pop and whine of rifle fire in the distance as his father dipped and rose, dipped and rose, straining under the weight of the crown prince with each flap of his wings. Artillery shells whizzed by, missing the moving target, exploding instead against the mountainside near where the survivors had landed.

Then he saw his father coming at him, commanding *grab him* before handing his cargo off and taking off again. *Now Champaigne*, he heard his father say."

In the confines of the little plastic house, Faucon found himself once again trapped in a nightmare, his mouth unable to utter the words he had been ashamed to speak aloud that terrible day. *Don't go back.*

But his father had gone back, heading directly into the oncoming artillery and into the teeth of the infantry fire. Faucon's heart pounded now as it had a hundred years earlier.

Drago didn't attempt a full landing. He scooped up Champaigne's body on his way past, needing only a few short steps before he was airborne again. Except this time his father didn't rise—he dropped over the glacier's edge into the chasm, disappearing from the enemy's sight. Faucon and the others saw the big *gargouille* dip and go even lower, close to the icy stream below.

Drop him, Faucon remembered thinking. The prince was too heavy for his exhausted father to carry. *He will take you down with him. Let him go.*

But then when he was three quarters of the way across, with the enemy fire stopped as they, too, held their breath, his father gave several tremendous wing flaps and rode the thermals up in a spiral toward the retreating band and Faucon.

Which brought his father and Champaigne once again into the sights of the German infantry and artillery. When he was ten feet from the precipice, Drago extended his hummingbird wings and relaxed his angel wings to make a hump on his back. His short wings vibrated at a fever pitch, humming loudly, and with the prince in his arms he rose and landed in front of everyone. He laid Champaigne down beside LeClair.

Which is when Faucon heard again in his sleep the whine of artillery shells—zeroing in on them. He felt a blast knock him back, saw his huge father tossed into the air like a leaf by a gust. He felt the hands of his comrades and heard their muted voices yelling at him to withdraw with them. He saw four of them pick up the princes under their knees and armpits, lugging them like stretcher-bearers without stretchers, then flying close to the ground in pairs using their short wings, skip-flying up the rocky terrain.

He felt himself, weak-kneed and stunned, his hearing muffled, standing and searching for his father, finally seeing him lying against a boulder, his body curled forward, hands holding his stomach. But alive.

Faucon, the not-quite-adult *gargouille* who was almost as large as Drago, placed an arm behind his father's lower back to try and help him stand. But when he pressed, he felt a gaping hole, and wetness. Another *gargouille* came and took the other side and together, with bullets ricocheting around them and artillery shells bursting nearby, they strained and lifted and used their short wings to lift and drag him up the mountain to safety.

They found a different ice cave farther up and got out of the sunlight. For three days and nights he heard LeClair and Champaigne coughing up pieces of their lungs. And then came the day when he and two others returned from foraging, and a kinsman from his Alps clan—the one who had helped him move his father— met them as they approached to say that Drago was dead.

In the porta-potty Faucon stifled a cry of agony. The plastic enclosure felt like a tomb. He could hardly breathe. Feeling suddenly full of pent-up power, he smashed his thick right fist against the door. It exploded open and he stumbled forward, gulping the cool air. Then he balled both hands into fists and let out a tormented, bloodcurdling scream.

CHAPTER 18

Elly Stedman turned on his TV around seven-forty-five Sunday morning and caught the opening of the media circus. He was into his second mug of coffee and was about to pour milk on his cereal when his phone chirped.

"Stedman," he answered.

"Hi. Carol McCusker at the farm."

"Mrs. McCusker, good morning. Everything okay?"

"Yep," she said. "Fine. Called to see if you read your Portland paper this morning."

"Not yet. Why?"

"When you were here, I told you I'd read about the fisherman."

"I remember," Stedman said.

"You never mentioned the apple pickers at Stiller Farm."

He sidestepped the implied question. "Is that in the paper?"

"*Sunday Telegram*, front page. They connected the two stories—Drake's Island and Spiller's orchard—and printed the sketch artist's drawings. The reporters didn't sound an alarm. He spun it more as a silly woo-woo spook story about vampires, with historical references. Read it and you'll see that I mean."

"Your story's not part of it, is it?" he asked.

"No way. We're not talking about it except to you and your pals, and Buck Soule's report kept it at *bat reported*. And I put the video on a thumb drive and erased it from the phone."

"Thanks for the heads-up," he said. "I'll check the *Telegram*."

"One of their on-airs joked about seeing it in the *Telegram*. My guess is, there'll be more of that kind of stuff to come."

"Thanks, Carol," he said.

"You're welcome, Detective Stedman. And by the way, you still haven't told me what that is that flew out of our silo."

"I know," was all he said, a little apologetically, and they clicked off.

Stedman carried his cereal and coffee out to the garage shop and booted up his desktop computer to view the *Maine Sunday Telegram* article online. Carol McCusker was right, it was front-page, and there was an above-the-fold headline: *Vampires in York County*. A black-and-white Bela Lugosi *Dracula* movie poster had been placed is a teaser position under the lead.

The article came from a trio of reporters and was a mix of fact, fiction, and tongue-in-cheek skepticism. They cited the Spiller orchard and Drake's Island beach reports, both of which used the word vampire. There were quotes from Harp Gagnon, Max and Jorge, and the late-night fisherman. When the article continued on an inside page, Stedman saw Annie Fitzgerald's police sketches of a red-eyed demon.

There was a sidebar with background on *Dracula's* author Bram Stoker, Transylvania and Vlad the Impaler, and a brief history of book and movie vampires. Stephen King's *Salem's Lot*, about a fictitious vampire town in central Maine, merited a three-sentence paragraph.

A second boxed sidebar went into New England's vampire hysteria from earlier centuries, citing Faye Ringel's *New England's Gothic Literature* and Rhode Island folklorist Michael Bell's *Food for the Dead: on the Trail of New England's Vampires*. Both authors debunked vampires as non-human entities, explaining how consumption—now known as tuberculosis—and superstition played into the unearthing of family members who were suspected of returning from the grave to drain other consumption victims' blood. Twentieth century forensic excavations of graves solved the vampire mysteries.

Near the end of the article were two provocative images of posters reportedly tacked to trees, posts, and utility poles around Wells. One showed Downy, a missing cat, the other Beau, a missing dog. The caption begged speculation: *Are recent pet disappearances around Wells connected?*

Finally, the piece ended with police contact information and a photo of an 18th Century vampire hunting kit: a small open suitcase containing potions, bullets, pistols, daggers, and a selection of both crosses and crucifixes.

Stedman pushed his computer chair away from the desktop, swallowed a sip of lukewarm coffee, and mumbled, "Crosses and crucifixes. Crosses for Protestant vampires, crucifixes for Catholic ones." *Amazon'll be lighting up with orders for these.*

He could see the start of a media circus already. Soon the other local channels—Channel 6 and Channel 8—would also be cannibalizing the *Sunday Telegram* article. It would go beyond local then, and New England Cable News NECN would spread the seeds of insanity from Maine and the Canadian Maritimes to western Connecticut and beyond. Fox News would latch onto it, which would force ABC, CBS, NBC, CNN, and MSNBC to play catchup. It might even pick up steam internationally. It would only take one more Faucon sighting to get the news vans, field crews, and satellite dish trucks to Wells. They'd be out shooting beach footage, farm and orchard scenes, lighthouses and breakwaters, and views of the police station. On-air personalities would hold microphones in the faces of Town officials, the police chief, business owners, ordinary citizens on the street, and visitors.

All of which would thrill the motel owners. The Wells Police Department, not so much.

Elly knew the true story wasn't about vampires. It was about Faucon and *les gargouilles*, the ancient race—gargoyles. And it wasn't a story he wanted the media digging into. He was a voracious reader and from that had come to understand that human curiosity and human fear always gave rise to a need to dominate and destroy the other race or species.

The *Sunday Telegram's* titillating story would expand through the day and into the upcoming week until the print and broadcast media's thirsty and starving audience either became satiated or grew bored and moved on. True story or not, some would believe and some would scoff—but they would tune in. Some of the crazies might even come in search of vampires to kill.

He glanced again at the final photo, the vampire hunting kit in the little suitcase. He recalled Marcy Stonestreet's phone call about the Feds wanting the files. Would modern vampire hunting kits come with syringes and automatic weapons with extra clips?

Just a silly, tongue-in-cheek story, he told himself. *A fluff piece written to entertain. And yet, there at the end, they had printed police contact information.*

He picked up his cellphone and pressed Maryann Keegan's number.

CHAPTER 19

Keegan had committed herself to calling the three Orono numbers on Monday, so after school—with a tiny bit of hope and a lot of trepidation—she sat down with her phone and notepad. All of the numbers were from the 1990s and were probably longshots.

Her first priority was the number she'd found on the back cover of her mother's genealogy course notebook. Zelda had jotted it down next to the name Jan, which Luna had insisted was pronounced *Yon*, because he was from Holland. Luna had also said Jan had the same white streak in his brown hair. And more important—whether it was true or not—she referred to him as *your father*.

She called the number and waited.

"Arredondo's Pizza," a woman's voice answered. "How may I help you?"

Keegan's first impulse was to say, "Sorry, wrong number," and hang up. Instead she said, "I'm calling from Wells, Maine, in the southern part of the state. Maybe you can help me. I'm trying to locate a UMO classmate of my mother's from the 1990s. Mom died, but she left me her classmate's first name and your phone number."

"Hang on," the woman said. "I just work here. Let me put Angelo on. He's the owner."

Keegan could hear her request being summarized for someone else.

"Hi, this is Angelo Arredondo," said a man with a slight Italian accent. "I got pizzas in the oven so—no offense—I gotta be quick. Tell me the name."

"A Dutch student named *Yon*—it's spelled J-A-N but pronounced *Yon*. Attended UMO late 1990s. Older student. Probably already in his 40s or 50s then."

"Streak of white in his hair?" Angelo asked.

Keegan couldn't speak for a moment. Then, "Yes. He had the white streak."

"Delivery guy. Couple nights a week."

"What?" she asked, not knowing what to ask next.

"Nice guy. Post-grad, I think."

The questions tumbled out now. "Can you give me his last name? Any contact information? Did he go back to Holland?"

"Sounds like this is really important to you."

"Very important," she said, and blurted out. "He may be my father."

Silence on the other end as Angelo absorbed her words.

"Look, give Teresa here your name and number and I'll call you back tomorrow—well, maybe tonight. I got pizza in now and I turn things over to the kids at six-thirty. I'll see what records we can dig up and call you back. Tomorrow for sure, but I don't want to keep you in suspense, so maybe tonight after eight or nine. Here's Teresa."

Keegan gave her information to Teresa, who had answered the phone, and clicked off. She sat at the table, waiting for her heart to stop fluttering.

A few minutes later, after her pulse slowed, she tried the 1990s number for the Student Teaching Office. The number hadn't changed in 20 years. She explained that she was looking for a Dutch student named Jan who might have been a scholarship applicant or winner.

"He could have been after his teaching certification," she said.

After a quick check for the names Jan, Holland, and Netherlands, the woman reported she couldn't find anything. Keegan thanked her and clicked off.

She tried the third number, hoping it was still the Language Tutoring Office. If it wasn't, she'd look up the office and get the latest number. Such a service didn't disappear. Students needed language tutors.

A male with a slight accent answered. *German?* She pleaded her case.

"I am new," the student said. "The director, John Foresman, is here. He returns to the beginning."

"Returns to the beginning?" Keegan asked.

"*Jah*, he has been here since long ago."

"Since long ago? Great. May I speak with Mr. Foresman?"

"Wait, please."

A moment later she was telling the director about her mother and about the Dutch grad student.

"I worked in this office as a student tutor myself," John Foresman explained. "For four years. Then in 1998 I became the assistant director, later the director. Jan was in demand as a tutor because—being from Holland, which is not a country but a region of the Netherlands—was fluent in English, French, and German. He was an older student, forties as I recall. Shock of white in his hair. He was post-grad in botany or biology, I think, so we had him for two or three years."

"Do you remember his last name? Do you have any other information on him—address, phone number, overseas address?"

"Can you stay on the line a few minutes while I check the files? I'll put you on hold. Don't mind the music."

After five minutes of easy listening, Foresman was back. "Ms. Keegan? All I have is the old college address, which was a dorm. Nothing in the Netherlands. Don't even know if he went back there. Maybe the registrar has more."

"Last name?" she asked.

"I'll spell it for you," he said. "D-A-U-P-H-I-N-E."

Five minutes later she couldn't recall whether she had said goodbye or thank-you or anything else to John Foresman. What she knew was, Jan's last name was the same as her first name. The man who might be Dauphine Keegan's biological father was Jan Dauphine. Her name was a combination of two surnames, Jan's and Zelda's. She could search the Internet now.

But first she called a fourth Orono phone number, the UMO Registrar, and found out that an international student from Amsterdam named Janos Dauphine, born May 5, 1960, had attended the University of Maine from 1997 to 2000, earning not one but two graduate degrees *summa cum laude* in biological and botanical sciences.

Was he still alive? And if so, where was he now? Back in Amsterdam?

CHAPTER 20

At dusk Luna stood at the mouth of the cave, shook out her upper wings, took a few steps, and lifted off from the clearing. She sighted in on Mt. Katahdin to the east, crossed Baxter State Park, and a couple hours later came out near the tiny hamlet of Patten. She picked up the Fish Stream going south then turned west along one of the smaller streams that fed it. A familiar craggy hillside appeared ahead of her, a small dark cabin barely visible among the pines at its base. The site was far from a paved road and electricity or plumbing. In front of it was an open space that looked from the air like a postage stamp, a cleared area with weeds that could hardly be called a yard. On her previous visit she had made a vertical landing using her short wings. Now, with her injury, she faced a challenge.

It called for a modified dove landing. She slowed her speed and lined up on the cabin's roof—a skip move—barely touching it with her feet then continuing downward into the open area where, as her feet touched the ground, she drew up her glide wings vertically to brake her. She stumbled forward two steps, caught her balance, and stopped. *More like a duck than a dove. That short wing can't heal fast enough.*

"Pernod. Are you there?" she called. "*C'est moi.* Luna." Hearing no answer from the cabin, she called toward the woods in French then English, "*T'es ou, Punaise d'eau?* Where are you, Waterbug?"

"Hush, Luna," came a loud whisper from the dark forest. "You will wake the dead."

A shadowy figure stepped from the trees into a patch of moonlight. He was Luna's height and size except that his shoulders were square like a human's, not hunched like hers. On his round head was perched a dark-colored ball cap with gold lettering: Navy Vet. Some sort of fabric covered his body. *A blanket or a long-sleeved poncho,* she thought, *like the nun's habit I wore into the bookstore.* Whatever it was, it covered him from shoulders to toes. In one hand he held a sack.

"What is wrong with your short wings?" he asked, wobbling toward her like an arthritic old man.

"A wound. It is healing."

"A wound? You did not say an accident, you said a wound. What happened?"

"A battle. *Un poignard.*"

"Whose dagger?"

"Faucon's."

"Ah, the pretender, the son of the Alps leader."

"*Oui.* Unfortunately, before he died Champaigne—out of a misguided sense of obligation—adopted Faucon. With both of the twin princes dead and no apparent grandchildren, he insists he is next in line."

"No one will agree to that," he said. "But I'm asking purely out of curiosity, as you know I reject the kingdom or its traditions."

"It's a new idea, to consider an adopted child. Faucon not only has an older brother leading the Alps clan, but a second brother after that. Incredible as it sounds, if he were to succeed Cyrus as king of *les gargouilles* worldwide, he would leap over both elder brothers."

They hopped up a single step to the door of the rundown cabin. To one side of it were two posted signs: *Disabled Veteran* and *Do Not Disturb.* He opened the door.

Luna asked, "Do these signs and your new hat keep humans away?"

"*Oui.* Since we posted the signs, fewer hunters, fishermen, and hikers come near. Either out of respect for my military service or out of fear that I am mentally disturbed, they keep their distance."

"Your military service?" she questioned. "But you are not even a veteran."

"They don't know that. When they see the warning signs and the hat, they leave me alone."

She shook her head sadly, muttered, "Ah, my Waterbug," and they went inside.

The cabin was a single room with only a wooden table at its center. He lit a candle using a wooden match from a cardboard matchbox. He plopped the sack on the table and pulled out two fish.

"Stream water under the table, Luna," he said. "In the bucket, should you be thirsty." He used his sharp fingernails to shred the fish and handed one to Luna. He sucked greedily at its flesh. Hungry after her exhausting flight, she did the same.

"Candles and matches?" she said. "Where--

"The humans have camps not far away," he answered. "I know how to get in, and I take little, so they do not miss them. I am careful not to leave signs."

"I cannot believe you continue to survive here," she said. "Are you not lonely?"

Instead of answering, he asked her, "So why are you here this time, sister?"

She looked across the table at the one who was practically a mirror image of her, except for his red eyes. Hers, because she was a female, were green. His shoulders were also different. Since they'd been children his deformity—as their father had referred to it—had left him square-shouldered, not looking hunchbacked like all the other *gargouilles* whose angel wings folded down onto their shoulders. At their hatching, her brother had been without either upper wings on his back or hummingbird wings under his armpits. He had instead a grotesque pair of rubbery bat-like wings budded halfway between his shoulders and his hips, just above his mid-balance point. They were a combination of thin hide, sinew, and lightweight bone struts. When retracted against his sides, they fitted him almost as tightly as a second layer of skin.

Pernod had learned as a child that if he extended them in the middle of a run and flapped them rapidly, they would lift him inches off the ground, so that he could speed forward along a path like an airplane on a runway that couldn't gain enough speed for takeoff. But like a roadrunner, he could scoot straight ahead on forest paths and zigzag across meadows and make circles around the clan camp—all while racing along just above the surface. At first their clan was entertained and laughed at what they saw. Then when they saw little malformed *gargouille* skimming the surface of the ponds and lakes and streams—flitting here and there inches above the surface as if water-walking—they began to call him Waterbug.

Then came the Great War in 1917 and the departure of the twin princes and a contingent of 20 French-Canadian *gargouille* swordsmen for France. That left the deformed Waterbug behind while his father Alfred went with his comrades to fight in France. His and Luna's father perished in the mustard gas attack while they slept in the ice tunnel.

It was then, a hundred years earlier, that Pernod had left the clan to become a recluse.

"Luna?" a soft voice asked. She blinked herself back to reality.

"*Qu'est-ce que c'est?*"

"Why are you here?" her brother asked.

Trying not to sound embarrassed, she said, "I need a telephone. Do you have access to one?"

"*Oui*. My friend, who lives near here in the summer, has returned to Florida."

"Good. After we eat, can you take me there?"

He chewed another bite of shredded fish. "May I ask why you need a telephone this time?"

"We need help to survive the winter. Myself, Bronwyn, and Yvette."

"Ah, yes, I remember our friend Yvette from when we were young. Bronwyn I do not know."

"She came to us seeking shelter after the Wales clan that lived in the abandoned mines failed."

"Why can you not survive the winter? Is the Allagash clan in trouble?"

"We are not with the clan," she said, and sighed. "We struck out on our own. And we cannot go back."

"You *cannot* return?" he asked. "Or you *choose not to?* Is this about Faucon?"

She ran a fingernail talon idly through the meat of her fish, avoiding an answer.

"If all you need is shelter," he said, "you can winter over here. There are many empty cabins. And I can show you where to fish."

"That is kind of you, little brother," she said. "But it is not that simple."

"*Pourquoi?*"

"We three are not alone," she answered. "*Nous avons tres enfants.*"

"You have three infants?" he gasped. "That cannot be. You are alive. Mothers must die for eggs to hatch."

She stared blankly at him, waiting for him to make sense of it.

"So these are not your children. Whose are they? Have you adopted them?"

She rested her elbows on the table and put her hands together, steepling her chubby fingers. "*Mon frere,*" she said. "*Tu es leur oncle.*"

"I am their uncle?"

"*Oui.* These are the children of our sister Diana and her mate, Prince LeClair. They are three months old. I fought Faucon for them. He wanted to destroy the eggs."

"To eliminate his competition." Pernod's face went from not understanding to disbelief. "Diana's eggs survived? And there are three males?"

"One male."

"What? You hatched two females? And you let them survive? Why would you do that? You know the rules."

"The rules are unjust and need to be changed. They benefit only the males. They are barbaric and always have been."

Her brother began to laugh, a low, snorty *gargouille* laugh, and his red eyes watered. "You, sister, are insane. There are things in this world that cannot be changed. Male succession is one of them."

"Ah, so you see my point," Luna said. "In any non-royal nest the females are allowed to survive, because they are a threat to no one. And they are needed for breeding, to continue our race. But this is not so in a nest of eggs containing the royal bloodline. In that nest the females pose a threat to *les dauphins*, the male heirs, so that threat is dispatched at birth."

"So you have three," her brother said. "And if you could, you would return to the clan with our nephew, because he is the one male in the kingdom who can negate the pretender Faucon's claim. Yet you cannot return to the clan, because if you show them our nieces, they will destroy them."

"As you can see, Waterbug—

He interrupted. "It would appear that you are hoping that if you can keep them from the clan until they are older—and this means Cyrus must hang on—then you can present all three to the clan, and the clan will accept them and not cull the females."

"That is one possibility," Luna said."

"And the other?" he asked. When she didn't answer, he said, "Oh, no, no, no. You're not imagining female succession. Do you mean to say that one of the females is the firstborn?"

"First hatched," Luna said. "Regine was the first egg I slit."

"Regine? You have already named her Queen?"

"We have. And her brother is Paladin, the knightly companion. Their sister is Mathilde."

"Ah, Mathilde, *mighty in battle*," he translated, and shook his head in disbelief. "No matter what you do—hide them or present them as an alternative to Faucon—*les gargouilles* kingdom and the Council will be thrown into chaos, and more likely into civil war."

"Do you care?" she said, and he went mute.

Then, "No. Not really. I no am no longer invested. I left long ago."

"Then back to my original question. Can you take me to your friend's telephone?"

He removed the poncho and the Disabled Veteran cap and laid them on the table, blew out the candle, and walked to the door. "Follow me. I'll skim the path, you stay just above the treetops. Keep a close eye on me down below. You will have room to land in my friend's driveway."

She watched Pernod's ultra-thin waterbug wings peel away from his sides. He stepped off the porch and before his wings started vibrating, she heard him mutter, "If you eventually go back, I'd love to be there to see everyone's reaction when you show them Cyrus' only living heirs." Then he shot forward on the path like a cartoon roadrunner.

CHAPTER 21

By eight-forty-five Angelo Arredondo, the Orono pizza shop owner, hadn't called back. He had told Keegan if it wasn't Monday evening, it'd be Tuesday morning. But with fifteen minutes to go, she still held out hope.

She had spent the late afternoon and early evening searching the Netherlands and nearby European countries for addresses and phone numbers associated with the first names Jan or Janos and the last names Dauphine and Dauphin. The searches produced fifteen residential phone numbers and addresses plus another six business-related. Four of those six had websites that didn't pan out. She found links to twenty-six newspaper or journal articles, which she read through, finding no apparent connection to her Janos Dauphine, the biologist and/or botanist. She checked Facebook, Twitter, and the other social media platforms then hit the online business connection sites like My Life and Linked In, also to no avail. She tried the obituaries. Other than the list of phone numbers and addresses, she found nothing else promising. But just in case, she recorded everything in both her notebook and in a computer document file.

At eight-fifty-five Arredondo finally called. They exchanged the usual pleasantries.

"This'll be short," he said. "Because the file my wife had on Jan was short. He wrote his name, Janos Dauphine—he spelled it out—on our job application and listed himself as a UMO student who had studied in Amsterdam. No address, no phone number. I also remember now that he said he didn't have a bank account, and it would be hard to cash a paycheck. We agreed to pay him in cash. And of course, his tips were cash, too. He didn't list a wife or emergency contact person. So there wasn't much there."

Keegan's nerves were frayed, and she muttered sarcastically, "I don't suppose he listed himself as a sperm donor?" Her voice had trailed off at the end.

"A what?" Arredondo asked. "Didn't quite get that."

"An organ donor?"

"Organ donor? No."

Keegan heard a commotion on the pizza man's end of the conversation, a woman's voice.

"Wait, wait, one conversation at a time, Maria." Then he said to Keegan, "My wife is waving this picture at me. Hold on." He broke away for a moment, then returned to Keegan. "Maybe a little good news. She found a couple of shoeboxes of photos—college kids who delivered for us over the years. We used to keep them tacked up on the front walls. It was a team spirit thing—you know, the pizza family—but it was also in case somebody got in trouble and we had to show the cops a picture. She's got one of Jan. It's an old print, not a digital, so I'll have to take a shot of the print and text it to you. Hope the quality is good enough."

Keegan practically squealed.

"I'll send it after we hang up."

"Oh, thank you so much, Mr. Arredondo," she gushed.

"Wait," he said. "Maria says she just remembered something else. I'm going to put her on."

Keegan heard the bumping and shuffling of the phone from husband to wife, then a voice, "Miss Keegan?"

"Yes. Hello, Mrs. Arredondo. Nice to speak with you."

"I know you are looking for Jan, who may be your father. Here is what I remember. When he traveled on Christmas vacation, he took a bus to Pennsylvania. His relatives had a farm with no electricity and no cars. He showed us a picture. They dressed in plain farming clothes and wore big hats. And they rode in horse-drawn wagons."

"Horse-drawn buggies?" Keegan asked.

"Yes. Buggies."

"Sounds like the Amish," she said. "They're also called the Pennsylvania Dutch."

"That sounds right," Maria Arredondo said. "And the place had a funny name."

"Funny?" Keegan asked.

"Sex," she replied.

"Intercourse?" Keegan said. "Intercourse, Pennsylvania?"

"I think so," the pizza man's wife said. "That sounds familiar. It's a real place?"

"It is. It's a famous Amish community near another town with a strange name, Bird-in-Hand. Some of our Wells High School senior classes have gone there."

"It's a curious name for a town," Maria Arredondo said.

"Sure is. I don't suppose you'd have a family name or phone number there, would you?"

"No. Nothing. I just remember him coming back from Christmas with relatives and talking about the horses and buggies on the sides of the roads, and the oil lamps for light and the hand pumps for water. I wish you luck finding him."

Keegan heard the phone being handed back to Angelo Arredondo.

"I don't think we have anything else, Miss Keegan," he said.

"Thank you so much, Mr. Arredondo. You and your wife have been a big help."

"I'm glad," he said. "In a few minutes you should get my text with the photo of Jan. We hope you find him. Call if there is anything else we can do."

They clicked off and, while she waited for the text to arrive with the pizza deliveryman photo of Jan, she went to her computer and searched Intercourse, Pennsylvania for any families with the last name of Dauphin, Dauphine, Daufin, or Daufine. No luck.

The text arrived. She saw on her little phone screen the thirty-eight to forty year-old man she resembled, with their shared blue eyes and brown hair with the white streak down the upper right of the forehead. He wore an Arredondo's Pizza delivery shirt that was gray with red trim and had his name stitched over the breast pocket in black: Jan. His shoulders were bony, his arms in the short-sleeved shirt were thin, and across his upper lip she could make out a wispy mustache.

Did he and her mother have a romance or had she chosen him a donor? This picture was from twenty years ago when he'd been around forty. What might he look like at sixty? Even with the picture in hand, would she be able to pick him out of a lineup? Probably, if the brown hair hadn't gone totally white. What would he say and do if she found him? Did he have other children? Did she have half-brothers and half-sisters? And the big question: why hadn't he tried to contact her in the last seventeen years?

She stared at the image of man who in college had gone by the name Jan Dauphine. And she wept. *I need to find you.*

CHAPTER 22

About the time Keegan was talking to the pizza man, Luna was standing behind her brother Pernod by steps of a covered rocking-chair porch fronting a lakeside log cabin.

"Wait here," Pernod told her, and felt around under a porch support beam until he found the key. The two of them hopped up to the porch and he unlocked the front door. It was dark inside with all the window shades down and curtains drawn for the off-season.

"Let me turn on the battery lantern," he said, and did. "Rusty—John Rousseau, he's the owner—turns the power off when he goes to Florida. He returns in May or June. But he leaves several of these battery lanterns around the house for me to use."

"He knows you come in?" Luna asked, clearly surprised.

"*Mais oui*. The hidden key was his idea."

Pernod set the lantern on a coffee table that had been from a massive lacquered slab of wood. The front room was large and extended upward two stories to the peaked log roof. Above them, halfway up, Luna could make out a log banister, with three doors along the open hallway, which she assumed were bedrooms. The front room they were in clearly served as the living room, with furniture organized around the slab coffee table: two brown leather couches, a matching loveseat, a black leather recliner, and a couple of heavy end tables with lamps. The wall art was hard to see by lantern light, but it appeared to be a mishmash of Maine and New England scenes—Mt. Katahdin, a fly-casting fisherman in waders in a stream, a lobsterman at the helm of his boat, black-and-white cows on a hillside against a colorful palate of fall foliage.

Luna's brother led the way to the kitchen, where he snapped on a second battery lantern on a wood-laminated, roll-around center island. Above the island hung a shiny metal carousel with pots, pans, fry pans, and an assortment of large spoons and ladles. At the end of the island was a butcher's storage block, its slots filled with cutting, chopping, and carving knives. The black-speckled granite counters along the outside wall had light cupboards above and matching cabinets and drawers below. There was a double sink, stove with microwave above the burners, and a stainless steel side-by-side refrigerator.

The alcove window to one side had its shade and curtains drawn. A shiny honey-pine trestle table stood between four matching swivel chairs. On the table were four placemats featuring a cartoonish map of Maine with points of interest. The no-man's land between the mats belonged to a cardboard chessboard laid out with two sets of pewter chessmen, one side light-colored and the other darker. Also in no-man's land were a napkin-holder and salt and pepper shakers, beside which a navy blue ball cap like the one Pernod had left at his cabin: Disabled Vet.

"Yours, too?" Luna asked, indicating the hat.

"Rusty's. Both the hat and the chessboard. He loves to play. When we started, he was good but not great. Now he beats me half the time."

"Is it coincidence that you have the same hat?" she asked.

"He had two and gave one to me. He said it—along with the warning sign—would encourage strangers to stay distant. It was a brilliant idea, don't you think?"

"I sense there is more to this story," Luna said.

"*Oui*," he said. "Follow me." He led her to a center hallway behind the kitchen's interior wall. The hallway started at the living room, passed a set of stairs leading to the three second-floor bedrooms, and ended at the back door. In between were three doors.

"Out that back door is a deck that overlooks the lake. On occasion, if there are no neighbors using their camps nearby, we sit out at night. Rusty likes to smoke his pipe while I read to him by lantern light. If we don't sit out, we use the den."

"You read to him?"

"*Oui*. Of course, I am reading to myself as well, getting an education. We have read Plato, Aristotle, Norse mythology, Agatha Christie, Stephen King, even Danielle Steele. Oh, and Bram Stoker's *Dracula*."

"*Vraiment?*" she asked.

"*Oui, vraiment*. Really."

"I can see this has helped your English," she replied.

He pointed to one of the doors. "That is his bathroom. The next is a closet." He gripped the knob of the third door, pushed the door open and stuck the lantern inside to illuminate the room. "Is the den, what he calls his office and library."

Luna glanced around. The walls were nowhere to be seen. They were hidden by floor-to-ceiling shelves jammed with books. Thousands of books. Many thousands. In the middle of the room a red leather armchair faced a 1970s beanbag chair. Next to the armchair stood a 1950s standup ashtray and in the ashtray a pipe.

"I told him I didn't like hard chairs, so he ordered the bean-bag pillow chair on Amazon. I still prefer to squat or stand, but I tolerate the beanbag chair. When we play chess at the kitchen table, I don't use that kitchen stool, I stand. He never comments, because he can't see."

"He's blind?" Luna shrieked. "Your human cannot see?"

"*Oui*. Since Viet Nam, when he was wounded. Which is why he has the hat."

"And that is why you read to him?"

"Well, at first I read to him because he was blind. Now I read to him because he is my friend. And because I, like him, love to read. When he goes to Florida for the winter, he leaves me the key. I come here often and read."

Luna didn't know how to respond. She paced, trying to absorb what her brother had told her, and as she paced she stole glances at the book titles. She had seen some of them on college reading lists at the University of Maine while she was a pretend scholar in habit and burka, sneaking into classes with Zelda Keegan. She spotted *Madame Bovary, War and Peace, All Quiet on the Western Front, Exodus, Othello, Carrie, The Color Purple, Huckleberry Finn, The Count of Monte Cristo, Frankenstein,* and *The Stand.* She had read none of them. But her brother Pernod—Waterbug—their clan's deformed one who had walked away from his family, history, and culture, had read them.

"So," she said. "Have you told this Rusty about us?"

"The answer to your question is complicated. When we first met, Rusty was still able to see shadows. I wore my poncho and a knitted cap that covered my head and ears. He asked me if I was hiding my skin because of napalm. He thought I'd been burned in Viet Nam. I said that wasn't exactly my case, but I was suffering from deformities that I preferred not to talk about."

"Does he still believe that?"

"I've told him the truth."

"That you are *un gargouille*?"

"*Oui.*"

"And more?" she pressed.

"*Oui.* But he swore himself to secrecy. And I would trust him with my life."

"And with ours?" she prodded.

He didn't take the bait, and said evenly, "This is not the time to point fingers, Luna. You came to me because you need to call someone on the telephone, and we *gargouilles* do not have telephones. Humans have telephones. Which tells me that if you need to call someone, then you too must trust one or more humans—with your life. *N'est-ce pas?*"

She tried to glare at him, but she had no self-righteousness to stand behind. She stood convicted.

"*N'est-ce pas?*" he repeated, turning the screws, saying it slowly in English. "Isn't. That. So?"

"*Touche*," she said, and let out let out the breath she hadn't realized she'd been holding. "Waterbug, your friend's telephone, *s'il vou plait*?"

"Of course. The telephone. Rusty He leaves it connected so we can communicate when he is away. No heat, no electricity, but we have the telephone."

"Then may I use Rusty's phone to call my friends Maryann and Keegan? I will tell you my story. It's as strange as yours."

***

Pernod showed Luna the landline on the end of the kitchen table near the chessboard: a black molded-plastic two-piece telephone that was a standard in American homes fifty years earlier.

"Rusty and I use it when we play chess at a distance," he said. "He has a chessboard in Florida. We also use the telephones on the nights I read aloud."

Luna placed a thick hand on the phone and pulled the unit closer to her.

"No push buttons," Pernod said. "It is called a rotary dial. Do you know how to use it?"

"*Oui.* It is like the one I used to call my friends from the Christian Brothers monastery."

"You stayed at a monastery? You were in disguise, *certainement?*"

"You must remember the heavy robe and hood I use to protect myself when I must go out in the sun. I had traveled far from our clan home and needed a place while I searched for Diana's eggs. The monks were kind and believed they were sheltering a retired Catholic nun."

Pernod gave a sharp laugh. "I can't wait to hear the rest."

"And you will, *Punaise d'eau*—Waterbug—after I telephone my friends." She lifted the receiver from its cradle and used a thick index finger to rotate the dial.

CHAPTER 23

Maryann was dozing in her recliner with an open book on her lap when her iPhone on the lamp table woke her. She reached over, picked it up, and saw that the Caller ID had marked it Unknown Caller rather than Scam Likely. The area code was 207, the call coming from inside Maine. She clicked the green Accept icon and said hello.

"This is Luna. Maryann?"

"Luna? Oh my God, are you serious?"

"*C'est moi, oui*. And this is you, Maryann?"

"Yes, yes, it's me. Luna, where are you? Are you okay? Are the babies okay? It's been three months. We had no way to contact you. We've been worried."

"We are fine. Keegan is there, too?"

"Keegan? Oh, sure. Just a minute. Let me call her." Maryann climbed out of the recliner and yelled from the bottom of the stairs. "Keegan! Keegan! It's Luna. On the phone. Hurry."

Keegan took the stairs two at a time and sat on the coffee table facing her mother, who switched the cellphone to Speaker.

"Hi, Luna," Keegan said loudly. "Are you all okay? Where are you calling from?"

"I am on my brother's friend's telephone. *Les trois enfants* are fine, and my two friends are well. They are with the little ones now. You understand that we could not return with *les enfants* to our Allagash clan, so we found a safe location to hide. But winter will soon be upon us, and we need help with food supplies if we are to survive it. I am calling for your—what is the word—*ideas*? No, *suggestions*."

"First let me ask," Maryann said, "How is your inner wing, your injury?"

"It is slowly mending. Not strong enough to use yet. But my upper wings still carry me the long distances. My two friends, Yvette and Bronwyn—you saw them but did not meet them—they take turns at the fishing and gathering. Without my

110

short wings, those two tasks are almost impossible for me. Watching the babies, who move around all the time now, is tiring. And we must take turns standing guard against the coyotes, which are—how do you say it—out of control in the north country. I did not realize until now how important the clan has always been in sharing in the raising of our young."

"So how can we help?" Maryann asked.

"We need a place to hide while we raise them. As you know, we cannot return to our clan with the babies, all three, who are, in my opinion, the rightful heirs to their grandfather's throne. If we take them back, the elders will feel bound to cull the females. Normally, the crown prince—that would be my mate Champaigne's brother, Prince LeClair—would have returned to the place Diana went to ground with their eggs, and he would hatch them, smothering or smashing the heads of, or slitting the throats of the females, saving the males."

"Princes are required to murder their own daughters?" Keegan asked, although she already knew the *gargouille* race's tradition.

"*Oui.* As Cyrus did with LeClair and Champaigne's sisters. As Faucon's father, Drago, as a clan chief, must have done to Faucon's sisters."

After a moment, Maryann asked, "Is it possible to just take the females into hiding to raise them, letting the clan have the male?"

"That would change nothing," Luna said.

"It would result in two more females living," Keegan blurted out.

Luna ignored her. "Culling is murder, pure and simple. And the tradition—call it a law, if you must—is unfair to females. It needs to be challenged. I refuse to separate them. Together they will challenge the cruel traditions and change both clans and the Kingdom."

Keegan and Maryann could see it was an argument two outsiders could not win with Luna. She wasn't about to separate the babies, hiding Regine and Mathilde so that Paladin could ascend the throne.

Luna said, "Our immediate need is for a place to hide and food to get us through the winter. After that we will need a safe place to raise the little ones."

Maryann and Keegan waited.

Luna finally said, "Can we bring them back to Wells?" When they didn't respond, she added, "If not for the winter, then for a short while?"

Maryann and Keegan looked at each other, and Keegan threw up her arms, twisting her face into a silent question: *What are we supposed to do?*

"Give us some time to talk about this, Luna," Maryann said. "I've got your number. We can call you back soon. Stay there and we'll see if we can come up with a plan, okay?"

"Okay," Luna answered. Then, "One other thing. Faucon. Any word?"

Maryann hemmed, then admitted, "We think he's sick, like maybe his damaged wing or his missing toes haven't healed well. There have been a few sightings—encounters with humans—here and there this week. But we don't know where he is. The encounters are drawing attention to Wells. The media are buzzing about a vampire on the loose."

"A vampire?" Luna scoffed, and gave a scornful laugh. "You humans have mistaken us for vampires, dragons, and werewolves. They do not exist."

"I never said they did," Keegan said.

"Me, either," Maryann said.

Luna returned to the question at hand. "Faucon can't get away. If he does, where does he go? If he returns to our Allagash clan, it is without his sword and *poignard*. And there will be questions about his missing toes. He is too weak to cross the

Atlantic to his own clan in France. He is weak and he is hungry, otherwise he would not forage so close to humans."

"Regardless of where he goes to live, we need to get him out of this area," Keegan said. "We can't stand the scrutiny. And I don't think your King Cyrus wants the world to capture a *gargouille*."

"So the question remains," Maryann said. "If we somehow located him, where do we send him?"

Keegan said, "We'll call you back at this number in half an hour, maybe an hour. You think about Faucon's dilemma and we'll think about yours. Talk soon."

CHAPTER 24

Luna told her brother everything. How she had left the safety of the clan and traveled to Wells in search of three books that might help her find where Diana had gone to ground, so she might unearth her sister's and LeClair's eggs and hatch them. She told him how Faucon had followed her to Wells, hoping to beat her to Diana's nest so he could eliminate potential competition for the throne. She described her swordfight with him at Stonehedge. She explained that Maryann, her daughter Keegan, Keegan's best friend AJ, AJ's policeman brother Aaron, and Aaron's cop buddy Cliff Bragdon had all stood by her against Faucon, the threat ending only when Keegan slammed an ax home through Faucon's angel wing and shoulder. Then she told him about the three human females serving as midwives in hatching Regine, Paladin, and Mathilde. And how, in the end, Maryann, Keegan, and AJ had driven her and the babies four hours north to a release point in the wilderness where Yvette and Bronwyn met them and helped fly the children to a hiding place.

"I can see why you trust these humans," Pernod said. "That is quite a story. You leave me breathless." Then, "You really cut off his toes? And this girl stopped him with an ax?"

"*Oui,* Waterbug, *C'est vrai.* I owe them my life and the lives of Diana's children. I trust them more than I trust our clan."

The phone next to the chessboard rang, and Luna jumped. It didn't chirp or buzz like a cellphone, it actually rang. Luna picked it up.

"It's Maryann. We can hide and feed you short-term. Cliff Bragdon says he can tuck you away in his barn. But only for a couple of days. And you can't go out, you'll have to remain invisible."

Luna was speechless, then said, "Okay. And how do I get them there?"

"Call again tomorrow night. We need Tuesday to make a plan. The feeding part is easy. The travel logistics, not so much. The hard part will be finding something safe after Cliff's barn. A longer term solution will require some creative thinking."

"So you think it's safe there in Wells?" Luna asked. "You said everyone is looking for vampires."

"That's mostly media hype," Keegan said. "We hope."

"And Faucon?" Luna asked.

"Remains to be seen," Keegan said, and immediately regretted phrasing it that way. "We work on getting him out of the area."

"You'll just have to trust us for now," Maryann said. "Talk tomorrow. Call us at suppertime, maybe around 5:30."

CHAPTER 25

Faucon was on the move, taking advantage of Monday night's darkness to make his way north toward Canada, where he hoped he'd be fed and tended to by the clan. If they questioned his missing sword and *poignard*, he'd say he'd had to shed the weight and hide them.

For now there could be no long, high, quiet flights above the Maine woods, not with his right glide wing out of commission thanks to Keegan's ax. Foot travel on forest paths or along dark roads had never been a real option, not with his shuffling *gargouille* gait and short stride. Besides, with hunters and a few nighttime poachers around, there were no safe land routes. And there was his swollen foot with its three severed toes. He had severely underestimated the much smaller Luna's skills when he charged her.

Now Faucon found himself wondering. *Did Luna survive her wound?* His *poignard* had skewered her rib cage and continued through her hummingbird wing. She and her human ally Keegan had disarmed him and allowed him to escape by using his short wings. But he hadn't escaped the disgrace and the humiliation. What he'd said to Luna minutes before during their air battle— suggesting he'd considered making her his queen if she abandoned the search for her sister's eggs and helped him claim and ascend the throne—that had been nothing but manipulative goading, hadn't it, an offer manufactured in the heat of battle to draw her out of hiding?

Here he was, wounded, sick, and unable to use the powerful wings that would normally carry him home in a few hours. He was reduced to stealing fish from a drunken human and pilfering apples and eating what the humans had dropped on the ground while storing it for their livestock. And to add insult to injury, he'd been forced to seek shelter in one of the tiny shell-houses where humans relieved themselves. He had surrendered his weapons and to survive was dependent on his short wings for travel, his ingenuity for food, and his dream of the throne for motivation.

Faucon flew barely ten feet above the trees, keeping his speed slow so the vibration of his lower wings wouldn't create too loud a hum, in case there were campers below. Even so, the sound startled a few owls and hawks into flight. He crossed Route 25 near Cornish and in the distance saw a few humans along those streets that were lighted. They strolled in pairs and in small groups—mostly school-age teens—with occasional singles out walking their dogs.

Northward he continued, elevating another hundred feet so he could use the lights of Bridgton as a North Star. Before he reached the town, a little south of it, he dropped back down closer to the treetops over Sandy Point, a district he knew to be dotted with numerous church and secular summer camps. He'd seen it from higher up in July when he'd shadowed Luna on her way to Wells. He felt himself tiring now, thirsty and hungry. He'd either have to rest, eat and move on later in the night or he'd have to find safe haven for the balance of the night and the entire next day. A summer camp in the off-season might work either way.

He spotted a small lake with a cluster of cabins at one end—a camp for human children—and landed on the sandy shore near a building with an open shed on one side. The roof stood on poles and protected two vertical racks of bottoms-up canoes and kayaks stored for winter. Ten feet from the boats, on cement blocks, rested a swimming float covered by a tied-down tarpaulin.

Faucon dipped his hands in the water, drank, and stood staring across the silvery water. What appeared to be a small island lay near the far end of the lake. He guessed it wasn't much larger than the building that housed Annie's Book Stop. He would check out the camp buildings first, but it he needed a different place away from the threat of bears and coyotes, the island might work.

Uphill from the sand beach he saw two clusters of cabins near a central meeting hall that he assumed contained a kitchen.

Rather than wobble up from the beach on an aching foot, he activated his wings and buzzed up to the dirt and gravel driveway in front of the center building. A sign next to the door said FREE CAMP—a red capital K added after FREE to make it FREEK CAMP. Below the name was a Buddha-like figure, legs crossed in the lotus position, a third eye in its forehead above the usual two eyes.

Faucon expended another quick burst of energy and flitted over the four steps and onto the porch. The sign at the center of the door read Dining Hall. Above the handle was a padlock. He tried it to see if it wasn't locked tightly, but the lock didn't move.

His wings hummed again and he skipped from porch to driveway. Then he waddled along the right side of the building, checking for unlatched windows. At the back he turned a corner and found a large open porch which he hopped up onto. The door lock had already been broken and the door was open a few inches. He pushed open the door, peered into the darkness, and stepped in. His eyes, already accustomed to the night, adjusted quickly and he made out a high-ceilinged room with dining tables and chairs at its center. It was a space in which humans, he knew, would find comfortable chairs and couches nearer the walls, where they would congregate.

At the far end of the big room he could see another room, one he assumed to be a kitchen, with a pass-through serving counter between it and the big room. To one side of the kitchen was a dark hallway. He walked toward it and into it, passing the kitchen door on the right before he found another smaller room, one with a sign declaring it CAMP OFFICE. The heavier door in front of him, he realized, was the front entrance that he'd found locked on the front porch. The camp office wasn't locked, so he pushed the door open, took a quick look—it was too dark to make anything out clearly—and withdrew.

The kitchen had a large window with no shade, so some light shone in on the stainless steel shelves, sinks, and prep counters. He saw an industrial-size refrigerator and a six-burner gas stove. Mounted on a wall bracket a few feet away was a shiny cylindrical tank with a paper sign thumb-tacked to the wall beside it, a stick-figure illustrating the instructions: in case of fire, point hose and squeeze handle.

At one end of the kitchen were found shelves not quite empty. They still held a few canned items. He grabbed a family-size plastic jar of peanut-butter, spun the top open, and dipped his fingers in. The aroma made him salivate, so he began shoveling it into his mouth. It was heavenly, and before long the jar was empty except for what stuck to its plastic walls. He held it up to his mouth and stuck his long tongue inside it, licking it almost clean.

On another shelf he found silver industrial-size cans with images on paper labels—beans, corn, peas—but he didn't know how to open them. He discovered a cardboard carton containing nearly a dozen small cans labeled Vienna Sausages, with pictures of what looked like his severed toes on the label. He didn't know what Vienna sausages were, but he saw there was a pull-ring on the top of each can. He figured out how to pop the tops and pull off the metal lids, then ate all of the soft, slippery, flesh-colored fingers.

He returned to the hallway and across from the CAMP OFFICE found a different door labeled INFIRMARY. Under the word was a red cross. He understood both the word and the symbol. He might be able to use what was stored inside.

The door was already partway open, so he pushed it and stepped in. Like the office, it had an outside window with drawn curtains. When he drew them back, the support rod across the top broke free and crashed to the floor, letting more light in. He saw a shelf with boxes and a few small plastic bottles on it. On the floor was a small trash can. He picked it up and scooped everything from the shelves into it and carried it back out to the big dining room, where he dumped everything onto the table that caught the most moonlight from the big windows. He didn't know most of the names on the bottles, but he was able to figure the ones that were aspirin or similar pain and fever products. He put them back in the little trash can.

There were tubes of salve—some for burns, some antiseptic, some that he didn't understand. He deciphered what he could and dropped them into the trash can. A medium-sized brown bottle said Hydrogen Peroxide, and something in the English description indicated its foaming action was meant to cleanse wounds, so he grabbed it. The boxes contained bandages, which he added to his haul. Then he grabbed the can and left the way he had come in. He made his way to one of the clusters of cabins, found a picnic table with good moonlight, and removed the medical supplies again so he could reexamine them.

He started with the foaming Hydrogen Peroxide, pouring it on the festering skin where his toes had been lopped off. The basic idea was: flush the wound. Next, not knowing which salve did what, he dabbed several different ones on his foot. He couldn't reach the ax wound in his wing or his shoulder, so he switched to the pills, swallowing a half dozen aspirin.

There was half a bottle of a pink liquid—he didn't know the word Pepto or the word Bismol—but he read the words stomach upset and relief and figured it couldn't hurt, so he lifted it to his lips and drained the bottle.

Then he checked the cabins and found none had been broken into. Vandals didn't need to break in, they were all left unlocked. One contained four bunk beds—eight mattresses—so he piled the eight together on the floor in a strange little mountain that would allow him to lie on his side and sleep.

Which he did. For sixteen hours. Uninterrupted. His last waking thoughts were: *Did Luna survive? Where is she now?*

CHAPTER 26

Luna was exhausted and slept the rest of Monday night and half of Tuesday in Pernod's beanbag chair. She awoke and got to her feet and stretched then shuffled to the kitchen area, where she found her brother standing at the table with a book.

"*Bon soir*," Pernod said, and set his on the table. "I trust you enjoyed my special chair?"

"*Ah, oui*," she replied. "*C'est tres comfortable*."

"You must be very hungry. There are three fish in that bucket in the sink, and three apples. Leave the bones and later when it is dark I will dump the scraps and rinse the bucket in the lake."

She carried the bucket to the table. "What about you? Have you eaten?"

"I fished before dawn and ate midday. Whatever is there is for you. You cannot fly back to your little family on an empty stomach."

"*Merci, mon frere*." She bit into an apple, chewed then asked, "What are you reading?"

"*The Red Badge of Courage*. It is about a young man who must go to war. It is painful to read, but I cannot stop."

She shredded the flesh of a fish and ate it. "Have you been reading it aloud to your friend Rusty? You must have spoken while I was sleeping. The chess pieces have moved."

"I called him this morning. We played three games and then began *Red Badge*. After he hung up, I had to read more to find out what happens. Tomorrow we will start again where we left off. But I could not wait. I am almost finished."

She ate another handful of fish. "Did you tell him about our nieces and nephew? Our dilemma?"

The old phone rang, and Pernod answered. "Rusty?" he asked.

Luna heard a female's voice say her name.

Pernod handed her the receiver. "It is Keegan."

"Keegan, it is not yet your suppertime," Luna said. "Your mother said five-thirty. It is not even four."

"The plan is coming together fast. Mom's busy on the other phone, getting a couple of friends to help."

"Friends?" Luna asked. "Do you mean AJ?"

"Well, yes, AJ. But also AJ's brother, Aaron, And Aaron's policeman buddy, Cliff. You didn't really get to meet them at Stonehedge, because Faucon disabled them. But they were there to help."

"Aaron is the tan one, like his sister AJ, and Cliff is the large one, *n'est-ce pas?*"

"Yes. And it is Cliff who is offering his barn as a hiding place for a few days. And there's one other policeman Mom mentioned—his name is Elly Stedman. Faucon bowled him over on a stakeout in York and put him in the hospital. You can trust Stedman. You can trust all three of these guys."

"So now, in addition to you and your mother and AJ, there are three *gendarmes* who know?"

"Yes. Three policemen. Even before you called us, they were trying to locate Faucon so they could help him get out of our area."

"Keegan, there are few choices for Faucon. Without his glide wings, he must travel north using his short wings. He cannot go far, because he must move after dark and also forage after dark. He will be lucky to travel thirty miles. Then he must find places to hide and sleep in when the sun is out. If his wounds are not healing properly, he will be further slowed."

"Stedman, Aaron, and Cliff understand that. They're monitoring police reports around the state, in case Faucon shows up on a wildlife camera or someone's outside security system. They want to get to him before some nervous homeowner pulls out a shotgun."

"And if they do somehow find him," Luna asked, "how will they communicate? What will they say? How will your friends help?"

"They'll explain that they want to give him a lift, get him home faster."

"Faucon has a strong will to live. In time he will make it back to the clan."

"Yes, in time. But right now, what he cannot do, is return to Wells. His close calls have people in this area on edge. They don't know who or what they are dealing with. We don't want them to respond with violence."

"Keegan, I cannot worry about Faucon. How do you say it in English—I have my hands full with my two friends and our three little ones. What must we do next?"

"If we drive to your cave to pick you up, how soon can you be ready?"

"You cannot reach our cave by automobiles. We chose it for its isolation."

"How about where you are now?" Keegan asked.

"I am with my brother Pernod's friend's house east of the big mountain."

Keegan heard Luna's brother say, "Mount Katahdin. The cave is west of Katahdin. Two hours flying time."

"Can you get the others to Pernod's?" Keegan asked.

"Tomorrow night. I will fly back tonight. Tomorrow we will eat, sleep, and prepare. We can travel tomorrow after dark."

"And our team needs tomorrow to get the barn ready and pick up your transportation. So you and your two friends can fly while carrying the babies? I'm sure they're heavier now than when we hatched them."

"*Oui.*" Then she asked, "Pernod, may we bring the little ones here tomorrow night? Our friends will meet us and take us to a safe place."

Her brother glanced around the room. *Gargouilles—trois enfants*—in a human's house, his friend's house? He thought of one of the phrases he'd read in a book: *a bull in a china shop.* Wouldn't toddlers do less damage if they were corralled in his Beware-of-Crazy-Veteran cabin? But there would be no dirt-road access, something the lake house had.

"Of course," he said. "They won't be here long." Then, directing his voice to the phone, "Will they, Miss Keegan?"

"Not long at all," Keegan assured him. "Can you give me an address for our GPS?"

Pernod knew what a GPS was—he had learned a few basics about the modern world from Rusty—but he didn't know the address. He'd never been asked such a question.

"How would we know the address?" Luna asked.

Keegan grasped their dilemma immediately. Luna and her brother might be able to find a home or business if they knew the address, but they had no experience giving out a location.

"Is there any mail or paperwork near you? Look for a bill or an envelope, even a catalog. If it came in the mail, the name of your friend is there with his address under it."

"Wait," Luna said.

Pernod looked over the kitchen counters, found no paperwork, and moved on to the den. There he found nothing on the desk but saw something in the wastebasket. He pulled out a catalog and returned to the kitchen.

"L.L. Bean is having an end-of-summer sale," he said toward the phone. He read the address out to Keegan.

"Sounds like an RFD box," she said, but got no response. RFD wasn't in the *gargouille* vernacular. "Okay, let me ask you this. When your friend's mail is dropped off in the little aluminum box with the red flag on the side, does he walk out to get it?"

"He must," Pernod answered. "No one brings it here to the house. I do not know because it happens in daylight hours."

"Is the RFD box close to the house? Usually they are at the end of the driveway," Keegan prompted.

"I can go outside now and find out," he said. "Won't take me long. I can't fly high but I'm fast near the ground. You can talk with Luna while I'm gone." Before Keegan could object, the brother with the malformed wings whom Luna's clan called Waterbug was gone.

"Mom and Elly Stedman will arrive at Pernod's sometime Wednesday—probably in the afternoon. They can wait with your brother. AJ and I have to be in school, so we can't make it. Cliff and Aaron will be getting things ready on our end."

"Your mother and this Elly Stedman, will they have room for six of us?"

"They'll have Aaron's red Jeep, and they'll be towing some kind of an ATV trailer, sort of an enclosed plastic pod. Cliff says he can borrow one from his cousin. It's designed to hold off-road vehicles like four-wheelers, motocross bikes, and snowmobiles. Don't worry, we'll throw in plenty of padding so it won't be too bouncy on the way here."

Pernod returned. "Rusty could walk with his white cane to his mailbox in five or ten minutes. The driveway is dirt and gravel but the grasses and weeds along the sides make it feel narrow. The man from town who delivers food and supplies in the summer is the only one who uses it. The road at the end of the driveway by the mailbox is dirt. The nearest crossroads is more than a kilometer away.

"Sounds like three-quarters of a mile," Keegan calculated. "Any other houses around? Close neighbors?"

"No," Pernod said.

"Okay," Keegan said. "Luna, it sounds like we have a plan. Wednesday afternoon for Mom and Stedman, Wednesday night for you six. Can't wait to see how the babies have grown and to meet your two friends when you get to Wells very late Wednesday night."

"Keegan," Luna said before her friend could click off. "*Merci beaucoup.*"

"*De nada,* Luna," Keegan replied, and clicked off, instantly feeling foolish. She realized she'd said *de nada—it's nothing, no sweat*, Luna—in Spanish.

CHAPTER 27

It was full dark Tuesday night when Luna got ready to start her return flight to the cave. On the table between her and her brother sat the rotary phone and the chess board.

"*Merci beaucoup*—to you and your friend Rusty for this," she said, and patted the telephone, "and for tomorrow night's hospitality for me, my friends, and the babies. *C'est tres genereux.*"

Pernod nodded. "I will tell him. He says he hopes you will return when he is here so that he can meet you."

"Rain is coming. I can smell it," she said. "I must be off. *Les enfants* are always hungry. And Bronwyn and Yvette have only the two *poignards* for protection—mine and Faucon's, which he left in my side. My friends are brave and would defend the little ones to the death, but they are not practiced in battle arts. If a bear arrives in search of a winter cave, their shrieks and shouts will do more to frighten it off than their blows."

They laughed. Then Pernod's eyes went to the hilt sticking out of the scabbard behind her neck. "I see that you have a sword."

Luna reached up, gripped it, and drew it from its sheath. "It is one of the pair that were the twin princes'. The other, which Faucon was forced to surrender, is with my friend Keegan. I could not carry all four weapons when I left Wells, so I kept this and the daggers." She laid the sword next to the chess board. When Pernod opened his mouth to protest, she said, "I could fly with it now, but tomorrow night we three must carry Mathilde, Paladin, and Regine. And because I am the one with a scabbard, I will also carry the *poignards*. I should have no need of the sword tonight or tomorrow."

Her brother looked from her to the sword on the table. "I have never lifted one."

"Go ahead," she invited.

127

"*Merci, non.*"

"As you wish, Waterbug. But sometimes it is necessary."

He didn't answer.

She glanced now at the chessboard, studied the positions of the pieces. "Your friend has black and you have white?"

"*Oui.*"

"And it is his move?"

"*Oui.*"

"And you plan to checkmate him in four more moves?" she said.

"*Oui.*"

"So you have taught your friend the basics, and a little more. But you have not shared our father's best advice?"

"What would that be? Help me remember," Pernod said.

"If I tell you, and you share it, your friend will improve. And you will not win as many games."

"That may be true. But if he improves, our games will be even more enjoyable. Tell me. What advice have I forgotten?"

"Before you continue, tell him: Yes, the king is the endgame, but in reality the queen is the most valuable. She has the most power. Consider the king, but don't dwell on him. *Protect the queen.*"

Pernod nodded. "I do it automatically when I play, but I had forgotten the source of it. I will share it with Rusty, and though I will lose more games, I will enjoy our matches more as my friend becomes more skillful."

Pernod walked her to the door that led to the deck on the lake. Moonlight and raindrops were creating a rippling light show on the water, and in the distance they could see Katahdin hulking. Hearing no thunder and seeing no lightning, Luna took a few steps and lifted off toward the dark western skies.

***

The rain was light over the lake, and by the time Luna reached the trees rimming the shoreline she was able to flap and

128

glide fifty feet above them. She turned west, encountering stronger head winds, and angled south below the big mountain. The rain came in torrents then, sapping her strength. But she faced into it, shoulders and ribs aching. About the time she reached Chesuncook Lake the rain slacked, and headed north up its center. An hour and a half behind her, less than an hour to go. She passed over the north shore of Chesuncook and zeroed in on the high pines and the remote area where their cave was, her mind shifting into worry mode as she drew nearer. She wondered if *les enfants* were hungry and if the winds and rain had frightened them, driven them into a huddle in the deepest recesses of the cave. Had they missed her?

The rain stopped and the winds lulled. Whatever weather disturbance had buffeted her little family—the one she had flown directly into—it had made its way from west to east over the big mountain and was by now passing Pernod's friend's place.

The familiar skyline came into view first—the jagged pattern formed by ancient pines, firs, and oaks on the meadow's south end. They resembled the spires and cupolas and roofs looming over a town's center. Even with her heart pounding from hours of exertion, she breathed a sigh of relief.

Then she heard the screaming and the snarling and the yapping. She pressed her tired wings down hard, felt their heaviness in her back and shoulders when she lifted them—*whoosh, whoosh, whoosh.* She saw the center of the meadow come into focus in the moonlight. A *gargouille* stood in a defensive crouch—it was Bronwyn—both arms extended as if balancing. In her right hand she held one of the *poignards* Luna had left behind. She swished the blade back and forth, warning the pack that was advancing on her.

In her left hand Bronwyn brandished a stick too light to work as a club. Eight coyotes took turns lunging in, trying to sink their teeth into the slight *gargouille's* legs so they could topple her. These were experienced pack hunters who knew their prey could spar with only one or two or three of them at a time, which gave the others behind her access to her Achilles tendons.

Bronwyn turned in a slow circle, cursing loudly at her assailants—*goading them*, Luna thought—while slicing the air with her dagger, moving it side to side, back and forth, not committing her weight with a forward thrust. Luna saw that the strategy was to keep the pack's attention on the lone figure in the middle of the meadow while gradually shifting the battleground away from the cave and toward the trees at the far end.

Luna began a descent that would take her right to Bronwyn. As she glided she reached her right arm across her chest to her left shoulder. But her dominant hand felt no hilt. No weapon. Bronwyn had one *poignard,* Yvette the other. And the lone sword was lying next to Pernod's chessboard. Luna was not only unarmed, but was burdened by a pair of short wings not yet fully healed. She couldn't hover in the air above the hungry coyotes. The most she could do would be to fly over Bronwyn or land somewhere.

"Bronwyn, use your short wings!" Luna yelled, swooping lower and closer to the battle. "Fly up! Escape them!"

Bronwyn's eyes met Luna's, but they were full of sadness and regret. She turned her attention back to the coyotes, calling back to Luna, "I can't. I have to keep them from the cave. Go help Yvette."

Luna lifted her eyes to the cave and saw five more coyotes on their bellies outside the entrance, inching their way forward. The pack had split, and the eight attacking Bronwyn weren't the only danger. Yvette stood bravely before the five, gripping her *poignard* in her left hand while she plucked rocks from a small pile at her feet with her right and threw them. One or two occasionally struck a coyote, but didn't hurt them or scare them off. They were hungry and they smelled food.

To Yvette's side stood the three innocents—Paladin and Mathilde, the two younger siblings, instinctively forming a battle triangle by fronting Regine. They were living up to their names—the knight and the one mighty in battle knowing their priority: protect the queen.

Luna had only twenty yards left between her and the embattled Bronwyn, which gave her a split second to decide her own priority. She had two choices: pull up and stand beside Bronwyn or give a hard flap and pass over so she could help Yvette and the children.

Then a desperate third option jumped into her mind—a crazy, grasping-at-straws compromise. Ten yards from her friend she ordered Bronwyn, "Retreat to the cave. We'll all fight them there." As she passed beside Bronwyn and veered off, she extended her foot talons and her hands gripped one of the coyotes while giving a tremendous flap that took Luna higher and lifted the animal two feet off the ground.

But seven snarling, salivating coyotes remained, darting in and nipping, gnashing their teeth. They hardly noticed the loss of their comrade.

"Fly!" Luna yelled back at Bronwyn. But the coyote in her clutches was too heavy, and when it squirmed and rolled, she was forced to let go. It hit the ground running and rejoined its brothers and sisters.

"The cave, Bronwyn! Fly!" Luna again. But she knew it was too late.

The returning coyote picked up speed and launched itself at Bronwyn's back, its forepaws slamming into her shoulders between her angel wings. She stumbled forward, off balance, into the midst of the advancing coyotes. Her short wings came out from her sides and for a brief instant she may have thought she could activate them and lift off. But two coyotes had clamped their jaws around her ankles, so that even as her wings began to vibrate, she wasn't able to rise. Another sank its teeth into the meat of her thigh. Another one—or was it two, she couldn't tell by the feel anymore—latched onto her furled broad wings. She felt herself sinking.

With only her arms free, she had a moment of clarity. *It's over. But Luna and Yvette will save the children.* She dropped the stick in her left hand and used both hands to reverse the *poignard*, pressing the sharp point of the blade to her heart. Then she fell forward on it.

The coyotes didn't care how she went down. They simply wanted her on the ground, dead or alive. They were hungry and tore the little *gargouille's* body apart.

Luna couldn't see behind when Bronwyn went down. She was focused on the cave entrance, where Yvette waved her blade weakly and tossed stones, somehow deterring the advance of her advancing foes, the children close to her, watching, eyes wide. Without the heavy coyote in her grip, Luna flapped once more and came in behind the five slinking coyotes.

Yvette saw her coming, heard Luna order her, "Yvette, toss me the blade!"

The five coyotes also heard her voice and, startled by a rear attack, looked over their shoulders to see what they'd heard. Luna passed over them, pulling her wings almost vertical to brake herself, the spread of them causing the cave's mouth to go suddenly dark. It was only a moment, but that was enough to confuse and slow the attackers.

"Throw it now!" Luna yelled, and Yvette lobbed the *poignard.*

Luna caught it, turned a pirouette in midair and landed between Yvette and the coyotes, facing them. Before they could react, she hopped forward onto the back of the nearest coyote and sank her toe talons in. It howled and tried to shake her off. But Luna extended her hummingbird wings for the first time in months, and though the wounded right one would not allow her to go airborne, it was well enough that she could vibrate them, steadying herself atop the beast's back. Now she was in a fighting position and could slash or stab downward. Unlike Yvette and Bronwyn, Luna was skilled—deadly—with the *poignard*.

The four coyotes around her had no choice but to turn their attention from Yvette and the babies to this new threat: a larger, winged, humming *gargouille* perched atop their yapping comrade.

With a single lightning-fast thrust she stabbed one of them in the eye, then slashed the snout off the coyote next to it. Both howled in pain. She thrust the blade into the open mouth of a third, piercing the back of its throat and slicing its tongue on the withdrawal. The howling intensified. She reached to her side and placed the *poignard's* tip in the ear of the writhing beast under her, then jammed it into its brain. The coyote collapsed on its chest.

Luna hopped from the carcass onto the hardpan, swished the sword side to side in front of her, and unfurled her great wings again as wide as she could, making herself huge, at the same time keeping up the vibration and hum of her short wings. And all the while she screamed.

The defeated coyotes, tails between their legs, whimpered as they slunk away to seek comfort with the larger pack.

Luna collapsed on her haunches, her short wings silent again. She kept her great wings spread so the cave entrance was filled with her dark, threatening shadow, in case the retreating attackers should choose to reverse themselves.

A series of swift practiced movements had turned the tide, thanks to the covert training she and Diana had received from their mates, Champaigne and LeClair, the Night Hawks who had terrorized the Confederates by night. What was important now wasn't their Civil War exploits but the fact that they had secretly instructed their lovers—two females—in how to defend themselves with the efficiency of assassins.

Luna stood between the two carcasses and stared at the pack in the meadow. They were too occupied with Bronwyn, satisfying their hunger, to mount an attack on the cave. She furled her angel wings against her shoulders and faced the trembling Yvette and the three tiny *gargouilles*.

"Bronwyn?" Yvette asked. She folded her own broad wings and her arms around Regine, Paladin, and Mathilde, drawing them close.

Luna shook her head sadly. "She bought us time by dividing the pack. Even when I told her to fly back here and fight with us, she stayed. That pack would have followed her here and joined the ones you held off. She knew they were hungry, and that once they took her down they would not need to come here."

Yvette began to weep. "She was our closest friend. She—

"She loved Regine, Mathilde, and Paladin," Luna said. "She was not afraid to die for them. You and I would have done the same."

Yvette rocked with the babies. "I have no skills with a blade, Luna. Had you not returned when you did …"

Luna placed a hand on Yvette's trembling shoulder. "But you have courage, my friend, which counts for many blades. You held them off just long enough."

The little family of *gargouilles* stood there as if praying together, each connected physically as well as invisibly to the others.

Yvette said, "Did you see Mathilde and Paladin? They had only courage. They stood in front of Regine, protected her. Three months old, barely ten kilos each, their wings not yet out—and no weapons, no weapons—yet they were ready to stand and defend each other."

"I saw," Luna said. "I saw." Then she reached out her arms and wrapped them around Yvette's neck and shoulders and extended her great wings to cocoon the four others within herself. She wept softly for a moment, then said, "Take them inside, feed them, and soothe them. I will stand guard until the pack leaves."

"And Bronwyn?" Yvette asked.

"When the time is right, I will go out and retrieve my other *poignard* and care for her bones—when you and the little ones are not watching."

"And if the pack returns while you are doing it?"

"I will have a *poignard* in each hand and I will unfurl my wings. If that doesn't frighten them, they will pay a high price."

"And what will we do next?"

"My brother is expecting us tomorrow night. My human friends will meet us there. They have arranged for a safe place to hide us."

"And how will we travel—to your brother?"

"We will fly. We will each carry a baby," Luna said. "As we did when we brought the babies here in July."

Yvette stared at Luna. "There were three of us then, and three babies. How will two of us carry three children?"

Luna stepped back. "I will find a way. Take the children inside. Feed them if they will eat, encourage them to sleep. I will keep watch and think."

CHAPTER 28

Several hours later Luna realized she had only three hours of darkness left before the humans—hikers, fishers, coyote hunters, kayakers and canoeists, whitewater rafters, autumn leaf peepers, and the hundreds of guides and helpers who showed them the area—awoke in their campgrounds to eat and spread out around Maine's North Woods. The colors of the leaves were vibrant and the weather promised to clear. Which meant that a *gargouille* venturing forth in daylight would be spotted quickly and pursued. Centuries—millennia—had taught Luna's race that it was essential they remain invisible to *homo sapiens*. And yet, here she was, ironically, scrambling to deliver three children—the remaining royalty of her race—to the safekeeping of human friends she had met barely three months earlier. She had to act now, even if it meant leaving Yvette and their three charges for a while.

Luna found Yvette in near darkness that was lit only by a small circle of hazy moonlight that beamed through the cave's entrance. Yvette was attempting to feed Regine, Mathilde, and Paladin, but it was early, not quite their feeding time. The main dish Yvette had prepared for them sat untouched on three separate slabs of bark. She and Yvette had pounded potatoes into a paste then added crushed nuts with the juice and flesh of pulverized, sweet, juicy apples. But these were rambunctious early toddlers—three months out of their shells, stronger and more coordinated in their arms and legs now—and they were ignoring their food, rolling and pushing and pulling, and wrestling on the cave floor. If the attacking coyotes and the death of one of their caregivers had traumatized them, they didn't show it now. Luna watched a moment, wondering if they would even remember Bronwyn later.

"Yvette, I must go out. Take one of my *poignards*." She held it by its point.

Yvette wrapped her stubby fingers and thumb around its grip. "Will I need it? Are the coyotes gone?"

"They are still feeding," Luna said. "It will keep them occupied. They have no need to come up here."

"But if they do?"

"If they do, take the children to the back of the cave where it narrows. Back the children and yourself into the crevasse. It is easier to defend. If they try to poke their heads in, don't move your blade in sweeps, and don't slash down. Thrust forward in quick short jabs—to the nose, the eyes, and the mouth—not hard enough to bury the blade. Imagine a snake bite. Use your thrusts to annoy, and conserve your energy. I am quite certain they will not come, but in any case, I shall return in less than two hours. You have a plan and you have a purpose."

The three little wrestlers giggled and squealed, and Luna turned to leave.

"Where are you going?" Yvette asked.

"Chesuncook Lake and the little settlement there. There are campgrounds and boat launches around the village and along the nearby shores."

"Be careful," Yvette cautioned. "The humans have made coyote hunting a business. There are many guns near that settlement."

"Two hours," Luna said, and walked toward the moonlight at the mouth of the cave. A few running steps and she was gone, soaring out and over the sated, drowsy coyote pack lounging amongst Bronwyn's remains. *Whoosh, whoosh, whoosh*, and she cleared the treetops.

***

Luna descended in a widening circle over Chesnuncook Village, census population ten. She remembered when the third of three dams was built in 1916, the Ripogenus Dam, flooding the lands around Ripogenus Lake, Caribou Lake, and Moose Pond to create the Chesuncook reservoir, Maine's third largest lake, twenty-two miles north to south and one to three miles west to east. With the decline of the logging industry and Maine's paper mills, the once remote logging lands had become a four-season recreation area. With the state's wolf population now nonexistent, the displaced *gargouilles* found themselves pushed north and west almost entirely out of Maine.

Luna located the West Branch of the Penobscot River and the point of land formed by the river and the lake. There was a beach and a boat launch that promised a perfect landing strip. She came in low, scanning the area for any humans who might be awake and watching, then landed on the grounds behind the Chesuncook Lake House and Cabins, furling her wings near one of its outbuildings. She wobbled among the buildings, rental cabins, and the beach, exploring, looking for ideas. She didn't know exactly what she was after, but she knew that the next night she and Yvette—two of them, not three, since Bronwyn was gone—would need to transport the three babies two-plus hours around Mt. Katahdin to Pernod's friend Rusty's lake house. Three children but only two adult *gargouilles*. And her with lower wing damage that diminished her weight-bearing capacity.

They had three options: air, land, or water. The land option, negotiating south around the lake and along the river roads like Golden Road to Millinocket and back up to the Patten area, made no sense. Too much exposure. And they had no ground transportation. Nor did the water option work, because she and Yvette—even if they had access to a boat or kayaks or canoes—weren't sailors or paddlers. And the lake, the dam, and the open river with its occasional rapids, would prove nearly impossible. Not to mention the probability—if they were caught on the open water in early daylight—of running into river rafting companies, canoeists, kayakers, and fishing parties.

Which left her with her original plan: flying. Flying perhaps two and a half hours, maybe three or more. But that plan had depended on the three of them, three healthy adult *gargouilles*, each carrying a fifteen-pound infant. Neither Luna nor Yvette could handle a double load for long. And alternating meant Luna, with her injured short wing and her chest wound—would have to land and take off several times. Which meant finding long open landing and takeoff strips, all of it in the dark while over unfamiliar terrain.

Our only chance is to share the load and not stop.

She came around a hedge and found herself facing a campsite with four pop-up tent trailers with cars and pickups parked in front of them. Glowing embers in a fire pit told her where the camping party's center was. Nearby someone had strung a double clothesline between two white birches, with an assortment of bathing suits and beach towels hanging on it.

Luna heard snoring in all of the campers, but she saw no one no one outside. She crept toward the clotheslines, keeping part of her attention on the trailers' doors. She found an assortment of towels and bathing suits clipped to the lines, and several pairs of swim goggles. There was a floppy, bright blue, Trader Joe's ice bag—the plastic zip-up kind for picnics—at the end of one clothesline. She pulled it free of the clothespin and waddled on.

A few meters farther she came to three cabin tents. Two were dark, the third glowing because someone had left a lantern burning inside. But no humans stirred.

On the ground she saw five one-person kayaks side-by-side, two adult-sized, three smaller. There were paddles beside them, and life jackets. Only one of the life jackets was child-sized. The others were either for adults or youths. She scooped up the child's preserver, a chest flotation device with hard plastic straps, then moved on through the campground, searching for whatever else might help her with her wild plan. She saw nothing.

But then, at the end of the beach, as she was about to take off for a different campground, she spotted a Jeep with no doors. A backpack rested on one of the rear bucket seats. She reached in, untied the boots that were lashed to the frame, and set them on the floor. She pawed her way through the pack. It was mostly hiking clothes, which she emptied onto the seat. On the vehicle's center console she found a small box of protein bars, which she slipped into the now empty backpack. To that she added the folded Trader Joe's ice bag and the child's life preserver. She zipped the backpack, looped its strap over her wrist, and walked like a holiday shopper out onto the floating dock. Seeing no one, she untied a twenty-foot line from a cleat, coiled the rope, and stuffed it into the backpack. Then she spread her broad wings and made a running takeoff off the end of the dock—*whoosh, whoosh, whoosh.* She skimmed the lake, dipping her feet in the cool water before elevating, then banked north and followed the reservoir on her way home to the meadow and the cave. Soon she'd be able to tell Yvette her plan for Wednesday night. In between they'd all need a good day's sleep.

CHAPTER 29

Wednesday morning arrived and with it came sunshine and daylight, which meant the earliest New England foliage was bursting with fall colors. Daylight also meant that the two ancient races—*homo sapiens* and *les gargouilles*—were on opposite schedules. Maine's humans were awake and active, going off to school, work, and the marketplace, while its *gargouilles* slept or engaged in indoor activities that kept them out of the direct rays of the sun.

Keegan and AJ, being Wells High seniors, had to go to school. They connected in the hall before homeroom, where Keegan again talked to AJ about the Orono pizza shop owner and the new information she'd learned about the Dutchman who might be her father. She showed AJ the eighteen-years-earlier photo Mr. Arredondo had texted her: a 39- or 40-year-old grad student with a white streak in his hair like Keegan's, who delivered pizza, volunteered as a UMO language tutor, and spent his holiday and semester breaks in the Pennsylvania Dutch farm country. And who had likely been Zelda Keegan's lover—or at least her sperm donor—making him a leading contender for Keegan's biological father. Now she knew the man's name—Janos "Jan" Dauphine, pronounced Yon—and what he had looked like around 1999.

She and AJ also talked about Wednesday night, when Maryann and Stedman would return from the Baxter State Park area with Luna and the other *gargouilles* they were picking up and delivering to Cliff Bragdon's barn.

"I can't wait to see the babies again," AJ said. "Remember how amazing it was to hold them right after they were born?"

"Correction. *Hatched*," Keegan said.

"Hatched. Born. Whatever. One minute they were these rubbery eggs, the next they were these living little things, crying and squirming."

"They were softer than I expected," Keegan said. "I had more of a turtle or an alligator idea, something hard and scaly."

"Remember how we tried to feed them and keep them quiet—first above the tunnel, then again in your mom's car on the way home, and—oh, my God—there in your living room that night?"

"What I remember," Keegan said, "is how they got to their feet first thing, almost as soon as Luna cut them out of those shells. They plopped on the ground—like calves do, or foals, or fawns—and in no time were struggling to stand. They wobbled and fell and got back up and took a few steps. Human babies don't walk for like, what, ten months or a year."

"I wonder how much they weigh at three months. And when do their wings pop out? And how long before they try to fly?"

"How long before *what* fly?" asked a boy passing in the hall.

"Um," Keegan said, then recovered quickly. "Bats. We were wondering if baby bats can fly right after birth."

"No idea," the boy said. "They're marsupials, aren't they—like kangaroos? Seems like bat babies would ride in the mother's pouch for a while. Maybe they're like birds, and instead of jumping out of the nest, they jump out of the pouch."

AJ looked at the boy with her best puzzled face, just wanting him to move along. "Think so?"

"I have no idea," the boy shrugged. He shook his head in a way that said duh, and said, "Ask your phone," and walked away.

"We don't discuss any of this again," Keegan said, "until we're out of school and sure we're alone."

***

142

Because it was Tuesday, Maryann didn't have to open the Book Stop. Once she'd gotten Keegan off to school, she had a free day. She picked up Elly Stedman, who was nearing the end of his paid medical leave from the Wells PD. They pushed two shopping carts into the Hannaford supermarket and began stocking up for their guests: mostly large containers of basic food staples like peanut butter and oatmeal, plus potatoes, apples, green bananas, and giant boxes of raisins.

When Stedman stopped and, with a questioning look, held up a large package of Pampers, Maryann shook her head and smiled as if to say, "Thoughtful but silly, Elly." He shrugged and grinned sheepishly, as if to say, "Hey, what do I know? I'm new at this. This is our first gargoyle. And it's triplets."

"Bread?" he asked in another aisle, holding up a family-sized economy loaf of white. "Will they eat bread?"

A seventyish lady pushed her cart between Maryann and Stedman and said in passing, "If the kids and grandkids are coming to visit, they can eat whatever you put out or they can go hungry. Don't cater."

Stedman and Maryann suppressed their chuckles until she was out of earshot.

"She thinks ..." Maryann said.

"Never mind what she thinks," Stedman said. "Bread or no bread? White or wheat?"

"Go for quantity," Maryann replied. "White'll fill 'em up. And we're only talking a few days to a week until they move to a long-term location."

They grabbed ten huge boxes of Corn Chex, Wheat Chex, and Rice Chex.

"Again, volume," Maryann said, and added several large boxes Saltines.

"Will they need milk for the cereal?" Stedman asked.

"Let's keep it finger food, Elly," she said. "I doubt they're into bowls and spoons yet, if they ever will be. And cow's milk might give 'em the runs."

They grabbed two twelve-packs of paper towels, each of them adding one to the mountain of groceries in their carts, then headed for the front registers. Maryann steered her cart into the checkout slot first, and Stedman followed with his.

The cashier, who knew all the locals, looked up, saw the two heaping carts, and asked, "Together or separate?"

Maryann stood there dumbly, as if she'd been asked if they were smuggling in gargoyle babies. Before she could answer, Stedman calmly said, "Separate, Cathy," and the cashier called a young man over to do the bagging while she scanned the first cartload of groceries.

Maryann paid for hers with her Visa, then pushed her cart, now loaded with bagged food and paper goods, away from the checkout. She glanced at Elly emptying his cart and called back, "Nice to run into you, Detective Stedman," and steered her shopping cart toward the door.

When he caught up to her outside in the parking lot, she had the rear hatch of the Subaru up and had finished unloading what she'd bought. Her shopping bags were neatly tucked into the left half of the cargo area. Stedman approached with a twinkle in his eye, saw the layout, and barely suppressed a laugh.

"*Nice to run into you, Detective Stedman?*" he said, over-dramatizing, and stood there without unloading his bags.

She shrugged and smiled coyly. "I'm sometimes awkward in social situations."

"A grocery store checkout line is hardly a cocktail party."

"I know, I know. But Cathy thought …"

"She didn't think anything," he said. "If she did, she may have thought we were buying two carts of groceries for the food shelf and was asking if we wanted to put it all on one ticket."

"Do you really believe that, Detective Stedman?" she asked, and before he could answer, she went on, "I know what she thought. So do you."

He lifted his bags and started transferring them into the cargo area, then stopped and smiled warmly, nodding at the cargo space. "Should we put a divider down the middle between your side and mine? Can we trust the cereals back here?"

She returned the smile and said, "You're funnier than I thought you were. Finish unloading and I'll take both carts to the corral."

Which he did. Then, grinning, he watched her push the shopping carts—first side by side then one inside the other—to the pipe-framed cart rack.

***

Cliff Bragdon was, like Stedman, almost finished with his medical leave. He got up early, fixed himself breakfast, and hit the road—a man on a mission. The firewood truck creaked on its springs as its load shifted side to side in the rutted driveway, groaning under the load of hardwood Aaron's volunteer army had loaded onto it on Saturday morning. Cliff had been deeply touched by the efforts of so many friends. But now it was time for the wood to be unloaded—not to the woodpile of a paying customer but to his cousin Dexter— because Cliff and Stedman and Maryann Keegan had hatched a plan to secretly move six *gargouilles* from Mt. Katahdin to Cliff's barn under cover of darkness. The *gargouilles'* wheels— his stealth transport—called for a Yankee swap. Dex wanted a load of Cliff's wood in exchange for the use of his ATV trailer.

Cliff pulled into Dexter Rasmussen's place in Arundel at eight-fifteen. He tilt-dumped the wood in a pile near the back door of Dex's workshop, knowing that his cousin's woodstove was just inside the door. Dex had also risen early—the wood-for-trailer swap was a late-night, last-minute deal—to make sure both of his toys, a snowmobile and a four-wheeler, were out of the trailer and stored in the shed before Cliff arrived.

The cousins clamped the trailer hitch onto the steel ball and hooked up the wiring package.

"So who's this friend you're moving?" Dex asked, curious. "Somebody local?"

Cliff momentarily forgot the story he'd pitched the night before when he worked out the deal, but he recovered fast. "Single mother. Can't stay where she is or where we're putting her."

"Domestic abuse?" Dex asked.

"Can't say."

"I'm guessing it's nothing official, not cop stuff, right? A good Samaritan thing on your part?"

Cliff managed a shrug and a goofy aw-shucks grin.

"Okay, didn't mean to pry. Just be careful lifting her furniture. You just got out of the hospital for those ribs. Let 'em heal. Let others handle the heavy stuff." Then he added, "Sure you don't want some help?"

Cliff shook his head. "I've got volunteers on both ends, thanks. I'm just the driver."

"Kids?"

"What?" Cliff asked.

"Kids. Does she have kids?"

"Who?"

"The woman who needs to disappear, Cliff."

"Oh. Yeah, one. They just need to move, get off the hot seat."

"She's not moving into your place, is she?"

"No, Dex, she's not moving into my place," Cliff said impatiently. "She's just needs someplace safer." Cliff fished his truck keys out of his pocket. "Look, Dex, I appreciate this on such short notice."

Dexter Rasmussen reached into his back pocket and pulled out a flat leather wallet molded like the curve of his butt. He fingered the billfold part of it and extracted a hundred-dollar bill, then handed it to his cousin.

"Here, Cliff. Buy her and the kids some food."

Cliff accepted the hundred, folded it and slipped it into the breast pocket of his flannel shirt. "Thanks, Dex. This'll help a lot." He shook his cousin's hand, climbed into his empty firewood truck with the attached trailer, fired it up and shifted into gear. "I'll have it back in a couple of days."

The cousins waved goodbye to each other and Cliff drove off, tickled to remember Dex handing him the hundred dollar bill.

***

Aaron had completed his shift and changed out of his uniform in the locker room. Now, in his black and red-striped jogging sweats and fluorescent yellow running shoes, he stood in the Wells PD station with a hot coffee and a cruller in his hand.

"How's the craziness, Zenny?" he asked Arsenia LeGuinn, who hadn't gone off dispatch yet. "Just because it wasn't a full moon, it doesn't mean the loonies weren't out."

"The chief's going on the news this afternoon," she said. "About this vampire nonsense."

"Seriously?" Aaron said, taking a bite from the dry cruller and moistening it with a swig of coffee. "Why?"

"She needs to tell the public to lighten up. She's afraid that with all the media hype some people may take it too seriously. *An ounce of prevention is worth a pound of cure,* she said."

"Did something happen? I mean, why now?" He applied his patented stare, knowing she'd crack.

"Got to promise ..." she said.

147

Aaron gave her the zipped lip sign. "Between you and me."

"Howie Gardner called last night."

"The high school history teacher?"

"*Retired* history teacher. He works nights on the desk at the Hampton Inn."

"And?"

"He wanted the chief to know two guys from Virginia checked in carrying gun cases."

"Hunters? We see them every year."

"Hunters spend their time farther north around Moosehead or Rangeley or the Allagash. If they stop here in Wells, it's usually a one-night stayover en route to those other paces."

"And?" he asked.

"These guys booked a week."

"There's got to be more than that," Aaron said, prodding her.

Zenny dropped her voice to a loud whisper, as if someone might be listening. "Howie said he heard them waiting for the elevator, laughing about vampires."

"But everybody's laughing about vampires lately," he said. "We've got the fish story and the apple tree. That hardly warrants a press conference."

"Think what you want. She's taping at four o'clock. You can count on bits and pieces making the news at suppertime with all the Portland stations, maybe the morning, too."

"No harm in calming the public's fears, I suppose. But she doesn't think the two guys at the Hampton Inn are here for a vampire hunt, does she?"

"Serious or not, she said it's time to say something to head off any *Walking Dead* or *Buffy* crazies, tamp it down before somebody gets hurt."

Aaron shook his head in disbelief and signed out.

CHAPTER 30

Tired as she was, Luna couldn't sleep. She woke Wednesday afternoon around three o'clock, thinking about Bronwyn, whose bones she hadn't had time to bury while it was dark, because the pack was still feasting on them when she made her raid on the campers at Chesuncook Village.

She made her way from the darker reaches of the cave to its mouth and stood gazing out onto the meadow where her friend had gone down. Most of the big pieces of her flesh had been stripped away and eaten. But the coyotes had left, turning the feeding ground over to the turkey vultures that now hopped around the carcass. They stepped forward and back, latching onto bits of meat they swallowed in chunks and strips. The bones, Luna could see, were pretty much picked clean, and what remained was the skeleton—the foot and leg bones, the hips, pelvis, and rib cage, and the backbone, shoulders, and skull. She made out the tip of the *poignard* blade pointing skyward out of Bronwyn's back from a spot between her angel wings.

Luna closed her eyes and choked back a sob. When she opened her eyes, the sunlight on the meadow reminded her that she'd soon have to expose herself to retrieve whatever remained of her friend, not just out of respect but because she knew sport hunters, who paid guides to find them coyotes, would in time follow the pack's trail to the meadow. She couldn't leave a *gargouille* skeleton for them to find. They would not mistake it for *homo sapiens*, despite the similarities. They would note the four wings—the angel wings on Bronwyn's upper back and the hummingbird wings at her sides. The hunters would see her stripped skeleton as a thing new and different, something they wouldn't mistake for a crusty prehistoric skeleton, but would see as a fresh kill. They would know that a winged creature they had only read about in fairy tales and movies was real—existed. Which meant there could be others. And the hunters would summon investigators and scientists. Luna knew that for the safety of her little family and for her clan and all the other clans around the world, for the preservation of her *gargouille* race, she had to make Bronwyn disappear. Now.

She drew out the *poignard* and shook out her broad wings. Her short wings still ached from fighting the five coyotes, but the wounded wing hadn't bled. That was progress. But even so, she knew it couldn't take much more stress. She had to rely on her angel wings.

At the mouth of the cave she took three steps then leaned forward and flapped. She felt her toes push off the ground and her body lift skyward. Another long, slow flap sent her into a short glide that would take her to the gathered vultures.

The turkey-faced buzzards sensed her before they saw her. They glanced up indifferently but didn't move. They had seen hawks and ospreys and eagles swoop toward them with wide wingspans, but experience told them single raptors seldom attacked groups of feasting vultures. They didn't flinch.

So Luna screeched and slashed the air with her dagger, and when the vultures didn't disperse she aimed her hurtling body directly at them. They left the rib cage and scattered—but backward, not skyward, their retreat only eight or ten feet away.

Luna lowered her legs and straightened her body, tilting her wings to catch the air and brake. She couldn't stop as with her short wings, but managed to stabilize in two steps. A small oval of Bronwyn's face remained—cheeks, chin, and the bony brow of her forehead pockmarked by the vultures' incessant pecking. What was left of her flat, rubbery, gorilla nose was dry, no longer glistening around the nostrils. Her eye sockets were empty.

Her green eyes were so lovely, Luna thought. *And so fierce at the end. We will tell the children about her.*

Below the nose, jutting downward and upward, was a sad rictus of exposed white teeth. The only body parts that remained untouched were Bronwyn's four wings—the angel wings and the hummingbird wings—all left uneaten because they were leathery and tough and had no meat on them.

The vultures kept a safe distance, waiting to see if Luna, this giant winged creature, would claim her part of the meal. *The pecking order.*

Luna landed near the carcass—it was too picked over to be called a corpse—and laid her free hand on Bronwyn's fleshless torso, now free of flesh and internal organs. She turned her friend's skeleton onto its side and removed the *poignard* that had saved her from being torn apart alive. *Thank you, Bronwyn, for your sacrifice.* Now Luna had a dagger for each hand.

The vultures, no longer sensing an imminent threat, hopped and flapped nearer. Several who had taken flight dropped lower, tightening their flight circles as they descended.

Luna raised both arms and, when they continued to advance, spread her broad wings, not to fly away but to make herself more menacing. She puffed up her chest, feeling the grief and anger animate her. She hissed like a protective goose then screed like a hawk. She waved her arms, slashing slowly at first, then faster, not able to slow herself. The air whistled around her slicing blades. Two bold vultures stepped in too close, imagining they and *la gargouille* could share the carrion, but with a flick of Luna's hands both vultures' heads toppled from their necks onto the ground. Their bodies stumbled aimlessly for eight or ten steps before they fell over. Two other vultures moved closer, as if to see that their comrades had indeed lost their heads. They never saw Luna's blades, and in a flash their heads, too, lay on the ground.

The flock hopped backward, away from Luna and the carcass they had been stripping. A few lunges by Luna and they retreated farther until they were no longer a threat.

Luna sheathed both *poignards* and—hands and arms and shoulders free—grasped Bronwyn's spine below the base of her

151

skull and with all her strength lifted the skeleton off the ground. She ran and flapped again and again and again, barely clearing the hardscrabble, working her shoulders and wing muscles as hard as she had in the storm over Katahdin. Miraculously, she lifted not only her own body but Bronwyn's remains, keeping them eight feet above the ground. She lowered her left shoulder, dipped her straining left wing, and made a wide turn so that she was lined her up with the mouth of the cave. The outraged vultures yawped behind her but didn't dare pursue. They had their four comrades' carcasses as consolation.

Luna leveled off and put all her strength into several long, slow flaps that got her to the cave. There might be bits and pieces of Bronwyn left behind that vultures could finish, but she had the important part. While Yvette and the babies slept—true to her word—she carried Bronwyn deep into the cave and helped her disappear under both dirt and a mountain of rocks where neither humans nor animals would find her. Once the little ones were awake and fed, she would reveal to Yvette the details of the evening's escape plan that would take the five of them—on a wing and a prayer—south of Mt. Katahdin to Pernod's friend's cabin, where they would meet up with her human friends from Wells.

CHAPTER 31

The six co-conspirators had arranged to meet at 4:30 Tuesday at Cliff's farmhouse for a quick supper and a final check-in before the mission launched.

Maryann, Keegan, and AJ parked the Subaru in the dooryard next to Cliff's firewood truck and carried a huge aluminum casserole pan full of warm lasagna into the house along with a tub of salad, three loaves of French bread, and two six-packs of cold Snapple drinks.

Aaron and Cliff met them at the door.

"Didn't see your Jeep, Aaron," Keegan said. "Or Stedman's car."

"Jeep's in the barn, all gassed up," Aaron said. "Cliff's cousin's trailer is hooked to it and ready to go. Stedman must be running a little late."

"We took the queen mattress off what used to be my parents' bed before they moved to Florida," Cliff said. "And I grabbed a twin mattress from the attic. We put them on the trailer floor so Luna's gang won't loosen their teeth on the way down from Katahdin. Who knows what those backroads are like before you get on the Interstate?"

"Very thoughtful, Cliff," Maryann said. "And thank you for getting your cousin's trailer."

"Wait'll you see the barn setup," the big man replied. "Mom and Dad's old Shasta travel trailer that we used for vacations was gathering dust and rust in an old horse stall. Been sitting there for years. The tires are dry-rotted and flat, so it's not road-worthy. But I hooked up the truck and dragged it out of the stall. Aaron helped me knock the cobwebs off it, and we vacuumed it out. We hooked up the electric but there's no water because it's a graywater tank and there's no place to dump. I figure gargoyles don't use toilets or toilet paper anyway. There's half a tank of propane if we need to turn on a little heat for the kids. Queen bed in the rear, double bed if you drop the back of the couch, single bed overhead in the front. That makes for a tight six, but it should work."

"Wow, Cliff," Keegan said, and AJ added, "Impressive."

Aaron said, "We also got rid of any of the old farm implements or sharp tools, anything the kids could get hurt on. We pulled 'em outside."

"You two are like grandparents," Maryann said, "childproofing the house."

Aaron said, "We also fixed the door latches in the barn and added slide bolts higher up so the littles ones can't break out. This way, when they're outside the Shasta but still inside the barn, they'll have the run of back part of the building—like a big playpen. We don't want them outside if somebody stops to order firewood or deliver a package."

"The two of us lugged the old fridge from the mudroom out to the barn and plugged it in. We can keep stuff cool in it for the time they're here. The one in the Shasta won't cool anymore, it's still good enough for dry stuff."

Maryann, Keegan, and AJ shook their heads in wonder.

When Stedman still hadn't arrived ten minutes later, they busied themselves laying out paper plates, napkins, and plastic utensils then set the food on the table. Maryann divvied up the food, filled a plate for Stedman, and covered it with foil.

As they were about to dig in, Keegan said, "Wait," and lifted her glass. The others followed her lead. "To safety—for all of us. And God bless our *gargouilles*." They clinked glasses, bottles, and cans and dug in.

When they were well into the meal, Aaron said, "Ms. K, all you have to do is transfer whatever part of the groceries you need up north out of your car into the Jeep and you and Stedman'll be ready to go. My suggestion is, after you pull that snowmobile trailer for four and a half hours, you might want to gas up again before you get to that lake house. You don't want to run out along the interstate on the way home, not with the cargo you're hauling back."

"Good to know, Aaron," Maryann said. Then, "You're dying to go, aren't you?"

"I am," he admitted. "But I'm on shift later tonight."

"AJ and I would love to go, too," Keegan said. "But we have school and a cross-country meet tomorrow."

"Also," Maryann said, "there's no telling how late we'll get back. Luna's group has to travel at night, but what time of night they'll do it, I have no idea. All I know is, Elly and I will be there from about midnight on, and we'll hit the road for Wells when they're ready. My guess is, we'll be home close to the time you two leave for school."

They talked and ate, the females trying to describe to the males what the three infants had looked like when they'd helped Luna hatch them. And they speculated on what they looked like now, how much they weighed, how much they'd grown, whether they had teeth or wings." They were so caught up in talking about gargoyles that they almost forgot about the vampire presser Stedman and Chief Warren were doing for the Portland stations. Cliff turned on the TV news.

***

Portland's Channel 13 opened up with five teasers in descending geographical order, biggest to smallest: North Korea, Hurricane Irma's impact on Puerto Rico, the Red Sox and the final stretch of the American League East race, a hand-printed Portland Restaurant sign announcing No Clams Due to Algae Bloom, and a uniformed female cop at a Town of Wells podium, the on-site reporter next to her saying, "Here in Wells, Maine, authorities say vampires aren't just a pain in the neck, they're a public safety issue."

"There's Sandy," Cliff said, pointing at the screen.

Headlights lit up the front window and a car parked close to the house. They heard a car door slam and a moment later

155

Elly Stedman came through the front door. He wore black jeans and a black hoodie.

"Too late for supper?" he asked, and walked toward the table.

"What're you, Black Ops?" Cliff asked. "No balaclava?"

Stedman ignored the question and sat down. Maryann pulled the foil off the plate of food and set it in front of him. "The chief on yet?" Stedman asked.

"Any minute," Keegan said. The hurricane story was on, the pictures of Puerto Rico's devastation gripping. "Chief Warren didn't need you after all?"

"It's all taped," Stedman said. "We did it at four o'clock."

"And how'd it go?" Aaron asked.

"Let's watch and see," Stedman said. "You be the judge."

They cut to a commercial, but not before a quick tease about the Red Sox pennant race. A 10-second Reny's ad played first—a high school chorus singing the famous phrase "Reny's, a Maine Adventure," followed by a man swearing that Prevagen had helped improve his memory.

"We all set for tonight and tomorrow?" Stedman asked, and began forking food into his mouth.

"All systems go," Keegan said.

"We'll show you the barn layout after the news," Cliff said.

Four more commercials before the Gulf of Maine algae bloom story came on. A reporter laid out the basics while standing on a dock between a man in fishing gear and a woman in a white chef's apron and hat. The reporter poked a microphone in the man's face, got a quick couple of sentences about the algae wrecking the clamming industry, then turned to the woman, a seafood restaurant owner, and let her speak briefly about the impact on her menu and her customers. The reporter ended with a few statistics and a quote from a University of Maine professor then signed off.

Three more commercials then the screen showed a young Asian-American woman in front of a podium bearing the Wells town seal. She gave a synopsis of the vampire situation—napping late-night fisherman awakens and looks up to see someone—a vampire, perhaps?—towering over him, the fisherman's two bass in its clutches. Fearful fisherman shuts eyes, hears hum, feels gritty swirling sand biting his skin, and opens eyes to no one—and no fish. The reporter shows the police sketch and fisherman swears to it. It looks like a trick-or-treater. The reporter continued.

"The night before, also in Wells, barely three miles away, at Spiller Farm and orchards, three workers saw—from a distance of thirty yards—something or someone hovering around the top of an apple tree, picking the fruit. They also heard the hum. They lay flat on the ground, hiding under tarps until the noise stopped. They peeked out to find no one in sight." Then she added, "These are the facts as presented. In neither case were fangs reported or blood sucked."

Stedman lifted his Snapple bottle toward the TV. "Here's where she introduces the chief."

"We've got Wells Police Chief Sandra Warren with us to say more about southern Maine's vampire sightings."

Chief Warren spoke into the podium microphone, from time to time glancing down at her prepared notes. "At first these two misdemeanor stories—stolen fish and pilfered apples are not felonies but misdemeanors—were interesting, even cute, especially after the artwork came out. But then speculation has gotten a little crazy, suggesting Maine is being invaded by vampires. Certain media have taken the idea and run with it, and local gossips and conspiracy theorists have embellished and promoted it—all in about a week. The next thing you know we've got a snowball rolling downhill, gathering loose snow and rocks and branches. Whether folks realize it or not, this has become a matter of public safety. By this I mean, not everyone can distinguish between reality and fiction. It would only take one nervous trigger finger to turn a comedy into a tragedy here. Rather than just throw words at you, though, let me do what my niece, an elementary school teacher, might do—treat you to a Show and Tell."

Chief Warren nods at the area in front of the podium where, barely a minute earlier, the Asian-American reporter had stood. In the reporter's place is a burly figure dressed all in black. It has a black hood drawn up over its head, and the face is clearly a vampire's. Or maybe it's one of the thieves in a Las Vegas bank or casino heist movie. The figure also rotates a quarter turn so the audience can see there's a backpack strapped to its shoulders.

"Is this a real live vampire?" Chief Warren asks the viewing audience, pausing for effect. "Halloween is four weeks away. Maybe this is a trick-or-treater—one of your kids or grandkids or neighbor kids. Or an adult chaperoning them but acting like a kid, wearing a costume. Who's waiting behind the door of the next house on Jack-o-lantern Lane? Is it somebody who's been stressed out by the Wells vampire rumors? Is their finger itchy?" Another pause for effect. "Do we see a public safety issue now?"

The black-clothed figure in front of the podium draws back the black hood of the sweatshirt, lets it bunch at the neck, then grips the vampire mask by the chin and lifts it off.

"It's you!" AJ exclaims. "It's Stedman!"

The five of them start to clap, and the in-the-flesh Stedman at the table holds up a hand. "Wait, wait. Watch."

"Of course this isn't a real live vampire, nor is this an adult trick-or-treat chaperone," Sandy Warren says into the mike. "Those two weren't our only options. If you had attacked this man, you'd have assaulted Detective Elly Stedman of the

Wells Police Department's Criminal Investigation Division. Detective Stedman, do you have something to add?"

The on-screen Stedman faced the camera and said, "This summer there was a story going around about an independent movie company—maybe a handful of college kids or older, who knows—filming a few scenes around Wells. Probably not a whole movie, but interesting scenes. If it's true, they failed to register with us. We heard from several residents that there was an actor in a scary rubber mask and a special suit." Stedman pulled off the backpack and held it in front of him. "They also say he flew with the aid of a jetpack." He made a loud humming sound. "Maybe that summer story was true, maybe not. But I'm sure glad nobody panicked and shot down some kid wearing a jetpack and a monster mask. Reality and the movies are sometimes right next to each other, sharing space. Seeing isn't always believing." On-screen Stedman gave a little bow, the chief gave him a nod of appreciation from the podium, and she ended with, "We hope you enjoyed our little Show and Tell. But please, please, please, as a matter of public safety, stop promoting the vampire rumors. Thank you."

The reporter, knowing she couldn't top what she'd just seen, simply signed off. "Reporting from Wells, Maine, I'm Marcia Kim."

The gang in Cliff's farmhouse applauded again and chanted, "Oscar. Oscar."

Then Maryann said, "Okay, so Sandy knew you were going to unmask, because they supported her point about trick-or-treaters and adults chaperones in masks. But did she know you were going to wear the backpack and adlib that fact-free speculation about the indie movie?"

"Fact-free?" he replied. "Let me remind you, Mrs. Keegan, that it was you and your daughter and her friend AJ here who first floated the jetpack idea this summer—out at Stonehedge."

She rolled her eyes. "Yesterday's news," she said. "My question was: did Sandy Warren know you were going to wear the jetpack—I mean backpack—and say what you said?"

Stedman held up his Snapple. "Hey, I'm just the actor. She's the director."

"Oh, come on," Keegan said. "Are you saying it was her idea?"

"We worked out the mask part on the phone earlier in the afternoon. She said she'd get the mask while I went home and changed into the black outfit. We met at the station before the reporter arrived, and Sandy pulled out a Reny's bag and handed me the mask. I was set to be her prop. I would have yanked the mask whenever she said to—with no dialogue from me. Then she showed me the backpack—also Reny's—and said, 'Do it. Just don't make it sound like it was a police report we took. Be honest. Tell them it was just a story we heard floating around.' Misdirection, I told her. 'Yep,' she said, which to me sounded like permission. So I ran with it."

They all shook their heads and chuckled as they cleaned up the table. Then everyone followed Cliff to the barn to see *les gargouilles'* transportation and their temporary living quarters.

Maryann, Keegan, and AJ inspected the interior of the old Shasta travel trailer and thanked Cliff and Aaron for the thorough cleaning. Stedman poked his head in the door and said, words muffled by the Reny's Halloween mask, "Hey, Maryann, do I look like an uncle or a cousin?"

They laughed, and Keegan pointed out, "Doesn't matter. They're *gargouilles*, not vampires."

"All right, Keeg," Aaron said. "Keep in mind that Stedman and I really haven't had a good look yet, and Cliff only got his glimpse as Faucon's smashed a sword across his chest."

"Stedman'll see them tonight," Maryann said. "You and Cliff tomorrow. AJ and Keegan tomorrow night. Let's remember that we're all feeling a little giddy at the moment. This is a crazy, even dangerous scheme. Loose lips and all that."

They transferred any last-minute groceries to the ATV trailer, said their goodbyes, and then they were ready. Maryann and Stedman fired up Aaron's Jeep and hit the road for some back road south of Patten, a more than four-hour drive pulling the ATV trailer.

Keegan dropped AJ and Aaron at their mother's house.

Cliff climbed into his firewood truck and headed for the PD to see if anything new had come in from around the state. Getting Luna, her friends, and the baby *gargouillles* moved from wherever they were now into their new short-term housing might prove to be the easy part, he thought. Keeping a wounded and maybe sick Faucon out of the area could be something else. He chuckled aloud again, recalling Elly Stedman on the evening news, and wondered if Reny's had more of the vampire masks, and if they had gargoyle masks as well. And were they realistic looking? And how much did they cost? He asked his phone what time Reny's closed.

CHAPTER 32

It was almost dusk Wednesday when Faucon woke up to find his upper body sliding down a mountain of bunk mattresses, his legs and feet on the cabin's bare floor. He tried to clear the cobwebs out of his head and remember where he was and how he'd gotten here.

Summer camp for human children. They sleep in this box, this cabin, on these metal frames with the flat pillows— mattresses—on these beds, one child stacked above another. I pulled these down and piled them together so I could sleep on my side instead of squatting—out of the sunlight—to help heal my wing, my shoulder, my aching foot.

He glanced down and squinted at the scabs where three of his toes had once been attached. The pain felt less now than in previous days.

The human medicines from the big building, they may have helped.

He got to his feet and stretched his arms then shook out his great wings. They reached from the bunks on one side of the cabin across to the bunks against the opposite wall. Less pain in the right wing and shoulder, but still enough a long flight was still out of the question. Even a running takeoff with a flap or two would leave him in a heap. But maybe a cliff dive and glide that let him extend the wings without the strain of flapping. He could catch and ride the updrafts. But it wouldn't all be updrafts.

Hungry. Thirsty. I need to continue the medicine.

He opened the cabin door and stuck his head out. The other three cabins in the grouping were dark except for the light on their roofs and glass windows. A quick check of the grounds, the ballfield, and the driveway told him no one was around, no caretaker or security service patrolling the camp. Past the ballfield the little lake glowed and rippled under a faint breeze. The forest behind the far shore was already a wall of darkness, and the little island he had seen when he arrived blended in against it.

He shuffled to the driveway and the little parking area by the front porch of the big building. He saw the sign next to the door: *FreeK Camp.* He remembered now. It was actually Free Camp on the sign, but someone had added the capital K. Now it was coming back to him.

He made his way down the side of the building to the back door he had used the day before. It was still ajar. Someone—probably teenagers—must have broken in between the final week of summer camp and Faucon's arrival. Whoever it had been, they hadn't trashed the place, which suggested they were locals with some measure of respect for the camp.

Everything was as Faucon had left it—the dark dining room, the kitchen, the office, and the camp nurse's office. In the kitchen he found several more large plastic jars of peanut butter like the one he had devoured earlier. He opened one and twirled his index finger around in it, eating until the jar was empty. He removed a black plastic liner bag from the kitchen trash can and stuffed the remaining jars of peanut butter in it. There were three bottles of apple juice on a shelf—*these will freeze and explode in cold weather*—so he drank one down and placed the other two in the black bag.

In the nurse's room he scooped up two bottles of hydrogen peroxide—*the foam helped cleanse my wound yesterday*—and grabbed sterile bandages and any pill bottles that mentioned infection or fever, adding them to his bag. Before he left, he hit the pantry shelves again and confiscated a half dozen bags of dried cranberries and apricots. He left with the bag the way he'd come in and made his way to the swimming beach.

Fly north a few hours on my short wings again and look for another safe place to stay the daytime? Or spend another night here?

His answer came when headlights cut through the dark pines. Humans coming up the driveway!

Faucon's hummingbird wings popped out and in seconds he was zipping over the surface of the lake, trying to make the little island before the visitors could hear the hum of his wings. He landed and retracted them as the vehicle appeared in the parking area, its headlight beams shining across the water. He dropped the bag and let himself fall face-first into the high reeds and bushes, unceremoniously landing like a soldier leaping into a foxhole in a mortar barrage.

Did they spot me? Are they here because of an alarm system?

He lay still, face down in the undergrowth, heart thumping fast, relieved that he had identified the island as a potential hiding place when he first arrived.

Behind him, across the lake, he heard the vehicle door creak open then slam shut. *A truck.* Then a second door. *Two humans, maybe three or four.*

"Bring the ice chest," one of the distant voices ordered.

Faucon raised his head, daring to look. Two humans standing. Then two more climbed down from the bed of the pickup.

"We left the back door open," one of the front-seaters said.

Faucon watched the four shadowy figures walk where he had minutes earlier. They winked out of sight behind the building.

Four males.

A faint light leaked through the glass pane in the locked front door. He realized they were inside and had lit one or more lanterns. Their voices were indistinct now that they were in the main hall. He heard occasional hoots and bursts of raucous laughter. He pictured them lounging around in the easy chairs, love seats, and bean bag chairs he'd seen near the wall.

It was a party, and it went on for almost three hours.

He didn't want the noise of his short wings to give them reason to come outside and investigate, so he did his best to get comfortable sitting up against a tree. He cleansed his stinking toes with the hydrogen peroxide and tossed down three aspirins and a tablet of something called Tylenol, then ate some of the dried fruit.

Around nine-fifteen the four partiers emerged, swearing loudly and slurring their speech.

"Gotta get the truck home by ten or my old man'll have my ass," one said. "Saddle up. Time to hit the trail."

Faucon heard a truck door open and saw an interior light go on, followed by the opening of a second door. Two slams and the light went out. A pair of dark shapes climbed into the truck behind the cab and settled down. "Home, Jeeves," one of them called, and the engine started. The headlights flashed on and the revelers wheeled around out of the parking lot and out the driveway the way they'd come.

Faucon peered across the lake at the dining hall. The window pane in the front door still glowed slightly.

They left their light. He had no idea if it had been an oil lamp, a wax candle, or a battery lantern. He waited.

An hour later he got his answer. The light in the front door pane grew brighter. The floor-to-ceiling windows along one side of the building were letting light out, too.

Fire.

Faucon stood quickly, fired up his hummingbird wings, and practically danced across the lake, over the beach and parking area, not stopping until he reached the unlocked back door. He lumbered inside. The dining room was hot, the light blinding. Flames danced on the wood floor, the furniture and table covers smoldered then ignited, and a ribbon of yellow fire snaked up one of the thick drapes. Two or three smoke detectors sounded the alarm to no one except Faucon.

165

He hurried to the kitchen and located the fire extinguisher on its bracket by the gas stove. When he'd seen it earlier, it had been dusk and some light had come through the large window. Now it was dark and he couldn't read the wall sign with the stick figures and the printed instructions. Hadn't it been simple—point hose and squeeze handle? He'd hoped so. He yanked it free and raced back into the burning room, aimed the side hose at the burning table with the melted candle on it, and squeezed the trigger grip. Foam shot forth, and as it smothered the flames he broadened the area the spray covered, attacking the easy chairs and beanbags then the couch and the knotty pine wall paneling behind it. He turned and followed the other path the fire had taken, laying down a coating of foam across the wood floor to the room's opposite side, where he doused the disintegrating drapes. He put out the last of it and stood there coughing as the extinguisher spewed forth the last of its contents and ran dry. He dropped the tank, staggered exhausted out the back door onto the porch, and began sucking in the sweet night air.

A few minutes later, after his breathing had evened out, he gave a last backward glance inside the dining hall in case anything had restarted, then skip-flew across the parking lot to the waterfront and over the lake to his island hideout. His decision—stay or move on—had been made by the fire and his decision to fight it. He knew, though, that he was too tired now to fly, forage, or find a new location to spend the next day. He rested his head on the black plastic bag and fell asleep.

Not long after—how long, he couldn't be sure—he was jarred awake by the sound of sirens and fire engines. He looked up and saw flashing lights in the parking area where the pickup had been. They stayed an hour, checked out the scene, and left.

Half an hour after that, the camp was dark again. But the incident didn't go unnoticed. Almost immediately, police departments across the state received Bridgton's report about responding to a fire at a summer camp south of town. The main building had been broken into and there was evidence of a fire that was apparently extinguished by someone before they left the scene. Empty beer cans and alcohol bottles were found, and the food pantries and nurse's office had been ransacked. No one was found at the scene.

CHAPTER 33

The king and the other *gargouille* stood on opposite sides of the high plank table, a small candle between them illuminating their round faces above the chessboard.

"Checkmate, Ronsomme," the king said, and pushed away from the table. "You do not challenge me the way Angeline did."

"Chess is not my game," the king's attendant said. "I am no match for you."

"King Cyrus?" a male voice asked from outside the king's chamber.

"Qu'est-ce que c'est, Guillaume?" the king said. "Step in."

Guillaume entered and stopped five feet from the table.

"News about Angeline?" Cyrus asked.

"No. Nothing about her. She left and has not returned. We do not know where she went."

"Then what is the news?"

"Gregoire is back."

"Gregoire? *Ah, oui*, Gregoire. Has he found Faucon?" The king straightened, his ancient eyes glowing bright crimson again in the candlelight.

"He has not told me. He is waiting to report."

"Then send him in. Now."

Guillaume turned and left.

"Do you want me to stay?" Ronsomme asked.

"You are my captain of the guard," Cyrus replied. "Stay."

A moment later a short, very thin *gargouille* limped into the king's chamber. His right eye was the same red as most males' eyes, but the left eye had long ago shriveled, having died in its socket. Now only a black shadow occupied the crater. What remained was a long battle scar—a bayonet slash from nose to temple across the center of the dead eye—that had accompanied the German bullet that left Gregoire with a limp. *Le gargouille* had sustained both wounds protecting Cyrus's sons, LeClair and Champaigne, in the French Alps. Because the one-eyed *gargouille* was uncomfortable with closed-in spaces like the clan cavern and its labyrinth of caves, Cyrus had assigned him and another mentally broken soldier, Toulouse, as lookouts in the Maine and New Hampshire territories. They lived in the field and occasionally returned to the clan to report. They were less spies, more forward observers or fire tower lookouts.

"You've found something?" the king asked. "Luna or Faucon?"

"Not Luna. Maybe Faucon."

"Where?" Cyrus asked. "Is he alive?"

Gregoire's facial expression and eye seemed to ask whether he should report in front of Guillaume.

"You may speak freely," Cyrus said.

"*Oui, monsieur.* Luna left here in June, Faucon less than a day later. We lost track of both. A week later, Luna's friends Yvette and Bronwyn left. We assume they joined Luna. For three months they have been invisible. It is unlikely—given the bad blood between Luna and Faucon—that he is with Luna's group."

"So, assuming they are all alive," the king said, "they are feeding themselves and avoiding contact with humans."

"The females, *oui.* They are invisible. But Toulouse and I believe Faucon is injured or sick. He is crossing paths with humans too often. He is putting us all at risk."

"Crossing paths with humans?" Cyrus asked.

"*Oui, monsieur.* Toulouse and I have found a way to learn what is happening in the world of the humans. In Bethel, Maine, behind his house, a man sits in a tub of steaming water each night. He eats and drinks and watches television. We hide in the trees and watch it, too. Last week the man on the television told of a human on the beach late at night who was robbed of his fish. The man on the television said it was a vampire with a horn. Then he showed a drawing. It looked like Faucon."

"Faucon?" Cyrus said.

"*Oui*," Gregoire replied. "It sounds like he cannot feed himself."

"Which would only happen if Faucon were sick or injured."

"*Exactement*," Gregoire said.

The king held up a hand. "You said there were other encounters with humans?"

"In the same town—Wells—several orchard workers saw Faucon—another drawing suggests it is our Faucon—hovering over a tree, picking apples at the top. They described the hum of his short wings. That drawing was also shown on the television of the man in the water tub. We saw it. In both drawings, we saw the rhino horn."

"So Faucon is in Wells," Cyrus said. "That is where my son LeClair and his mate Diana were during the American Civil War, along with his brother Champaigne. If Faucon is there, it is likely that Luna went there first."

"Why would they go there?" Guillaume asked.

"There are rumors," said Cyrus, "that she believed her sister Diana went to ground much later than the end of the Civil War, that Diana and LeClair could have delayed nesting until just before he left for the Great War in Europe."

"Which could mean," the captain of the guard said, "that Luna's sister's eggs might still be hatched this year—giving you a male heir."

"An alternative to Faucon, who is not even of your bloodline," the one-eyed Gregoire pointed out.

Gregoire and Guillaume stood by quietly while Cyrus paced. Finally the king said, "If Luna was right about when her sister went to ground—and there is a male heir—where is she?"

"A more pressing question is," the field observer said, his single blood-colored eye glistening, "do we find Faucon and bring him home before the humans capture or kill him, or do we help him disappear?"

"Either way you must find him," the Captain of the Guard said. "He is a danger to us all."

"Then I have more to report," Gregoire said. "Tonight Toulouse and I were fishing above Sebago Lake when we heard fire sirens near Bridgton. We followed them to a summer camp for young people but saw no flames. We hid in the trees and heard someone yell that the fire was already out. When we left we crossed the camp lake and saw a small, dark island. When we looked down, we saw red eyes in the moonlight. It had to be Faucon, but was he alive or dead? Could he see us? I ordered Toulouse to stay and monitor the island and Faucon. Tonight I flew hard to get here to report to you."

Cyrus paced again, then stopped and said, "If Faucon is alive, he's endangering the clan. If he's dead, we need to keep his body out of the hands of the humans."

Gregoire asked, "My question is, do we treat him as the heir to your throne? We do not know if Luna is alive or has hatched a grandson."

"Let Faucon think what he wants to," Cyrus said. "Do what you must to stop his encounters with humans. Keep your eyes and ears open for Luna."

"For Luna?" Gregoire asked. "Or a grandson?"

Cyrus stepped to the chessboard and placed his stubby fingertips on the crown of the red queen. "If you find one, you are sure to find the other," he said, and pressed the queen onto its side, leaving it to roll on the board.

CHAPTER 34

At eleven-thirty the IGA parking lot was practically empty. There were only two vehicles in sight, both running. Aaron sat in one of them, his patrol SUV. In the other, a State Police sedan, was Trooper Alicia "Smitty" Smith. They were parked driver window to driver window, and both cops had their left elbows crooked on the open windows so they could chat. It was mostly business but with a little innocent flirting woven in—a way to pass the time when their shifts overlapped and the night was slow.

Their vehicles had been in exactly the same spots three months earlier, in late June, when they'd responded to a silent alarm at Geoff Swett's Toil & Trouble office, from which he ran online book auctions. A rare Civil War journal had been stolen, and no one was caught. But Aaron figured the thief had been Faucon, who was probably also the one who broke into Annie's Book Stop a few nights later and then into Maryann Keegan's house the following morning. But he couldn't tell that to Smitty.

Aaron was saying something about the TV show *NCIS* when she raised an index finger—*wait a sec*—and zipped her window up. Two minutes later she lowered it again.

"Sorry," she said. "Suspicious fire in the area I used to cover, at a at summer camp close to Bridgton. Same camp where the five camp kids were kidnapped seven or eight years ago. I'm familiar with the camp and know the director, the staff, and the kids."

"Bad fire?" Aaron asked. "Nobody home this time of year, right?"

"Shouldn't be. My guess is, teenagers used it for a party and got careless with a candle. At least they managed to put the fire out before they left. They tossed the place. Kitchen, pantry, office, nurse's office."

"What's there to get? No money. No prescription drugs. Canned goods, maybe."

"One of my buddies says they ate peanut butter." Smitty laughed. "I'll bet their jaws are tired. When I was in elementary school, our school cafeteria got surplus peanut butter from the government for school lunch programs. There was so much peanut butter and not enough jelly to match up with it, so when the lunch ladies made PB&J sandwiches, it was an inch of PB and a light glaze of J. We called 'em *chokes*."

Aaron laughed at that. "That's all they took? Peanut butter? No crackers?"

"Sounds that way. Looks like they also went through the nurse's supplies, which would be at most a few bottles of aspirin, Tylenol, and Advil. My buddy said they found an open tube of antiseptic and a spilled bottle of Hydrogen Peroxide— like one of them got a burn from the fire. Our people will send out a BOLO to Bridgton Hospital and area Urgent Cares in case somebody shows up with a burn."

Seemingly out of the blue, Aaron changed subjects. "I've got to run back to the station, Smitty. Just thought of something I've got to do." He zipped up his window, drove past the traffic signal to the Wells PD, and five minutes later was printing out the overview report of the Bridgton camp incident.

***

"Cliff, the place is called Free Camp," Aaron said into his cell phone, and gave the address. "I'm sending you a scan of the Bridgton report as we speak."

"And you think this might be Faucon?" Cliff asked.

"Good chance. Given his wounds, if we plotted his path north on a map—let's say he's headed home to his clan—we'd put a pin in Wells then the McCuskers' farm in Springvale. Give him a night or two without making contact and where would he land next? After the silo fiasco, he could've made Limerick or Cornish, so the next logical stop could be Naples or Bridgton.

But both towns are busy with leaf-peepers and boaters, so where does he lay over? How about a kids' summer camp?"

"Not all that farfetched. It might explain the peanut butter and the meds."

"The meds are for his wounds," Aaron said. "He may not know exactly what each thing does, but if stole a book, it means he can read—including the instructions on the bottles."

"Let me play devil's advocate for a sec," Cliff said. "Teenagers might do the same thing: eat peanut butter and, if they got hurt putting out the fire, try to treat their own burns? And, by the way, none of this explains how the fire started or how it got put out."

"You're right. And if it was Faucon, we don't know for sure that he's still there. There's one detail in the report that suggests to me this was him, and that he might hang around. Did you see the part about the cabins?"

"I was focused on the dining hall and offices."

"I was, too, at first. But you have to read that last part."

"Looking at it now," Cliff mumbled. "Four girls' cabins in a quadrant with a girls' bathroom and shower building near them. Same arrangement at the other end of the ballfield for the boys: four cabins with toilets and showers."

"Check the last line. One of the boys' cabins has four bunk beds—that means it'd sleep eight. Whoever wrote this report said they found all eight mattresses piled in a little mountain in the center of the cabin floor. They also found an empty hydrogen peroxide bottle in that cabin."

"Somebody flushed a wound," Cliff said.

"Exactly. But if it was the teenagers who started and then put out the fire, why would they go to a cabin to treat it? And why would teens pile up mattresses? Wouldn't they lie on the bunks on top of the mattresses and springs?"

"I see it, Aaron, I see it. Did you call Stedman?"

"I did. He and Maryann are north of Bangor almost to where they're meeting Luna. They've already got their hands full."

"Did he have any suggestions?"

"Let Faucon go, is what Stedman said, he's on his own."

Silence on the line for thirty seconds.

"Cliff?" Aaron asked.

"Yep."

"Well?"

"We ought to get Faucon out of there," Cliff said.

"I can't," Aaron said. "I'm on shift all night."

After a moment's hesitation, Cliff said, "I can go. It's only an hour and a half to Bridgton."

""And do what? Even if you found him, he doesn't know you, might not trust you."

Cliff replied, "Three humans know him: Maryann, Keegan, and AJ."

"Maryann's busy with Luna," Aaron pointed out.

"That leaves Keegan or your sister. Or both."

"I'm not crazy about sending either of them into the breach," Aaron said.

"Not much choice," Cliff said. "Soon as we're done, I'll call Keegan. She can call or text AJ."

"Okay, Cliff, before you hang up, let me make a couple of suggestions."

***

Keegan drove the family's Subaru and picked up AJ. They drove to Cliff's and waited in front, as Cliff had instructed. Ten minutes later he pulled in with his truck and parked. He climbed down from the cab and began transferring things over from the truck to the Subaru's way-back. Then he then slid into the back seat and gave Keegan the GPS address. "Okay, let's do it," as if he were in a movie.

175

It took them an hour and twenty to reach Free Camp's RFD box on the left side of Route 302, a few miles north of Naples. The aluminum mailbox was dented and had long ago been defaced by a graffitist so the lettering read FreeK Camp.

"I checked the camp grounds on Google Earth before I left home," Cliff said, and held out a square printout made up of four taped-together pages of copy paper. "It's about a hundred acres. This driveway snakes uphill to the main building, where the fire was." He pointed and said, "Here are the four boys' cabins and showers, the ballfield, and the four girls' cabins and showers. Maintenance garage here, waterfront building by the end of the beach, and here's the lake. Kayaks, canoes, and the swimming float are beached or stored for the off-season. Trail on the north end leads up to a waterfall. The lake is about twenty-five acres, two to twelve feet deep. There's a little island out here that's a couple feet above the water level, has trees, bushes, and some kind of camping lean-to with a fire pit. Closest neighbors are two abutting summer camps. There's a turnout ahead on the left where we can hide the car."

"Then what?" AJ asked.

"We get our equipment out of the back and we walk in. Find Faucon and convince him to save time by taking a ride north with us. We get him close to home and turn him loose."

"You're assuming lack of transportation is what's keeping him around," AJ said.

"Correct. If we need leverage to convince him, we mention the vampire mania he's responsible for, and which could get him killed."

"Okay," Keegan said. "And we have no reason to fear him, right, Cliff? He'll be happy to hear us and to take our advice and go for a ride with us?"

AJ said sarcastically, "So Faucon's fine with that ax Keegan stuck in his back and wing?"

Cliff ignored their comments and had Keegan drive to the turnout. He got out and opened the rear hatch then began unloading their gear.

He handed out black sweaters, sweat pants, and watch caps. "I shopped at the station before we left." "Night vision goggles for each of us. Put the clothing on and I'll explain how the goggles work."

He strapped on his service pistol but didn't offer AJ or Keegan a weapon. "This is for emergency only. Our voices will be our first persuaders." Then he pulled out a cargo net and a body bag. "In case we have to transport him." Keegan and AJ looked at him in horror. "Hey, we don't know if he's conscious or unconscious, alive or dead, at the moment. He's wounded and may have a serious infection. We have to be prepared."

Lastly he pulled out a rifle with a scope.

"What's that for?" Keegan asked.

"Relax. It's a C2 X-Caliber dart projector. Basically a CO_2 gas-fired pellet gun that fires tranquilizer darts—*if we need to.* I've got it set for a 250 to 300 pound human or a bear."

"Will it hurt him?" AJ wanted to know.

"No. If he doesn't want to go voluntarily, the dart will chemically immobilize him. The drug class is called dissociatives; they distort perception of sight and sound and disengage the ability to use voluntary muscles. Mostly game wardens and animal control officers use them. There's a light anesthesia in with the immobilizer. Ideally, if this were an animal like a moose or a bear, you'd shoot for the back of a rear leg, a fleshy spot like a buttock so you don't bounce the dart off a bone and miss the shot. In Faucon's case—*if we have to*—if I can't get a buttock or a thigh, I could try for the meat of the shoulder. Which tells us our strategy. You two have to talk to him, call him out—assuming he's on the grounds—and I'll stay behind you out of sight. I promise I won't dart him if you can

177

talk him into leaving or accepting our ride-share. But if he won't go, or if he's a danger to you …"

"Understood," Keegan said. And the three of them started up the long driveway to the camp.

CHAPTER 35

Luna squatted at the cave entrance, awake but motionless but awake, looking like a cement gargoyle in a flower garden. She felt that way, too, like stone, her emotions hardened, her body and spirit lacking animation. The stormy flight from Pernod's and the battle with the coyotes had left her bone tired. She wanted to grieve the loss of Bronwyn, whose coyote-and-vulture-stripped carcass had lain in the meadow for hours before she could retrieve it and bury it. But she couldn't spare any emotion or energy for grief. She needed all the strength and resolve she could muster if she and Yvette—two adult *gargouilles* instead of three, with Bronwyn gone—were to move the three babies back to Pernod's.

"Luna?" a soft voice asked from behind her. "Are you all right?"

"*Je suis tres fatiguee et mon coeur souffre,*" Luna replied without glancing back.

"I, too, am tired and sore of heart," Yvette repeated, and squatted beside her friend. "I am glad the babies are not old enough to ask where Bronwyn is or why she is gone."

They sat quietly for a few minutes, watching the clouds play peekaboo with the moon.

"Mathilde and Regine went to sleep after they ate," Luna said, "but Paladin wanted to tumble and wrestle and explore. How did you finally get him to slow down?"

"An old trick I learned from others who tended clan babies. I gently massaged a spot above the bridge of his nose, above the eye. Humans say it's the spot between a child's eyebrows."

"Hmm. Perhaps you can show me next time. I know nothing about mothering. I must learn quickly."

"*Mothering,*" Yvette said. "It's strange that we even use that word, *n'est-ce pas?* None of us who raise the little ones are actually their mothers. The mothers go to ground and die. Their bodies nourish their eggs until the trees attach their roots and sustain the nest. She never sees them, never knows if her mate has returned and hatched them, or if they survived childhood. The male who raises his children experiences fatherhood, but the female . . ." Her voice trailed off in a sigh. "It is an act of faith, they tell us. But I think it is cruel and unfair. It is the curse of *les gargouilles*."

Luna put an arm around her friend's shoulder. "My sister knew I would mother these children. What she did not foresee was her mate's death. She did not know LeClair would not live to raise them."

"What if you could remain a *gargouille*," Yvette said, "without having to go to ground, without having to become the food source for your eggs? What if you could live to raise your own children, like the humans do?"

"That's an easy choice," Luna answered. "But it cannot be." She went silent a moment, like a child deciding whether to share a secret. "I once described our dilemma to a human, a student at a university. He told me that before the Second War in Europe, some—not all—human females who bore a healthy first child were doomed to die bearing the second. It had to do with their blood. He called it the RH factor."

"You said that was true *before* the Second War?" Yvette asked.

"*Oui.* Scientists and doctors corrected it. They developed a drug they could inject after the first birth. It prepared the mother's blood for other births. It was miraculous, he said, and saved countless females' lives."

"That's wonderful for the humans," Yvette said. "What does it have to do with our race?"

"He said, 'What if science and medicine could duplicate the nutrients our eggs need? And what if that food source took the place of the mother?'"

"So she didn't have to go to ground!" Yvette said. "Mothers could live to see their eggs hatched then raise their own children."

"They could enjoy a long life with their mates," Luna added. "As it is now, if a female goes to ground at one hundred fifty years, her mate may live to reach four hundred. Diana and LeClair chose one way, Champaigne and I hoped to spend our lives together, maybe to age four hundred."

"Did this student believe it was possible? For science and medicine to help *les gargouilles*, I mean."

"He said we wouldn't know until we tried," Luna answered. "When I asked what was stopping us, he said our *gargouille* population would quickly be out of control."

"Out of control?" Yvette asked.

"We would multiply rapidly and compete with humans for space and food and water. He said he couldn't imagine the human race would help make that happen."

A squawking came from deeper inside the cave.

"Paladin," Yvette said. "The forehead massage only works for so long. They're not used to sleeping after midnight. He's sure to shake his sisters awake soon."

"Then it's time to go," Luna said. "Last chance for them to eat potato and apple paste. I'll prepare our transportation."

***

Stedman and Maryann exited I-95 at Medway and gassed up Aaron's Jeep at the 24-hour Circle K. They made pit stops and bought large black coffees, pizza slices, and a couple of pastries. Fifteen minutes later they were driving north again, looking for the turnoff that would eventually lead them to Pernod's friend's house

Maryann had learned little she didn't already know about Stedman in their four-plus-hour drive. Stedman had been a high school football star and a good boxer in the Navy. She knew he loved being a detective and that he read a lot of mysteries that he bought used at her bookstore. In his off hours he worked in his garage woodshop. His college education was thanks to the GI Bill and his home was thanks to a VA loan. He was more likely to ask questions than to answer them.

She said, "Tonight's press conference with Sandy suggests you may have a second career waiting for you in either acting or clowning."

"Doubtful. I'm not totally introverted, but I am one of those quiet guys who keeps to himself."

"But admit it," she said. "You enjoyed doing that for the cameras."

"I did," he said. "I actually did."

"Ever married?" Maryann asked. "Divorced? Widowed? Kids? Brothers and sisters? Parents still alive?"

"No. No. No. No. Yes, one sister, a veterinarian named Rainey, married to another veterinarian, Dr. Tom. They have a farm and clinic in Tamworth, New Hampshire. Yes to parents alive. Mom and Dad live in northern New Hampshire, both still working. I think that covers everything."

"The vets have kids?"

"Only the goat kind. They also have cows, dogs, cats, birds, fowl, llamas, donkeys, burros, and a couple of miniature horses. Don't know if they were unable to have kids, decided not to, or were too busy with rescue animals."

"Do you dance? Go to musicals—like at the Ogunquit Playhouse? Do you run into the ocean in winter for the Polar Bear swim? Republican, Democrat, or Independent?"

"Not much of a dancer, but I can do the basics at a wedding reception. Been to quite a few Ogunquit shows. No swimming, no matter the water temperature. What were the other questions?"

"Political," she said. "But you don't have to answer."

"I don't mind. None of the above. That's my answer, and I'm sticking to it. Why don't we reverse things and you tell me about yourself? You'll have to make it fast. I think we're at the edge of Grindstone, getting close."

"Never married but raised a daughter. As you know, Keegan was born here at York Hospital, which is when my sister Zelda—Keegan's birth mother—died of a brain aneurysm. So I adopted Keegan, made my niece my daughter. Before that, I had a Boston-area librarian job after college but moved back here when our father died. He left us everything, so we used part of our inheritance to buy Annie's Book Shop and part of it for Zelda's expenses at UMO. I spend a lot of time at the bookstore in the summer, attend Keegan's track meets and other sporting events when I can, and give some time to the Historical Society. Like you, I read a lot. Oh, and I've been working on a novel for ten years. I think I'm in the twentieth revision, with the tenth different ending."

"Anything else?"

"Yes, other than taking Keegan into my arms when my sister died, and falling in love with her, my second greatest experience has been hatching three *gargouille* eggs with Luna, Keegan, and AJ. I can't wait to pick those babies up in my arms."

"Not excited, are you?" Stedman asked playfully.

"How astute of you to perceive that, Detective."

He laughed. "Okay. I think we're close to the road we want. We need to concentrate on the directions. Anything you'd like to add before we shift back to our mission?"

"I'd love to go dancing."

Stedman grinned and mumbled, "Okay then," and let his words hang. A moment later he said, "And here's our turn."

CHAPTER 36

Free Camp was dark and quiet. All the cars and firetrucks were gone, and the only evidence of their earlier presence was a waist-high barrier of plastic warning tape around the parking lot and the main building. But even with no human presence, Faucon didn't move. He lay motionless on the island, sick and weary, still as a corpse. He rested on his right side with his head on a mound of scooped-together leaves. This position let him view the lake, the distant camp structures, and the high pines south of the boathouse, which was now his preoccupation. High up in one of the oldest trees he could see a recently arrived shape with a pair of glowing red eyes like his own. *Un gargouille. Watching me.*

Earlier he'd seen three red eyes. They had belonged to a pair of familiar shapes circling the lake. The single red eye had to be Gregoire and the two eyes Toulouse, the pair who spent months at a time away from the clan, gathering information, mostly on the movement of the humans, for King Cyrus. The king could also count on these two if intimidation or assassination was called for.

Are they here to eliminate me? They could have done that by now—unless they think I still have my weapons. If they've been trying to find me, Gregoire has flown home to inform Cyrus, and he left Toulouse behind to watch, in case I move again. But I haven't moved a muscle, and Toulouse can't tell if I'm alive or dead.

***

Cliff, AJ, and Keegan advanced up the driveway like a squad on patrol, walking noiselessly while scanning the dark woods on either side. They carried penlights but kept them turned off now that they'd adjusted to the night-vision goggles. Cliff led the way, service pistol on his belt, dart rifle in his right hand. When the driveway opened into the parking area, Cliff gave Keegan and AJ hand signals to halt while they scanned the area. They split up then, AJ and Keegan skipping under the police tape and skirting the main building along its right side, Cliff surveilling the ballfield and the clusters of cabins.

Keegan climbed the steps to the back deck and poked her head in the dining hall. It was very dark, and she could smell char from the fire. But nothing inside registered in the light-gathering goggles. She felt sure Faucon wasn't inside, dead or alive, or someone would have found him. She backed out and rejoined AJ, and the two of them met Cliff at the one of the cabin quads. Cliff indicated an open door on one cabin and peeked in.

He whispered over his shoulder, "The report said mattresses were piled together."

They checked the bathroom/shower building, found nothing, and checked out the other cabins and shower buildings. Nothing. No one. No sign of forced entry. They sneaked single-file toward the waterfront, Cliff leading, but he froze when he felt Keegan grip his shoulder. She motioned him to the ground, and the three of them dropped to a crouch then lay flat like toy soldiers.

Keegan put an index finger to her lips, then added a middle finger to make a V that she pointed at her eyes and then across the water. Cliff looked where she had indicated and saw a pair of close-set, glowing red eyes. They seemed to be almost at ground level on the far shore. Their goggles gathered in enough moonlight to reveal a prone figure with something protruding from its forehead.

Cliff mouthed two words that reached AJ and Keegan's ears as a very faint whisper. "The island."

Cliff fumbled to make the F sign, but Keegan rolled her eyes and thumbs-upped him.

AJ poked them both and gave her own two-fingered sign for Look. She pointed to the left, toward the high treetops. Two more red eyes. A fuzzy hunchbacked shape sat on a branch like a giant owl. Was it a mate, maybe a guardian? They hadn't anticipated this.

After five frozen minutes, Cliff signaled a retreat to the cabins. They slow-crawled back to the cover of the cabins then entered the one with the mountain of mattresses where they whispered softly.

"Who's that?" AJ asked.

"My guess is, the search party left a guard behind to keep track of Faucon. If that's the case, more *gargouilles* will be arriving."

"Which solves our problem," Cliff said. "Why hang around if they're sending help?"

Keegan said, "We should make sure they actually evacuate him, because if they don't, he'll just go searching for food again, which means more human encounters. I say we stay a while."

"But Faucon no longer needs us," Cliff protested. "We should go."

"Okay, you go first then," Keegan said. "We'll meet you back at the car."

"But—

"Another thought," AJ cut in. "If that bird in the tree is here to help, why isn't he on that island—caring for him, reassuring him, and waiting for the medevac with him?"

Cliff had no answer, and two minutes later was crawling on his belly alongside Keegan and AJ to the grassy area in front of the girls' cabins, where they waited.

After about twenty minutes, a voice came across the lake from the island. "Toulouse? Can you hear me?"

Keegan recognized the French accent and the speaker. *Faucon.*

No answer from the treetops.

"Toulouse, I can see you on that high bough, and I know you can see me."

Still no answer.

"Toulouse, where is Gregoire? I saw his eye earlier when you circled the lake. Has he gone home for help?"

No answer for a moment, then simply, "*Oui.*"

"Toulouse, I am injured. Why did you two not come and see what was wrong?"

"You are armed, Faucon," the *gargouille* in the tree answered. "If we startled you, you might turn your sword on us."

"A weak excuse," Faucon replied. "There are two of you, and you could have approached with talk. You have your hummingbird wings, and if I tried to attack you, you could have escaped easily."

"I do what Gregoire tells me."

"And Gregoire does what the king tells him. Has he gone to Cyrus for orders, asking what you should do with his adopted grandson, his heir?"

"You, Faucon, are an outsider, and ..." Toulouse checked his tongue. "I do what Gregoire tells me."

"The devious one-eyed Gregoire, you mean? Will he bring other assassins to do the king's dirty work, the work you two dared not attempt when you first circled this evening?"

"I do what Gregoire tells me. He told me to watch you until he returns."

"Then come closer and watch me, Toulouse. Come land on my island and bandage my wounds. Are we not brothers-in-arms? It was my father, Drago of the Alps clan, who died rescuing Cyrus's sons from the Germans."

No response.

Then, "It is time for me to move north to a new hiding place for the night, Toulouse." Faucon rose to his feet. "I will cross the water to the big building where the fire was. I will take what I need for food and I will leave. When your friends arrive, tell them I appreciate their concern for my wellbeing, but I will find my own way home."

"Stay there," the voice in the treetops said, more desperate than commanding. "Gregoire will—

"Gregoire will what—scold you, punish you?"

Cliff, Keegan, and AJ heard a loud hum come from the island, and saw a figure lift off from its shore and cross the lake surface, feet almost skimming the water. Faucon appeared to be making a beeline toward them. They ducked, flattening their bodies against the dark ground.

Faucon passed inches above the beach until he reached the parking area then landed, the hum of his wings ceasing. He ducked under the police tape and headed for the dining hall's back door.

They raised their heads to see how Toulouse would react. The sentry's glowing eyes were no longer in the treetops, he was flapping over the lake and coming their way. No hum, just the *whoosh, whoosh, whoosh* of his broad angel wings. The speeding *gargouille* dropped lower, zoomed over the beach, and at the parking lot tilted his wings to brake himself, stopping where they'd seen Faucon slip under the police tape. Toulouse furled his wings tight and with both hands reached over his shoulders, drawing his sword and *poignard.* He followed the path he'd seen Faucon take down the side of the building.

Keegan whispered, "Faucon's not armed."

"How do you know?" Cliff asked.

"Luna took his dagger and I have his sword at home."

None of them moved, so AJ said, "Cliff, we've got to do something." When he didn't move, she said, "My brother would."

Still no decisive movement.

"Cliff," Keegan pleaded. "You've got your pistol. Shoot him. You've got to. Maybe not kill him, but take him down. Cliff, please, Faucon is unarmed."

"Thinking," Cliff said, and seconds later stood up. "Better idea." He held up the pellet gun in his left hand. Then with his right he reached to his holster, flipped off the tie-down, and withdrew his service pistol. "AJ, here." He handed her the weapon. "I know Aaron showed you how to use it, and I know you've fired other pistols. You shoot only if it's to save yourself or me."

"Or me!" Keegan said.

"No. Not you. Because the minute we go in, you've got to be the one to make a run for the car. Lock yourself in. If things go bad, somebody's left to tell the story. Got it?"

"But—

"No buts and no time to waste. Let's move."

They hustled to the parking lot, whispered good luck, and split up. Keegan took off down the driveway while Cliff set the projector dart pressure for something a little thicker than human skin. He crept alongside the building with AJ three steps behind. She had the pistol in a two-handed grip, pointed skyward.

Cliff whispered, "If you do have to shoot, remember that the bad garglee is the one holding the weapons. Hopefully I'll tranquilize him first."

They mounted the steps onto the wood decking. Cliff stepped to the left side of the door frame, AJ to the right. The big cop peeked around the door molding into the dining hall, moving his head slowly from side to side. The night vision goggles showed no outline of a *gargouille*.

"Faucon," a voice from the kitchen called. *Toulouse.*

Cliff raised the dart rifle to his shoulder and aimed across the big room toward the hallway. Had Faucon been smart enough to hide in a walk-in cooler or under an office desk? And if Toulouse couldn't find him, would he leave by way of the hallway and return to the dining room? If he did, Cliff could try to talk him out of his mission and let him leave. But if he had to, he was prepared to dart him.

"Faucon," Toulouse called again.

Cliff heard heavy pots clang. *He bumped into an overhead carousel.* Next the sound of a refrigerator door opening, the seal around its edge breaking the suction. Then the sound of a squeaky oven door. But no fighting.

Feet padded from the kitchen into the hallway, and for a moment Cliff could see through the goggles the outline of the armed *gargouille*—long blade and short blade out in front of him. He was moving away from Cliff, though, not toward him, investigating the smaller rooms. Still no fight sounds. *Maybe I won't have to dart him, after all. Maybe Faucon didn't come in here, and AJ and I can back out.*

Then from behind, as close as the porch steps, Cliff heard Faucon's taunt. "Toulouse? *Au revoir.* I must be on my way now."

Which brought the noise of Toulouse's scrambling from the camp office. With no room to spread either his short wings or his broad wings, he charged along the dark hallway as fast as his stubby legs could move, and burst into the dining room, assuming it was a straight path to the door and out.

Cliff was surprised, but not caught totally off guard. He already had the shot lined up and instinctively took it. The dart struck Toulouse in the meaty part of his diaphragm, puncturing the skin and depressing the plunger, delivering the tranquilizer cocktail. But the drug's effect wasn't instant, and the sword-wielding *gargouille's* forward movement didn't stop. Nor did he drop to the floor. Cliff fired again, aiming lower in hopes of hitting softer flesh around the hip or thigh. But Toulouse continued, stumbling slightly on unsteady legs, his great wings unfurling as if opening them might help him regain his balance. The drug's disorienting properties were confusing his muscle responses and before he could reach the door or Cliff or AJ, who had the pistol pointed directly at him, he stumbled forward. Cliff saw the sword arm go up then start down at him. Without thinking, he shifted his hold on the pellet rifle, gripped its stock in one hand and the end of its barrel in the other, raising it like a weightlifter's bar in front of him.

Toulouse crumpled, the sword blade clanking on the breech of the rifle, its impact causing the swordsman to lose his grip on his way to the floor.

Cliff stood there with his heart pounding, unable to speak. The tip of the sword, still in the twitching *gargouille's* grip, was between the big man's ankles.

"*Merci beaucoup*," said a voice behind Cliff. "I am forever in your debt." Then the voice added, "The others will come. Where can you hide me?"

CHAPTER 37

"Call Luna's brother," Stedman said. "We're five minutes out."

Maryann pressed the green call icon, heard it dial, and switched to speaker. Someone answered but said nothing.

"Pernod?"

Still no voice.

"It's Maryann, Luna's friend."

"*Oui*," a male voice replied. "*C'est moi.*"

"We're almost there. We have a red Jeep with a trailer. Did Luna and the others get there yet?"

"*Non.* Probably in a few hours. I will wait for you where the driveway enters the road. Look for my lantern and follow me to the house."

Five minutes later they crested a rise and spotted a dim light in the near distance. Whoever held it was small, and as they drew closer they could see that he was hiding behind the mailbox post.

"One if by land," Maryann said.

Stedman gave a flash of his brights and slowed. Rather than step out to show himself, the figure disappeared down the driveway with lantern in hand. Stedman turned in and saw the light far down the dirt and gravel path now.

"Luna's brother's like a bottle rocket," Stedman said.

"Roadrunner, I was thinking," Maryann said. "Luna said they call him Waterbug. Born with odd wings and can't fly high, but he can really skim the surface."

They bumped and creaked along the driveway and stopped in what passed for a parking area in front of the house. The yard was weedy but Stedman had no problem rolling over it when he circled the Jeep and trailer. He left them facing the driveway and the road. The two of them climbed out, stretched and worked the kinks out, and glanced up at the porch, expecting to see a *gargouille* holding a lantern. But he wasn't on the porch.

"Pernod?" Maryann called.

"*Ici,*" said the voice they had heard on the phone. "Behind your trailer."

They walked to the back of the Jeep and a little farther and saw a small shadowy figure with an unlit lantern hanging at his side.

"Conserving the battery," Pernod said. "I have several lanterns and some extra batteries, but they will be better used inside the house. We will also need them when Luna's *entrourage* arrives."

The three of them stood for an awkward moment.

"Would you like to see how we have prepared the trailer?" Maryann asked, and Stedman followed her lead. He reached for the handle and turned it, then lifted the clamshell roof. "If you snap on the lantern for a moment, you can see. We have mattresses on the floor, so it won't be so bumpy for the little ones."

Pernod pressed the button and the lantern came on. He peered into the ATV trailer.

Maryann and Stedman sneaked glances at their host. Stedman hadn't seen a *gargouille* before except for the blurry video of Faucon exiting the silo. Maryann had seen both Luna and Faucon, and noticed that Luna's brother was about her height and weight, but he lacked the broad upper wings that made her shoulders look hunched. His frame appeared straighter, more erect.

"Very thoughtful," Pernod said. "*Merci.* Luna and her friends and *les enfants* will be comfortable on the drive to wherever you are taking them." Then, aware that Stedman was staring, he said, "I know you are curious." He lifted his arms slightly so the lantern illuminated his flanks and back. "I have no angel wings, only these short wings, and they are not like my sister's or other *gargouilles'* hummingbird wings." He unfurled them. "I cannot soar and I cannot hover or go backwards. But these wings allow me to move forward very quickly. I am slow in the forest, especially in the tangles, but on an open path like this driveway—or even on top of the water—I travel very quickly. Just not very high."

"Thank you," Maryann said, "for explaining. Having seen only Luna and Faucon, I was very curious."

"Yes, thank you, Pernod," Stedman said. "Looks like fun. And it beats jogging."

Their host chuckled. "Shall we go inside?"

"We have some supplies to carry in from the Jeep," Stedman said. "Maryann figured the kids would be hungry when they got here." He opened the Jeep's back door and the three of them hauled things inside.

***

"It's time," Luna told Yvette. "Wake them and bring them here to the cave entrance. I will have everything ready."

Ten minutes later Yvette appeared with *les enfants*.

"This is called a lifejacket," Luna said. "Humans strap them on when they canoe. This is a small one made to fit a child." She handed her friend the life preserver she had stolen from the Chesuncook Village campsite. "Mathilde's arms go through these holes, then you tighten it here and snap these pieces together at her chest. I will check it when you are finished."

Luna grabbed the pilfered backpack she'd brought back from the village and beckoned to Regine. "We're going for a ride, little queen. Come here." She opened the flap of the backpack, lifted the baby *gargouille* then lowered her into it. "That's it, let's pull your little feet through these holes I cut at the bottom." She leaned the improvised infant carrier and its passenger against a small boulder. "Wait here soon and we'll go for a ride."

She found the bright blue Trader Joe's insulated bag, which now also had two leg holes. "Your turn, Paladin. In you go." She lifted him into the bag and zipped the zipper as tightly as she could over one shoulder and against his neck. Then she checked Yvette's work to be sure the life vest was snug and its clips secure.

"But you and I are still only two," Yvette said. "And they are three."

"Patience, my friend." She took a short length of rope she had cut from the stolen dock line and tied the lifejacket to Yvette's chest, the baby facing forward. "You'll fly with Mathilde."

Yvette looked puzzled.

Luna picked up the backpack with Regine in it and turned it so the baby was also facing forward. "Fasten the snaps on my back," she said, and Yvette did.

"That's two," Yvette said. "How do we carry Paladin? I can carry one, you can carry the other. Even without a third, if there is an emergency, I can change from my angel wings to my hummingbird wings. You cannot."

"This is the tricky part," Luna answered, and pulled out the remaining length of dock line. She slipped it through the straps of the Trader Joe's cooler so it was above Paladin's exposed head. There were loops in either end, one for Yvette, the other for her. "It goes over your wrist." She demonstrated by slipping her own wrist into the loop at the other end of the rope. "We share Paladin's weight. We each carry a baby and a half."

"He will hang between us?" Yvette asked.

"*Oui*. His weight will threaten to pull us together, so be vigilant. If we touch wingtips or tangle, we crash. Ready?"

The two *gargouilles* took their loops and separated until the rope was almost taut. Then like two mothers on a park stroll—Regine and Mathilde facing forward in their strange child carriers, Paladin facing forward with a zipper over his shoulders and his bare legs sticking out of the ice-blue Trader Joe's bag—the two adults started a takeoff run, flapping. *Whoosh, whoosh, whoosh. They* passed over the center of the meadow where Bronwyn had given herself for them, then they cleared the skyline of trees and gained altitude, turning toward Katahdin's south end and hopefully the sanctuary house of Pernod's blind friend Rusty.

CHAPTER 38

Stedman and Maryann tripped twice inside the house before Pernod relented and turned on a couple of battery lanterns.

"Sorry," he said. "My friend Rusty is blind and, because I am *un gargouille*, I have good night vision. So neither he nor I have need of the lanterns unless I am reading a book."

They made several more trips to the Jeep carrying in what they thought might be good for feeding *les trois enfants* once they arrived. Pernod showed them the kitchen and suggested the best combinations of mashed vegetables.

"I have never been a father," he admitted, "so I am no expert."

Maryann spread the food items on the kitchen counter and island, then started chopping, pounding, and mixing.

"We appreciate you providing a place for us to meet them," Stedman said. "And for letting us in."

Maryann saw that the conversation was awkward and changed it. "How long have you lived here, Pernod? Or should we call you Waterbug? Luna told us how you got your name."

"I do not live here," he replied. "My cabin is close by, and I come here to read and to use the telephone to call Rusty when he is in Florida. During the summer, I come to visit and we play chess or I read to him."

"So he knows you are a *gargouille*?" Maryann asked.

"*Oui.* And I suspect that he is a human." Pernod smiled slyly.

"Sorry," Maryann said.

"Does Rusty know we're meeting Luna and the others here?" Stedman asked.

"*Oui.* I told him. He is happy to help."

"If this works out," Stedman said, "I'd love to meet him sometime and thank him."

"Let us see how it works out," Pernod said. "And to your previous question, Maryann, "Call me Pernod for now. Waterbug is more for close family."

"Pernod it is," she replied. "And what can you tell us about Luna? I can tell you that she was my sister Zelda's friend twenty years ago at the University of Maine. Zelda died in childbirth and I adopted her baby, whose name is Dauphine, though she prefers to be called by her last name, Keegan. Luna disappeared about that time, then reappeared this summer. My daughter Keegan, her friend AJ, and I helped Luna find your sister Diana's nest and hatch her eggs this summer. Luna and her two friends have been hiding the babies in the wilderness ever since."

When Pernod didn't say anything, Stedman prompted him. "Your turn."

"My sister is not doing this because she wants children, but because she wants reform. No doubt she cares about the little ones, but there is the risk of using them like pawns. If she had to sacrifice one of the three now, which do you think she would sacrifice?"

"Honestly, I have no idea," Maryann said.

The conversation lulled, then Maryann asked, "Are many of your females trained for battle?"

"Not in our clan. In other clans, if there are too few males, females have learned to fight. But it is rare. Luna and Diana learned the secrets of battle from their mates, Champaigne and LeClair."

"Colonel Chamberlain's Night Hawk scouts," Stedman said. "The American Civil War."

"*Oui.* Who died as a result of the mustard gas the Germans used in France. Had they lived, this question of heirs would not be before us."

Another long silence as they pondered things.

"I find it interesting," Stedman finally said, "that both you and your sister have developed friendships with humans. For an ancient race that has always tried to be invisible, to not even leave a footprint, it's ... well, it's odd."

"It is," Pernod admitted. "Mine, as you may see, is about isolation and loneliness. My physical differentness, though somewhat accepted by my clan, made me feel like an outcast. In time I decided to make that reality become actual. I left and became a hermit. But fate, this blind human—an outcast in his own right—befriended me. He helped me find a way to keep the less friendly humans from invading my privacy, and I helped him solve his problem of not being able to see his books—by reading aloud to him. Out of our needs we created a bond, a friendship, a genuine appreciation for each other. So, I am still careful about leaving a *gargouille* footprint in the larger human world, and he is careful to not expose me."

"Then let me ask you a question," Stedman said. "Given your breakthrough and Luna's breakthrough, do you think there's hope for more interaction between humans and *gargouilles*? I mean, we both read books, we both play chess, and we both care about children. The Night Hawks and Colonel Chamberlain fought together against slavery. We both fought against German occupation in the Great War. It's a start."

Pernod answered, "Both are possessive of the earth's resources, fearful, territorial, and prone to violence. What do you think?"

"A different question, Pernod," Maryann said. "It's on a more personal level. Your friendship with this blind man is beautiful. But how old are you, and how old is he?"

Pernod said, "We all die, humans and *gargouilles*. Our race's lifespan is four times yours. Rusty and I have talked of this. We will enjoy each other's friendship for as long as we can. He has an embroidery in a frame on the night stand in his bedroom. His wife—she died thirty years ago—made it for him—a sort of motto, words to live by. She knew he could not see it, so she made the embroidery thick, so he could read it by feeling it. It reads: *Live until you die.* He reminds me of it whenever I tell him I am worried about his health. Ours is not a complicated friendship, but it is a deep one. We look forward to our phone calls, our long-distance chess games, my reading aloud to him and our book discussions. Even though he is human I feel closer to this man than I ever did to *les gargouilles* of our clan. When his last breath leaves him, my own chest will heave and shudder with grief."

Maryann's phone broke the tension. "Keegan?"

"Mom? Got a situation here. Need advice."

"Here? Where is here? You're at home."

Stedman motioned for Maryann to switch to speaker so he could hear. She did.

"Don't worry, Mom, I'm okay. I'm with AJ and Cliff, and we're all fine."

"Where are you?" Stedman asked.

"Near Bridgton, at that camp that had the fire earlier. We're about to leave."

"Can Cliff hear me?" Stedman asked.

"Wait a sec." Keegan switched to speaker.

"Cliff here."

"What's going on?" Stedman asked.

"We have Faucon. He surrendered to us."

"What?" Maryann asked.

"He's sick, barely keeping it together," AJ chimed in. "We've got him in the way-back, lying down."

"But we don't know where to take him," Keegan said. "We can't just drive him to the wilderness like we did with Luna. She was at least able to fly. Faucon's a mess. I don't think he'd be able to get up, and wild animals would get him."

"Should we take him back to Cliff's?" Keegan asked.

"No way!" Maryann said. "No way."

"I need to make a phone call," Stedman said. "I have an idea. I'll call you back soon. In the meantime, drive west on 117 toward Tamworth, New Hampshire. Don't speed and don't get stopped."

They clicked off. Stedman brought up a number from his contacts and hit the call button.

"Who're you calling?" Maryann asked.

"My sister Rainey in Tamworth. Maybe she and Dr. Tom can treat Faucon."

"But they're vets."

"Can't take Faucon to a hospital ER. They can do the basics and keep it under wraps."

After a half dozen rings, a man answered.

"Tom, this is Elly. Sorry to call so late, but I've got a big, big favor to ask of you and my sister."

CHAPTER 39

Les enfants couldn't yet fly on their own, but they loved being airborne immediately—Regine in her makeshift baby carrier with her legs forward through the backpack's cutout leg holes, feeling secure with her back against Luna's midsection, Mathilde in her life vest, her back pressed against Yvette's chest, and Paladin in his Trader Joe's bag with its top zipped over his shoulders against his neck, him the only one not physically touching an adult because he was hanging suspended at the center of the long rope connecting Luna and Yvette, the rope like a clothesline drooping slightly between the two flapping-then-gliding *gargouilles*. The three babies gurgled and giggled with delight as the cool night air rushed past their faces and chilled their cheeks, the pits of their tummies giddy at the rising and falling they experienced in the air currents, their eyes wide at the new view of the sky and the moon above and the ground and the trees and lakes below.

Luna and Yvette spent the first mile working out the bugs of flying with   what felt like a fifteen-pound baby in each of their bellies, with an extra fifteen-pound boulder—Paladin—suspended between them, pulling them down and also toward each other. But they made the adjustment.

About five miles out Luna called to Yvette, "We can reverse sides if you switch the loop onto your other wrist and I do the same. Cross ahead of me and I will drop back then move into your position. It will reduce the stress we are feeling when we try to keep ourselves apart."

They managed the aerial maneuver, but with one unanticipated consequence. They each had a baby in a pouch in front of them, but poor Paladin in his cooler bag was now left facing backward. He didn't like it, and soon began struggling to turn himself around inside the bag so he could see forward. The wiggling turned him from an almost dead weight to a twice-as-heavy cargo, stressing Luna and Yvette. So rather than land and start over, they performed the aerial reversal again and reclaimed their original positions. Paladin settled down.

They followed Chesuncook Lake's eastern shore south, seeing on the western shore the occasional campfire and the dim light of lanterns. A few electric lights on tall poles marked the Ripogenus or "Rip" Dam of 1920, where they veered left and moved to a higher altitude.

"It is called the Golden Road," Luna said. "Great Northern Paper Company built it to link the North Woods and their Millinocket mills. If we stay high, it will resemble a dry creek bed, but no one will see us. After we pass what humans call the Nesowadnehunk Deadwater we will be able to see in the distance the light of the Millinocket Airport. When we see them, we leave the road and fly due east close to the north shore of Millinocket Lake. Then we leave landmarks behind and cross the wilderness to a small town called Grindstone. If we miss it, we still run into the Penobscot River and can follow it north until we find the town. Waterbug's friend's lake house is near there, not quite in Patten. So, from here, another two hours. Can you continue without stopping to rest?"

"The night is clear, the updrafts are perfect, and *les enfantes* are content. I am fine. *Et toi?*"

"I am fine, too," Luna replied. Then she added, "*Pour le moment*," and they laughed. They were overcoming obstacles and they felt a sense of hope. Finally things were going well.

When the airport lights came into view they turned toward Millinocket Lake, skirting the north shore. Porch lights and yard lights glowed below all around the lake.

One of the babies screamed. Paladin.

Luna felt the danger before she saw it—a strong pull on her right wrist, her connection to the clothesline and the Trader Joe's bag carrying Paladin.

"Owl!" Yvette cried out. "Owl!"

The pull on Luna's wrist was stronger now, threatening to draw her to the center where her wingtips and Yvette's would touch and force them into a downward spiral. They both fought to keep stable and fly straight ahead.

"It's attacking Paladin," Yvette screamed.

Luna glanced right and saw between them the yellow-gold eyes and head tufts of a great horned owl, its wingspread matching theirs, its razor-sharp talons sunk into little Paladin's scalp. The owl's wings weren't flapping, it was using them only for balance, letting the two *gargouilles* carry the load. The added drag was slowing their airspeed and the clothesline was drooping. But the great horned owl couldn't drag its prey away from the tether line.

Paladin screamed again. His sisters cried out in sympathy.

Instinctively Luna reached for one of the *poignards*, but she immediately sheathed it again. "If I go after the owl, the owl and Paladin will drop lower, and I will not be able to reach them."

Paladin cried out again at the pain of the talons in his thickly crowned head. Regine responded, howling and kicking her tiny legs against Luna's belly. Yvette screamed at the owl, "Let him go. He is not food."

They were dipping, losing altitude, and the owl showed no signs of loosening its grip.

"Yvette, Yvette. Listen to me."

Yvette stopped screaming.

"You fly higher and I will fly lower. Paladin will slide toward me on the rope. I need Paladin close to me." She reached back and drew out the thrusting dagger with her left hand again. "Higher, Yvette. A little at a time."

They adjusted—Luna down, Yvette up—until the clothesline tilted and Paladin's bag started to slide on its handgrips. Luna prepared to slash or stab the owl.

But the great horned owl felt the weight of its prey increasing as Paladin slid downward, gravity pulling at the bird's legs and talons, transferring more weight over to it.

"What now?" Yvette yelled.

"The lake. Drag them over the surface. Scrape the owl off. Now."

The two *gargouilles* leveled off and reestablished their distance, leaving the wailing Paladin and the owl atop his head three-quarters of the way across the clothesline on Luna's side. Luna and Yvette, with the two females crying and kicking in their stomach pouches, descended as if approaching a short runway. When their cargo was five feet above the surface they moved together a little and the Trader Joe's bag skimmed the water. But the owl was on top of Paladin, not under him, the talons of both feet embedded in the child's crown, as if ready to pull apart the two halves of a walnut and peck out the tender meat inside. It wasn't about to let go or be scraped off. Oblivious of the attached rope, the owl flapped its powerful wings, lifting its prey in hopes of escaping the bodyguards.

"Goose landing!" Luna yelled. "Pull up. Switch to short wings. Attack the owl."

Both *gargouilles* turned their angel wings then and stood straight up, catching the air and braking to an almost full-stop. Luna settled and began to sink. Yvette didn't, because in the same moment she used her angel wings to brake, she fired up her hummingbird wings, which made it appear that she was walking on water. The side wings vibrated at an excited speed that was almost deafening. With the soles of her thick feet slapping the water, she both hovered and ran towards the owl, her own sharp foot talons out, her arms and hands gesturing wildly, menacingly in front of Mathilde.

Not knowing what sort of creature was closing in, the owl released its death grip on Paladin, flapped backwards twice as if astonished and afraid, then made a 180-degree turn and flew off.

Luna paddled to the water-filled Trader Joe's bag that was sinking below the surface with the zippered-in Paladin unable to escape. But the owl's attempt to lift the baby and fly away with him had actually been a blessing. It had kept his head above water for a few extra precious moments, so that now, barely seconds after his small, moon-shaped face dipped below the surface, Luna was able to dip her hand underwater and snag the bag and pull him to the surface. She clutched the sputtering infant, pulling him against Regine.

The hum of Yvette's wings ceased and she settled into the lake, one arm around Mathilde, the other starting to tread water.

"It is shallow," Luna said, moving closer. "My feet are touching the bottom."

Yvette found her footing, the water and the cool night air meeting halfway up her ribcage and at Mathilde's waist. She opened her arms to embrace Luna and they pressed the three infants between their two bodies. They wept and had to separate a bit to give the babies breathing space. They stroked them and cooed like mourning doves, whispering words and sounds of comfort, calming them and taking turns licking and kissing Paladin's bloody scalp.

After a while Yvette asked, "What now?"

Luna answered, "A small adjustment. I will fly above you using my great wings. My short wings are not much help, as you saw when I fought the coyotes. They will not support the added weight of one of these three. Yours are strong and you can lift."

"What will be different?"

"I will carry Mathilde, who is the lightest, and I will do the hard flapping—above you. I will hold the upper end of the rope and you will hold the lower end below and little behind me.

206

We will strap Regine to your back and Paladin to your chest, and you will channel all of your strength into lifting with your hummingbird wings. You can still use your great wings to glide, but no flapping. I will tow you. The journey will be slower, but it is the best use of our energy."

"And all three babies are protected," Yvette said. "Even a great horned owl will not attack an adult *gargouille*."

They rearranged the baby carriers so that Yvette was sandwiched between Paladin and Regine.

Yvette asked Luna, "Are your short wings strong enough to lift you for a few seconds, holding Mathilde?"

"No choice," Luna answered. "Ready?"

"Ready," Yvette said.

Both *gargouilles* extended their short wings then activated them. The noise was deafening as they strained and lifted, each rising straight up from the lake until they were poised, ten feet apart, a few inches above it.

"Here we go!" Luna said. And while supported on a cushion of air over the water, they unfurled their great wings and slapped their soles on the surface, flapping through a tandem takeoff and rising gracefully above the lake. Luna retracted her short wings and flapped harder, rising faster than Yvette, who stayed with her short wings, using her angel wings now only for gliding. They angled east toward the slightly reddening sky that promised dawn, and by the time they cleared the at the lake's end, they were configured for the long haul. Luna's strong upper wings moved rhythmically in long graceful strokes. She was comforted by the feel of Mathilde's back against her chest, the hum of Yvette's wings below, and the drag of the rope that connected the five of them.

If some early-morning fisherperson or caffeine-seeking night owl happened to glance up then at their silhouettes, they probably think they were seeing some sort of National Guard or Air Force mid-air refueling maneuver.

CHAPTER 40

Stedman called Keegan back as she was slowing for a village speed zone. AJ took the call and put it on speaker.

"How far'd you get?" he asked

"Just entering East Denmark on 117 west," Keegan answered.

"East Denmark? That's all?" he asked impatiently. "You should be past Brownfield, maybe even close to Eaton, New Hampshire."

Cliff leaned forward from the back seat. "We had a complication."

"A complication?" Maryann asked on Stedman's phone. "Is everybody okay?"

"We're fine, Mom," Keegan said.

"Then what's this complication?"

"Wait," Stedman cut in. "Let me give you my sister's address, so you don't miss the switch from One-Seventeen to One-Sixty." He read them an address in Tamworth, New Hampshire, and AJ put it into the GPS.

"Got it," she said. "Would you mind telling us who your sister is and why you're sending us there?"

"Lorraine Garrison," Stedman said. "Everybody calls her Rainey. She and her husband, Dr. Tom, are vets with a clinic on their farm. They also board animals. And it's more or less a rescue sanctuary. They're near Hemenway State Forest. I told her Faucon was sick and needed treatment. She and Tom agreed to help."

"Did you tell them Faucon is a *gargouille*?" Keegan asked.

"I did."

"And they believed you?"

"Your mother helped. She convinced them I'm not off my meds."

"Meds?" Keegan said.

"He's kidding, Keegan," Maryann cut in. "When you said you had Faucon we had to think fast. Rainey and Tom understand our situation and can keep a secret."

"That's great, Mom, but as we said, there's a complication."

"Okay. Explain."

Cliff said, "We have two."

"*Two* complications?" Stedman asked.

"No. *Gargoyles*. Or *garglees*. Or however you pronounce it. We have two of them."

"Where?" Maryann asked, her voice rising. "Not in the car?"

"Yes, in the car," Keegan said. "Under a tarp in back."

Silence. Then Maryann said, "You talk, we'll listen."

Keegan started. "When we got to the camp where the fire was earlier, we saw Faucon lying down half-dead out on this little island, and there was this other *gargouille* watching him from the treetops. They didn't know we were there."

"How'd you spot them?" Stedman asked.

"Cliff's night-vision goggles," AJ said. "He borrowed them from the PD."

Before Stedman could jump on that, Cliff confessed, "Sarge, I also borrowed one of the G2 X-Calibers, in case I had to dart Faucon."

Stedman kept his voice calm. "And did you? Tranquilize him?"

"No. What happened is, as we sneaked in from the road Faucon said something to the bad *garglee* and made his move. He used those hummer wings and scooted across the water to the camp lodge. Which drew the bad guy in. He swooped down and pursued Faucon into the building. He was armed, Faucon wasn't, so we followed them."

"But Faucon wasn't inside," AJ said. "He tricked the other *gargouille* and hid under the back porch. Cliff stayed by the door and when the bad guy came out with guns blazing—swords, actually—Cliff dropped him with the dart rifle."

"At which point," Keegan said, "Faucon gave himself up."

Stunned silence on the line for a moment, then Stedman said, "Which doesn't explain why you have two *gargouilles* under a tarp in the back of your car."

"Oh, that part," AJ said. "So, remember how my brother said there were guests with guns at the Hampton Inn, and they were laughing about vampires?"

"Howie Gardner called it in," Stedman said. "It helped the chief decide to do the press conference."

"Exactly. Well, if we figured out Faucon's flight path and stops, why couldn't they? Or maybe the Bridgton cops or CID or the Staties were on their way. We didn't want to leave a *gargouille* for them to find."

"So we dropped the wider of the Subaru's seatbacks down," Keegan explained, "and found a boat tarp to cover Faucon and this other guy."

Cliff said, "Don't worry, I cuffed him, duct-taped his mouth, and tied his arms and wings. And I'm in the back seat next to him, XP loaded and ready if he gives me trouble."

"What about Faucon?" Maryann asked.

"He's sick and exhausted, sleeping," AJ said. "Faucon wasn't crazy about lying next to his attacker, but we said he had to if he wanted a ride."

"So do we have to call Rainey and Dr. Tom," Keegan asked, "and see if they can handle a two-fer?"

"It's not that they can't handle it," Stedman answered. "The problem is, we don't want to deliver Faucon's enemy to wherever Faucon goes for rehab. You need to set him free along the way, as soon as possible, and hope he finds his own way home. Find a remote place to drop him off. Take the cuffs off, untie him, and get out of there. Get Faucon to Rainey and Tom and head for home. If you're lucky, you'll get in by dawn."

"Here it comes," Keegan said, not quite under her breath. "Mom's going to say it. 'You girls have school in the morning.'"

Maryann said, "I heard that." Then she added, "You can call in sick and go back to bed. We'll call you when we're close to home with Luna and the others. We expect them here soon."

"Thanks, Ms. K," AJ said.

"Thanks, Mom," Keegan said.

"See you at the barn in the morning," Cliff said. "I'll text you once we accomplish our catch-and-release."

They clicked off.

CHAPTER 41

They didn't waste time dumping Toulouse.

"The GPS map shows Moose Pond Road coming up on the right," AJ said"

Keegan slowed and took it. It was an unlit blacktop road hemmed in on both sides by old trees and thick undergrowth. A half mile in she spotted what was either an old logging road or a dirt driveway.

"No mailbox," Cliff said from the back. "Fire lane."

Keegan turned and followed it a hundred yards to a rutted wide spot then made a three-point turn so she faced out again.

AJ and Cliff jumped out and lifted the hatch door.

"I don't think he's ready to wake up yet," Cliff said, and grabbed Toulouse by his thick ankles and pulled. By the time he had the sedated *gargouille's* legs out, Keegan was beside him and AJ.

"Same way we got him in, but in reverse?" AJ asked, and prepared to grab an arm.

Keegan took the other arm and each of them looped their hands under Toulouse's arms near the armpits. Cliff wrapped his forearm under Toulouse's knees.

"On three," Keegan said. "One. Two. Three."

They grunted, lifted the drugged body out, and set it three feet to the side by the underbrush.

"That was easy," Cliff said. "Ready?"

"Wait," Keegan said. "We can't leave him tied up. Wolves could eat him."

"No wolves in Maine for decades," Cliff said.

"So, you think he'll wiggle himself loose?" she replied.

""Maybe," Cliff said.

"How about we loosen the ropes?" AJ asked. "When he comes to, he can figure it out."

"I need my handcuffs," Cliff said, and removed them. He loosened the rope binding Toulouse's wings.

"What about the sword and dagger?" AJ asked.

"Leave them," Keegan said. "But not in his scabbards. Put them close by so he can find them. He may need them. And he'll need to save face with his friends. He won't want them seeing him disarmed."

"Just so he can't use them on Faucon or us," Cliff said.

"He may not even remember getting darted, right, Cliff?" AJ asked. "He'll have a hard time figuring out how he wound up out here."

Cliff stuck the two weapons in the dirt ten feet from Toulouse and said, "Let's get out of here before he wakes up."

They walked to the car and Cliff climbed into the back seat again. "Faucon, if you're awake," Cliff said, "you can stretch out a little more."

No answer from Faucon.

AJ and Keegan opened the front doors. "Less than an hour to Tamworth," AJ said, and climbed into the shotgun seat. "The sooner we check Faucon into rehab, the sooner we get home." Keegan started the car, and they took off.

Behind them on his side, Toulouse had a sense that his tormentors had left. His eyelids fluttered and his mouth twitched as he fought to clear the cobwebs from his brain. His arm and leg joints felt creaky and stiff, but his arm and leg muscles were no longer spasming and felt like they belonged to him again. He had no idea who these three humans were—he thought he had heard two females and a male—but he'd caught a place name at the end. Tamworth. Which he was sure was in New Hampshire. He repeated in his mind like a mantra so he wouldn't forget it. He'd have two useful bits of information when Gregoire returned. He had seen Faucon alive, and the humans had a connection to Tamworth.

Steve Burt

CHAPTER 42

The final leg of Luna and Yvette's flight was an exhausting but uneventful two hours. No night hawks or barred owls, and thankfully no great horned owls like the big one that had tried to carry Paladin off in its talons, nearly sending them all crashing to the ground. Their path took them from Millinocket Lake to the Grindstone Road to Stacyville then above the Fish Stream. Luna steered them toward the dirt road and the spot where the RFD box marked the driveway.

Luna called down, "When we leave this road I will glide to the house and when you let go I will circle back to the road. Then I will come in by the same path."

Inside the lake house Pernod's ears had pricked up at the hum of Yvette's wings. "They're here!" he exclaimed, and tromped out the front door. Maryann and Stedman sat up on the little couch in the study, shook off their sleepiness, and followed.

Pernod stood on the steps, staring up the driveway and waving his battery lantern like a railroad signalman. The three of them had to resist the urge to run out to the dooryard.

Luna slowed her forward speed and made the turn with Yvette and her double bundle in tow below. She sighted in on the building at the far end of the driveway gave one flap then glided, Yvette fifteen feet above the ground then ten then five. Yvette let go her end of the rope and came to a hover stop, settling in the little yard. Luna pulled up, banked left then returned to the road.

Maryann and Stedman stared down at Yvette with a baby on her back and another on her chest. If they had expected something like three-quarters of a Blue Angels flyover, a triumphant return to base that would leave them looking up open-mouthed at the undersides of three adult female *gargouilles*, each carrying a precious payload in its arms, they were disappointed. The worn-out Yvette sank to her knees and

214

fought to stay in an upright squat. They ran to her and held her up.

Maryann, not knowing why there were only two adults or why the pair had approached in over-and-under configuration, yelled toward the road, "Luna, come back. We're here. It's safe. Bring your other friend."

Yvette barely had enough breath to speak, but croaked out, "Bronwyn did not make it. Watch Luna. She has Mathilde."

Regine and Paladin began to fuss and cry, so Maryann and Stedman lifted them out of their carriers and held them close.

They saw the V of Luna's angel wings going away from them toward the road, and knew she had only to turn and make a fresh approach. She would follow the driveway and coast at the end like a waterfowl then pull up short and land.

But the tow rope still hung from her wrist, and when she made the tight turn, what had been Yvette's loop snagged on the mailbox's handle. She didn't even know it had caught, and before she could shake either the top or the bottom loop free she felt herself being dragged into a tight spiral that, in the blink of an eye, dragged her face-first onto the road's gravelly shoulder.

"Luna went down," Pernod cried out, but in the dim light Maryann's and Stedman's eyes hadn't been able to make out the crash. In no time Pernod's feet moved and his stubby roadrunner wings popped out. They watched him sprint-fly away out the driveway toward Luna and her vulnerable passenger Mathilde.

Pernod reached his sister in seconds. She lay face-down, her right broad wing fully extended, her left bent under her, Mathilde crying in the carrier.

"Luna," he said, and helped her sit up. "Are you hurt?"

The extended broad wing began to move, then like a hand curling into a fist, slowly furled against her shoulder. With Pernod's help she rolled onto her side.

"Legs, arms, anything broken?" he asked. "Left wing?"

She slowly folded the left wing, then sat up.

Pernod unstrapped the carrier and removed the baby. He leaned the sobbing baby against his shoulder and she calmed down. "Your face is bloody, Luna. There is also blood on the left side of your head. We can rinse the gravel out at the house."

"Help me stand, Waterbug," she said, and when she was on her feet he faced her and looked her over.

"Both legs are bloody," he said. "Your knees. And your hands. Some skin is gone."

"Skin will grow back," she said. "Yvette and the other two? How are they?"

"They did not crash," he said, and she forced a chuckle. "Maryann and Elly are with them. Let's see if you can walk."

She took a tentative step, then another. "I can walk."

"You will be sore tomorrow."

They started down the driveway on foot, Pernod holding his sister's hand to steady her, the baby on his other shoulder. "This is Mathilde? She likes the walking motion."

Maryann and Stedman met them halfway, each with a tiny *gargouille* hugging them like chimpanzees, the couple back-patting the infants as they walked.

"Yvette?" Luna asked before anything else could be said.

"Yvette is fine," Maryann answered. "She's on the porch steps. She wants to hear from us that you're okay."

"A little scratched up, but I will recover. The rope caught on something and I—how do you say it, *corkscrewed*—I corkscrewed myself to the ground."

They all laughed lightly, then Maryann said, "She told us Bronwyn didn't make it. I'm so sorry."

"*Oui.* She ..." But Luna couldn't finish, and her tears of sadness over Bronwyn mixed now with her tears of joy and relief at having arrived safely at the blind man's lake house to find waiting friends eager to help.

CHAPTER 43

The GPS guided Keegan through Tamworth, New Hampshire and up the Chinook Trail with its road signs featuring the famous sled dogs from the Antarctica expeditions. Six miles from the town's four corners they passed the historic site of the Chinook Kennels, and two miles beyond that the GPS announced they had arrived at the final turn before they reached their destination. An RFD mailbox stenciled with the name of Rainey and Tom's Farm and Vet Clinic stood at the intersection of the Trail and a hard-packed dirt road that would in a few months be riddled with frost heaves and pot holes. They started down it and immediately spotted a sign: WATCH FOR ANIMALS, 5 MPH.

"*Ou suis-je?*" Faucon mumbled, waking. Then in English, "Where am I?" He found himself on his side now, hands bound behind him by the handcuffs Cliff had taken off Toulouse.

"*Chez le medecin,*" Keegan said in her best French. "At the doctor's. You need help."

"*Et Toulouse?*" he asked. "*Il est mort?*"

"No, Toulouse is not dead. We left him sleeping in the forest. He'll find his way back to his . . . um, friends."

Faucon made a sound of disapproval.

A quarter mile beyond the sign was another larger wooden sign to the left that announced the veterinary clinic. The second and third line each had a name followed by the letters DVM, with a phone number and hours below.

From the dirt road a narrow blacktop driveway to a log cabin that was clearly a residence. A man and a woman got up from porch rockers when Keegan turned in. They wore white lab coats and walked into the headlight beams of the Subaru.

To the right and slightly behind the residence was a paved parking lot with a split-rail fence between it and a large two-story building that could have been stick-built or possibly delivered pre-fab and assembled like Stedman's little house. Connected to the right side of it was a long, one-level block structure that had outdoor chain-link pens along its front and presumably the same across its rear. Farther down the road beyond that stood an old dairy barn with several silos and sheds.

Keegan parked in front of the log house. She, AJ, and Cliff climbed out and introduced themselves to Stedman's sister Rainey and her husband Tom.

"Should I leave the car here or is there a better place?" Keegan asked. "Faucon's lying down in the back, tied up."

"Is he violent?" Rainey asked.

"Depends on the day," Cliff said. "Right now he's happy to get a ride and medical attention. I think he'll be cooperative."

"How about if we help him out of the car and take a quick look?" Dr. Tom said. "That'll tell us which building to take him to next."

"Okay," Keegan said. "Let me tell him first so he's not startled." She opened the driver's door and stuck her head in. She spoke quietly, and the others could hear her voice but not the words. A moment later she backed away and shut the door.

"Cliff," she said, "can you remove the cuffs and ropes. He promises he won't make trouble."

"After he's out of the car and on his feet," the big cop answered.

She opened the door again and relayed Cliff's answer, then shut it. "Fair enough," he says.

Cliff raised the rear hatch door and helped Faucon out. As soon as the *gargouille* was on his feet Cliff slipped the handcuffs off and helped Faucon untangle himself from the ropes.

Faucon turned to face the two vets.

"Monsieur Faucon," Tom said. "I am Dr. Tom and this is Dr. Rainey. We're here to help you."

"Merci, Dr. Tom *et* Dr. Rainey," he said. "*Je suis malade.*"

The couple tried not to gawk, but here before them stood a living, breathing gargoyle, a creature they not only had never seen but didn't know existed.

"May we approach?" Rainey asked. "Where does it hurt?"

"My foot," he replied. "Three toes are missing. There is great pain when I walk."

"Luna did it to him with a sword," Keegan interrupted. "They may be infected."

"Thank you, Keegan. We'll check it out," Dr. Tom said. "Anything else, Monsieur Faucon?"

"My back and my wing are not working well."

"Which wing?" Rainey asked, and took a step toward her patient.

Faucon raised a hand to hold her off. "Wait, please. I do not wish to startle you. If you give me room I can show you my wings. I know you are curious."

"Very well," she said, stepping back.

Faucon spread his angel wings from his shoulders then, without firing them up, extended the pair of hummingbird wings from his sides.

"Wow!" Rainey said.

"Stole my words," Dr. Tom said. "Amazing."

"Again, which wing is injured?" Rainey asked.

Faucon pulled the short wings close to his sides again. "The right great wing and the right shoulder. A wound."

"A firewood ax," Keegan added.

Faucon managed to furl his left angel wing while keeping the right one spread. The two vets moved closer and behind the *gargouille*. She examined the shoulder, he the wing.

"Definitely infected," she said. We'll need to get you on some antibiotics for a while. And it's going to take some stitches."

Her husband said, "The wing is a different story. There's still a hole there but it's not normal skin covering flesh like the shoulder wound. The wing material is thin, without flesh under it, so imagine trying to fix a drum with slice in it. If you try to play it, it'll tear further. Even if we immobilize it, it's not going to naturally heal itself. This is going to take some very creative patching, a graft maybe."

Rainey squatted down and examined Faucon's foot. "We've got to get going on this right away. No time to lose."

"Will I lose my foot?" Faucon asked, furling his wounded angel wing.

"Too early to say," Rainey answered. "We'll save as much as we can. But it looks like an operation, for sure." She stood up and looked directly into his sad red eyes. "I'm sorry."

Cliff broke the awkward silence. "So where do you want him?"

"Monsieur Faucon," Dr. Tom said. "If it's all right with you, I'd like Cliff to help me walk you over to the clinic building there. We have several exam rooms with better lighting than we have out here. I'll string an IV antibiotic right away, get some pictures of your injuries, and finish my examination. We have a small building out near the back of the property where you can sleep all day. We can draw the shades to keep out the sunlight. We have clients bringing their animals in all day, but usually not at night. So we'll treat you after business hours. How does that sound?"

"This is very kind of you," Faucon said. "How long must I stay?"

"At least a few days," Dr. Tom said. "Depends how you respond to the antibiotics and what we're able to accomplish patching you up."

"Very well," Faucon said. "Merci."

Dr. Tom said, "Cliff, can you give me a hand. I'd like to keep the weight off his bad foot."

Laney said, "Keegan, AJ, while they do that, why don't I give you a quick tour of the clinic, the boarding building, the barn, and building that will be Monsieur Faucon's B & B while he's our guest. By the time we finish, Cliff will be finished helping Tom and you three can hit the road for home. We'll walk far out the driveway first, past the barn, so I can show you where Faucon will be staying. You'll see why I called it a B&B."

CHAPTER 44

Rainey shined her flashlight on the dirt road ahead so they could pick out the depressions and potholes. They walked three across with the trees and stone walls on their right and a string of buildings on their left: house, clinic, kennels, barn and silos. Behind the buildings were sheds, old farm implements, and more stone walls, and beyond them an expanse of dimly lit fields that stretched a hundred yards or more to another tree line.

"Excuse the potholes," Rainey said. "The road's not town-maintained, because it's all on the old farm. We've got a friend with a road scraper who'll hit it again before the snow flies. He also plows for us in the winter."

As they neared the curve in the road where the barn and silos were, Keegan said, "You and Tom didn't seem all that shocked to see a *gargouille.*"

"Shocked, no. Curious, yes," the vet replied. "My brother sketched your situation out for me on the phone after you left Bridgton, including the two sets of wings. He said Faucon's eyes would be red, but your friend Luna's are green."

"I guess all female *gargouilles* have green eyes and males red," AJ said. "There are variations by clan and where they come from geographically. Luna told us Faucon's Alps clan has the rhino horn above the nose. Her Allagash clan doesn't. We don't know about the others."

They neared the ancient dairy barn which was two stories high and double that in length. Its weathered shingles had once been yellow but had over the years been bleached by the summer sun and sandblasted by the winter winds.

"So, tell us about yourself and Tom," AJ said, changing the subject.

"Straightforward story. Two veterinary students, one from Pennsylvania and one from New Hampshire, meet at Cornell, fall in love, marry, and buy a practice here together. No kids—our own animals and those we either take in or board seem to fill that need. I do more of the general stuff, Tom does a little of that and most of the big surgeries."

"And your brother Elly?" Keegan asked.

"We grew up in Walpole, New Hampshire, near Keene. Elly's two years older. Our father was a large-animal vet—cows, horses, mules, donkeys, moose, deer, and a few llamas and alpacas—once a circus elephant passing through. Mom was a seamstress. They're retired to Florida now."

"We hear Elly was an athlete," Keegan said.

"Football. Then boxing in the Navy."

"He looks like he could box," AJ said.

"Technically, yes," Rainey said. "But Mom said he lacked the killer instinct."

"I'll bet he had no problem finding dance partners," Keegan said, grinning. "He's a nice looking man."

Rainey stopped and faced them, also grinning. "Are you two vetting him?" A soon as she saw their deer-in-the-headlights response, she gave a little laugh and said, "For Maryann, right? I'd have to be deaf and blind to not notice her name sneaking into Elly's phone calls."

"Has he said anything about my mother straight out?" Keegan asked. "He seems a little …"

"Shy?" AJ finished.

The vet raised the index finger of her free hand. "I'm not going to play some high-school gossip game. We need to finish this tour and check on Faucon so you and Cliff can get back to Wells. So here's the one thing I'll say. My brother's a forty-something-year-old man who just hasn't met the right person yet. Okay?"

Keegan and AJ nodded their heads, mouths knotted in resignation at the limited information.

"Okay?" Rainey repeated. "Can we move on now?" But she didn't turn and AJ and Keegan didn't move forward.

"I think you can say little more," Keegan pressed. "Like, how'd you know my mother's name was Maryann?"

"All right," the vet sighed. "But then we go."

Both girls nodded.

"Elly visits us a couple times a year—the holidays—and helps our daytime staffers with things like feeding, grooming, and walking the dogs. For the last couple of years he's dropped this lady bookseller's name into the conversation: Maryann. Which I now know is your mother, Keegan. He never said it, but it was obvious to Tom and me that there was an interest. Not that Elly would come out and say it. Hey, I'm not sure he even recognized it. But my guess, from what he reveals in phone conversations or in our small-talk when he's here, is that he's reading more mysteries and buying more books—know what I mean? And though they may be mysteries and police procedurals, I don't think he's buying them for continuing education and professional development."

"For years?" Keegan said.

"He's a slow mover. It's probably what got him into trouble in the ring." She placed her hands on her hips like a schoolteacher and said, "Are we done?"

"We are," Keegan said, and she and AJ smiled. "Resume the tour."

They set out again along the dirt road and passed the barn and the silos. Rainey turned left and led them across a field that had clearly been hayed not long ago. Fifty yards farther, along the back border of the field near the trees, she shined her flashlight beam on a chain link pen that looked like a mini-prison. It was a rectangle thirty or forty feet long and almost as wide, with fence walls ten feet high. The top was attached to forty-five-degree angle irons that turned the fence in over the yard at the top. At one end was something like a doll house, maybe fifteen by fifteen feet with an open porch that was covered by a roof.

"The B&B," Rainey said. "No cooking facilities but there are a pair of twin mattresses inside. And believe it or not, it has heat and air-conditioning. And a push-button fountain."

"TV?" AJ asked. "Hot tub? Chocolate on the pillow?"

Rainey laughed. "Not that extravagant. And no indoor bathroom."

"What was it?" Keegan asked.

"The last owner of the farm—before we bought it—was an advertising executive from New York City. He got here a few weeks a year. But he had farm staff who took care of his animals. This was for his two prize boxers, who were a little pampered."

"A little?" Keegan said.

"He loved our idea for a vet clinic and rescue shelter here, and sold it to us for almost nothing, then financed our building of the clinic and the kennels. For our part, we treated his boxers during their lifetimes and buried them here near the woods. There are two stone markers near here."

"So this is where Faucon will stay?" Keegan asked. "While he's recuperating?"

"Tom and I will handle his meals, and we'll make sure the staff don't come down this way. All he'll have to do is stay inside during the daytime, which he'll do anyway." Notice there are privacy shades on the little windows and door."

Rainey shined the light and, sure enough, they were there.

"I can see why you call it a B&B," AJ said. "All he'll be lacking is a good book to read."

"Somehow I think we can handle that," the vet said. "Okay, now we'll go back by way of the barn and the kennels. The dogs will be quiet while we're in the barn, but expect them to bark when I open the kennel door on this end. They'll quiet down again when we leave through the door to the clinic. By then Tom should be ready to tell us something."

They entered the barn and Rainey flipped on the center overhead lights. What had once been a cow barn still had a cement center aisle that the wooden-wheeled grain cart had rolled down, hay and grain troughs that would have been under the milk cows' noses and mouths along either side. The wooden-yoke stanchions that held the cows in place by their narrow necks now hung open, and the stalls where the animals stood while being fed or milked were clean. They hadn't been occupied in decades. The gutters behind the cows were long ago sanitized and no longer stank of urine and cow manure. The rows of small-paned windows that lined the exterior walls beyond the gutters were clean, not dust-covered. The barn looked like a museum that visitors might come to every weekend.

"Part of our promise to our friend who sold it to us. Keep it like new," Rainey said.

"When's the last time it was used?" Keegan asked.

"Six or eight years ago when a dairy barn in Warren burned. It happened during the day, and all the cows were in the field. So we kept them here until a replacement barn went up. They even brought in milking equipment, so it was a working farm for about six months. That's when we added these overhead sprinkler systems. It's the only improvement to the original dairy barn."

They exited at the end near the kennels and Rainey held them in place just outside the door. "Look back there." She pointed at a pasture that stretched from the barn to the woods. It looked from the evenly spaced posts as if it was fenced in with barbed wire. There were dark figures in the distance, four-legged ones. When Rainey shined her light at them, they were staring back, their eyes glowing.

"Horses, two llamas and two single-hump camels—yes, they do spit in your face—a half dozen Holsteins, some sheep and goats, and two Nevada burros and a pair of Wyoming donkeys."

"And they all get along?" Keegan asked.

"Far as we know. Might be some inter-species hanky-panky out there, for all we know. After dark we don't intrude."

"Not worried about wolves or coyotes?" AJ asked.

"Not with donkeys and western burros in the mix," Rainey said. "That's why farmers adopt rescue equines and add them to the mix. They bond with the herds and protect them when they're out at night. We have coyotes, but we don't have coyote problems."

They crossed the little area of open space between the barn and the first concrete kennel building.

"Here we go," Rainey whispered. "Plug your ears. And if they beg you to let them out, don't fall for their sob stories—unless you're ready to take a dog, car, or potbellied pig home with you." She put a hand on the knob, and even before she turned the handle, the barking began.

CHAPTER 45

Dr. Tom's clinic wasn't an average vet practice. Because he was a surgeon, he and Rainey had more than x-ray machines. They also had ultrasound equipment, an MRI, a Doppler Electrocardiogram setup, and a CT Scanner. Between himself and his wife, who also handled the anesthesia during endoscopies and surgeries, they were prepared for almost anything.

"Your first *gargouille?*" Faucon asked, looking up from where he lay on the exam table. Two plastic bottles hung from a steel frame beside him, a pair of IV drip tubes connecting to his arm.

Cliff Bragdon sat on a chair in the corner of the room, observing. Standing by, really, in case there was trouble.

"So far," Dr. Tom said. "Are there more of you waiting in the wings? Pardon the pun."

"Depends if you cure me," Faucon replied. "If I die, they may be reluctant."

"Now I have to add to my notes," the vet said. "Bipedal, opposable thumbs, similar bone structure to humans but with the addition of wings—two sets. Capable of complex thought, speech, problem-solving, emotion. And now—dry sense of humor that leans toward sarcastic."

The vet's hands and fingers, sheathed in thin surgical gloves, felt gently around Faucon's discolored foot, ankle, and leg. "This hurt?"

The weakened *gargouille* responded appropriately at each pressure point.

"I'll close off this exam room to my day staff and lock you in tomorrow. I understand you normally sleep during the day anyway, but to be sure, I'll add a mild sedative to the IV to help you relax and make sure you sleep through. Given the shape you're in, we can't move you out to the guest house tonight. Dr. Rainey and I will take turns monitoring the IV drips. If the room is off limits to staff and if you can keep quiet, we'll get you through the day and do more exams after our employees and volunteers go home."

"And my foot? My leg?" Faucon asked.

"I'll have a better idea in twenty-four to forty-eight hours. The drugs should help, but we're not out of the woods yet. Tomorrow evening Dr. Rainey and I will go over your wing and shoulder." Dr. Tom scribbled more notes on his iPad. "Anybody you want us to notify?"

"*Pardonnez moi*?"

"Is there anybody—other *gargouilles*," the vet said, "family or friends—that you want us to notify that you're here for treatment?"

"I want no one to know," Faucon said.

From the corner Cliff added. "If they find him, his life could be in danger. We got him out of a jam before we brought him to you."

"I understand," Tom said. "We'll protect your privacy, Monsieur Faucon." Without a second thought, the vet gave Faucon's thick hand a squeeze. "I'll be back with something I think you can eat—no meat—and some fresh water. Next time I'll get more information about your diet."

"Again, *monsieur, merci*."

"Come on, Cliff," the vet said. "I think it's safe to leave him. You and your friends need to get home to Maine."

***

Tom and Cliff found Rainey, Keegan, and AJ sitting in the waiting room, munching some of the clinic's stash of Nutrigrain cereal bars. The docs and the staff didn't always keep regular lunch hours.

"Good tour?" Tom asked the three women.

"Quite a spread," Keegan replied. "A little loud at the end when we walked through the kennels."

229

"They were happy to see you," he said.

"They all said *take me, take me*," AJ said.

"It's a state-of-the-art facility," Tom pointed out. "Only a few like it in the country. If some emergency happened—say a fire or a flood—all the inside pen doors lift and the big fire doors on either end of the building pop open so our guests can escape."

"Rainey used that word, too," AJ said. "*Guests*. I like it."

"So, what's the verdict on Faucon?" Keegan asked.

"He needs a couple days of rest and medications. He'll sleep through the day. Then tomorrow night, when everybody's gone home, Rainey and I can get x-rays and whatever other tests we need. It's possible we can move him to the little B&B house the day after. He's got a long road ahead."

"And the foot?" Keegan asked.

"It's wait-and-see," Cliff answered. "We can call and check. Right now, though, I'm ready to hit the road. Hour and a half, maybe two, to get home. And we need a quick coffee-and-donuts stop. I'm starving. We can call Maryann and Stedman from the road, see if Luna made it there yet."

Rainey opened the front door and, after everyone filed out, hit the lights and locked it.

CHAPTER 46

The flying wedge of King Cyrus' *gargouilles* flapped south from the clan home, the one-eyed Gregoire on point. Bat-faced Grondin flew slightly behind to the leader's left and Percheron, as horse-faced as his name implied, occupied the right side. They were pushing hard to reach the summer camp south of Bridgton, so none of the three noticed they weren't alone: a small Argentinian female followed a mile behind them.

Once they passed high above Bridgton's lights they descended quickly, skimming the treetops that watched over the dark forest below. When they cleared the last of the trees everything below opened up so they could see Free Camp's lake. Swooping low, Grondin and Percheron broke farther to their leader's flanks so the three of them could survey the lake and shores as they glided across to the camp's beach. Gregoire, in the center, glanced ahead and down at the water, as if searching for floating logs or submerged bodies. When the lake ran out they all angled their great wings to brake themselves and settled onto the beach, folding their wings tightly against their shoulders. They scanned the buildings and shadows behind the police tape, saw no threats, and turned to face the lake again.

"Faucon is gone from the island," Gregoire declared.

"And I did not see Toulouse where you left him," reported Percheron, whose prominent jaw gave him the face of a chess knight. "There is no one roosting at the top of any of the grandfather pines above the shore to the right." Percheron reported.

"Do you think Faucon left?" the beady-eyed Grondin asked Gregoire. "Perhaps Toulouse followed him."

Gregoire looked thoughtful then said, "If one had killed the other, there would be a body."

"So, we wait for Toulouse to return?" Percheron asked.

"We look around," Gregoire replied. "We will see if we can figure out what happened."

They turned awkwardly, wobbled up the sandy incline to the police tape, and ducked under it. Gregoire led the way to the front porch of the admin building then started down the right side to the back porch, where they found the back door ajar.

"Wait here," he said, then drew his sword and *poignard* and went inside. Several minutes later he came back out to the porch. "Nothing new. "It is as it was earlier."

"What now?" Grondin asked.

Gregoire sheathed his weapons. "We have some time before sunrise. You wait in Touolouse's tree. Percheron, hide near the boathouse. I will check the island where Faucon was lying down. If neither Faucon nor Toulouse returns soon, we will fly to our Kezar cave near Lovell. We can safely sleep the day there and see what tomorrow night brings."

They split up and took their assigned positions.

Half an hour later a *gargouille* flapped up over the trees from the west and descended, skimming the lake then landing near the beached swimming float.

Percheron stepped from the boathouse shadows. "Toulouse?"

Toulouse drew his sword and *poignard*. Something in the challenger's voice put him on the defensive. *"Qui est-ce?"* he called, and turned toward the boathouse.

"C'est moi, Percheron." The big horse-faced *gargouille* showed himself. His weapons were also drawn.

"Ou est Gregoire?" Toulouse asked, glancing around for the one-eyed *gargouille* who had assigned him to keep an eye on Faucon.

"Ou est Faucon?" came Percheron's answer. Toulouse heard a challenge, perhaps an insinuation, in the where-is question.

"I answer to Gregoire," Toulouse said. "Not to you, Percheron." His body fought to throw off the hangover from the tranquilizer dart and was doing its best to muster some defensive tension.

Both *gargouilles* heard the hum of fast-beating hummingbird wings and glanced toward the lake's center. A single glowing red eye sped across the water, coming from the island.

"Lower your weapons, idiots," Gregoire loudly commanded, and both the groggy Toulouse and the aggressive Percheron sheathed their blades.

A second figure, this one with two red eyes, glided down from his treetop perch and landed on the gritty sand. He furled his great wings as his leader pulled his short wings into his sides. The hum ceased and the four fiery-eyed *gargouilles* stood glaring at each other.

"I left you to watch Faucon," Gregoire said, and took a few steps up the beach until he was in Toulouse's space. "Where is he?"

"I believe some humans took him."

"Humans? What humans?"

"I do not know. I did not see them."

"Yet you are sure these were humans?"

"*Oui*," Toulouse answered.

"Very well," Gregoire said. "And these humans—did they take Faucon himself or did they take his body? When I left, we did not know if he was alive or dead."

"I do not know."

"How can you not know?" Grondin snapped from the high ground behind Toulouse.

"Silence, Grondin," Gregoire ordered, and Toulouse's shoulders sagged. "Toulouse, tell me what happened."

Toulouse sighed and let out a loud breath. "I watched from there." He pointed to the roost Grondin has just flown down from in the grandfather pine. "I thought I heard a human vehicle in the distance, near the road, but I did not know if it was coming here or passing by. A moment later I heard the sound of short wings and saw Faucon racing across the lake. He yelled something about going into the building where the fire was last night, so I left the trees and followed him to the rear door of that building. I went inside and checked all the rooms, but Faucon was not there. When I started to leave, I saw him on the porch. But there was another figure—a large human, a male, I believe—just inside the door, in front of Faucon. There may have been a second human as well, a female. I could not make them out, because they had strange protectors over their eyes."

"What did you do?" Gregoire asked.

"I charged them. They were blocking my only way out."

"Did you engage them?"

"I tried. But the large human had a firearm—a small rifle, I think—and he fired it. Sometime later I woke up miles away from here in a forest, sitting against a tree. My wings were bound and my wrists hurt. They must have transported me there and left me."

"And your weapons?" Gregoire asked.

"I found them near me when I awoke."

"But the humans were gone?"

"*Oui.*"

"And you think they took Faucon?"

"*Je sais pas.* The humans removed my memory."

Gregoire put a thick hand to his chin and pondered this, then said, "They have special guns they use to subdue animals— moose, bear, deer, coyotes, wolves, cattle. They did not know you were here, so they must have brought it to help them capture Faucon."

None of the four *gargouilles* spoke for a moment. They simply stood waiting for Gregoire to finish whatever he was mulling in his head.

Then Toulouse said apologetically, "I returned here as soon as I was able to fly again."

"After they shot you," Gregoire asked, "Do you recall seeing or hearing anything?"

The rattled *gargouille* thought hard, aware that the beady-eyed, bat-faced Grondin was behind him. Then a name popped into his head and onto his tongue. "Tamworth," he said, and repeated it. "Tamworth."

"The town in New Hampshire?" Gregoire asked.

Toulouse shrugged and shook his head.

Gregoire pressed him. "Are the humans from Tamworth or were they going to Tamworth?"

Toulouse shook his head once more. "All I have is the one word."

"And when you last saw Faucon," Gregoire said, "he was alive?"

"*Oui*. He was standing behind the two humans when the big one shot me."

"If they brought a special gun to capture Faucon, why was he standing when you saw him?" the horse-faced Percheron said. "They subdued you, not Faucon."

"He must have gone with them voluntarily," Gregoire said. "He is sick and has turned to the humans for help, not to his own kind."

"Is it not possible he is not with them?" Grondin wondered. "He could have escaped and may still be trying to get home. Would he accept captivity with the humans?"

Toulouse responded slowly but in a soft, clear voice. "I. Do. Not. Know. All I know is, the human shot me with the memory gun and I woke up in the woods. As soon as I was able, I flew back here."

Gregoire made a command decision. "Here is what we will do. We all need rest. Daylight is nearly upon us, and we cannot risk exposure to the sun or to humans. Tamworth is to the west, but we do not know what these humans look like or if they are there. And we do not know if Faucon has gone there. So for now we will fly over Bridgton to the Kezar cave and sleep there. When darkness falls again, you three go to Tamworth and take up positions around the town. If Faucon is there, he will have to come out at night to fish and forage. Stay three nights. If he appears, two of you stay and one of you comes to get me. On those nights I will be watching Faucon's island from the grandfather pine."

"And if none of us find him?" Grondin asked.

"It will mean either that he is dead, or heading north on his own, or he is a prisoner of the humans who no doubt would love to have *un gargouille* to display and to experiment on."

"So we fly to the Kezar cave now?" Toulouse asked.

"On our way out we will check two other parts of this camp. I saw a sign beyond the cabins pointing to a trail that leads to a waterfall. Grondin, you and Percheron check it. Toulouse and I will search the shoreline behind Faucon's island, in case he has decided to hide in plain sight. We will all meet at the Kezar cave."

The four *gargouilles* split up, one pair setting out across the lake, the other following the waterfall trail, all of them worn out from their long flights and thinking about sleep.

CHAPTER 47

At the same time, almost five hours away at the lake house, little Paladin lay cradled in Stedman's arms, wincing and whimpering as Maryann dabbed his scalp lacerations with an alcohol compress. The great horned owl's razor-sharp talons had inflicted a good deal of damage around the crown of the baby's head. The blood had clotted during the flight and Stedman's swabbing was removing some of the crusting scabs. The alcohol cleaned the exposed scratches but also stung, so Stedman responded by clucking and cooing then turning his knee into a rocking horse to distract the baby as Maryann worked.

Luna and her brother stood nearby, Pernod watching Maryann's example so he could wipe Luna's scraped and bloodied road-rash areas. She sucked in her breath whenever he touched the skinless patches but didn't cry out.

"Antibiotic ointment next, Pernod," Maryann said. "The little tube between us. Use your fingertip." She demonstrated on the baby, and Pernod followed her lead.

"Everything okay in there, Yvette?" Maryann asked.

From the little den/library came an answer, "Mathilde and Regine are asleep in each other's arms on this strange mattress. Pernod, you called it a bag chair? They love it."

"A beanbag chair," he called back. "I love it, as well."

When Maryann and Pernod had finished up the wound care, she said to Stedman, "Maybe an hour or two of sleep for everybody, Elly? It's almost light outside. When we're rested, we can say goodbye to Pernod and get Luna and Yvette and the babies settled into the camper. Then we can hit the road for home, get there by one-thirty or two."

By now Elly had the dozing infant against his chest, its small head sideways on the cop's shoulder, the big man's large hand under the baby's bottom.

"Stedman, you're a natural grandfather," Maryann said, and lay down on her side on the plank floor, a kitchen towel under her cheek. She was asleep almost before her head hit the towel.

"These are good humans," Pernod said.

"Good *friends*, Waterbug," his sister answered. Then she and her brother went into their sit-squat positions and fell asleep.

***

Bacon and eggs were not on the menu at Pernod's friend's lake house, nor were pancakes and sausage. With the power and the cooking gas shut down for the winter, there were no fixings in the refrigerator or in the pantry. There was cold cereal in the cupboard but no milk for it. Luckily Maryann had thought ahead. She brought in a box of chocolate-chip protein bars from the Jeep, opened it, and dumped the contents on the table. She picked one up and Stedman, who had traded Paladin for Mathilde and Regine, sat with them clutched to his broad chest, rocking them.

"Can you peel two of those things for me?" he asked. "They look kind of small, but I'm starving."

She unwrapped two of the bars and handed them across the chessboard in his direction.

"Haven't got a free hand," he said. One palm was cupped under Mathilde's little fanny, the other under Regine's. He grinned sheepishly. "Can you feed them to me?"

"Isn't it supposed to be grapes?" Maryann countered. "Never seen a protein bar in Italian art."

She got up from her chair and walked around the table to his side and held up one of the bars up to his mouth. When he leaned forward slightly to bite it, she eased it away before he could bite.

"Don't tease," he said. "You can see I've got my hands full here."

She smiled and let him have a bite.

He chewed and made an exaggerated *mmm* sound. "Gourmet," he said. "You've outdone yourself."

Pernod returned from the library with Paladin against his shoulder. "Luna and Yvette are asleep on my beanbag, leaning against each other like sisters." When he saw the wrapped protein bars spilled out on the table, he asked, "May I try one of those?"

"Be our guest," Maryann said. "Here, take this one. It's already unwrapped." She handed him Stedman's second protein bar. "I'll get Elly another one. How can I resist two males with their arms full of babies?"

Pernod accepted it with his free hand and bit off the top third and chewed. "Mmm." He swallowed, then said matter-of-factly, "Know what I miss?"

"What?" Maryann asked.

"My mug of fresh, hot, black coffee."

Maryann laughed out loud, and Stedman's head tilted slightly as his eyebrows went up in surprise. "Oh, my God," she said. "Are you serious? You drink coffee?"

"*Mais oui.* My friend Rusty has a Keurig. It is under the kitchen island because he is in Florida and there is no electricity. It started with him having a cup and I would smell it across the chessboard. One night I remarked on the aroma and he asked if I wanted a cup for myself. He made it and I found it bitter. But I tried it again the next night and then again, and I grew to love it."

"But you only have it in the summer," Stedman said, "when the power and water are on. Ouch."

"*Oui, monsieur.* Ouch. *C'est difficile.*"

"Difficult doesn't half describe it," Stedman agreed.

"No coffee," Maryann said, "but I do have bottled water" She pulled three plastic bottles of Poland Spring out of a canvas book bag. "Better than nothing."

They drank it down with their protein bars.

"Save these last two bars and waters for Luna and Yvette," Maryann said, and set them on the counter.

"So, Pernod," Stedman said. "How'd you come to live out here in the boondocks?"

Pernod held the sleeping Paladin close and peered across the chessboard at Stedman, who sat rocking the sisters. Not just good *humans,* Luna had assured him, good *friends.*

"Our father—Luna's, Diana's, and mine—was Wolfgar the fire-worker. You humans would call him a blacksmith. He was the fifth generation to work with fire. Our ancestor was the first in the *gargouille* world to heat and shape metal."

"So, plows and hoes and rakes?" Maryann asked. "When I think of blacksmiths, horseshoes come to mind."

"None of those," Pernod replied. "While your race farmed and domesticated animals and turned to eating animal flesh, *les gargouilles* did not. We continued to fish and forage, living off the land and waters. Perhaps fire-worker is not the best word. Your word would be *swordsmith.* Our father's line forged blades—swords and *poignards.* In fact, the first fire-worker, our ancestor, was the only one in the entire *gargouille* world."

"Which must have made him invaluable to the king," Stedman said.

"Very valuable," Pernod said. "At that time there was no king. We were a race with hundreds of separate tribes and clans, each with its own leader. In times of plenty, there was peace. In times of want, they battled each other for territory. It was my ancestor the fire-worker's clan chief who united them all into a kingdom."

"Because he had all the swords and all the swordsmen," Maryann said.

"*Exactemente,*" Pernod said.

"Which is probably how the Allagash clan chief came to also be the king of the *gargouilles* worldwide," Stedman said.

"*Oui.*"

"And the power of the king has never been challenged?" Maryann asked.

"Several times. Many other clans, of course, gained knowledge and skill in the making of swords. Faucon's father Drago led a force from his French Alps clan against the Germans in the Great War. But he fought under the command of our Allagash clan's twin princes, LeClair and Champaigne. The Alps clan did not challenge ours, perhaps because they were suddenly forced to face a common enemy. Other rebllions over the centuries have been crushed, their leaders executed."

"And you, representing your generation of esteemed fire-workers, decided to stop contributing to the slaughter?" Stedman asked.

"*Oui.*"

"So you didn't leave because you were different?" Maryann asked. "The different wings?"

"My deformed wings gave me an excuse, not a reason. Everyone assumed I left because I was different, an outcast of sorts in my own community."

Stedman and Maryann sat pondering what their new friend had told them.

"But you do know the art of fire-working?" Stedman asked. "You're a swordsmith?"

"*Oui.* But I choose not to fashion weapons. That is what every king will want from the males in my line—sharp steel blades—so they can remain in power."

"What about Luna and Diana?" Maryann asked.

"Our father created two swords and two *poignards* for King Cyrus's twin sons. Females have never been allowed to handle weapons. But LeClair and Champaigne courted my sisters, who convinced the princes to teach them the way of the sword in secret."

"And thank God they showed them," Maryann said. "It saved Luna's life and helped her defeat Faucon."

"I'm seeing something different here," Stedman said. "I'll bet King Cyrus and your father, the master weapons-producer for the dominant clan in the kingdom, encouraged that double match: LeClair and Diana, Champaigne and Luna. What an alliance between the two families. It would provide both strength and loyalty."

"Including loyalty from the next generation of weapons producers—you!" Maryann said. "Cyrus must have been betting that if your sisters paired off with his sons, there was no way you, the male who would become the next master swordsmith, could walk away from it."

"Except that—*luckily*—I was born with a deformity. So, while the clan at first taunted me but slowly came to accept me, no one ever truly embraced me. I never had a friend until I fled here to the Katahdin wilderness, eventually meeting Rusty, a blind human, whose house we are in." Pernod's voice swelled with emotion. "Rusty is my first true friend in more than two-hundred years."

"Which must also make you sad," Maryann said. "Because a human's life expectancy is, at most, a quarter of a *gargouille's* lifespan."

Pernod's mouth had drawn tight, his face taut in the light of the battery lantern.

"But there is good news, isn't there?" Stedman said, and Pernod glanced across at him, his face puzzled. "Rusty isn't gone yet, and hopefully you'll enjoy each other's company for a good many more years. Also, you now have a few younger friends, don't you—Maryann and me. And hopefully you'll someday meet Cliff and Keegan and AJ and Aaron. So you're expanding your friend circle sevenfold."

Pernod's mouth curled into something that looked a lot like a human smile.

"Elly's right," Maryann said. "In fact, here's an idea. We're moving Luna, Yvette, and the three babies into to Cliff's barn in Wells so we can get them out of the wilderness. They can't stay here in the lake house, because you three adults would be worn out trying to fend for yourselves and care for the little ones. Cliff's barn is a short-term measure—what we call a Band-Aid—that lets the rest of us help until we can figure out a longer-term solution, until we can settle them in a more permanent place."

Elly saw where she was going with the conversation and stole her punchline.

"Rusty won't be back from Florida for six months, right, Pernod? So why don't you come with us to Wells? Luna and Yvette could use your help caring for your nieces and nephew."

Pernod hesitated.

"And you could spend time with friends," Maryann said.

Waterbug, the undersized *gargouille* with the deformed wings, patted the back of the even smaller *gargouille* resting on his chest—the infant with the scabbing, talon-shredded scalp—and slowly nodded his head.

Maryann and Stedman waited.

The baby snuggled into the hollow between his shoulder and neck.

"Two things," Pernod finally said. "First, we need to pack the chess set. Second, I have to call Rusty and tell him where I'm going. Since I won't be here to answer the house phone, can you get me a cellphone?"

"Easy peasy," Maryann said. "We'll get you on the family plan."

Chapter 48

As soon as Keegan's Subaru was out of sight, the two tired veterinarians returned to the clinic.

"I'd love to just fall into bed," Tom said, "but I promised our guest I'd bring him something to eat. I'm thinking that fresh water and some of that high-end vegetarian dog chow we fed for that allergic Pomeranian will be the safest to start—until we find out what *gargouilles* eat."

"Makes sense," Rainey said. "If he's awake, let's get a quick history, make sure he's settled in, and go get some sleep before the staff arrives."

They went inside and found Faucon on the floor beside the exam table in his squat-sleep position, his eyes dull.

"Monsieur Faucon?" Rainey asked, and the membranes covering his eyes slowly lifted, disappearing under his eyelids. The red was once again brighter and more vivid.

"Not a back sleeper, I take it?" Tom asked. "Hurts the wings?"

"It does not hurt them," Faucon answered, "but it is not comfortable. Same with lying on my side, where my short wings are. I was able to tolerate it while you completed your examination, but I prefer sleeping upright." He stood up at full height, which Rainey would note later was about six and a half feet. "Our race sleep upright, but not standing. We squat, which may be why the early French sculptors—who modeled their drain spouts after us—showed us always crouching. I have often wondered if the sculptor's model grew tired and fell asleep." He held out his arm to show the IV tubes that ran to the metal stand. "And do not worry, I did not disturb these medicines you are putting in me."

Rainey said, "We thought we'd try you on this food to start with." She handed Faucon a large glass of water and a large shiny steel bowl half-full of something resembling a wheat germ and granola mix. "Just until we zero in on your food preferences."

Faucon accepted it, took a handful and put it in his mouth and chewed. The vets heard the dog food crunch in the *gargouille's* mouth as he chewed.

"The water will soften it," Tom said, and Faucon took a big gulp from the glass, let it moisten the pellets into more of a paste, and swallowed. "Mmm. Good both ways."

Rainey pulled an iPad out of a wide pocket in her lab coat. "I know my husband did a quick assessment when he checked you in. Now I'd like to get a little more information—not too much, because we're tired, too, and need to get some sleep. We start work in a few hours."

"More questions?" Faucon said. "How can I say no?" He nodded, almost smiled.

Tom said, "I don't think you want what's referred to as a paper trail, monsieur, so we'll list you as *unknown large raptor with injured wing dropped off by motorist.* We need some sort of treatment record for ourselves, but if you're in hiding we don't want to be too specific."

"*Merci,*" the gargouille said. "The fewer who know I am here, the better. Proceed."

Tom moved closer and began examining his patient again. "The wings are membranous," Tom said, and his wife took notes. "Thin but tough, like a fruit bat's. Lightweight and stretch to over six feet, maybe over seven, when extended, but they retract tight against the shoulders. When the tops of the two wings meet, it looks like there's a hump near the top of the spine. Even though they're membranous, they must be able to handle a tremendous volume of air if they lift our friend here."

Dr. Tom had Faucon stand on a large platform scale he used for dogs and small animals, and Rainey recorded the weight. He took blood pressure, pulse, and other vitals that she also entered on the iPad.

"Without a standard," she said, "we have no idea if the numbers are high, low, or in an acceptable range."

Dr. Tom pointed a small plastic device at Faucon's forehead and gave the other vet the reading. "Don't know what's an average temp, but I think it's safe to say he's running a bit of a fever." Then to Faucon he said, "Do *gargouilles* sweat?"

"*Oui. Un peu.* With extreme exertion. Perhaps after a battle. But not usually while flying or after landing. We tolerate a wide temperature range, so hot summers and cold winters have little effect."

Dr. Tom said to his wife, "Take a note that when I brought him in, the wound to his right shoulder was still pink, but it appears to be healing."

Faucon volunteered information. "You need not note this, but our broad or great wings are sometimes called angel wings. They are not feathered like those of eagles, hawks, and condors, but they have similarities. We can flap and glide, rise high and travel long distances. Our shorter wings vibrate at high speeds—you can hear the hum—also do not have feathers, because we are not birds. Yet the way we use them is similar to hummingbirds or to your mechanical helicopters. We can go up, down, sideways, backwards, forward, or hover in place. But the short wings take more energy, and they are not good for covering long distances, which is why I am here now."

"Overall, how's your appetite?" Tom asked.

"Poor. For quite a while now."

"Are you a carnivore?" Rainey asked.

"Do you mean, do I eat human flesh?" he replied with a hint of a grin.

"I meant, do you eat animal flesh, what we humans call meat? Beef, poultry, pig, squirrel, raccoon."

"No."

"Eggs?" Tom asked.

"No. We have heard of *gargouille* clans that have taken to eating animals and birds and eggs, but ours has not. Fish, yes. But not animal flesh or bird flesh. Our primary diet is plants— vegetables, fruits, berries, nuts, roots and bark, leaves. Very few grains—especially what you humans call wheat. As a result, because we use most of what our bodies take in, we produce very little waste."

The two vets looked at each other, considering the diet options.

"Okay," Rainey said. "I think what you just sampled is a good start, and we can put together an organic package from the foods we have on hand or can order on short notice. We can get some that include fish for protein—and we'll see if we can get fresh fish in town for a few meals. We'll avoid wheat, meat, poultry, additives, and preservatives. Those last two would be something totally new to your system, and I'm not sure how you'd react."

Faucon remained silent for a long moment then said to Rainey, "Has Dr. Tom told you about my foot and leg?"

"He said it's too early to tell. He'll know more tomorrow night after some x-rays and other tests."

"Be honest, *s'il vous plait*. Will I need surgery to remove part of it?"

The vets looked solemnly at each other, as if deciding how much to share.

"Probably the foot," Tom said. "Not positive, but it doesn't look good. Maybe below the ankle, maybe above it. Let's give the drugs a chance, Monsieur Faucon."

Faucon looked downcast, so Rainey responded with, "If you can sit on the exam table again, we can take another look."

They helped the wounded *gargouille* hop up onto the table and looked at his foot, ankle, calf and shin, knee, and thigh. He winced as Rainey used several Q-Tips to apply something to the toe stubs where Luna had severed three of them with her sword. He sucked in his breath when she pressed against his swollen foot and ankle.

"The good thing is, you still have feeling," she said. "The bad thing is, I can tell from the smell, from your low-grade fever, from the necrotic tissue, and from your exhaustion that gangrene set in while you were out wandering, and it's pretty far along. You're going to lose the foot for sure, maybe the ankle halfway to the knee. If we don't amputate soon—tomorrow night—you could lose the whole leg, even your life."

Faucon's shoulders slumped, which made the hump shape of his great wings even more pronounced. He was too fatigued to protest.

"We will evaluate you again tomorrow and then tomorrow night," Rainey said. "Whatever happens—keep the foot or lose it—while you are here with us you cannot hunt or forage outside. You cannot risk exposure to the human world or to those of your own race you say may be after you. Tom and I will feed you and tend to your medical needs to the best of our abilities until you are ready to leave on your own. Is that clear?"

Faucon couldn't find a voice to answer.

"Agreed?" Tom asked, and when their patient whispered softly, sadly, "*Oui,*" Rainey said, "We'll do our best to save it, I promise."

They stood quietly then Dr. Tom asked, "Is there anything else before we go to sleep?"

Faucon thought a moment and asked, "What about Luna?"

"Luna?" the vet said, looking puzzled. "Who is Luna?" He glanced at his wife, who simply shrugged and shook her head.

CHAPTER 49

The lake house door opened and a wide shaft of sunlight streamed in onto the wooden floor. Then it winked out.

"Next," Maryann said, and walked toward the table with the chessboard. The drawn curtain in front of the picture window allowed enough filtered light that she could make out furniture and objects again. "The toilet paper's on the porch railing."

"I'm guessing she means me," Stedman said to Pernod, and groaned slightly as he got to his feet with Regine and Mathilde in his arms.

"Pick a spot with no poison ivy," Maryann said.

"Funny," Stedman said, and handed her first one baby then the other. "Almost time to wake 'em up." He headed for the front door. "Be right back."

"I'll get Luna and Yvette up first," she said. "While you're out. I want to make sure we have extra hands when we turn these buckaroos loose."

Stedman stopped with his hand on the door handle. "*Buckaroos?*"

"I always wanted to use that word for a herd of toddlers."

"Really?" he asked.

"No. But he word popped out. I have no idea why. Just go."

The door opened, sunlight streamed in for a moment then the rooms were dim again.

"He likes you," Pernod said.

"He's a nice man," she said, and changed the subject. "When he comes back in, we'll wake your sister and Yvette. You three watch the babies while Stedman and I get breakfast on the table. I made two cookie trays of peanut butter and honey sandwiches. And we've got sliced apples, grapes, and raisins."

"Water?" Pernod asked.

"Got it covered. Brought two cases of Poland Spring. We adults can drink out of the bottles. Stedman wasn't sure about the babies, so he bought some baby bottles with nipples."

"Nipples?" Pernod said. "What are nipples?"

"You know," Maryann started, then remembered that Luna had no breasts. She changed course quickly. "So, you think the kids can drink out of bottles, too? Or will they have to lap it up from bowls?"

"I do not know," Pernod answered. "Ask Luna. They probably drank from springs and streams. Bottles will be new, but they should learn."

They heard the front door open and blinked when the sunlight burst in then breathed a sigh of relief when it closed again.

"Ready to let the buckaroos loose?" Stedman asked.

"Go wake Luna and Yvette," Maryann told him, and he disappeared through the door into the dark den where the deformed little *gargouille* Pernod read great books aloud to his blind Viet Nam veteran friend Rusty. A moment later the bulky detective emerged, followed by the two adult female *gargouilles*.

All three babies awoke on their own and stretched, as if they smelled the pair of females entering the dining area. They wiggled and wormed until Pernod and Maryann let them plant their feet on the floor and released their grip. The sisters toddled to Luna and Yvette, hugging the adults' thick legs. Paladin—was he confused—wobbled across the room to the hallway and did the same with Stedman, wrapping his short arms around the cop's left calf. The three with babies attached to them stood motionless.

"Freeze," Maryann ordered. "Don't pick them up. Stand right there." She pulled out her phone, found the camera icon, and snapped a quick photo. "Let 'em run a few minutes before breakfast, burn off some energy. I'll get the food on the table."

The house was beginning to smell like sliced apples and peanut butter.

Les trois enfants, as if they understood, released the legs each hugged and wobbled in different directions to explore.

Paladin's hands went up to shoulder height in front of him, as if he needed them for balance. The three-month-old *gargouille* looked no different than a one-year-old human poised to take its first step. Then he executed a Charlie-Chaplin little-tramp turn and teetered into the front room. Stedman walked behind him, peering into the dimness, checking for booby traps because there'd been no time to childproof the house before Luna's troupe arrived. Not that Stedman knew how to do it, anyway.

Mathilde let go of Luna's leg and pivoted, circling back to enter the library/den. Was she seeking the comfort and security of the beanbag chair she'd enjoyed upon their arrival, or did she need a darker room away from the light? She made for the standup ashtray with Rusty's pipe on it, with Luna a step behind, arms out to the baby's sides in case she had to catch Mathilde if she fell over.

Regine pushed away from Yvette's leg and put on an unexpected burst of speed, wobble-sprinting down the hallway toward the bathroom at the end.

"Come back here, you," Yvette said in baby-chase language. "I'm gonna get you."

Regine disappeared into the dark bathroom and, before Yvette could get to her, slammed the door.

"She doesn't know how to lock the door," Maryann said, in an effort to be reassuring.

So Yvette stood at the door and knocked. "May I come in, Regine?"

"Time for breakfast!" Maryann announced. "It's on the table. Let's eat."

A crash came from somewhere near the front door, followed by Pernod's whimpering cry of regret.

"He's fine," Stedman said. "Pulled over the table with the battery lantern on it. All plastic. Nothing broke. Just scared him."

The others could hear the grunting sound of Stedman picking Paladin up, followed by cooing and comforting sounds. They couldn't see the big cop, but they knew he was rocking the upset toddler. "It's okay, we'll go eat some breakfast, Pal," they heard him say, the nickname for Paladin coming out of Elly's mouth effortlessly.

"Come and get it!" Maryann announced loudly.

"Smells good," Pernod said.

Another crash, this time from the den.

"Waterbug," Luna called from the dark room. "Your friend's round glass dish has fallen over, the tobacco plate he uses when you read to him."

"Did it break?" he called back. "The glass ashtray?"

"No. It fell onto your special chair."

"The beanbag?"

"*Oui.*"

"No harm," he said, but there was annoyance in his voice. "Bring her to the table to eat."

Then came the unmistakable sound of books hitting the floor—several at a time—Mathilde pulling them off the bookcases, one shelf at a time.

"Luna, do not let her tear the pages, *s'il vous plait*," Pernod pleaded, trying unsuccessfully to control himself. He got to his feet. "Mathilde. Mathilde, leave the books. We must eat, Mathilde. Yum, yum, yum." He scooped his niece up and, as he was crossing back over the hallway, there came another crash, this time from the bathroom. Breaking glass.

"Regine?" Yvette called, and flung open the door.

Regine began to cry, a child's cry of embarrassment and shame.

Pernod shuffled down the hall and stood beside Yvette. It was too dark to see inside the windowless little room.

"Don't let Regine move," Maryann said. "She could step on broken glass. Wait right there. I'm on my way." She scooped up the lantern she had used while spreading peanut butter on two loaves of white bread and was behind Yvette and Pernod in a flash. Stedman, with his arm around Paladin's stomach, came up behind her, and Luna, holding Mathilde in the same way, stood beside him.

Maryann held out the lantern so it lit the bathroom. It spotlighted Regine, who sat atop a closed toilet lid facing them and looking like a teary little queen on her throne. On the floor between her and the vanity sink were chunks of broken glass and a tiny rigged sloop. It looked like the vessel had been birthed from a glass egg.

"Rusty's ship-in-a-bottle!" Pernod moaned. "He made it when he was a child."

Stedman said to Maryann, "I'll trade you Paladin for that lantern. You take him and the rest of these buckaroos and have breakfast. I'll clean this up. I can save the pieces and take them home with me, see if I can put Humpty Dumpty together again in my shop."

Yvette plucked Regine from her throne and everyone except Stedman retreated to the dining table, where they gathered around the bowls of fruit and the trays of peanut-butter and honey sandwiches.

"Elly's brainstorm," Maryann said, as everyone dug in. "PB&H on white. A poor man's feast."

While Stedman swept up the broken parts to their host's childhood project and placed them in a shoe box, Maryann played waitress to a party of six homeless *gargouilles* having breakfast out as a family—three adults striving to raise three infants, none of whom were their birth children. And feeding three toddlers who hadn't yet cut a first tooth. Her heart swelled as she watched them—the six—having a brand new experience as they pressed Stedman's white bread against their mouths and chins and cheeks and noses, the peanut butter and honey going onto their fingers—which they licked—and into their mouths and stomachs, dabs and clots of it sticking to their cheeks just out of tongue's reach. They loved it—the food, the taste, the holding and being held, the family experience. They giggled and burped and belched, their breath and chatter spreading the fragrance of peanut butter and clover honey everywhere.

Stedman came in, announcing he had all the pieces picked up, and stood beside Maryann. Together they watched their ragtag bunch of *gargouille* friends eat and bond.

"Did you get a sandwich for yourself?" he asked.

"I'm eating crow," she said. "I laughed when you suggested we load up on white bread."

He set the box, the broom and dustpan, and the lantern aside. "Let me risk an arm and grab a couple for us."

"I've got two bottles of water for us over here," she said, and gave his hand a quick squeeze. "I'll save you one."

He stepped to the table, asked, "Mind if we have a couple?" There were still a dozen half-sandwiches on the tray.

All six *gargouilles* glanced up when they heard his voice and saw his arm and hand.

"*Merci,*" Luna said, and Yvette added, "*Merci beaucoup.*"

Pernod looked at him and then at Maryann in the kitchen. "*Merci,* Elly. *Merci,* Maryann. Thank you so much, *mes amis.* You are good humans and good friends."

254

CHAPTER 50

They finished breakfast around eight-thirty and Maryann announced that she wanted to be on the road by nine-thirty, giving everyone an hour to do whatever they needed to do.

Luna and Yvette found paper towels in the kitchen and cleaned the peanut butter and honey off the babies' fingers and faces, then took them outside to the side of the house that hadn't yet caught the sun's rays. The three toddlers delighted in waddling to the trees and hiding from each other. But they didn't stray far from Luna and Yvette, who let them play peekaboo in the shade until there the light breeze brought whiffs of something that smelled faintly of peanut butter.

Pernod packed the chessboard and pieces, then used the lake house landline to call his friend Rusty at the Florida house. He told him about Bronwyn holding off the coyotes at the cost of her own life, and of the refugee family's harrowing flight around Mount Katahdin and their near-disaster with the great horned owl.

"They had to crash-land in the lake to get rid of the owl. Poor little Paladin's got deep talon scratches on his head."

Maryann, who was shelving the fallen books on the bookcases, overheard sounds of sympathy and understanding coming from the Florida end of the line. She did her best to put the toppled ashtray and pipe back in place, and called toward the kitchen, "Tell Rusty we look forward to meeting him."

Pernod passed the message on and replied, "He says, '*Moi aussie.*' Me, too." Then to Rusty he said, "Oh, this is funny. Let me tell you about the peanut butter breakfast."

Stedman did the final checks of Aaron's Jeep and the ATV trailer. He opened the clamshell pod and arranged the mattresses that had slid around during the trip from Wells. Then he rummaged through the groceries in the back of the Jeep and pulled out a plastic bag of grapes, a dozen ripe bananas, and a box of Cheerios. With his jackknife he notched the tops of the bananas so they'd be easy to peel then opened the Cheerios box and the inner plastic bag. He set aside the nippled nursing bottles he'd bought and instead switched to the five large bicyclists' squeeze bottles. He filled them with Poland Spring water and screwed the caps on. Their built-in straws required a combination of suction and squeezing, so the water wouldn't drain out if one of the infants set it aside or held it upside down. He put the food and water in a cardboard box and set it in the trailer alongside the mattresses.

With hands on hips he stared inside the hard-shelled little room. *Should they have something to hold onto—like a grab bar in a shower? Too late now. Got to go with what we've got. Remember to explain the bananas, cereal, and bicycle bottles to Luna.* He walked around to the lake side of the house and climbed the steps onto the deck. The trees around the shoreline were afire with the reds, golds, and oranges of autumn with Katahdin in the distance, rising over—dominating—the landscape. *What a view. And even if he were here, poor Rusty wouldn't be able to see it.* He went back to the driveway and let himself into the house by the front door, where Maryann immediately handed him the remains of the ship-in-a-bottle that had shattered on the bathroom floor.

"Don't forget your winter project," she said, and when he took it from her, she grasped his hands in hers and drew him close for a light kiss. When she pulled back, she said, "You're a good man, Charlie Brown. A damn good man."

He gave her a sheepish grin.

"That I cannot say," they could hear Pernod saying into the phone. "We can hide in the barn in Wells for a week or two, perhaps a month. But after that, where?"

Luna and Yvette came inside carrying the three little ones and set them on the floor.

"They are ready," Yvette said.

Maryann handed Luna her cellphone. "In case you need to call us in the Jeep."

"Rusty," they heard Pernod say. "I must go. It is time." Then, after Rusty's response, Pernod said, "*Oui*, I will take a box of books with me, and I will read to you when I get my new cellphone." After some mumbled words, he hung up the old house phone.

"Pernod," Maryann said. "You will not lack for books. I have a whole bookstore full. And we have the Wells Public Library, which gives us access to every library in the state. You will be amazed."

Pernod nodded. "*Merci.*" Then he gathered more than a dozen of the shelved books into a cloth bag. He held the bag in one hand and the flat boxed chess set in the other. "That is everything I need."

Stedman and Maryann helped the *gargouille* family into the trailer, with Stedman explaining to Luna as he lifted babies, "You don't have to eat the banana skins."

She laughed and answered, "I have eaten bananas before, Detective Stedman."

"Elly," he said, and repeated, "Elly, *s'il vous plait.*"

Luna accepted his offer of a hand and climbed in. When she let go she curtsied and smiled again then said, "I have eaten bananas before, Elly Stedman."

When the *gargouilles* were settled on Cliff's mattresses, Stedman said, "Oops, wait just a minute," and trotted back inside the lake house. He returned a minute later carrying Pernod's beanbag chair from the den and set it next to the mattresses. Before Pernod could shift over to it, the three little ones jumped onto it and made themselves comfortable. "You gotta be quick in this family," Elly said, and closed the shell. Then he and Maryann climbed into the Jeep and he fired it up and steered them out the driveway, their passengers safely in tow behind them. When they got to the RFD box, Stedman turned and looked at Maryann, one of his eyebrows raised in a question, a sly smile curling the corner of his lip.

"I know what you're thinking," she said, and smiled back.

"What?" he asked innocently.

"First McDonald's drive-thru. Large black coffees and four egg McMuffins with sausage."

"My thoughts exactly. But I'll never forget the peanut butter."

"Same here," she said wistfully. Then, as if leading a charge, she said, "McDonald's!"

"McDonald's!" he echoed, and eased the Jeep forward onto the bumpy dirt road. "Home by three."

CHAPTER 51

Maryann ended up driving the last hour and pulled the Jeep and trailer into Cliff's driveway. She saw her Subaru parked in the dooryard next to the firewood truck, so she continued past the barn until she saw Cliff. Stedman zipped down the passenger window and Cliff leaned close to speak.

"Good trip?" Cliff asked.

"Uneventful," Stedman said. "Would've been more stressful if the kids were in the back seat."

"Don't make me pull over!" Cliff said in a stage voice.

Maryann put her head down a little so she could see Cliff's face. "Just your usual, boring, in-state *gargouille run.*" Then she added, "I see you've got the big doors open. Want me to back the trailer in?"

"Sure. Get it far enough inside so that I can crank the trailer's foot down and disconnect you. Then pull out again and leave it about where you are now. Keegan suggested we close the doors before we pop the top and turn 'em loose."

"And where are they?" she asked. "Keegan and AJ?"

""Decorating. Crepe paper streamers."

"Sounds like them. Elly, you can get out. I got this."

Stedman opened the door, unfolded his bulky body, and climbed out without a word.

Maryann pulled up close to the firewood staging area, cut her wheels and put the Jeep in reverse. Using only her side mirrors, and without hand signals from either Cliff or Stedman, she lined up with the barn's open back doors and backed the trailer in like she was in a Peterbilt truck competition.

"That's good," Cliff called and made a closed-fist stop-there hand signal she could see in her mirror. He cranked down the metal foot, disconnected the trailer from the hitch ball, and unplugged the lighting package. "Take it away."

She pulled forward, parked the Jeep, and came back to the now narrow opening in the barn door. She stepped through and Cliff closed it and latched the big door from the inside.

It had once been an old cow barn, and the back quarter was one huge, high room that reached from outside wall to outside wall and from the dirt floor two stories up to the pitched roof. The front three-quarters of the building was separated from the big back room by a wall and was two stories: a hayloft above and a bottom-floor milking barn with a raised cement center aisle that ran between feeding troughs and headlock stanchions for the milking cows who faced each other like opposing football lines. Behind them were gutters that Cliff had shoveled clean thousands of times. He and his sister and their friends had made many tunnels in the overhead loft by stacking bales to create mazes.

The big room everyone was in now had once housed tractors, choppers, and balers out of the weather. Now it was home to two trailers: the beat-up Shasta travel trailer with its flat tires, and Cliff's cousin's ATV trailer with its cargo of *gargouilles* waiting to be released.

The lighting was purposely dim, thanks to Aaron and Cliff. A few low-wattage bulbs were now in the big room's wall sockets, with several more rigged on overhead lamp cords they had strung from the old hewn support beams. Keegan and AJ's thumbtacked crepe streamers made the room look more like Little-House-on-the-Prairie barn dance than a high school prom. They had also hung a few accordion-fold bells and some Halloween witches and pumpkins.

"We had to go with what we had available," Keegan said when the two cops questioned the décor choices.

The Shasta's side door was open and pinned back, and the single metal step in front of the entrance had been pulled out. The guest suite was ready for inspection, for occupancy.

Between the Shasta and the newly arrived pod trailer sat a card table with a small Hannaford sheet cake on it. Across the white layer of frosting was a hand-scribbled pink word: WELCOME.

"Open it!" Keegan said excitedly, gesturing to the pod. "Set 'em free."

Stedman did the honors. First he knocked on the fiberglass shell. "Luna, we're ready." Then he popped the clamshell cap open, raising it on its carriage hinges like a suitor presenting an engagement ring in a felt box.

Three adult *gargouilles* huddled close together at the center of the queen mattress, each hugging an infant close to its midsection, all three babies' faces shyly pressed against their protectors' paunches, eyes closed against the light and any new threat.

"*Un moment,*" Luna cautioned. "Allow them to adjust."

Maryann and Stedman stepped forward ahead of the others.

"It's okay, Mathilde," Maryann cooed. "I'm right here. And Elly's here, too."

Stedman tried to soften his deep voice to something more child-friendly. "Paladin, Regine, come on, you can sit on Grampa's lap. We can eat peanut butter. Yum."

Maryann looked at him, surprised. "*Grandpa's* lap?"

He shrugged. "What're they going to call me— Stedman?"

Luna turned Regine around so she was facing the gawking newcomers. She pointed to individuals and put names to human faces. Luna said, "That's my friend Keegan. You already know Maryann—she pointed—Maryann is Keegan's mother. Those two are AJ and her brother Aaron."

Keegan moved next to her mother and they hugged theatrically and smiled at Regine. "Hi, Regine," they said together, and waved.

Steve Burt

AJ and Aaron mimicked that, also embracing and saying in baby-talk tones, "Hi, Regine."

Regine made a hand motion back at the four of them—not exactly a wave, but a raised hand in front of her confused face. She glanced around at the others.

Paladin and Mathilde sensed something was going on behind them and squirmed and turned until they too were facing out, eager now to see what was going on, sensing from the calm that there was no threat.

Luna said, "Maybe if you back away, my brother Pernod and Yvette and I can come out of this box. Elly and Maryann, wait a few minutes and then we will hand you the babies. Once they are comfortable, set them down and see if they will explore. They will be ready to eat soon. The Cheerios were—how do I say it—a hit. And they loved the bananas."

Everyone backed away, and given more space, the three adult *gargouilles* climbed out onto the barn's dirt floor, the babies clinging to their wrists and arms, not yet feeling fully secure.

"Want to see the inside of the big trailer?" Keegan asked, motioning with a sweep of her arm toward Cliff's parents' recently cleaned Shasta. "At first we thought you'd all stay in it, but now that I see how the babies have grown, I'm thinking we should keep the ATV trailer for a while. It's already got mattresses. Oh, and a beanbag chair, I see."

Paladin, facing forward, spotted Stedman, who extended his big arms from ten feet away. Paladin's arms went out in response, and he wiggled and squirmed for Yvette to set him down. She did, and he wobbled unsteadily toward the big cop, who reached down and scooped him up and hugged him. He rested his chest against Stedman's for a moment then turned his body to check on his sisters.

262

"Oopah," the toddler said, as if calling his siblings' attention to Stedman, whose mouth and eyes went wide with surprise.

"His first word," Pernod said.

"Is Oopah French or English?" Cliff asked.

Pernod shook his head. "Ask Paladin."

"You want to get down, buddy?" Stedman said softly in Paladin's ear, and lowered the little one to the floor.

Paladin stood beside Oopah, his small arm and hand reaching up to the giant warm hand of the human who gently clasped his. Together they took a tentative step, then another, until they stood before the metal step of the Shasta. Stedman bent down and supported the toddler's butt with a thick hand, still holding the other hand in his own, and gave him a little boost onto the step. He let him wobble and balance at this new height for a moment, then boosted him to the doorsill so he could peer inside. Faint ceiling lights and a wall dome lit the interior but kept it dim enough for the *gargouilles'* comfort. Paladin wobbled in, steadying himself on walls and faux pine cabinets.

Regine and Mathilde watched their brother disappear and squirmed until they got what they now wanted: to be placed on the floor. Maryann stepped forward, bent and took Regine's hand, and they started for the Shasta. Mathilde stayed between Luna and Yvette, who each lent a hand, and they got in line. At the door Maryann put her hands on Regine's hips from behind and hoisted her to the threshold, then backed away and stood beside Stedman. Luna and Yvette did the same with Mathilde. The three fast-growing *gargouilles* explored their new quarters together, and the adult humans and the adult *gargouilles* laughed together when they heard the shower curtain rustle and the plastic toilet seat's lid creak up and crash down several times.

"Curious as cats, aren't they?" Maryann said, and paused as the back of her hand brushed against Stedman's. "Oopah?"

His fingers spider-walked over the bridge between her thumb and forefinger, his fingertips tickling her palm.

"The party is on, everybody," Keegan announced. "Before we cut the cake, we have carrots, raw broccoli, and celery sticks with an onion dip for those who are able to eat it. Maybe not the kids."

Maryann stepped forward. "But first I'd like to thank you all for your efforts that made this possible. We welcome Luna, her brother Pernod, and their friend Yvette. Sadly, another dear friend, Bronwyn, made the ultimate sacrifice for her adopted family. I hope Luna and Yvette will be able to tell us more about her in their time here."

Luna and Yvette's heads sagged slightly, so Maryann switched gears.

"We also want to thank Cliff Bragdon here, who not only lined up that little ATV trailer that we used to get Luna's family here from the lake house, but also provided this barn and this Shasta, which give us a short-term fix for housing. Thank you, Cliff."

The humans clapped and the three adult *gargouilles* each raised an arm as if they were holding champagne glasses.

Maryann placed her palms together, fingertips straight up, and bent slightly, giving Cliff a *Namaste* thank-you. But her own words—*short-term fix*—still echoed in her head. *Long-term*, her mind argued, *we need long-term. We can't hide them here for long.*

From inside the Shasta came the sounds of the plastic toilet lid clapping shut, clapping shut again then clapping shut yet again. Paladin had his sisters' attention, an audience of two to pass this new skill on to.

Maryann locked eyes with Stedman then and nodded toward the Shasta. The toilet lid clapped again. "Oopah?" she repeated. The nagging earworm repeated *long-term, long-term.*

CHAPTER 52

Friday morning Maryann called Cliff to say she'd be stopping by to do a wellness check.

"I'll drop Keegan and AJ at school on my way over. I won't be long. Got to open the bookstore this morning."

He met her in the dooryard and together they walked to the barn, opened the door, and stepped inside. None of the barn lights were on, but the Shasta's door was open and the interior contained a soft glow.

"Luna?" Maryann called softly. "It's Maryann and Cliff."

"In here," a muffled voice to their left answered. *Pernod.* From inside the ATV trailer. But the clamshell cover was closed.

"Where are the others, Pernod?" she asked.

"In here sleeping," he answered quietly, and the hinged cap creaked up, leaving Luna's brother peeking out as if from under a quilt. "Shh," he said, and slipped out, carefully lowering the fiberglass lid behind him. "*Bonjour.*"

"Good morning," Cliff said. "They didn't like the travel trailer?"

"The beds there were so far apart. It is about both comfort and security. They—*we*, now that they have drawn me in—prefer to ... what's the word ... *huddle* together. We all feel warmer and the little ones feel safer. So we gathered together on the mattresses and closed that top so the babies could not wander."

"But aren't *gargouilles* nocturnal?" Maryann asked. "You didn't sleep through the night, did you?"

"We let the three little ones explore this room. To them it is very big. And new. And they occupied themselves. You would call it playing together. Mostly wrestling and pushing and hugging. We also fed them several boxes of Cheerios and those little tomatoes."

"Was it hard to stay in the barn?" Cliff asked. "I mean, it's not a prison but it's got to feel a bit closed-in."

"We took turns going out," Pernod replied. "I stayed with the babies while Luna and Yvette went out. They brought back two fish that we three adults ate."

"Tell me they didn't steal two striped bass from a fisherman!" Cliff said only half kidding.

"Freshwater pond," Pernod answered. "They told me where it was and I returned with another. "

"Did the kids eat it, too?" Maryann wanted to know.

"No. But soon, when their teeth come in. I can feel them pushing up in the front. If we had a salmon, they could handle the soft pink flesh."

"I'll put salmon on my shopping list," she said.

Cliff said, "Hate to play the spoilsport here, but I'm thinking you and Luna and Yvette shouldn't be out and around, not even on short trips. There's too much risk that somebody will see you and it'll reignite the fuse on this stupid vampire mania. We're trying to hide you. Why don't you let us feed you until we figure where else to move you?"

Pernod's face was unreadable.

"We just want you to be safe," Maryann said.

Pernod said, "I appreciate what you have done for us. I will speak to Luna."

"Tell you what," Maryann said. "Let's all talk about it tonight over supper. Do any of you adults eat pizza?"

Pernod shook his head.

"But salmon works for all six of you, right?"

"*Oui.*"

"Okay, pizzas for six and salmon for six. Anything else you need between now and then?"

"They will mostly sleep," he answered. "We may feed them once—they love the white bread with honey. It will make them run around the two trailers until they tire, then they will sleep the afternoon."

"Mental note," Maryann said. "More bread, salmon, and honey. Sounds like we have a plan, Pernod. I've got to get to work and open the bookstore now. See you for supper."

"*Merci*, Maryann. *Merci*, Cliff," the little *gargouille* said, then lifted the top on the ATV trailer, climbed back in, and pulled it down again.

Cliff closed up the barn door and walked Maryann to her car.

"Not sure the barn is going to work after all," she said, "at least not for long. It'd be hard enough to keep the secret if they were cooperating and staying inside. But they snuck out on the first night. What're we going to do?"

Cliff didn't respond to her question but stood there stone-faced.

"What?" she asked.

"The chief called this morning. My medical leave is up."

"You're kidding."

"Nope," he said. "I start back Monday. Days for a few weeks. So I can still be the on-site caretaker at night for a while."

"Which is great," Maryann said. "But we have to cover the days, too, even if they're sleeping. Keegan and AJ are in school during the week, and Keegan's in the bookstore with me on Saturday, but I can be here Sunday through Wednesday. Aaron's on shift some nights but not all, right?"

"Right," he replied, his face still stone serious.

"So our flex guy is Elly," she said.

"Not as flexible as you think," Cliff said. "When she got off the line with me, she was going to call Stedman next."

"Don't tell me his medical leave is up, too?"

"Also Monday."

"Damn," she said.

They stood beside her car door a moment. Just as she opened it, Cliff said, "On the bright side, Pernod says they like the pod."

"The pod?"

"Yeah, the ATV trailer. You know. *Peas in a pod.* If we had to make a quick getaway, we could slap it on a hitch and take them overnight camping. A little food and they're good to go."

"Good to know," she said. "But my mind is scrambling for something longer-term. Any suggestions would be appreciated."

"I'll think on it," Cliff said. "See you back in the barn for supper with the kiddies."

She nodded, slid into the driver's seat, and almost made it out of the driveway before her cellphone pinged. *Stedman.* She put the car in Park.

"Elly?" she answered.

"You at the bookstore?" he asked.

"Not yet. Just leaving Cliff's."

"Everything okay there?" he asked. "The babies asleep?"

"They are. But Luna, Pernod, and Yvette needed some time away during the night."

"As in, they left the building?"

"Yep. The whole group abandoned the Shasta so they could sleep close together in the ATV trailer—what Cliff calls the pod. Then the three adults took turns exploring the woods and ponds around Cliff's place. They brought back some fish."

"Aw, geez, if they're seen..."

"Preaching to the choir, Elly. Cliff and I have been over that. So I told Pernod we'd talk about it tonight over supper. Six of *us*, six of *them*. Hopefully it'll become twelve of *us*. If we can't rein them in—if they can't see the importance of staying hidden—this hideout won't last a week. And then what'll we do—send them back to the blind man's cabin? There's no way we can supply them if they're four hours away."

"I know, I know," he said. "Look, things just changed on my end."

"The chief called?"

"Yeah. She said she called Cliff, too. I guess he told you."

"He did. Monday, huh? Having you guys on medical leave was a luxury too good to last. We'll just have to work around it."

"Need company at the bookstore today?" he asked.

Not help but company, she thought. "Give me a couple hours to catch up on things. Bring lunch. I left my pasta salad in the fridge."

"Deal," he said. "See you then."

She clicked off and drove toward the Book Stop, her heart surprisingly light despite her *gargouille* concerns.

At the other end Elly Stedman whistled a tune for the first time in years and made his way to the shower, already thinking about lunch.

CHAPTER 53

Except for Faucon—whose Thursday night operation left him with a heavily bandaged right leg—Friday was everyone's first somewhat "normal" day in more than a week.

AJ and Keegan were back in school and Maryann opened the bookstore. Aaron was sleeping so he'd be ready for another evening shift. Stedman and Cliff Bragdon were thinking ahead to Monday, when they had to return to work after long medical leaves. Cliff was playing nervous host to the nest of *gargouilles* hiding in his barn.

It wasn't business-as-usual, however, for Luna and the other five displaced *gargouilles* who were trying to adapt to their new surroundings. To start with, it was clear they weren't about to take to Cliff's parents' old Shasta travel trailer. They didn't like the hard flat beds, the narrow center hallway linking the kitchen to the bathroom/shower area, or the tiled floor that defined the living/dining area. As Pernod had pointed out to Cliff, they preferred to huddle in the ATV pod together, with the pod for sleeping and the pod open when they were active and the little ones were climbing in and out of it. When it was bedtime Regine, Mathilde, and Paladin fought over Pernod's beanbag chair—fought not for who would get it, because it was just big enough for three toddlers, but fought over who got the center slot between the other two siblings. The adults slept in pairs with them, leaning against the three little ones in their squat-sleep positions like a pair of cast metal gargoyle bookends. The third adult kept watch outside the pod, occasionally chatting with Cliff when he left the farmhouse to come out and check on them. Pernod set up his chessboard beside the Shasta on the little card table that had held the welcome cake, and told Cliff he couldn't wait for Maryann to get him his own cellphone so he could call his friend Rusty in Florida and start a new game.

"I think she's ordering three new phones today," Cliff said. "For you, Luna, and Yvette. She's at the Book Stop today and tomorrow, but she's got Stedman picking them up. Should have them after work."

***

Stedman arrived at the Book Stop before noon with sandwiches, chips, and drinks. He also had the three new phones, which he handed to Maryann.

"I programmed in the main contacts by name," he said. "You, Keegan, AJ, Aaron, Cliff, me, Luna, Yvette, and Pernod. For Pernod's I added his friend Rusty. Anybody I've forgotten?"

"Not that I can think of at the moment. We can teach them the basics of how to use them tonight."

"Just make sure they know they shouldn't dial 911," he reminded her.

"Funny."

"Kind of, yes. But I prefer *thoughtful*."

She gave him a serious look that might have been apologetic. "You're right. Thoughtful. You're a thoughtful guy."

He smiled. "Nobody in the shop. Lunch? Work room?"

The bookstore phone rang. She stepped to the register and picked it up, waved Stedman to the work room and made a one-minute signal with her finger. He took the food bag and headed for the back room.

"Sorry," she said into the phone. "I've been on the road for a couple days. Her fingers tapped at the counter computer's keyboard. "I see the email. Yep, attached files. I'll review them this afternoon. Yes. Yes. Sure. Okay, Marlene, thanks for calling. I'm on it." She hung up, clicked on the Word files to open them, and hit Print. A dozen pages accumulated in the printer's output tray. She scooped them up and carried them to the work room.

Stedman had their sandwiches on paper plates on opposite sides of the big work table, the bag of chips open

272

between them, and a Snapple Lemon Iced Tea by each of their plates.

She stopped and stared at the table setting then grinned. "We're not going to play a board game, Elly. We can sit on the same side, next to each other."

He rearranged the plates and came around the table.

"Sit," she said, and he sat on the stool, his forearms resting on the edge of the table. She set the sheaf of papers on the table and took the stool next to him. "Thanks for bringing lunch," she said. "And for picking up the phones."

"My pleasure," he said, and gave her a sideways glance.

She gave a coy smile. "I'm not good at this."

"Neither of us is," he replied, and added, "I'm patient."

"Elly, look at me."

He turned slightly on his stool, turned his head even more so he was looking almost straight at her.

"Breathe," she said. "You're holding your breath."

He drew a deep breath.

She placed her hand on top of his and leaned in.

He responded, kissed her without placing his arms around her, without moving off his stool or her moving off hers. Yet it was a moist, passionate kiss that ended only because the shop phone rang again.

She broke off, started to get off the stool to go to the phone.

Stedman held her hand and asked, "Doesn't the voicemail say you're with a customer, so leave a message?"

"Actually, it does," she answered.

"Well, I'm a customer, aren't I?" Stedman said.

She smiled and her cheeks blushed. "A good one." She moved the stool closer and settled onto it again, this time so the sides of their legs and arms were brushing up against each other.

The phone rang two more times then went to voicemail.

CHAPTER 54

Late Friday afternoon King Cyrus' scouts squatted or paced in the Kezar cave between Bridgton and Lovell, eating raw fish and apples. At dusk it would be safe for them to return to the observation posts where each had spent the night Thursday. There had been no sighting of the missing Faucon, not at the Free Camp island where the one-eyed Gregoire had sat perched in the grandfather pine, and not over the three rural expanses around Tamworth, New Hampshire that Toulouse, the bat-faced Grondin, and the horse-jawed Percheron had divided up. They sat and watched their sections of fields and forest, periodically patrolling—watching and listening. Faucon had to eat, they knew, and he couldn't use his damaged angel wings to soar or glide. So they themselves used only their quieter broad wings and waited for the hum of the injured *gargouille's* short wings or the outline of his body against the moon or the night sky.

This would be night two. Gregoire had said they'd try it for four. After all, all they had to go on was the word Tamworth, which Toulouse thought he might have heard humans say when he was coming out of the anesthesia the tranquilizer dart had put him in. For all they knew, Faucon could have gone on his northward tack again, with the humans returning to or passing through Tamworth.

Shortly after dusk they launched out of the cave, flapping as noiselessly and as little as possible, gliding twenty feet above the treetops, watching for powerlines, and taking advantage of updrafts above streams and forest paths. After five minutes Gregoire continued south and the other three veered west southwest toward New Hampshire.

The fifth *gargouille*, the small green-eyed one who had slept the day in a nearby hayloft, didn't try to catch up. She knew from the previous night where the three were going—

Tamworth—and she knew where each had set up watch stations. Toulouse's was in the Hemenway State Forest, not far back off the Chinook Trail. She'd observed him in secret all Thursday night, and although Faucon had not appeared, her money was still on Toulouse. Now, with her in an old nest in a tall pine a half mile from him, watching him and the skies, she had two sets of eyes and ears on the job.

***

At the vet clinic Dr. Tom and Dr. Rainey said goodbye to the owner of a late-arriving Black Labrador that gotten too cozy with a porcupine. The two vets and an assistant had stayed past closing to remove nearly seventy quills from the dog's lips, snout, cheeks, and tongue. Several had skewered the animal's eyelid and one had pierced its eye. They gave care instructions, offered reassurance to the owner, and told the veterinary assistant to go home. When everyone had left, they secured the doors and went to see Faucon in the exam room they had kept closed-off all day.

"You're stable enough that we can move you tonight, Monsieur Faucon," Tom said. "To the B&B at the far end of the property."

Faucon tried to sit up and swing his legs around to the side of the exam table, but there were two raised metal railings on either side preventing him.

"Patience, sir," Rainey said. "We want to tell you what's happened, give you some instructions, unhook you from the IVs, and help you up."

Faucon tried to relax against the pillows he was propped up on.

Dr. Rainey said, "You may recall us telling you today that in last night's operation we had to take some bone and remove the necrotic tissue—the dead flesh—from your leg. We couldn't save the foot or the ankle, but we were able to save the knee and most of the shin, which is now heavily bandaged. In time we should be able to create a prosthesis—an artificial but working leg, ankle, and foot so you can walk fairly normally. It'll take a lot of physical therapy and hard work on your part, but you should be able to resume a normal lifestyle. But it'll all take time."

"And my wing and shoulder?" Faucon asked.

"The shoulder is healing slowly," Tom said. "What you need most is to do some exercises—stretching and strengthening—which we'll recommend and show you. The wing—well, that's different. My wife and I need a little more time to figure out a patch that will hold it while the natural material fills back in. So, no definite answer tonight. But we're hopeful, and confident, and we have time. You're going to be our guest for at least a month."

"So, how will I walk?" Faucon asked.

Dr. Tom began removing the tubes, needles, and wires from the *gargouille*.

"For now, with these," Rainey said, and reached behind her for a pair of crutches. "When Tom drops the side guards and helps you up, we'll adjust these for your height. You can't put any weight on the stump, of course—your good foot and leg, and your armpits, will carry the weight—but at least you can walk. It'll be just like anybody else with a broken leg or ankle. Until we design a prosthesis."

Dr. Tom dropped the nearest side brace and helped Faucon sit up and swing his legs to the side. "Just sit for a minute," he said. "Clear your head, get your balance, catch your breath." He took the crutches from his wife and placed them in Faucon's hands. "When you're ready, stand up but don't try to walk. I'll adjust the height for you. Then we can try walking."

Faucon slid from the table and balanced on his good foot. He put the rubber-tipped crutches on either side of him, shifted his weight so he was standing without the support of the exam table, and let Tom adjust both crutches.

"You're going to swing that short leg and it'll feel funny without the weight of your foot on it. Crutches under your armpits. Let's try a few steps. You'll have to adjust your balance with only one foot touching the ground. It'll take practice. After we get a prosthesis you can switch to a walker and then a cane."

With support from Tom on one side and Rainey on the other, Faucon planted his crutch tips on the tile floor and clumsily wobbled forward.

"Practice," Rainey said. "Trust me, you'll master it in a day or two."

They walked out to the clinic waiting room.

"So, the gangrene?" Faucon asked.

"Your body responded well to the antibiotics we started yesterday," Dr. Tom said. "But even antibiotics couldn't help the dead tissue."

"*Merci*," Faucon said solemnly. "*Merci beaucoup.* I owe you my life."

"If you owe it to anyone, it's the three who brought you in," Rainey said. "Just in the nick of time, as we say in the movies."

They stood a moment, and Faucon said, "Are we walking to the guest quarters?"

"I think we'll wait until tomorrow night to move you in there," Dr. Tom said. "For tonight we'll go next door to our house. We'll put you in the guest room. Rainey can take you over. I'll grab a stand and couple bottles of saline and antibiotics so we can keep you infused tonight. I've also got a pair of portable side rails for the bed. We can take turns checking on you. Clinic is closed tomorrow and Sunday except for emergencies, so we'll give you some walking practice, see what else we can do for the shoulder and wing, and hopefully move you out to the B&B Saturday night."

"Any questions?" Rainey asked.

Faucon looked thoughtful. "Do you have any salmon?"

The two vets laughed.

"How about a couple of cans of Albacore tuna and a green salad?" Rainey asked, smiling, and offered him her hand.

CHAPTER 55

Friday supper at Cliff's had the feel of both a barn dance and an extended family picnic. The little ones played and the adults multi-tasked—keeping a watchful eye on the babies and laughing at their antics while at the same time chatting with other adults and setting up the food, drinks, paper plates, and plastic forks on the table Cliff had put together by laying a sheet of plywood across two saw horses. The only thing they lacked was a campfire and some hot dogs and marshmallows.

Maryann and Stedman had closed the Book Stop and made a grocery run on the way over. She had promised fresh salmon for the six *gargouilles*, who would eat it raw, and got a bargain at Hannaford's seafood counter. She also picked up honey and a half dozen loaves of white bread. Stedman, without consulting her, added two bags of pears, four bags of apples, and five bunches of bananas.

When Maryann shot him a questioning look as he unloaded the fruits from his mini-basket onto the checkout conveyer belt, he said, "Hey, it's expensive raising kids."

Cathy, the cashier they'd had days before, looked up from the groceries she was scanning and said, "I didn't know you had kids, Detective Stedman."

"I don't," he said, attempting to recover. "I meant grandkids."

"Well, that's quite a trick, isn't it?" Cathy said. "No kids. Grandkids." When the red-faced cop didn't reply, she let him off the hook by turning back to the bags of fruit she'd been scanning. She told him his total and he inserted his credit chip into the reader and paid.

Maryann said to the cashier, "Visiting grandnieces and a grandnephew. They call him Oopah. He thinks of them as the grandchildren he never had. Likes to spoil them."

Cathy said, "I understand," and with a sly sideways look at Maryann, added, "So, does this make them your grandkids, too?" The cashier gave a tight-lipped smile and her eyes twinkled with mischief.

Maryann shook her head and replied, "Mmm, maybe."

Keegan and AJ had been assigned to pick up the human food, and after school had walked down to the IGA. They bought a mixed meat-and-cheese cold-cut platter, two packages of hard rolls, and a bag of Asian salad mix that came with all the ingredients including dressing. AJ remembered to grab a small bag of freebies: condiment packets of mustard, mayonnaise, and relish. From the IGA they had walked over to the police station to rendezvous with Aaron, whose Jeep's back seat held a case of six-packs of soda and iced tea plus a case of Poland Spring water and a cooler of bagged ice.

Cliff was the only hot food guy because he had access to the kitchen stove in his farmhouse. He brought out a tray of crispy egg rolls and two thin-crust DiGiorno pizzas.

They all ate, drank, and made merry, including Pernod, who now had in the Shasta's kitchen a brand new Keurig coffeemaker and a box of Green Mountain coffee pods. Dessert was leftover Welcome cake from the day before when Luna's group arrived.

After supper—on Maryann's cue—Keegan, AJ, and Yvette took the now slowing toddlers for a lantern-light tour of the old milking barn, with Cliff, who knew the building intimately, acting as guide.

"Luna, Pernod, we have to talk," Maryann said, and invited them into the Shasta with her, Aaron, and Stedman. The three humans took the living room seats, knowing the *gargouilles* would be more comfortable standing or squatting. When everyone had crowded in and gotten situated, she said, "Two things we need to discuss: first, we have to come up with a better, safer place for the long run, and second we need an emergency plan."

"An emergency plan?" Pernod asked.

"Yes," Stedman said. "What if lightning struck and this barn burned tonight? Or the townsfolk got wind that you were here and came with guns? Where would we move you on short notice?"

"For an emergency, we can return to Rusty's lake house," he said. "He and I have already discussed it."

"But that not a plan," Aaron said. "That's a place. That's one part of it. Where would you escape to if you had to leave the barn at a moment's notice? And while the lake house makes sense, it's four and a half hours away. How would you get there? We'd have to be sure of a trailer—the ATV pod or something similar—and we'd need to be sure we had the tow vehicle to pull it. And then there's the *who*—who hooks it up, and who drives? See what I mean? There are details to be considered for it to be a plan and not just a place."

Pernod and Luna looked tired, overwhelmed. But not defeated.

"Perhaps we should learn to drive," Luna said. "If I had my disguise again—and pillows to sit on—why couldn't I drive the vehicle that pulls the pod? Or maybe I could drive a van with the others hidden in the back."

"Do you know how to get to the Interstate?" Aaron asked, a hint of exasperation in his voice.

"Wait, wait," Maryann said. "Let's not discount the idea. We're brainstorming and we can hold that idea for later. The plus I see in it is, it could work if all of us humans were unavailable. Luna's group isn't dependent on us. A genuine emergency could mean we're not here to help."

"Let's work on that more tomorrow," Stedman said. "How about we talk about the next place? Maryann and I have come up with a possibility. Not for the long term but for the short to medium."

Luna, Pernod, and Aaron looked blankly at him.

"You have?" Aaron said.

"Yes. This one presented itself in the last few hours," Maryann replied. "And it comes with pictures." She passed her iPad to Aaron.

He looked at the photo, said, "Looks like a deer camp," and flicked his fingers across the screen to view the second, third, and fourth photos. "Cast iron cook stove in one shot. Outhouse in the next shot. And what's that in the last one—a metal Quonset hut? Don't think I'd call it a garage. Storage, maybe. Big enough for a couple snowmobiles."

Maryann held up a sheaf of papers. "The place is the Sarah Orne Jewettt Writers Retreat, and it's not just remote, it's ultra-remote, up north of Moxie Lake and a mile in from the nearest road. Oh, and no running water. You haul in bottled water or get it from a spring or a stream."

"Sarah Orne Jewett," Aaron said. "In her time she was as famous as Stephen King. Her house is right out Route 9 in downtown Berwick, a National Historic Landmark and open to the public for tours. Wrote essays for the big national magazines of the late 1800s. Best known for a collection called *Country of the Pointed Firs,* which was a little boring for us school kids who were forced to read it. But she was a force. They credited her with putting Maine on the map as a destination. She almost single-handedly jump-started the tourist industry. Out-of-staters came by carriage, train, and steamboat to the lake lodges and big turn-of-the-century hotels."

"Well done, Aaron," Maryann said. "You might want to work for the State Tourism Office."

"The point here is," Stedman said, "Guess who's on the Sarah Orne Jewett Writer's Retreat's applicant screening committee? Four to six people—an editor, a published poet, a published novelist, a published nonfiction writer, a literary agent, and a bookseller—have the task of vetting a few dozen applicants and awarding four one-month residencies and four stipends."

"And you're the bookseller?" Luna asked Maryann.

"I am. I'd forgotten about the Jewett cabin until today. One of the other committee members called and reminded me that we needed to review next year's candidates by October 15th, so I printed out the list she sent me."

"And how does this help us?" Pernod asked. "Luna and I are not writers."

"We don't need any more writers," Maryann answered. "The four move in and out in succession during the warmer months: June, July, August, and September. It's vacant October through May. So the last writer, a female Montana essayist, just moved out. Nobody wants to hunker down during those months in a poorly insulated cabin with no water and difficult winter access. There's no electricity to run a computer, no Internet or TV, a sketchy cellphone signal. A writer would have to use pen and paper, and they'd risk their fingers freezing off."

"Sounds like a dream come true," Aaron said sarcastically.

"Okay," Stedman said. "It's far from ideal. But there are three things worth consideration. First, Maryann is the primary caretaker. Second, she has the keys. And third, it's all we've got. For now, at least."

"Quick question," Aaron said. "If we have to shuttle food and water in, and there's snow, what do we do about our tracks: boots, skis, snowshoes, snowmobiles?"

"*Gargouilles* fly," Maryann said. "We meet them at a designated turnout off the road and they airlift it themselves. They won't need shopping carts of food later, because Luna, Pernod, and Yvette can do their own fishing and foraging at night. If they need something, one of them can fly to where they can pick up a cellphone signal and call us."

No one had anything else to say at the moment.

"For now you stay here in the barn," Stedman said. "We can do this for a while. It also gives us a few weeks to check out the Orne Jewett cabin and make sure it's ready for you. I can put something in my front windshield indicating I'm the caretaker and park by the road and walk in. I'll get some signs made up that we can post—it's a hundred acres or more—so people won't be bothering you. This gives us time to work out the details. And if they need a vacation, we sneak them back here for a week or so."

"Any questions?" Maryann asked. "Good for tonight?"

"I have a question," Pernod said. "If we go there, where will I plug in my Keurig coffeemaker?"

CHAPTER 56

On Saturday morning the skies between Wells Beach and Route 1 were overcast and misty to start, but the Weather Channel promised afternoon clearing. At eight-fifteen, in front of Annie's Book Stop, Keegan and her mother sat in the Subaru with AJ, waiting for Stedman. The usual Saturday plan was for the three of them to open the bookstore, which, now that they'd moved to the fall schedule, was only Friday and Saturday. But the possibility of hiding Luna's family at the remote, tumbledown Sarah Orne Jewett writer's retreat had changed things. Now it was divide and conquer. Keegan and AJ had handled the bookstore alone before, and if Aaron brought lunch around eleven and stayed until one-thirty, he could help if there was the usual midday rush.

Meanwhile Maryann and Elly would drive three-and-a-half hours north to the donated cabin that for the four warmer months of the year housed those writers-in-residence who were willing to rough it. With the last occupant gone, it was time for Maryann as one of the six board members and unofficial caretaker to attend to the end-of-year inspection and buttoning up. She was a week ahead of the usual schedule, but it was the perfect time to see that it was suitable for Luna, the other two adults, and the three little ones to lay low there for the winter.

"Elly made up a bunch of Posted notices," she told the girls, "to warn hikers and hunters away. The signs make it clear that the place will be occupied by a writer this winter and asks them to please give it a wide berth. We'll walk the perimeter of the property after lunch and tack them up to create a buffer zone."

"You think you'll get there by noon?" Keegan asked.

"Closer to one," Maryann replied. "We're making a quick stop at Biddeford Crossing Walmart for four more of those beanbag chairs to go with Pernod's old one and a set of walkie-talkies. We'll hit a drive-through for lunch. A couple-three hours on site to clean and to put up the signs, then grab supper on the way back and get home by eight or nine."

"Walkie-talkies?" AJ asked.

"One for us, one for Luna. We won't want to leave tracks when we go up with supplies, but we probably won't have cellphone coverage. Walkie-talkies are good for a mile or more, so from the road we can talk to them in the cabin."

Stedman drove in then and swung a wide arc so his passenger door was next to the Subaru. The three of them got out and Maryann switched over to Stedman's car. AJ went to the bookstore's front door and waited for Keegan to follow and unlock it.

Keegan moved to Stedman's open driver-side window and said, "When you scope the place out, pretend you're grandparents checking out daycare providers for your grandkids."

Stedman smiled, said, "Thanks. Your Mom and I got this," and zipped up his window and drove off.

Once in the bookstore, Keegan set the little zippered bank bag on the checkout counter and said, "Lights, register, action. I'll fill the till and set up this computer, check for emails. You boot up the work room computer and log in whatever FedEx Freddy dropped off last night. Since we're alone today, we'll want to be ready before we open." They split up and got to work. A steady stream of rainy-day customers in search of a good read started as soon as they flipped the sign from closed to open.

***

At Cliff's barn Luna and Yvette and the little ones slept in the closed pod. Pernod sat at the card table across from Cliff, each of them sipping a mug of steaming black coffee as they stared at the chessboard that lay between them. This wasn't the chess board Pernod and his friend Rusty used for the long-distance phone games. That one was set up on a kitchenette table in the Shasta now. This set was Cliff's, a boxed plastic chess and checkers combination in a frayed, worn old box that Cliff had brought out from his attic. He and his father had played it when he was a kid, so it had been gathering dust for ten or more years.

"Didn't see that coming," Cliff said, and moved his queen out of harm's way.

"*En garde*," Pernod declared, the courtesy phrase alerting an opponent that their queen was in danger of being taken off the battlefield. In Cliff's mind, hearing *en garde* for a queen was better than hearing *check*, announcing a challenge to one's king, or even worse, the endgame phrase *checkmate*."

But Pernod moved another piece and said once more, "*En garde*."

Cliff moved a small round-headed piece—a pawn—forward a space to block the threat.

Pernod moved a third piece, didn't say anything, and simply waited for Cliff to assess the situation. Cliff saw no threat and moved his knight. As soon as he took his hand off the horse's mane and sat back, Pernod moved his bishop diagonally and announced, "Check." Cliff studied the board, saw his dilemma clearly, and realized the only piece he could use to block the threat to his king was to block with his queen. But it meant sacrificing her to the bishop, and things would rapidly go downhill from there until it was over.

"I concede," Cliff said. "I don't believe it can avoid the eventual checkmate." He put his fingers on the crown of his king and tipped it over, signifying surrender.

The two of them sat silently staring at the board, and Pernod lifted his mug of coffee to sip.

"There was a way," Pernod said.

"A way to what?" Cliff asked. "Avoid losing?"

"*Oui*. Do you want me to back up so you can see to see it?"

"Please," Cliff said.

Pernod righted Cliff's king, then backed up several plays. "Remember when I threatened your king?"

"I do."

"You were so focused on the king that you forgot about your queen. And while you were thinking about that, look where I had left my own queen—in a vulnerable position. I was so intent on my attack that I didn't notice I placed her where your second pawn could have threatened her in a way I could not have blocked. You'd have had my queen and in time you'd have had the game. See it?"

"Yes," the cop said.

"And you could have laid your trap with that tiny pawn. My heart was in my throat when I saw that I had presented myself to you in that careless move. I waited to see if you would catch it."

Cliff shook his head. "Even when I was at my best playing my father, I wouldn't have seen that. Very instructive, my friend."

Pernod nodded, said "My pleasure, *mon ami*," and raised his mug to Cliff.

CHAPTER 57

The earlier cloud cover had lifted and the sun was brilliant overhead, lighting up the fall foliage at its peak: glowing yellows, golds, oranges, and reds. The dirt and gravel road was bumpy, and Stedman had slowed his Rav 4 to twenty miles an hour while listening to Maryann's instructions.

"After this ledge of rock," she said, emphasizing *this*, because it was the fourth ledge of rock she had claimed was her first landmark. "Definitely, this time. It's got the red paint mark. See it?"

"Red paint?" he said. "Or the blood of the last writer who tried to find this place?"

"Oscar Wilde said: sarcasm is the lowest form of wit."

"Often quoted without the second part," Stedman said. "Sarcasm is the lowest form of wit, but the highest form of intelligence."

"*Touche*," Maryann said. "I didn't see that coming."

"How about seeing that pole gate over there on the right?" he asked. "Right there." He pointed out through her side of the front windshield. "That's it, right? Splotch of red paint on the big pine where the branch was sawed off?"

"Yep. Another smear of the same writer's blood. Pull past it on the shoulder and I'll get out and move the branch. Then back your car in and park it." She placed a cardboard sign on the dashboard and got out.

DO NOT TOW
Sarah Orne Jewett Writer's Retreat
Volunteer on Site

Stedman parked his Rav 4, climbed out, and opened the tailgate door. "Let me try my cellphone," he said, and punched up Maryann's number. No coverage.

"Glad we got the walkie-talkies," Maryann said. "Leave 'em in the car for now, but they'll definitely help when we're here and Luna's in there." She nodded toward the narrow path that led into the woods.

Stedman grabbed the four beanbag chairs from the cargo area, each of them taking two and holding them at arm's length like sacks.

She faced him and looked him up and down then asked, "Santa?"

He smiled broadly and used one of his beanbags to bump her butt. "Onward, elf. To the chimney." They set off down the path leading into the woods.

When they arrived at the cabin Stedman checked the Pedometer app on his phone. The night before at Cliff's barn Maryann had guessed the walk in was a mile. It was almost half a mile but felt longer, perfect for communicating with the cabin from the road later after the *gargouilles* moved in.

Maryann checked to make sure the most recent writer-in-residency had returned the key to the magnetic holder hidden under the circular charcoal grill on the weathered picnic table out front. The guest had followed the checkout instructions. The key was there. She pulled an identical one from her pocket, unlocked the padlock on the front door, and swung the door open.

"If this didn't work," she said, "the window latches around back are easy to jimmy. Don't tell anybody."

They stepped in and set the beanbag chairs on the rough board floor of what was essentially one big room with a wooden table, a pair of wooden chairs, and a wooden deacon's bench. Against the far right wall was the woodstove from the photos on the Orne Jewett website, its stovepipe disappearing into the roof. The washtub sink had a plank countertop next to it, one which sat a large nearly empty plastic water jug. The washtub had a drain in the bottom and underneath it a PVC pipe that exited through the outside wall of the structure. There were no handles or faucets on the sink.

"Kind of bleak, don't you think?" Stedman asked.

"Hey, they were living in a cave near the Allagash," Maryann replied. "They know how to drink from a spring and manage the basics. If we supplement their food and water periodically, they'll be okay."

They walked outside.

"Outhouse," Stedman said, pointing. "Don't think they'll use it. They have their own ways."

"What do you think of the Quonset building?" She walked toward it, he followed. It was an arc of corrugated aluminum—probably surplus from the Second World War—its roof caked with years of leaves and moss. A few small branches rested on it. There was no front wall or back wall, and they could see straight through the semi-circular tube. The only thing in it was a knee-high stack of firewood and a pile of kindling twigs that had probably come from the woods around the place.

"Like I said, you might park a couple of snow machines in it," she said. "But other than that, what do you do with it?"

"If it was a deer camp, they may have hung the deer here. And as we can see, it works for dry firewood storage. Probably just got a bargain on a Quonset."

"The advantage of this place is, it's available and it's a long way from people," Maryann said. "But those may be the only two pluses. Are we wrong to send them up here?"

He placed a big arm around her shoulder and drew her close. "It's what we've got."

"Maybe you could cut some boards in your shop and make some rope swings for the kids."

He gave her shoulder a squeeze. "Next you'll want a couple of Adirondack chairs for the adults."

"*Gargouilles* can't sit in Adirondack chairs," she said. "But maybe two for us when we visit."

"In snowmobile suits?" he kidded.

"Maybe."

They traipsed out about fifty yards, keeping the cabin in sight, then walked in opposite directions, making a wide circle and posting the laminated Winter-Writer-in-Residence notices as they went. They met back at the cabin, made one last check, took a bunch of cellphone photos so they could consider what they'd need later, and locked up. They left on the path they'd taken in, but this time, without beanbag chairs to carry, they walked hand in hand.

***

It was three-thirty when Stedman pulled his Rav 4 back onto the dirt road and Maryann secured the gate behind them. She'd barely gotten into the car when he turned to her and said, "Got an idea for the Quonset hut."

She clicked her seat belt. "Oh, yeah? What?"

"I know that if *gargouilles* live in caves, they can handle a wide temperature range. But that cabin—and maybe I'm projecting myself into things here—will be bitter cold in December, January, February, and probably March. They love to sleep huddled together, right?"

"Right."

"So we buy a used snowmobile pod. Cliff's cousin's has to go back to him soon. But we can find one on eBay or in the local want ads. One a little smaller than Cliff's cousin's ATV trailer is what I'd suggest. I can double insulate the walls and ceiling. We add two more beanbag chairs to make six, so they fill up the floor—and insulate it."

She heard his excitement, said, "But if we move it into the little Quonset garage, won't somebody steal it? Thieves can just hook up to it and tow it away."

"Which is why we unbolt the pod from the chassis and drive the chassis away. All we want is the container. And to add to the insulation, we dig the inside of the Quonset down about three feet and set the pod into it. When they pop that clamshell top, they're at ground level. I can also close in the two ends and put in a door. The six of them can keep each other warm."

She reached across the Rav 4's console and patted Stedman's leg. "Elly Stedman, you're a mad scientist and a thoughtful grandfather. What a combination. I love the idea."

***

Five minutes later Maryann's cellphone chirped.

"Back near a cell tower," Stedman said. "Who is it?"

"Keegan," Maryann replied, and clicked the green button to accept the call. "Hi."

"Mom, Mom, I've been trying to call." Keegan's voice was beyond excited.

"What is it?"

"AJ and I were super-busy all day. When we closed she finally got around to checking the voice messages. You had one yesterday at noon and didn't pick up."

"I remember. I was so caught up in going to have supper with Luna's family that I forgot to go back and listen."

"Okay, okay, so let me play it for you now. It's easier than me explaining it. Ready?"

"Ready," Maryann said, and put it on Speaker.

"Hello, this is Doretta Schussler calling from Lancaster, Pennsylvania. I'm trying to reach the Keegans in Wells, Maine, and I saw the name in connection with this bookstore. Friends are telling me someone named Keegan has been calling folks in Bird-in-Hand and Ronks and Intercourse—asking if they know my father, Janos. Call me back if I have the right Keegans." The caller left a number.

"Call her back," Maryann said. "Call her back."

"I did," Keegan said. "It's a landline. I got her answering machine. She's gone for a week. If you'd picked up the message yesterday, Mom, I might have reached her before she left."

Maryann said nothing. The recrimination was simply frustration and pain. "Try to calm down, Keegan. We can talk when Stedman and I get back."

No response, so Stedman said, "Do what you do best. Check her out on Google. This is amazing news. You could have a sister."

Chapter 58

Saturday night over western New Hampshire was clear with a bright yellow moon and an ocean of stars. No muddy dirt road to impede Faucon's move from the vets' house to the B&B at the far end of the clinic and farm property.

Rainey and Tom had spent an hour that afternoon helping Faucon get used to walking on crutches.

"Resist the urge to plant that right leg," Rainey had said. "When they first lose a limb, amputees work by feeling and muscle memory and tend to forget that the foot and ankle aren't there anymore. And distributing your weight on your hands and onto the grips of the crutches—that takes practice. Eventually we'll make you a prosthesis that will feel in some ways like you're walking on solid ground again."

Dr. Tom offered Faucon a wheelchair the clinic made available to pet-owners who had human mobility issues. "It'd be the easiest way to transport you to your new quarters beyond the dairy barn. We can push you along the road and you can put the crutches across your lap."

"*Gargouilles* don't sit well," he said. "*Merci, mais non.*"

So, as soon as it was past dusk, with Faucon's amputated right leg bandaged at mid-shin, the three of them left the vets' home and started down the dirt road. Faucon soon gained a rhythm, jabbing his crutches forward, shifting his weight onto his palms on the cushioned handgrips, and swinging his legs forward under him. Several times the rubber tips of the crutches faltered when they bit into the crusty edges of a recently dried rut, and he had to catch himself. Each time the vets were at his side, though, and quick to lend a supporting hand so he didn't fall sideways.

Then came a shadowy stretch where the road ran beneath an overhanging swamp maple and an oak that were shedding their leaves, many on the road. Faucon's right crutch touched down on a layer of leaves and slipped. His reaction was to lift the tip of the crutch up, away from the problem, which left him with no right crutch and no right foot to plant on the ground. He fell to the right, too heavy for Rainey to catch. But she tried, and he went to down on his right side on top of her.

Tom swung into action immediately, helping Faucon up by lending him a shoulder to put his arm around.

Rainey dusted herself off and got to her feet, handing Faucon his lost crutch. Faucon waved it away and let go of his left one. It clattered to the ground.

"Bring them when you come," Faucon said, and as he pushed away from Tom he raised both arms slightly and extended his hummingbird wings. Tom and Rainey couldn't speak to him over the loud hum. They could barely hear him over it when he said, "Last building after the barn. I will meet you there." And he lifted off the ground and flew at five feet above the road ahead of them.

***

The loud hum did not go unnoticed. A mile away, in a roost at the top of a pine, the lookout Toulouse's ears pricked up. He wasn't expecting company. Gregoire was on his third night watching the Free Camp island, and both Grondin and Percheron were scouting other parts of Tamworth. And it was short wings, not the silent glide wings of a night hunter. This must be Faucon finally on the move. Toulouse launched himself and used several soft, quiet flaps to get him to an updraft then, staying close to the treetops, followed the sound, looking for both Faucon and a new place to spy from.

The other *gargouille*, the exiled Argentine female Angelina, who had been watching Toulouse from a hidden nest barely a hundred yards away, also heard the hum. She, too, knew it had to be Faucon, so she followed the scout at a distance.

She was no match for any of the battle-hardened males trained in the use of swords and *poignards*, but thanks to the coup she survived in Argentina, she knew all too well the value of the mini-dagger in the sheath hidden beneath her left hummingbird wing.

***

Two hours later Angelina was once again in a position to observe and eavesdrop on Toulouse, who had made a beeline back to Maine to the summer camp. From a safe distance she heard him report to Gregoire that Faucon was in the tiny structure beyond the big barn on the farm property in Tamworth. Toulouse had heard him fly using his short wings and had seen that his foot was gone, the leg bandaged.

"Two humans carried sticks to him—I think they call them crutches—and treated him like a guest. Then they returned to a log house at the other end of the road. I think they are animal doctors."

"So he really is injured," Gregoire said. "He cannot use his angel wings, and now he has half a leg. This is not a *gargouille* who would make a good king."

"So do we leave him?" Toulouse asked. "He is no threat."

"It seems he will not escape tonight, so fly back to Tamworth and bring Grondin and Percheron back to the Kezar cave with you. We will rest tomorrow and go after Faucon tomorrow night."

"Will we kill him or take him back to Cyrus?"

"That depends on Faucon."

***

It was a few hours before dawn, and Angelina was confident that Gregoire's three underlings had left Tamworth and returned to the Kezar cave. She perched on the ridgeline of the old dairy barn and looked beyond it at the fenced exercise yard and the little house inside it at the far end. It had clearly been a fancy dog pen at one time.

"Faucon," she called. "Faucon, come out."

Minutes later the lower ends of a pair of crutches poked out a square door, followed by a full leg and foot and a half leg with no foot. A figure swung himself up on the crutches and stood balanced on an unnatural tripod: one foot and two rubber crutch tips.

"*Qui est-ce?*" he asked.

"*C'est moi, Angelina,*" she answered, and glided down and landed close but outside the fence.

"Ah, Angelina. And where is Cyrus?"

"I preferred my independence," she replied.

"He asked you to leave?"

"He banished me in one of his fits of anger. *Et toi?* It appears that you also have chosen independence. Have you given up on becoming king?"

"*Pour l'instant,*" he said, and when he caught her staring at his crutches and bandaged leg stump, added, "A temporary setback. These humans say they can make me a new one."

"And your great wing? I watched you earlier on the road. Can they repair that, too?"

"They say they can." He adjusted the crutch pads under his armpits and flexed his fingers on the handgrips. "Why are you here? And how did you find me?"

"I followed one of the king's scouts, Toulouse."

"Ah, the slow-witted one who follows the cyclops around. So he and Gregoire know where I am?"

"Toulouse has been watching this area for several nights and earlier heard the hum of your short wings. He reported to

Gregoire, who pulled his other two soldiers back to the Kezar cave until tomorrow night."

"They will come for me?"

"*Si.*"

"Did you recognize the other two?" he asked.

"Percheron, the bully with the horse face. And the one they call the little bat, Grondin."

"Do you have your weapons?" she asked.

"Only these," he said, wiggling his crutches. "And my tongue, my powers of persuasion."

"Which leaves two options: retreat or hide. Your wing is damaged, your leg slows you, and there are four of them, all armed and not eager to take you back to Cyrus if there is a chance you might succeed him."

"Where will I hide? The woods?"

"Your friends in the house have many buildings. They know all the hiding places. It is almost morning, and they will check on you. Tell them your life is in danger."

"If they hide me, they will also be in danger," Faucon said.

"*Sans doute,*" Angelina said, and unfurled her great wings, ready to fly off.

"Wait," he said, and when she paused, he asked, "Why did you come here?"

"During the coup in Argentina, a friend warned me that assassins were coming for me. I barely escaped. A month later they killed her. I have owed her for a long time. Now my debt is paid." *La gargouille* nodded, said in his language, "*Bon chance,* and flew off.

CHAPTER 59

Maryann was still tired when she woke up and trudged downstairs Sunday morning. She had enjoyed Elly's company, but the Orne Jewett writer's retreat trip had eaten up twelve hours, after which she'd listened for several hours as Keegan vented her frustration and impatience about the woman on the Book Stop voicemail who had said she was Doretta Schussler. After hours on the Internet, Keegan's searches had turned up the physical address in Lancaster, Pennsylvania that was associated with the landline. The phone was registered to Mary Broere, age 95, with no mention of any other household members, and no one with the surname Schussler. When Keegan ran a search for Mary Broere, nothing came up, nor did the search term *Mary Broere obituary*. The woman who had left a message saying she might be Keegan's sister was, it appeared, a very private person who didn't put a lot of information out on the Internet.

"Got coffee?" Maryann asked sleepily.

"Fresh brewed. Milk, cereal, and half a banana on the counter," she heard a male voice say. Then "Good morning."

She looked up to see Aaron Stevenson sitting alone at the trestle table, hands around the coffee mug in front of him, his police officer ball cap to the side.

"More coffee, Aaron?" she asked without missing a beat. "Keegan gone already?"

"She just left on a run. I'm good on the coffee. This is already my second cup."

"Who ate the first half of the banana, you or Keegan?"

"I did," he said. "On my cereal. I rinsed my bowl and spoon and put them in the dishwasher."

Maryann walked to the table balancing a mug of coffee and a bowl of cereal, set them on the table across from him, and sat down.

"How'd the trip with Stedman go?" he asked.

"We think the place will work. He has an idea for modifying it—half-burying a pod in the ground and insulating it. He can tell you about it at the barn tonight, over supper. You're off, right?"

"For three days. Stedman and Cliff go back to work tomorrow, so they're free tonight. AJ and Keegan have school in the morning. Another picnic in the barn?"

"Enjoy them while we can." She sipped her coffee. "So, how many times did you stop by while you were on patrol?"

He gave her a sheepish grin. "Just twice."

"Nighttime. Bet the babies were active."

"Oh, they were," he said. "They're watching the adults and figuring out how things work—like door latches. And they're starting to climb."

"Problem is, without wings they can fall and break an arm or a leg or their necks just like human kids."

"Miz K, I think *gargouilles* have been surviving childhood for a long time."

"Words of wisdom," she replied, "from a man who was only recently a kid himself."

Aaron pushed back the bench he was sitting on and stood up. "Look, I've got to get home and grab a few hours of sleep. Is the plan to meet for supper at Cliff's around six?"

"I think so. We can discuss the writer's retreat and Elly can outline his idea for half-burying an ATV trailer at the retreat house for Luna's family to sleep in. He wants to buy a used one and unbolt it from the frame and chassis, just use the box and lid. We'll need to set up shopping and babysitting schedules, now that everybody's back to work or school."

Aaron carried his mug to the dishwasher, came back past the table and grabbed his cop cap, and walked to the door.

"She told you about the Pennsylvania woman?" Maryann asked.

"She did. I hope this isn't some opportunist doing a shakedown."

"I hope not. She's on an emotional roller coaster."

"That's how they work you," he said. "See you at the barn."

***

Ten hours later they gathered at Cliff's again. A dish-shaped charcoal grill on aluminum tripod legs stood near the Shasta, tongs and a wide spatula on a cement block next to it. The briquettes glowed white hot and were ready to cook on. Stedman brought several huge pieces of cod he'd picked up at Mike's Fish Market, figuring part of it could be grilled for the humans, the bulk of it presented raw for the *gargouilles*. It was something the adults and the little ones could eat. What wasn't consumed at supper Cliff could refrigerate for the next day or night.

AJ and Aaron brought chick peas, raw broccoli, and sliced white potatoes, some of which was cooked. Maryann and Keegan picked up an assortment of fruits and Cliff contributed a large bottle of merlot, two six-packs of Allagash White. For Pernod he had a Green Mountain Coffee Roasters variety pack of Keurig cups.

The little ones were glad to see their surrogate grandparents, aunts, and uncles. Not only Paladin but Mathilde called Stedman Oopah when they ran to him and he picked them up. After a few seconds of hugs and mugs they slipped to the floor and raced around the big room. The adults—human and *gargouille*—stood chatting and watching the energized toddlers' escapades while discussing Stedman's idea for a half-buried fiberglass car-top carrier for the Writer's Retreat's Quonset shed. The atmosphere was that of an extended family gathering over a meal.

Cliff had just put the fish on the grill when Rusty called from Florida. Pernod chatted with him on the new cellphone

301

Stedman and Maryann had brought. Then when all the adults closed in, he switched to speaker and they introduced themselves to Rusty. Maryann brought Paladin, Mathilde, and Regine close to the phone as Rusty tried his best to entice them into a conversation.

"They only know one word so far, Rusty," Maryann said, "and that's Oopah. It's what Paladin and Mathilde call Elly."

They three toddlers were fascinated by the phone. They could hear Rusty but they couldn't see him. Each of them babbled a few nonsense words, until Regine, with coaxing, eventually mouthed *Wusty* loud enough for Pernod's friend to make it out. Everyone laughed and clapped.

Both chessboards were set up. Rusty's from the lake house was still in the Shasta, waiting for Rusty and Pernod to start a new phone game. Cliff's childhood board was on the tray table between the charcoal grill and the Shasta's door. The game Cliff and Pernod had started that morning was nearing completion, with Cliff clearly on the defensive.

They had raised the ATV trailer's hinged top and locked it open so it couldn't accidentally drop and crush one of the kids' hands or fingers or toes or worse. Keeping it open allowed them easy access to the beanbag chair and mattresses if they tired. The adults' minds were all focused on childproofing and safety.

The *Saturday Night Fever* soundtrack had been repeating on Aaron's old CD player, and had come back to the Bee Gees' *Staying Alive*. Even the babies bobbed their heads and dipped their hips to it.

And then came a godawful scream. Everyone turned from Pernod's phone toward the broiling fish and froze, horrified. The charcoal grill lay on its side, white hot coals spilled on the ground and on three sets of baby feet. The little ones stood with the embers searing their flesh, in too much pain to step away from the pain holding them to their spots.

Maryann, Yvette, and Luna leapt to their sides and scooped them up, the two barefoot *gargouilles* scorching their own feet before they pulled the children back. The adults cried out in pain but the babies screamed and wailed and cried, and each clutched the adult who had rescued them. Their pained cries pierced not only the air but everyone's hearts.

"Call 911," AJ shouted, an automatic response.

"No!" Stedman ordered. "No 911. We can't." His fingers poked at his cellphone. "Cliff, Aaron, get a First Aid kit."

"Cabinet over the fridge in the Shasta," Cliff said, and Aaron was moving. "It's got burn ointment and bandages. Bring the whole kit. AJ, run into my house and get all the ice in the freezer. Plastic bags under the sink to put the ice in." AJ was out the door.

A moment later Aaron was back, popping open the First Aid kit. He looked around for a place to set it, then with a single swipe of his hand cleared the pieces off the chess board and set the kit on it. He pulled out the tube of Bacitracin ointment, a packet of gauze pads, a roll of adhesive tape, and a small pair of scissors.

"Keegan, start cutting tape strips. This long," he said, and cut one and stuck a tiny edge of it to the edge of the chess board. He handed her the tape and scissors and she started in. "Cliff," he said, handing the ointment to his friend, "Don't smear it on the burns. Dab it on the center of the gauze pads." To the three holding the wailing babies he said, "I'll tape the gauze with the Bacitracin on it loosely over each burn. You hold their feet out away from you while I do it."

"AJ's bringing ice," Luna said. "What's that for?"

"For the three of you to hold against your burns. We're not going to have enough Bacitracin for everybody."

Keegan cut tape strips while Cliff squeezed dabs of antibiotic ointment onto the gauze patches, which Aaron then gently applied to the tops and sides of the babies' feet. None of them appeared to be burned on the soles, only Luna's and Yvette's.

They heard Stedman talking loudly as he paced back and forth by the big barn door.

"Yes, three. And three adults. But the babies have the worst burns. Yes, they know you've got him there, but we can't do anything about that." Then, "Okay, we're on our way. Hour and a half. Thanks, Rainey. See you soon." He clicked off and trotted back to the group.

"We're taking them to Tamworth?" Keegan asked. "To the vet clinic?"

"No choice," Stedman replied. "Two vehicles. Maryann, is your Subaru gassed up? My Rav 4 is low from yesterday's trip."

"I filled it today," Keegan said.

"Good. Aaron, your Jeep good to go? We need it to pull this ATV trailer. They'll be more comfortable in it and they won't be seen."

"As soon as I finish these last bandages," Aaron said.

"Ice is here," AJ announced, and held up a white kitchen trash bag.

Stedman said, "You three just climb in the pod with the kids and settle in. Luna and Yvette, just stick your feet in the ice bag for about five minutes at a time. Let's hook Aaron's Jeep to the trailer and hit the road."

Cliff got a barn shovel and scooped the still hot charcoal back into the grill, then hit the area with the kitchen fire extinguisher from the Shasta.

Pernod took a baby from Maryann and climbed into the ATV pod with Luna, Yvette, and the other two little ones. Stedman lowered the clamshell top and latched it. He felt a slight thump from the front and knew Aaron was securing the trailer's metal tongue to the hitch on his Jeep. He heard the turning of the crank handle that raised the settle foot that had been planted on the ground.

"Ready?" Aaron called back.

"All tucked in tight," Stedman answered. "You take Cliff and AJ, I'll ride with Maryann and Keegan."

Two minutes later they were bumping out of Cliff's driveway onto the road. Behind them in the barn, like fallen soldiers on a battlefield, lay the plastic pieces that had fallen from Cliff's cardboard chessboard, which still had a gauze patch at its center and a strip of tape stuck to its edge.

CHAPTER 60

Despite Maryann telling him from the shotgun seat urging him to hurry, Stedman kept the Subaru at seven miles an hour over the limit.

"If we get stopped it'll take even longer," he said in a level voice. "And if Aaron gets stopped behind us and the cop hears kids crying in that trailer, what then?"

They passed through Tamworth and drove north on the Chinook Trail, looking for the clinic's mailbox that marked the turnoff onto Rainey and Tom's private road.

"She said not to come to the clinic," Keegan said. "Don't turn in. One of them will meet us by the mailbox. I texted Aaron, so he knows, too."

A minute later Stedman recognized the landmarks and slowed. His headlights caught the strip of reflective tape marking his sister's mailbox. She stood waving two flashlights like she was on a carrier flight deck, directing him into a narrow path in the pines behind the mailbox. He started easing the nose of the Subaru in along the soft dirt path that was covered by fallen leaves, zipping his window down as he passed her.

"What's with the parking?" he asked.

"You want these babies treated?" she asked. "Pull ahead. I'll explain in a minute. Get in close to the old stone wall and leave room for the Jeep and trailer behind you. They've got to squeeze in there, too. Turn off your lights and all of you sit in the cars and wait for me."

Stedman did as ordered while Rainey instructed Aaron and guided him forward. When he had the Jeep side-by-side with the Subaru, he doused his headlights.

"Open your windows—both cars—so you can all hear," she said, and their windows dropped. She leaned down close to the windows and said in a clear, level voice, "We have a complication. Faucon is here recuperating from a foot amputation. You knew about him, but he didn't know about you. That changed two hours ago. He knows about you now."

"How did he find out?" Keegan asked.

"When my brother called in your medical emergency a couple hours ago, we were at the doggie B&B where we're keeping him, and he overheard some of the call. He called us about an hour ago and insisted we move him into the barn loft, and while we were doing it, he asked if Luna's babies were okay—you know, sounding concerned. Tom told him we can't discuss clients."

"But he does know we have babies," Stedman said.

"Yes," his sister answered. "But that's not the only complication. He also told us why he wanted to move. He says four of King Cyrus' goons are coming for him tonight."

"To take him back to the clan or to kill him?" Keegan asked.

"Not sure," Rainey said. My point is, he knows there are babies. If they take him prisoner, he may tell them. If they threaten to kill him, he's got the information as a bargaining chip for his life."

"So what do we do," Aaron said sarcastically, "pray that the king's men assassinate him before he can open his mouth?"

Nobody laughed.

"So you can see why I had you park out here in the woods," Rainey said. "You can follow me up this path to our back porch and sneak into the house then use the connector to get into the clinic. We can treat you and you can get out fast. We don't want you caught in the crossfire if Faucon is right and those guys show up tonight."

"Which is fine," AJ said, "but it doesn't stop Faucon from ratting us out. Whether the king finds out about the babies sooner or later, he'll have his people after us."

Everyone sat mulling the new complications. Half an hour earlier they had all thought they were simply bringing a trailer of burned *gargouilles* to an animal ER.

They heard a click behind the Jeep—something unlatching—then the squeak of hinges. The ATV's fiberglass top creaked up. When the angled lid was secure, Luna stepped out, followed by her brother Pernod.

"I know Cyrus' four," Luna said. "The cyclops Gregoire and his lackey Toulouse. The other two are assassins, Percheron and Grondin, known as Horse Face and Bat Face." She reached behind her shoulder and pulled out first her sword then her *poignard*, then the second *poignard*.

"Hey, my service pistol is in my Rav 4 at Cliff's," Stedman said.

"Mine's at home," Cliff said.

"Mine, too," Aaron said. "We're a little short on weapons."

"Our aim is not to kill them," Luna said. "It is to stop them from learning from Faucon that there may be children. Perhaps we can keep them from reaching him, maybe drive them away."

"So because we and these four bad guys may all be at the farm at the same time tonight," Maryann said, "we don't just risk them finding out *about* them, but actually *physically* finding them. Maybe we should just pack up and head home."

"And fight them again on different turf at a later date, Mom?" Keegan said. "Because if they find Faucon and get it out of him, there will be a later date. And we won't know when they're coming next time."

The babies began to whine and mew in the open trailer, and everyone could hear Yvette trying to comfort them.

Luna said, "We must bring them to the clinic so the doctors can help them and get them back out here. But they and the doctors must be protected. While that is happening, I will visit Faucon in the loft."

Before anyone could ask what she would do when she reached Faucon, Pernod said, "I have an idea. Luna, give me the extra *poignard*."

CHAPTER 61

Just before eleven, Gregoire and the others arrived and alighted in the tops boughs of the pines that looked over the dirt road toward the B&B. The house was dark but there was still a light on in the clinic building. Had the animal doctors forgotten to turn off a light in an exam room before going to bed? Or were they dealing with a late-night emergency, maybe a dog who had faced down the wrong porcupine?

This was Gregoire's and the two assassins' first visit to the farm. Toulouse had been on watch for two nights in the Hemenway State Forest when he'd heard the hum of short wings and located Faucon at the last building of the five, the small one beyond the barn. He had told Gregoire that an extraction should be simple—no humans close, Faucon isolated.

Percheron and Grondin glided down from the treetops and over the high chain-link fence into the former dog pen exercise yard. They landed quietly and approached the big dog house, drawing their weapons as they went.

Grondin knocked and said, "Faucon, it is time to go home. King Cyrus would like to see you." No answer, so he knocked again, this time harder. "Come out, monsieur. Or do you need us to come in and help you?" A hint of a taunt. If he did exit voluntarily, the two of them would escort him out to the road so Toulouse could bring down the four-vine cargo sling they had fashioned to transport him back to the clan cave.

Grondin tried the latch handle and the door swung open. Leading with his sword and dagger he cautiously stepped inside.

"Is he in there?" Percheron asked.

Grondin emerged, shaking his head. He turned to the trees and showed Gregoire his upraised palms. *Empty. Gone.*

Gregoire motioned them to return, which they did.

"Has he gone out foraging or fishing?" Toulouse asked.

"Idiot," Percheron sniped. "He has only one leg. And we'd have heard his short wings if he was nearby."

"He moved to one of the other buildings," Gregoire said.

"Which means he is resisting," Percheron said, practically salivating.

"Perhaps," Gregoire replied. "So we will divide up and find him. Grondin, you search that barn. Percheron, take that long building with the outside pens. There are more pens inside. Be prepared for many dogs and cats. They will be noisy. You will need to look in each cage, in case Faucon is hiding with them. Toulouse and I will fly up this dirt road to the building with the light, where the doctors do their surgeries. Maybe his leg required further attention. We will wait outside to give you two a chance to find him first. If you do, we need not encounter the humans."

"And if we do meet a human?" Percheron asked. "Do we leave witnesses?"

"We are here for Faucon."

"But if they see us," Percheron persisted.

"If they see us, they will report it to the police, who will attribute it to the current vampire hysteria."

Knowing their assignments, the four pushed off and glided toward the buildings.

Grondin landed in the open space between the B&B and the barn. The door was open, and when he stared down the cement strip that ran the barn's length between the two facing rows of empty cattle stanchions he saw a bit of light at the far end. The door at that end was open, too. And beyond that, at the kennels, he could see Percheron drawing his weapons, poised to open that building's door and enter. Grondin drew his own sword and *poignard* and stepped into the barn. He felt a slight breeze coming toward him down the barn's spine and, when his eyes adjusted, saw that the entrance at the far end was also open. The moonlight outside gave an eerie glow to the rows of dusty windows on either side, behind the milking areas where dairy cows had once stood in facing rows or lain with their heads in the stanchions. Faucon, he knew, could be prone in any of the fifty spaces the cows had occupied. He crept forward, checking left and right, hearing a cacophony of barking and howling begin in the next building—Percheron setting the animals off. *If the humans were asleep*, Grondin thought, *they aren't now.*

***

Far out in the pasture there was movement, slow at first but picking up speed, moving toward the narrow fence opening close to the space between the barn and the kennels. Someone had rearranged the fence so it formed a narrow funnel that left animals no choice but to enter the barn from the kennel end.

The driving force behind the now-gathering, now-moving mix of herd animals was pressuring them from the fence. One was a human who, when he heard the dogs in the kennels begin to bark, had called to his *gargouille* partner, "They're inside. Let's get 'em moving." The *gargouille* had begun racing back and forth, his deformed but perfect wings humming like baseball cards in a bike's spokes, agitating, awakening, startling, and ultimately moving the cows, horses, llamas, alpacas, mules, burrows, steers, and ostriches toward the barn. His partner Aaron urged them forward with hand claps and words of encouragement like *c'mon* and *giddyup*. The cowboy pair were learning to rodeo on the spot, and the herd was moving without stampeding—toward the barn.

At first Grondin didn't hear them coming. He was busy looking left and right for Faucon, half-expecting to see him lying in a stall trying to hide under a covering of straw. The din of yapping dogs was more of a soundtrack for his search, since he didn't have to look toward the other end of the barn and the open door. But then he heard braying and mooing and neighing and oinking and lifted his gaze to see a torrent of animals tumbling toward him. He raised his arms to deflect the horde but found himself pressed between two large beasts—one he was sure was a tall horse. Whatever giant bird came through behind them was heavier and stronger than he expected, and thumped him sideways against a cattle stanchion, which saved him from being trampled by the beasts that followed. He pulled himself through the space next to the stanchion yoke and caught his breath while he waited for the river of animals to exit through the door he'd entered by, spilling out into the area surrounding the B&B exercise yard. He located his sword and dagger where they had fallen in the center pathway and resumed his search.

Percheron could hardly think in the kennel building. At least he had some light by which to search the cages—very tiny red and green and yellow bulbs on the walls and overhead. There were yapping and barking dogs and loud-meowing cats everywhere. Some of them were close to the fronts of their pens, as if asking him for attention, others growling and snarling with teeth bared, daring him to come near so they could take a bite out of his hand. Far at the end of the concrete center walkway he saw two humans standing by the last cages. Could these be the husband-and-wife animal doctors? Who else would be in the kennel so late?

"Turn around and go back outside," the man shouted over the insanity.

Percheron continued his advance, checking left and right so as not to miss a crouching Faucon under a blanket or curled up with a big dog.

"You're upsetting our animals," the woman screamed. "Go back."

The big *gargouille* swaggered toward them, swishing his blades before him as he went. "Faucon," he roared above it all. "I want Faucon." He saw the big human aim something at him—the heavy brass nozzle of a thick hose.

"You asked for it," Cliff Bragdon yelled, and manipulated the handle of the old firehose used for hosing the place down each day. The blast first hit at Percheron's feet, but Cliff raised it so it struck him in the chest and face, the force of the water pressure forcing the *gargouille* to turn sideway and shield his face with his forearm. The force of the water cannon drove him back a few yards at first, but then, without loosening his grip on his weapons, he leaned into the water stream, deflecting it to the side, and continued his relentless by sheer strength and will.

"We told you to get out," the woman screamed, and when Percheron followed the voice he saw AJ lift her hand and place it near the ceiling. She flicked her thumb and a spark appeared at the end of her fingers. She held it up to a ceiling fixture and waited. Seconds later water sprayed from spigots above him—spigots over each animal cage and in a straight row over him. The deluge showered every inch of everything below, making the air dense and difficult to breathe. At the same time the entrance doors on both ends of the building snapped open and the gates of all the animal pens lifted in unison. Dozens of soaking wet dogs and cats scrambled out, several bumping him. He grabbed the mesh of one of the cages and withstood the frightened beasts' bumping and jostling his legs as they slipped and sloshed to the exits.

In two minutes the building was almost quiet except for the sounds of water still hissing from the overhead sprinklers and the pressure hose's splatting against Percheron's powerful body. The kennels were empty of animals except for a few feeble dogs lying in an inch of water.

Now it was only Percheron and his human tormentors, the big man still trying to hold him back with the hose, the woman—or was it a girl, she seemed young—helping him with his improvised water weapon. The *gargouille* clutched his weapons, staying sideways to reduce his target area, and pressed steadily forward against the stinging surge.

Cliff ordered AJ, "Get out. Now. Run."

314

And she did. She took a step back, let go her hold on the hose, and ran out the door.

Realizing that Percheron would reach him soon, Cliff backed up until he felt the wall beside him. The water pressure hadn't changed, but Percheron was actually deflecting it with his biceps.

"No fair," Cliff yelled. "A water pistol fight isn't the same as a sword fight. Besides, you know it's against the rules for garglees to kill humans."

Percheron gave a throaty laugh. "Unless there is no one around to see it." He raised his sword arm, so Cliff tilted the nozzle up a little, blasting the exposed side of his attacker's head. Enraged, Percheron slammed in fist down hard—sword hilt clutched in it—in the hollow between Cliff's ear and left shoulder. Its force and the accompanying pain drove him to his knees.

"Where is Faucon?" the furious assassin demanded. When he got no answer, he drew his sword arm back yet again, prepared to deliver a downward slice that would cleave Cliff's skull. But before he could act, Luna leapt through the door and thrust her *poignard* into the assassin's heart. The astonished *gargouille* fought to keep his balance and stood in place a moment, towering over the crumpled cop and staring in disbelief at Luna. She felt the weight of him sagging and withdrew her dagger blade, then watched his hands relax and his weapons clank to the concrete beside him. With a final shudder he toppled like a felled pine and crashed onto the cement walkway with a thud and a splash.

"AJ," Luna called out the door. Come in and turn off this hose and the sprinklers. Then take care of Cliff. Aaron and Pernod should be in from the pasture soon to help. I have to get back to the babies."

CHAPTER 62

Gregoire and Toulouse stood in the clinic parking lot and heard a cacophony of barking, wailing, and howling dogs. They had expected it, and knew Percheron had breached the kennel building. Shortly after, on the heels of the canine sounds, came other noises that were difficult to make out over the initial din. Now, mixed in with the sounds of the upset pets, came the braying and mooing of large animals. Even from a hundred feet away the two *gargouilles* felt the vibration of hooves pounding the ground.

"Percheron upset the dogs," Toulouse said, "which frightened the herd animals in the pasture."

They waited another minute, hearing the clack and clatter of hooves on the cement floor of the empty barn. Yet another minute and still no word from Percheron or Grondin about the crippled Faucon. The large animal noises subsided as they exited the barn at its far end and fanned out on the dirt and grass, calming down after their mini-stampede. The kennel barking went on.

"Time for us to go inside," Gregoire said. "I will go in this way, you go around to the back."

"Do these humans have guns?" Toulouse asked.

"Probably not. These are doctors. They are trained to heal, not to harm. And because they helped Faucon, they will not be startled to see *un gargouille*. Remember, we are simply two concerned friends searching for our injured comrade."

While Toulouse wobbled out of sight around the corner of the clinic, Gregoire tried the front door and found it unlocked. He stepped in, felt the wall to his right, and flipped on a light switch.

The reception area was a large room with ten chairs, four end tables with lamps on them, and a low coffee table with ten years of pet magazines stacked on it. The walls were papered with animal photos and newspaper and magazine clippings about pets and pet owners. Behind the check-in counter was a small windowless office for the receptionist.

A sliver of light showed under a door to the right, so he knocked and said in polite English, "Doctor?" When no one answered, he turned the knob, cracked the door, and said it again."

"Working on a cat," a male voice answered. "Can it wait until tomorrow morning?"

Gregoire pushed the door wider found a stocky middle-aged man standing next to an exam table. He wore a white lab coat with a name tag above the breast pocket that said Dr. Tom. His arms were wrapped around a swaddling blanket and he was gently rocking what appeared to be a baby. He looked up, showed no surprise at seeing a *gargouille* whose angel wings made him look hunchbacked, and said, "Just a guess, but are you here to visit Monsieur Faucon?"

The one-eyed *gargouille* stared at him.

"I'm Dr. Tom. My wife Rainey and I own the vet clinic. We're the ones who did the surgery on your friend. He's staying with us while he recuperates. Last building after the barn, if you want to visit. It's got a tall chain-link fence around it."

Gregoire continued to stare.

"Not trying to give you the bum's rush, monsieur, but I've got a pretty sick Maine coon cat here—vomiting and diarrhea."

"May I see the cat?" Gregoire asked politely.

"Sure," the vet replied, and gently laid the bundle on the table. "Shh," he said, index finger to his lip. "It's taken a lot to calm her down." He drew back first one side of the blanket then the other, revealing a huge mass of tan fur. "Cannolli is her name. About eighteen pounds. She looks heavier because of all the fur, but eighteen pounds is an average weight for her age."

A hint of a smile crept to the corners of Gregoire's mouth. Was it amusement? It was the look of someone enjoying playing a game. He didn't back out of the room.

"If you don't mind me asking," the vet said, sounding empathetic, "how'd you lose the eye?"

"War. France. Nineteen-seventeen. German artillery."

"Sorry."

The *gargouille* didn't budge.

"I'm sorry, monsieur, but do you need me to walk you down to Faucon's quarters?"

With his left hand Gregoire reached behind his neck and slipped the poignard from the scabbard. It hissed as it slid from the sheath, the sound of a knife being sharpened. With his right hand he pointed below the coon cat's protruding belly. "Do you see that thing?" he asked, and moved his finger toward the area between its haunches.

The man in the white coat looked. "Did I miss something?"

"*Oui*, monsieur," he replied, practically grinning, as if they were sharing a joke. He drew back his hand. "Your Cannolli is a male." He drew back his hand and stood there, looking smug now. "I recognize you, monsieur. You are indeed a talented *acteur.*"

"Actor?"

"*Oui.* When Toulouse and I were in Bethel a few days ago, we saw the fat man who sits behind his house in hot water. While he soaks, he watches the television. We stood in the trees and watched with him. That night you were playing a policeman in a vampire mask."

The color drained from Stedman's face.

"Remember?" Gregoire continued. "The woman *gendarme* behind you warned humans not to kill children. Your performance made an excellent point. Tonight, I find you playing *un veterinaire, un docteur,* and you were very convincing."

Stedman jumped to his backup plan, slipping his right hand into the lab coat pocket and emerging with one of the clinic's tranquilizer darts. But before he could jam the spring-loaded plunger against Gregoire's body, the point of the *gargouille's* dagger was pressing against the soft flesh of his throat.

"Place it on the table," the *gargouille* said, and Stedman laid it down beside the cat. "I believe that is for a tranquilizer gun—like the one used on my friend Toulouse at the camp?"

"Don't know anybody named Toulouse except Lautrec, and don't know about any camp."

A little laugh escaped Gregoire's throat. "I think, *monsieur,* that you are acting again."

Gregoire picked up the dart with his thumb and forefinger, immediately understood how it worked. "Hold out your arm."

Stedman shot him a look of defiance, and the *gargouille* gave the dagger tip a little more pressure. The cop didn't yield to the pressure and felt the sharp blade break the skin enough to draw blood. "Monsieur, why would you give your life to protect Faucon?" When Stedman gave no answer, his tormentor said, "Your arm, *monsieur acteur.* You won't feel a thing."

Stedman reluctantly extended his arm and Gregoire jammed the dart hard against his muscled forearm, firing the needle that emptied the sedative and tranquilizer into his system. The last thing he was aware of was Gregoire mercifully pulling the blade back from his throat. Then he lost control of his muscles and collapsed to the tile floor, reduced to a helpless mass of jerks and spasms. In his foggy brain he heard one last statement—*a talented acteur indeed, monsieur. I was nearly convinced*—but the voice carried no words of comfort for the fate of the other defenders, those he loved.

CHAPTER 63

There were two other doors in the exam room. Still gripping his dagger, Gregoire cautiously opened the one labeled Lab and snapped on the lights. No Faucon. The second proved to be an adjoining door connecting to a second exam room. He turned on the overhead fluorescent and found it, too, was empty. The left door said To Reception, the right Pharmacy. He found no one in the pharmacy.

The final door said To Private Residence and was unlocked. Beyond it he found a narrow walkway four feet above the ground. It spanned the twenty-foot gap between the clinic and the house and had waist-high wooden handrails on either side. He crossed it and found the exterior door unlocked, so he let himself in. There was a table lamp on and a kitchen light above the stove. He checked all the rooms. No Faucon. No doctors.

He walked through a mudroom to back door, which was locked. He unlocked and opened it then stepped out onto a deck overlooking a backyard in need of mowing. On the grass were brightly colored fallen leaves. Above the high grass he could see concrete birdbaths on pedestals, birdhouses on tall wooden posts, and a dozen iron shepherd's crooks stuck in the ground, all hung with flower pots and a few wind chimes that tinkled in the light breeze.

Near one of the birdbaths stood Toulouse, looking down the gradually sloping yard toward the forested acres that separated the farm from the main road.

"Your job was to search the house while I searched the clinic," Gregoire scolded.

"The door was locked, and before I could break a window, I thought I heard voices in the woods."

The breeze tickled three or four sets of hanging chimes, each producing different notes.

"Perhaps that is what you heard," Gregoire said, half suggestion and half question.

"No, I think I heard voices. Female voices. And look, there is a worn path from here to the trees. The doctors must use it often. It must go through the woods."

Gregoire's single eye stared at the woods. "Someone warned Faucon and *les docteurs* that we were coming. It was not one of the four of us, but perhaps it was Angeline, the one Cyrus banished. I can think of no one else. When the dogs began barking and the pasture animals escaped, *les docteurs* knew we had arrived and begun our search. They escaped from their offices to the house then left by this back path. You nearly ran into them."

"So what do we do now?" Toulouse asked.

Gregoire said, mostly to himself, "That would explain the fake doctor—his job was to slow me down, to give the husband and wife time to run. But why would the television man be here? And why would he risk his life for them? If his ruse had succeeded and I went away, would he have then fled to join the couple and Faucon?"

"Gregoire?" Toulouse said, and Gregoire snapped out of it.

"They must have hidden a vehicle somewhere. Probably near the highway. Toulouse, you follow the woods path. I will go to the front again and follow the dirt road. Who knows, I may overtake Faucon on his walking sticks. I'm sure he would take the road, not a forest path with growth at the edges and slippery leaves on the path. We fly low and silent, and approach from two directions."

***

Gregoire glided like a turkey vulture down the dirt road, checking not just the road but the gullies alongside it. He caught up with no one and landed near the clinic mailbox just off the Chinook Trail. It took him less than a minute to locate the overgrown path Rainey had used to make Maryann's Subaru and Aaron's Jeep disappear. The vehicles were no longer invisible.

He heard Toulouse's voice first—the tone sounded threatening—so he crept. Had Toulouse somehow managed to capture Faucon, or *les docteurs*, or all of them? Or had they captured him?

There was enough moonlight for Gregoire to see side-by-side vehicles, one pulling a low trailer. He'd been right, the doctors and maybe their *acteur* had hidden their cars near the highway for a covert escape if required. But why hadn't they backed in so they could escape by driving forward? Sometimes things didn't add up perfectly.

Where the path widened ahead of the cars he saw Toulouse brandishing his weapons near the couple. No Faucon in sight. He squatted, practically hugging the back bumper of the ATV trailer so as not to give himself away, even to Toulouse, who might say something to expose him.

"Drop your weapons and come down," Toulouse demanded of someone. But Gregoire could plainly see the man and woman were unarmed—unless they had pistols under their lab coats. *If they did, they'd have used them by now against a fop waving a sword.*

"I never surrender my weapons," a female voice answered. The voice sounded vaguely familiar, but it wasn't Angeline's. He knew Angeline's from the years when she kept Cyrus company, before he expelled her from the clan.

"Drop them or I will be forced to hurt your friends," Toulouse ordered.

"No," she replied defiantly. "And what makes you think they're my friends? They're humans."

Gregoire leaned carefully around the trailer and saw a *gargouille* perched on the Jeep's roof rack. He questioned Toulouse's demand. Females didn't have weapons or training. If this one had a weapon, he couldn't see anything in her hands.

322

Was Toulouse sure *la gargouille* was armed, or was it the stress of keeping three prisoners at bay?

"Just like you, I am here for Faucon," she said without fear. "Where is he?"

Gregoire recognized the voice now. It was Luna, Prince Champaigne's mate. Toulouse was right to assume she had weapons and knew how to use them. She and her sister Diana were the exceptions to the rule; the twin princes had taught them to fight.

"The animal doctors are just trying to get out of the way," Luna said. "They are innocent humans who tried to sneak off in their automobiles until you and I are gone. Let them go and we can get back to searching for Faucon."

A baby cried. Luna, Tom, and Rainey all turned toward the trailer. Gregoire looked, too. The sound had come from his left, next to where he was hiding. Inside the closed trailer.

Gregoire acted quickly, gripping and turning the latch that kept the fiberglass trailer top secure.

"Our daughter," the quick-thinking Rainey said to Toulouse. "Your yelling woke her up."

It sounded plausible to Toulouse but Gregoire ignored her and lifted the travel pod's clamshell roof. As soon as he caught a glimpse of the contents, he drew both weapons from his back. "What have we here?"

"What is it, Gregoire?" Toulouse wanted to know.

"Two more humans and two *gargouilles*—baby *gargouilles*—the cyclops answered. Then, speaking into the trailer, he said, "Get out."

One of the babies gave a little cry as its caregiver shifted positions. Maryann backed out then leaned inside again and came up with a green-eyed *gargouille* child that she cradled in her arms.

"Take your little female and join *les docteurs*," Gregoire said. "Toulouse, watch them." Maryann did as ordered. Then

Gregoire tapped his dagger blade on the edge of the fiberglass box. "You next. Step out."

Keegan climbed out with a red-eyed *gargouille* baby riding her hip, and went to stand by her mother.

"Any more?" Toulouse asked. "Is Faucon hiding in there, too?"

Gregoire glanced back in, made out the flat mattress and Pernod's lumpy beanbag chair, and prodded them with his sword. "Empty," he said, and walked by the side of the trailer to join Toulouse.

"So, no Faucon?" Toulouse asked, as if he couldn't believe it.

"Anyone care to offer an explanation?" Gregoire asked.

Keegan said, "These two are Luna's brother's children. He's the one who was estranged from your clan and lived off the grid until he died this summer. Luna promised she'd raise them. Mom and I said we'd help."

Gregoire shook his head in disbelief. "Good, *mademoiselle*, but not as convincing as the man who pretended to be *le docteur*. Still, an entertaining attempt. What is your name?"

"Keegan."

"And this is your mother? That I believe. You resemble her except for the white streak in your hair. We once had a human visit our clan, he had a similar white streak."

Before Keegan could say more, he said, "Luna, I remember Waterbug, your deformed brother. These are not his children. I believe they are your sister Diana's. It was rumored that you left to search for her eggs."

Luna didn't deny it.

"Cyrus will be very interested. He may promote me when I bring him *le dauphin*."

"You're not taking them," Maryann said sharply.

"Not *them*," Gregoire said slowly. "*Him*." He gestured toward the red-eyed infant in Keegan's arms. "He will ascend. Have you named him?"

"His name is Paladin," Keegan said, and ran her palm and fingers tenderly across his scalp and the healing talon scabs.

"Ah, the knight," he translated.

"His sister's name," Maryann said, "is Regine."

"A queen?" he translated again, and pretended to stifle a condescending laugh.

From the roof rack Luna called down, "Only a fool would prefer a knight to a queen."

"Tell that to the king," Gregoire said. Then, "Toulouse, sheathe your *poignard* and take our little knight."

Toulouse put away the dagger and reached for the baby with his free hand, as if he might pick it up the way he'd move a kitten, by the scruff of its neck. But Paladin squirmed and wriggled in Keegan's arms, trying to cling to her while pushing Toulouse away with his bandaged feet.

"Hand him over," Gregoire ordered Keegan, and placed the tip of his long sword against the upper back of the female in Maryann's arms.

Keegan loosened her grip and passed Paladin to Toulouse, who awkwardly tried to balance his sword in one hand and Paladin on his palm in the other. Finally, he stuck the sword blade into the dirt beside him and used both hands to shift the squirming baby onto his left hip. He wrapped his forearm tightly around Paladin and held him in a sort of death grip, then reclaimed his sword.

"Will you be able to fly, Toulouse?" Gregoire asked.

"It will be easier after I put my sword on my back and can use two hands."

"Then it is almost time to go," Gregoire said. "One last detail and we are off." He looked up at Luna and said, his voice dripping with sarcasm, "I really hate to do this, but the law is the law. We cannot have female heirs."

Luna's eyes widened in terror. She knew what he meant, what he was about to do.

Maryann understood it also and screamed *Don't* while instinctively turning away from Gregoire to protect her baby from the forward plunge of Gregoire's sword tip.

The blade went through the child's back at an angle and came out the left side. Gregoire pulled it back out, but before he could strike again, Keegan lowered her head and ran straight at his stomach, knocking him back.

Maryann rolled away.

Luna grabbed her sword from the flat Jeep roof and launched forward on the power of her wounded hummingbird wings. She flew straight at Gregoire, who was pounding on Keegan's back with his sword hilt as he tried to keep from falling over backwards. Luna stopped short of his flailing sword.

There was also another sound—also short wings, but at a different pitch and vibration speed. Partway up the trail, hidden by a tree, Pernod had fired up his deformed wings and buzzed toward the assailants. He hit Toulouse in the back, jarring the baby boy off the *gargouille's* hip so the little one shot forward, landing at the feet of the two vets. Pernod wrapped his arms around Toulouse and clung to his back like he was taking a terrified piggyback ride.

From between the Jeep and Subaru, where she had hidden quietly, Yvette used her short wings, racing forward with Luna's *poignard*. She flew straight at Toulouse and never hesitated. While he reached with both his right and his left hand to grab his sword or his dagger from behind his shoulders, she plunged the dagger into his abdomen, her forward movement burying it to the hilt.

Gregoire had a headful of dark hair in one hand and his sword in the other. He saw Luna coming—sword in hand now, but no *poignard*—and yanked Keegan up in front of him as a shield. He turned his sword crosswise and held the blade close to her throat.

Luna braked to a stop in front of him, sword lowered at her side.

"Throw it in the bushes, Luna," Gregoire said.

She did, and he nodded down at Keegan and said, "This one will go in last."

"You are making a mistake, Gregoire," Luna said. "You will end up like Toulouse."

He glanced quickly to his right and saw Toulouse's body bleeding out on the dirt, a *poignard* protruding from his midsection. "Yvette," he said. "I have not seen you in a while. And Waterbug, it's been decades. You two join the others. Go get in that thing."

To Rainey, the vet, who had taken Paladin into her arms, he said, "When you get in, put him on the ground. I will treat him well."

As the others migrated toward the back of the ATV trailer, Luna extended the birthing talon in her index finger, the sharp hook she had used to slit open her sister's eggs at Stonehedge. She kept the hand at her side. A few seconds later she caught Keegan's attention and closed the lid over one of her eyes. When Keegan gave her a puzzled look, she did it again. Keegan opened her mouth to shape an O and gave a faint nod.

As Yvette and Pernod passed by him on their way to the trailer, Gregoire lowered his sword away from Keegan's neck.

"I can't believe you're all doing what he says," Keegan cried.

And Luna gave her the nod.

Keegan's right hand went up like a hitchhiker's and kept going. Sensing the position of Gregoire's lone red eye more than seeing it, she poked her thumb hard, praying she'd hit the gelatinous orb and sink in.

Gregoire screamed in pain and raised his sword hand to remove whatever fragment had violated his eye socket. Keegan jumped forward and flattened herself on the ground.

Luna ran straight at him, but he didn't see her, then dodged beneath his left arm, hooking her left arm under his armpit and swinging herself up onto his back like a trick rider quick-mounting a horse. Her right arm ended up over his right shoulder and around his neck as if she might choke him.

Gregoire howled at the eye pain while his sword arm flailed across his chest and up over his left shoulder as if he were trying to sheathe the weapon.

"I used this for birth and now I will use it for death," she said, and drew the razor-sharp finger talon across his throat.

He faltered, grew weak in the legs, and toppled forward with her still riding the bumps made on his back by his angel wings. She lay there a minute, catching her breath. Keegan rolled closer and pulled Luna off Gregoire's back and hugged her close.

Then the others came and gathered close, some crying in relief and gratitude. Except Maryann, who was already halfway up the woods path with the pierced, bleeding baby girl in her arms, racing for the clinic a few steps behind Rainey and Tom, and repeating, "Oh, Mathilde, Mathilde, I am so sorry. So sorry. Please don't die."

CHAPTER 64

"AJ, this is Keegan. Come in, AJ." She waited, got no response, and pushed the button again on the vets' walkie-talkie. "AJ? This is Keegan. Are you and Regine okay?"

"We're fine. It's dark and smelly down here, but we're fine. Is it safe to come out yet?"

"Tell her, not yet," Luna said. "I have to check on Faucon. We know Gregoire, Toulouse, and Percheron are dead, but we don't know where Grondin is."

Keegan didn't have to tell her, because she still had her finger down on the button, so AJ had heard it.

"I know Percheron is dead," she said. "I set off the kennel sprinklers and Cliff manned the fire hose. When the dude got too close, Cliff pushed me out the door. Thank God you were there to stab him, Luna."

"Stay in the root cellar," Luna said. "I am going to the barn."

She picked her sword off the ground then pulled her *poignard* out of Toulouse's gut, where Yvette had sunk it. She drew the flat blade across his body to clean off the blood then slipped both weapons into her scabbard. "Stay with Pernod and Yvette," she told Keegan. "Nobody is safe until we know about Grondin." She headed for the dirt road where she could launch using her great wings.

"What happened to the other two guys?" AJ asked. "Luna said they're dead, too. Are you all okay?"

"The vets are working on Mathilde now up at the clinic. Mom's up there with them. It was a helluva fight here, and the two bad guys Luna mentioned—the dead ones—one of them stabbed Mathilde. Mom turned her just in time or it'd have gone through her heart. We hope it's a flesh wound. I saw it sticking through—it was horrible. Scary. But it looked like it went in under the shoulder and came out the side. We're praying here, we're praying."

"Why'd he stab Mathilde?" AJ asked.

"That patriarchy nonsense Luna told us about this summer. The guy wanted to take Paladin back to the king, but wouldn't he consider a female. When he asked what her name was, Luna said it was Regine. We didn't know if Luna got it mixed up—she knew it was Mathilde—or if she intentionally told him that. So we all followed suit, we all went along with her. We figured he'd try to leave with Paladin, and Luna would follow, but we never expected him to try to kill a baby—a female baby. This male succession thing, they're pretty hard core, inflexible."

"So, we're glad he's dead?" AJ asked.

"Absolutely. I am, anyway—at least until the adrenaline wears off."

"Wow."

"Yeah, wow. And to think it started with a little hunchbacked nun walking into our bookstore. Anyway, Luna, Pernod, Yvette, and I are here and, I think, getting ready to walk up to the clinic to see how Mathilde and Cliff are doing. Mom's worried about Stedman, but we think he just got hit with some of his own tranquilizer juice. We're glad you two are both safe."

"Thanks. You, too." AJ said.

"Remember, Luna says to stay there until she says the coast is clear. You copy?"

"We copy. But hurry. It really stinks down here. I think the potatoes down here might be last year's. Or the year before. They're rotten. And the root vegetables they left on the shelves or hung on the walls-yecch! Over and out."

***

Pernod started up the woods path with Yvette and Paladin a few steps behind. Keegan saw him glance at the two dead *gargouilles'* weapons. But he didn't pick any of them up.

She knew he abhorred the weapons he had been trained to make, but she had seen him spring into action quickly when others' lives were in danger, giving no thought to his own safety. He might be a pacifist or a conscientious objector, but he was no coward. When she came to the weapons, she also passed them by.

When they reached the backyard, Aaron was there with an arm around Cliff's shoulder, walking him among the hanging plants and wind chimes.

"Shaking out the cobwebs," Aaron said. "Hoping he doesn't have a concussion. But I'm afraid he may have a broken collarbone. I'll get him to ER after we get back to Wells. Start thinking up a story about how he did it. The guy'll do anything to extend his medical leave."

Cliff smiled weakly and gave a little wave of acknowledgment.

The clinic was lit up, so Keegan took Paladin from Yvette and left her in the yard with Pernod, then carried the baby inside. She knocked on the closest exam room door and said, "It's Keegan." Rainey told her to come in, and when she opened the door, she found Tom and Rainey working on Mathilde.

"She's a fighter," Rainey said. "She's going to be okay. "We stopped the bleeding, gave her a sedative and an antibiotic and stitched her up. And a tetanus shot, of course." She shifted to baby talk, "She's a brave little girl who pretended she was her sister Regine."

"Will she be traumatized—you know, scarred for life, PTSD—by what she saw and went through? That was pretty brutal for all of us, but I don't know what it's like for a toddler."

"Time will tell," Tom said. "Loving families help."

"Well, she's got that going for her," Keegan said. Then, out of nowhere, said, "Three big bodies to dispose of. And we're not talking goldfish or parakeets, or even a Great Dane."

Rainey smiled. "From the sounds of that comment, Keegan, I'm thinking you may be experiencing some mild shock. If your mother says it's okay, I can give you a Zanax. We sometimes use them for pets with extreme separation anxiety. Why don't you ask her? She's in the other exam room with Elly. Through that door. She's sitting with him while he wakes up. His tranquilizer dart idea backfired on him. We can handle Mathilde. And don't worry about the bodies. We're the principals in the pet crematory."

Keegan knocked on the door to the other exam room, got a come-in from her mother, and entered with Paladin.

Maryann and Stedman were sitting on the floor with their backs against the wall. She was helping him sip water from a plastic bottle. He was groggy and when he looked up at his visitors, he looked drunk.

"Oopah," Paladin said from Keegan's hip, and stretched out his arm. "Oopah," he repeated, waving the hand and arm now, impatient for Keegan to set him down so he could run to the sleepy cop.

Keegan bent and knelt, then placed his bandaged feet on the floor.

He wobbled around the end of the exam table, made a Charlie-Chaplin-like turn, skidding without toppling over, and threw himself in the exhausted cop's lap. "Oopah," he said again, and snuggled against Stedman's chest.

On the exam table something stirred. The tawny Maine coon cat, all eighteen pounds of it, turned from its back onto its side to look at the little family of three on the floor below it, and in a hoarse voice, said, "Meow."

"I'm glad you're okay, Elly," Keegan said. "Mom can fill you in on our part of the story later. Thanks for giving us all a chance to get out of the house."

He nodded, and his eyes drooped. His head fell to the side and rested on Maryann's shoulder. Paladin clung to the big man, his head sideways on Elly's chest so that it looked like he was listening to Oopah's heartbeat.

"I'll be out back with the others, Mom," Keegan said, and backed toward the door. As she did, she ran her hand across the soft fur of the coon cat, which responded with purring. She stroked it for another thirty seconds, and the tears began to stream down her cheeks. She closed the door without going out after all and went and sat on the other side of her mother, who placed her free arms around Keegan's shoulder while the girl sobbed.

***

A while later Luna showed up. She had AJ and Regine with her. She had those in the exam rooms come out to the backyard so she'd only have to tell the story once. Everyone was exhausted, but they were all eager to hear what had happened to Faucon.

Luna gave them the essence of it. Faucon was alive and still in the loft. Grondin was on his way back to the clan but could possibly die *en route*.

How had it happened this way?

When the Wells group had first arrived, Pernod realized that Faucon—who had told Dr. Tom a hit team was on the way—would be left unarmed and exposed if they searched and found him. So Pernod had asked for Luna's extra *poignard*, which he took to Dr. Tom, who delivered it to Faucon in the hayloft. At least the disabled *gargouille* would have a chance. If they killed him, the search would halt and Luna and Yvette and the babies, all being treated for burn injuries in the clinic, wouldn't be discovered. If the search went farther, the plan was to escape into the house, then to the hidden vehicles. They would take only two babies in case they were caught, leaving one defender—it ended up being AJ—to protect the real queen in Tom and Rainey's underground root cellar. It was the only safe place that wasn't a building, so the king's team would be unlikely to search it.

Dr. Tom, as instructed by Pernod, told Faucon that "a sympathetic friend" had sent the weapon, but he didn't know who.

"When he saw the *poignard*," Luna said, "which had until recently been his, he assumed that I had sent it.

"As soon as he accepted it, he said, his realized that if the searchers split up, he might be able to outwit the one who came for him. But he had only the dagger.

"So when Dr. Tom left, Faucon unwrapped the end of his amputated leg and used the tape to secure the *poignard* to the end of his crutch—like a bayonet. He set himself up on bales of hay facing the opening where the ladder came up to the loft. He made the bloody stump of his leg the focal point for his visitor. He lay his left crutch straight down his middle on his chest and left leg. His bayonet crutch, he told me, he hid against his hay bed along the right side.

"When Grondin came up to the loft and saw his pitiful unarmed victim, he assumed he had an easy kill. He approached with only his dagger, and when he leaned in at Faucon's feet, Faucon lifted his left crutch and pressed the tip of it against Grondin's chest—which Grondin assumed was a weak attempt at holding him away. He pressed harder against the crutch tip so he could get closer with his dagger. And when he did, Faucon raised the right bayonet-crutch and stabbed him—he claims—near the heart. In the battle, Faucon now had two leverage points, which helped him push Grondin away. Faucon says Grondin fell back, clutched his wound to slow the bleeding, and disappeared down the hole.

"When I found Faucon a while ago, he said he owed me his life and he would pledge his loyalty to me. I did not mention any of you or the children. He believes I came and acted alone. And it appears that Grondin, if he makes it back to King Cyrus,

334

does not know, either. He only knows that Faucon is alive, and I'm not sure he dare admit that."

"How will Grondin explain his return without the others?" Aaron asked.

"I do not know. I am certain Faucon is worrying about this, too."

"So Tom and I have to get Faucon patched up fast," Rainey said. "Improvise a foot and maybe a patch for his wing— and while we do that, the rest of you will need to find him a new hiding place far from here."

"He's not coming to my barn," Cliff said. "He may say he'll pledge you his loyalty, Luna, but I'll bet that'll change at the first sign of trouble—or a better offer. And we can't let him know about these kids."

"For tonight," Keegan said, "we need to dispose of three bodies before we hit the road."

"That's right," a still drunk-looking Stedman slurred. "You and AJ have school tomorrow. And Cliff and I have to go back to work."

They looked down at their feet and saw the real Regine and her knight brother Paladin on the beanbag chair Pernod had brought up to the yard from the trailer. Both siblings were leaned up against Mathilde like a pair of gargoyle bookends, tight against their sister with the bandage wrapped all the way around her waist. All three were asleep.

A light breeze rustled the colored leaves in the yard and tickled the strings of wind chimes.

CHAPTER 65

It was Wednesday evening before the group could meet again. Exhaustion and shock from the battle at Tom and Rainey's farm had taken a toll.

AJ and Keegan skipped school Monday so they could sleep. They returned to classes Tuesday and Wednesday, which brought back a basic sense of normalcy.

Maryann also slept much of Monday. But with Cliff in a sling for his broken collarbone, and Elly back on detective duty, much of the care and feeding of Luna's crew—especially the wounded Mathilde—fell to her. She shopped, played nurse, and tried to strategize with Luna and Pernod. Elly stopped by the barn when he could and joined the strategy sessions. So did Aaron.

Elly was in regular communication with his sister Rainey and her husband Tom. Before their clinic employees arrived Monday, the two of them had lifted the bodies of Gregoire, Percheron, and Toulouse into three of the disposal bags they used for horses and cows, then later in the day cremated them. They hid the three *gargouilles'* swords and *poignards* in the root cellar. Rainey had asked Elly if there was a plan for Faucon's next hiding place, but he had no answer. He explained that not only was he back at work at Wells CID—with a more than three-month backlog of cases—but he was trying to locate a small camper he could insulate and half-bury at the Orne Jewett Writers Retreat to house Luna's crew for the winter and spring.

"Tom's going to try something with Faucon's torn wing," Rainey had said. "Before we disposed of that big *gargouille's* remains—the one Luna took down in the kennel—

"Percheron," Elly said.

"Yeah, I guess. Anyhow, he's almost as big as Faucon. So we removed the leathery lining of his right wing. Tom wants to try a transplant on Faucon—just the torn part, not the whole wing."

"It'd be great if that worked and you could set him free to find his own next hiding place."

"That's what we were thinking," she replied. "Also, Tom's got a prosthesis we used on a pony a few years ago. The pony's gone, but the prosthesis is in storage. We'll try to adapt it to fit Faucon. It's simply mechanical, no batteries or electromagnetic signals or anything. But it's a step up from a peg leg. He might need a cane or a crutch, too, at first, but he'll get better with it as time goes by."

"How soon on the wing and the foot?" Elly asked.

"Wing tonight, as soon as the help's gone home. Prosthesis in the next day or two. We're pushing, because we're afraid that bad guy who got away might return with reinforcements."

"We'll keep working on a place for Faucon," Elly assured her. "Good luck with patching that wing."

The Wednesday evening meal was take- out pizza again for the humans and cod and mashed pumpkin for the *gargouilles*. The atmosphere was somewhat subdued, not as jubilant as the week before when the little ones had run around and wrestled and played before tipping over the charcoal grill.

Stedman sat on a collapsible stadium chair with two slices of pizza next to him on a tray table. The pizza was cold now—he had taken a single bite out of one of the slices before Paladin climbed onto his lap, asking to be bounced on Oopah's knee.

Maryann sat beside them with a bandaged Mathilde on her lap. The little *gargouille* was letting Maryann feed her and seemed to enjoy being pampered.

Regine toddled from Luna to Yvette to AJ, begging scraps of food from the adults' plates—fish from the *gargouilles* and a small crust of pizza from AJ. She gummed the crust to soften it, then managed to eat the pasty dough.

Pernod and Cliff were at the card table absorbed in a game of chess, each eating and drinking between moves. When Cliff said something about being at a disadvantage—having to play one-handed because his arm was in a sling—Pernod said, "Okay, Cliff, I'll play one-handed, too."

"No luck on the half-sister connection yet?" Aaron asked Keegan, and sat down beside her. He held out one of the pizza boxes that had two slices left.

"No," she said, sounding tired and down.

"No to the Pennsylvania thing or no to another piece of pizza?"

She reached for the pizza box and lifted out a slice. "No to the Pennsylvania connection. I called yesterday and today, but still no answer, just the voice messages box. I made sure to leave my cell number and Mom's cell number. When she called the store, it was kind of luck on her part. She got word from somebody in the Amish Country that I had been asking around. But I guess the only thing the person could remember me saying was my name—Keegan—and something about us having a bookstore in Wells, Maine."

"Didn't she say in her message that she'd be away for a week?" Aaron asked. "Give her a few days. She's got your name and number."

They cleared away the pizza boxes and paper plates and drew together. Regine came over and climbed onto Aaron's lap, and AJ and Keegan took the other two.

"Saturday's a work day at the Writer's Retreat," Maryann said. "Like last Saturday, AJ and Keegan, you get the Book Stop. Elly, Aaron, and I will drive up to Moxie Pond to dig the hole for Elly's bunker—for lack of a better term. I'll rent a posthole-digger and a handheld trencher so we're not doing it all with shovels—which would take forever. Elly's got the dimensions for us."

"And when will we put this bunker in place?" AJ asked.

Stedman said, "The following Saturday, best guess. It's an older wedge-shaped aluminum snowmobile trailer I found on Craig's List. On Sunday the guy's delivering it to my house from Lake George. It's lightweight and has only a single axle—a Spam can on a utility trailer, the guy says—which means we won't have to unbolt it from the frame to plant it. We can leave the tires right on it and dig them into the ground, too. All it needs is a layer of insulation around the inside walls."

"I know somebody with one of those," AJ said. "The entire back wall drops down to become the ramp you use to load and unload the snow machines. How's Luna going to open the door if it's dug into the ground?"

"Don't need it," Stedman replied. "There's a walk-in side door, so we just need to make sure we dig a few steps below ground so it'll swing open. And the front gives us an emergency exit—the upper part of it flips up like an awning."

"And just out of curiosity, who's paying for it?" Keegan asked.

Stedman started to say something.

Pernod cut him off. "My friend Rusty is. It's his contribution to the Writer's Retreat, in case anybody asks about it."

"Everybody got their assignments?" Maryann asked.

Before she could answer, Stedman's cellphone chirped, and he answered. After a couple of uh-huhs and yeps, he got up and walked away from the group. After a few minutes of pacing near the barn door, he returned, his phone no longer in hand.

"Tom and Rainey," he said, and slipped the phone back into his side pocket. "Our Faucon problem is solved."

"What? How?" Aaron asked. "Is he dead?"

"Rainey says he's got a place."

"A place? Where?" Aaron asked.

"Seems a female *gargouille* paid Faucon a visit at the doggie B&B an hour ago. She told Faucon the assassin he stabbed in the hayloft—Grondin—didn't survive. He made it as far as some cave he and the others had been using near Kezar Falls. But he never got out of the cave."

Luna said, "So he cannot report to King Cyrus."

"How does this solve our Faucon problem?" Cliff asked.

"She says she has been seeking shelter for the winter, so she removed the body," Stedman said. "She invited Faucon to share the space until he is healed enough to go out on his own."

"But he can't fly and he can't walk," Cliff said.

"Tom said he's got a snap-on cover for his pickup bed. He can hide Faucon in the back when Faucon is ready to make the move, then he'll drive him to Kezar Falls some night and get him close to the cave. Faucon can use his short wings to get him the rest of the way."

Everyone was relieved to hear the news from Rainey and Tom, except Keegan wasn't so quick to accept it without questioning it.

"This female *gargouille* didn't just *happen* to find Grondin in that cave," Keegan said. "If she went to Rainey and Tom with a solution to Faucon's next apartment, she already knew Faucon was there. Was she watching the assault on the clinic, and did she follow Grondin from there to the cave? And how much else did she see? Does she know about us—and by us, I mean all of us here tonight, including the existence of three royal heirs? We're assuming four dead assassins means nobody knows about us, and our secret is safe. But maybe it's not, because even if Faucon doesn't know, this other *gargouille* may."

Luna said, "I believe *la gargouille* you speak of is Angeline. But do not let her name deceive you. She was a leader in the coup to overthrow the Argentinian clan chief. I do not know her motive in helping Faucon, but for the moment she is not our enemy. That does not mean she is our friend, either. When the time is right, I will speak with her. For now, let her have Faucon. We have enough to do here."

CHAPTER 66

At school Friday, Keegan found it hard to concentrate on anything but her phone and the fact that Doretta Schussler's week was up. But the phone didn't chirp or vibrate, and there were no texts. At lunchtime she called her mother at the Book Stop to see if Doretta had contacted her, either on the bookstore phone or on Maryann's cell.

At school Friday, Keegan found it hard to concentrate on anything but her phone and the fact that Doretta Schussler's week was up. But the phone didn't chirp or vibrate, and there were no texts. At lunchtime she called her mother at the Book Stop to see if Doretta had contacted her, either on the bookstore phone or on Maryann's cell.

"If she calls, I'll text you," Maryann said. "And I'll arrange for her to call back after you get home from school, maybe suppertime."

By the time Keegan went to bed Friday night, there was still no word from her potential half-sister in Lancaster, Pennsylvania. The last thing she did before going to bed was succumb to the temptation to call. When she got only the answering system, Keegan said she was calling to leave her email address, something she had forgotten to do the week before. As soon as she hung up, she realized she probably sounded not just eager but desperate. She slept with her phone plugged into the charger and turned on. She changed the sound options for the phone's ringtone, text, and email notifications to the loudest choices she could find. The phone made no sounds all night.

Maryann was out of the house early Saturday morning, before seven o'clock. She packed eight sandwiches, potato salad, and two six-packs of Gatorade for Stedman, Aaron, and herself, knowing they'd be starving after a morning of digging out for the bunker under the Retreat Center's Quonset shed. She left a note for Keegan to find when she had breakfast.

Don't obsess. She'll call. I'm interested, too. But we have to be patient. Love, Mom

Keegan called AJ and said she'd pick her up early so they could get to the Book Stop and check the messages, in case Doretta had called on the bookstore line. Without whining about the change of schedule by an hour, AJ simply said, "Sure. No problem."

When they arrived at Annie's, the only message was a canned pitch about extending a vehicle warranty.

The two of them worked the store like they had the previous Saturday, except Keegan kept her cellphone in her back pocket, never leaving it on the work table or on the checkout counter.

Cliff stopped by at noon and reported on Mathilde's progress—he was proud that he had changed her bandages after breakfast—and said he'd been told the sling could come off his shoulder Tuesday, and he could return to light duty Wednesday then to regular patrols ten days after that. He made a quick run to Subway for sandwiches for the three of them, which they ate in the work room when there was a lull in business, and left around two.

The store phone rang as Cliff pulled out of the parking lot, and AJ grabbed it. She listened a few seconds, turned toward Keegan, whose face was full of expectation, and shot her an eye roll while mouthing the name *Mrs. Barnes.* Keegan was disappointed, but she was also happy to have AJ handle one of the confused Mrs. Barnes's regular calls about books she hadn't ordered.

Then Keegan's cell rang and she checked the caller ID: *Lancaster, Pennsylvania.*

"Hi, this is Keegan—sometimes known as Daupine Keegan." She almost never used her first name. Even the teachers at school and all her friends knew that she went by last name, that she treated it like it was her first name or nickname. She waited, then heard the voice from the original phone message say, "Hi. This is Doretta Schussler. Is this Dauphine Keegan?" It was the voice of a young woman.

"Yes, but call me Keegan."

"Is this a good time to talk?"

"Hang on a sec." Keegan caught AJ's attention, pointed at her phone and gave an excited head nod and a thumbs-up. "Watch the front," she said. "I've got to take this in the work room."

AJ, still on the phone with Mrs. Barnes, nodded and hand-signaled O.K.

Keegan disappeared behind the break-room door, sat on one of the high stools, and said, "Now I'm free to talk. First thing, though, give me your contact information in case we get cut off." She wrote down several pieces of information on a large Post-It note and offered her own to the caller.

"Let's see if we can untangle this," Doretta Schussler said. "Last week I called and left a message at Annie's Book Stop in Wells, Maine."

"Which is where I am now. It's my mother's bookstore. Where are you?"

"I'm at my great-grandmother's house in Lancaster, Pennsylvania."

"And her name is Mary Broere. She's ninety-five."

"Ah, the power of the Internet. Your facts are generally correct, but she had to move into assisted living last month."

"Sorry."

"It was her idea. She knew she needed help to do some things. Overall, she's quite healthy and is still with it mentally."

"So you don't live there?"

"I'm only in Lancaster when I'm not in college. I'm a junior at Skidmore, in Saratoga Springs, New York. I stay at

Great-Gram's over vacations and semester breaks. I came down last week to visit her and check on her place. She had a bunch of phone calls on her answering machine—two from friends in the Amish Country, both saying someone named Keegan at a bookstore in Wells, Maine was asking about Janos Dauphine. The two friends remembered him and knew he had a connection to my great-grandmother, Mary Broere."

"So, do you know why I was calling?" Keegan asked.

"I didn't last week, I just knew someone was asking about him. Then when I arrived late last night, I listened to the new messages you left, including the one when you said your first name was Dauphine. That's when I knew I had to call you back."

"So, tell me who Jan—Keegan pronounced it *Yon*—is to you." She felt her heart make a little leap when she said it.

"Great-Gram's son was Henrick Broere. His daughter Deborah Broere—Debbie—was my mother."

"She married a Schussler?"

"Right after I was born."

"After?"

"I was born—as they say—out of wedlock. Fred Schussler adopted me. But I was born Doretta Broere."

Keegan was tempted to ask the paternity question, but instead said, "What year?"

"Nineteen ninety-six."

The workroom door opened and AJ stuck her head in. "Keeg, I need help. Customers."

"On my way," Keegan replied. Then into the phone she said, "Doretta, bookstore just got busy. Just one more question before we hang up."

"What is it?"

"Any chance you've got a white streak in your hair, probably above your right temple?" Keegan heard a little gasp on the other end of the line. "That's what I thought. Call me

345

tonight around six. Let's use Facetime, if you can, so we can see each other. We need to talk and pretty soon we're going to want to meet. We've got a lot of notes to compare."

CHAPTER 67

The trio got the excavation done at the Orne Jewett Writer's Retreat and made it back to Wells before supper. Aaron and Maryann dropped Stedman off first. He was worn out from handling the gas-fired trenching tool for four hours. He wouldn't admit how sore and tired he was, and insisted he wanted to get home so he'd be ready for the delivery of the snowmobile trailer Sunday at noon. He said he'd get the extra insulation installed Sunday afternoon, right after the seller turned the trailer over to him.

Aaron pulled into Maryann's driveway around five-thirty

"Home with a half hour to spare," he said. "Hope the Facetime goes well. Keegan sounded excited on the phone.

"I'm excited, too," Maryann said. "At this point, I have no idea what to say or do.

"It's mostly Keegan's show, anyway. Play it by ear."

***

Keegan had a list of questions and facts jotted on an old yellow legal pad. Maryann was still adding to the list when Keegan's phone alerted them to an incoming Facetime call. They looked at each other, took a deep breath, and Keegan clicked Accept.

The initial view brought shock on both ends. Both Keegan and Doretta were blue-eyed brunettes with the streak of white hair above the right side of their foreheads. Thought their facial structures, noses, lips, and jawlines were distinctly different, it was hard not to think they were either sisters—maybe fraternal twins—or first cousins. Both girls saw it and Maryann saw it.

Their voices were different, first by regional accent—southern Maine versus central Pennsylvania—and then by register. Keegan was an alto, Doretta a soprano. They were three years apart in age.

Doretta's mother, Debbie Broere, had been the daughter of a couple who owned a motor court in Pennslvania's Amish country. At eighteen and just out of high school, she had fallen for Jan Dauphine, a post-grad student from Holland who was studying at the University of Maine. He was twenty years older than she was. But proximity made a huge difference: on U Maine's vacations Jan came to stay with his distant cousins, the Deutzmans, whose house was barely a half mile from the Broere motor court. One thing led to another and nine months after Christmas break, Debbie delivered Doretta. Three years after that, Debbie married Fred Schussler, and shortly after that Fred adopted little Doretta Broere, giving her a new name, Doretta Schussler.

"My real father wasn't part of my life at all," Doretta said, "until about four years ago when my mother died. He contacted me and I met with him. He said he'd promised Mom he'd stay out of our life unless something happened. Marriage and parenthood didn't drive him, something else did—some crazy mission, or research, I think. But when Mom died, he said he'd pay for my college."

Keegan and Maryann told their stories. Zelda had gotten pregnant by Jan—whether through a sexual relationship or a sperm donation, they didn't know—and had died of an aneurysm before childbirth, with Aunt Maryann immediately adopting her sister's child, turning Aunt Maryann into Mom.

"Keegan's got applications in at eight colleges," Maryann said. "She'll be getting acceptances from some of them next month. Maybe you could mention her name to your father—her father. We're not too proud to take tuition help."

"Mom's kidding," Keegan said. "The Keegans have a dry sense of humor. But I would like to know how to get in touch with him. I've still got questions."

"I'm sure you do," Doretta said. "Problem is, I have no way to contact him—no address, no phone number, no email. I can't even shine a Bat signal in the sky. He insists on it. He pays my college expenses, but I have no idea how. It's like magic. Makes me think he's a Mafia don or something."

They shared about their lives for another hour, built some bridges and agreed to correspond by text and email until their next Facetime in a week, when Doretta would be back at Skidmore.

"Think Thanksgiving vacation," Keegan said. "It'd be a good time to meet."

They said their goodbyes and signed off, all three of their hearts fluttering. Neither Keegan nor Maryann said a word about *gargouilles*. Doretta didn't, either. One didn't tell everything on the first date.

CHAPTER 68

The next day the guy from Lake George, New York drove up to Stedman's house pulling the gently-used snowmobile trailer. He backed it into the driveway and unhitched it in front of the garage. Stedman checked it over and handed the seller two checks: one his personal check for half the total, the other half a check Rusty had mailed from Florida. The man was barely out of the cul-de-sac before Elly started installing the insulation he'd stored in his shop. The following Saturday, he and Aaron and Maryann had the trailer fitted into the ground at the Moxie Pond retreat property, ready to house Luna and her new family.

They set Sunday, October 29 for the *gargouilles'* move-in date. Foliage had just peaked and tourist numbers had passed their peak and were declining.

Which gave them Saturday night, October 28 for their goodbye party at Cliff's barn.

***

Cliff had red, blue, green, yellow, orange, and white Christmas lights strung around the barn's big room. Maryann and Keegan brought lasagna for the humans and striped bass with mashed potatoes and an apple-squash paste for the *gargouilles*. Aaron had hooked the trailer up to his Jeep so they'd be ready to move the six *gargouilles* to Moxie Pond the next day. They'd use the ATV trailer for the last time to transport them, move them into Stedman's bunker, and return the borrowed trailer to Cliff's cousin.

The mood was mixed. There was some excitement and expectation about Luna's group moving to a medium-term location, but there was also sadness about them moving out of Cliff's barn after so many family evenings involving the humans and the *gargouilles*.

They started supper without Stedman, whose excuse was a meeting in Portland. But he said he'd catch up. Everyone ate and afterwards Luna gave a thank-you speech of sorts. Yvette, not the public speaker, added a few humble words.

Tom and Rainey arrived from Tamworth shortly after.

"Nice to be able to make a house call," Rainey said. They checked out the babies and Yvette and Luna, and declared that both adults' foot burns were healing nicely, then said Mathilde's stab wound was healing well. It was time to stop the waist wraps and switch her to Band Aids. Paladin's scalp wounds were no longer scabbing.

"Once a month we'll visit you at Moxie Pond," Dr. Rainey said. "And Luna, your short wing is almost perfect. It's not due to anything we put on it. I'd say that whatever poultice Yvette was applying, it worked miracles. Stretching exercises and very short flights should return you to full strength in a month or so. We'd love to know what went into the ointment."

"Birch bark and something else," Luna said. "Only Bronwyn knew. She pounded it and mixed it and rubbed it on my side and wing every day."

"Well, here's to friends like Bronwyn," AJ said, and raised her glass of iced tea.

Aaron changed the subject to AJ and Keegan's college applications.

"Early acceptances mid-November," Keegan said. "U Maine's probably a sure thing, but I'm also considering applying late to a couple of New York schools: Skidmore in Saratoga Springs and Binghamton University on the Pennsylvania border. Both have great writing programs." She didn't explain the last-minute shift, and no one asked questions.

The babies were bored and made it clear they wanted to go to the pod and wrestle or play hide-and-seek. Paladin, not seeing Stedman, asked, "Oopah?" Maryann used the question to move them into a game.

"Oopah's not here," she said, and in baby talk asked, "Who's that?" She pointed to Keegan.

Regine and Paladin both said, "Kee."

This was a first. So far the only name had been Oopah.

"Very good," Maryann said, and clapped. The rest of the gathered group clapped, too. "And who's this?" She pointed to Yvette.

"Eee," Mathilde and Her sister said, and everyone clapped and oohed.

"And who's this?" Maryann hand-motioned toward Luna.

"Lu," all three said, and clapped themselves before the adults could do it. Everybody followed suit.

"And this?" Maryann asked, indicating AJ.

"A," was their shorthand answer.

"Yes," Maryann said enthusiastically, and put her hands together for a series of small claps. "Yay!"

"And who am I?" Cliff asked, taking hold of the conversation.

"If," they said, and he gave an abashed grin. "Close enough. Yes. If."

Aaron was Ar and Pernod was No. Rainey was Rae and Tom was Ta. They all laughed hysterically, and the babies, finding a receptive audience, kept babbling their variations of everyone's names, the laughter growing in intensity with each repetition. The little ones didn't know why it was funny, but they knew they were entertaining the adults.

"And do you know your own names?" Maryann asked. "Who's this?" She pointed at Paladin, and his sisters said Pal. "And who's this?" She put a hand on top of Mathilde's head, and the siblings said Til. When she did the same with Regine, Pal and Til said Jean. Everyone laughed.

Then they heard the crunch of gravel—a vehicle in the dooryard—and they hushed. Cliff and Aaron went to the big door at the back of the barn and poked their heads out to check.

A moment later they let Stedman in. Paladin shrieked Oopah and ran with open arms to embrace his adoptive grandfather, who scooped him up and hugged him. His sisters weren't far behind, also calling Oopah. Stedman scooped them up, too, in his wide embrace and hugged them close.

Behind him, feeling his way in tentatively, came a shriveled, bent-over man with white hair and a Veteran ball cap. He had a travel bag slung over his shoulder, and his smile was as wide as his face.

"Hello, everybody," he said.

"Rusty?" Pernod asked in disbelief. "What are you doing here?" He rose and walked to his friend and they embraced. "I wasn't expecting you until May. It's so good to see you. Everybody, this is my friend Rusty, who owns the lake house."

Rusty rested a hand on Pernod's forearm and waved. "Good to see you all—figuratively speaking. I'm blind, as you no doubt know, but I look forward to getting to know you."

Stedman said, "His flight was late getting into the Portland Jetport."

They set up an extra seat for the latecomers and made introductions all around. Maryann fixed a plate of food for Elly and their guest and got them drinks.

After they'd all talked a while and Rusty was up-to-date on everyone's recent history and the immediate plans, they turned to the gift-giving.

Maryann got everyone's attention and said, "Since Luna's group is leaving tomorrow—and tonight is probably the last time we'll all be together like this for a while—we thought this was the time for a few presentations. Keegan, do you and AJ want to start?"

The two girls stood up. "Rainey and Tom," Keegan said, "in appreciation of everything you've done for us and for Luna and Yvette's little family—most of it at the last minute—we'd like to present you with this garden statuary from Weathervanes of Maine in Wells." From behind her, AJ pulled out a heavy concrete statue of a crouching gargoyle. Tom and Rainey got up from their seats and, to much applause, accepted their sculpture.

Tom raised the heavy piece overhead like he was accepting an Oscar and said, "A new weapon for our arsenal in case of another attack." Mixed laughter, then he sat down. He passed it to Rusty, so he could feel it.

Stedman was next. He set the three little ones on the ground and said to Pernod, "You have the box?"

Pernod handed him a box from the card table.

"This is for Rusty," Stedman said. "It's not new, but you might call it refurbished." He handed the blind man the gift box.

Rusty felt it then unwrapped it. From the box he pulled a glass bottle with a fully-outfitted ship in it. "Feels familiar," he said. "Mine?"

"One of the kids dropped it and broke it open," Maryann said. "Elly put Humpty Dumpty back together again."

Rusty laughed.

"What?" Stedman asked.

"Funny story," Rusty said, and giggled. "It's solid again."

"Okay?" Stedman said. "What?"

"I dropped it and broke it a couple years ago. I couldn't see to fix it, so I put it on the top of the toilet tank. The top half was simply resting on top of the bottom half. I'm the one who broke it, not one of the babies."

"I've got something," Cliff said. "It's for Pernod. Oh, and maybe for Luna and Yvette, if they develop the habit." He pulled out an Amazon box and handed it to Pernod. "It's open because I already put it together, so it's ready to go."

Pernod opened it and pulled out something shaped like a metal box. It had a rubber tube attached and in a side compartment was a green cylinder with a brass fitting screwed onto its top.

"What is it?" Pernod asked.

"It's a camper's cook stove. Runs on either a butane or a propane cylinder. It's for heating pots and pans of food when you're away from electricity—like at a writer's retreat cabin. I've got it hooked to a little propane tank to start. Auto-ignition so you don't need matches. I'll show you how it works later. You can bring four cups of water to a boil in five minutes."

"I'm confused," Pernod said. "What is it for?"

Cliff reached into a large plastic shopping bag and brought out an aluminum camp coffee pot and handed it to his friend. "From Reny's. It's the poor man's Keurig. You can't use coffee pods. But you can use this." He reached behind him and drew from the bag a can of Maxwell House. "As Teddy Roosevelt said, it's good to the last drop. I'll show you how to make camp coffee later. I'd suggest you do it in the writer's cabin, not in your trailer."

Pernod was thrilled. "Thank you my friend," he said. "I hope you can come sometime and join me for coffee, conversation, and a game of chess."

Cliff reached behind him again and pulled out yet another box. "I call 'em diner mugs. Plain white china. Four mugs in the set. In case you convert Luna and Yvette, with one for a guest."

"Like me," Rusty said. "You never know when I might pop in."

AJ and Aaron went next. Aaron walked to the old Shasta and stepped inside. When he emerged, he was carrying a wooden box the width and height of a large pizza box but twice as thick. "This is for Pernod, but it also connects all of us— particularly Pernod and Rusty, and Pernod and Cliff, Pernod and

Luna, but maybe more." He placed it on Pernod's lap. The top lifted off easily.

"Oh my," Pernod said. "It's beautiful." Before he said what it was or showed it off, he wrapped his palm around something small in the box and handed it to Rusty. "Feel this," he said, and pressed it into his friend's hand. "Know what it is?"

Rusty worked it with his fingers then grinned. "Magnificent. Feels like pewter or bronze. Wonderful details. I'll bet it looks like you, Pernod."

"Not that one," Pernod said. "More like Luna or Yvette or Mathilde or Regine. That's the queen." He handed his friend another chess piece from the boxed set. "How about this one?"

Rusty felt the piece's detail. "The knight. Paladin." Then "Aaron and Cliff, where did you find such a beautiful chess set?"

"Amazon's got everything," Cliff said.

Rusty opened his hands and on his palms everyone saw two shiny metal *gargouilles*, a queen and a knight. Pernod passed the box around so they could all see and touch the striking set of *gargouille* chess figures.

"We have something, too," Keegan said. "Mom and AJ and I."

Maryann brought out three small flat white boxes, each tied with a red bow. "Yvette and Luna can open these."

The two *gargouilles* tugged at the ribbons binding the corners and opened the boxes. Inside the three boxes were tree slings. Luna and Yvette looked puzzled.

"Those are called Baby Hipseat Carriers," Keegan said. "Remember the rigs you improvised for the flight around Katahdin? Very inventive of you, Luna. These are the real thing. Put Regine, Mathilde, and Paladin in them, slap them against your tummies with their legs around your hips, and you're ready to fly. No more life preservers, backpacks, or Trader Joe's cooler bags."

The party lasted another two hours. They ate and drank and watched Paladin, Regine, and Mathilde race around the barn and pile on each other and roll over on the dirt floor. They laughed and clapped when the children tried to say names— Oopah, Kee, If, and Jean. When the little ones climbed into the ATV trailer and fell asleep on the beanbag chairs, they heard Luna and Yvette tell Bronwyn's brave story. They heard the details of the little family's harrowing flight around Katahdin and the encounter with the Great Horned Owl that tried to carry Paladin off. Then they all told their pieces of the clinic battle story.

The night ended with a mix of sobbing, tears, laughter, and little shouts of victory. Then it ended with hugs and well-wishes and goodbyes and promises to meet again. No one wanted to acknowledge that before dawn the Jeep and the ATV trailer would be leaving Cliff's barn and relocating to a remote location the little *gargouille* family that had become a big part of the little human family.

When Luna and Yvette and Pernod climbed into the pod to huddle with their children, the others left and Cliff secured the barn door. They made their way to their cars quietly, somberly.

Stedman walked Keegan and Maryann to their Subaru, and when Keegan slid into the front passenger seat and closed the door, Stedman and Maryann stood beside the driver's door.

"It's overwhelming, Elly," she said. "I am so exhausted. I need a month's vacation just to process it."

"Can't help with the vacation thing," he said. "I've got to work. A lot to catch up on. But if you're open, we could go dancing Thursday night."

She got up on her tiptoes, leaned into a kiss, and when she stepped back, she said, "You're on, Oopah."

THE END

Made in the USA
Middletown, DE
18 June 2023

32323350R00199